Sweater Girl
and Other Tales of Mondauk County

novellas & short stories

Also by Michael-Patrick Harrington

Deep Autumn

I See No Angels

Saving Magdalene

www.michaelpatrickharrington.com

Sweater Girl
And Other Tales of Mondauk County

Michael-Patrick Harrington

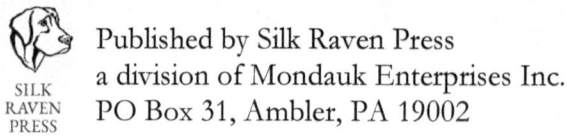

Published by Silk Raven Press
a division of Mondauk Enterprises Inc.
PO Box 31, Ambler, PA 19002

(SRP-004)

Dedicated to:
Raven,
my faithful companion and clown prince.
Another cookie is not out of the question.

There is no end to petting the Raven.

That was the original dedication
written before you passed away.

Helium Raven Teardrop
November 1, 1997—November 2, 2011
Hero to the Masses
The Basketball King
I miss you, Boo.
I keep thinking I hear you padding down the hall with your monkey.

There is no end to crying for the Raven.

My literary guardian angel:
Beth Meier

Thank you:
Nichole Kohler, Pepper Lillie,
Margaux Kent, Lorraine Grassi

Inspiration:
Michael & Karin Berson,
Cathie Gore,
Søren & Silas Kent

Always:
Ma & Kath

Cover photograph:
My grandmother Ro-Ro
on the day she received her driver's license.

TABLE OF CONTENTS:

"The past is never dead. It's not even past."
William Faulkner

"For aren't memories the true ghosts of our lives? Do they not drive
all of us to words and acts we regret from time to time?"
Stephen King

"Home is anywhere you hang your head."
Elvis Costello

Sweater Girl
and Other Tales of Mondauk County

Sweater Girl

"She was a sweater girl," my father said of my mother on more than one occasion. We didn't know what he meant for a long time, but my father was the authority on my mother, the final word, at least until he died in the garage during our one and only night spent with Kerry Mackenzie. We didn't understand what a "sweater girl" *was* until Kerry Mackenzie, and by the time we did, it was too late—too late for us; we were goners when it came to Kerry Mackenzie. Far too late too, it appeared, for my mother, although she was fully exonerated. And if my father truly knew the secrets of the sweater girl, of *his* sweater girl, he took them to his grave. Sweater girls haunt my family.

I don't have many memories of my father. Bobby Haber used to say that what we call memories are actually just memories of memories—we're remembering what we *think* happened: the pain is always worse, the jokes the funniest in the world. In one memory of a memory, my father was teaching me how to shake hands, a task that he treated with gravitas; shaking hands was important to my father.

"*Grab* my hand; don't be a fairy," is what I remember my father saying.

"Don't grip too lightly; that's how a girl shakes hands," was what my father more than likely said.

Or what I wished he'd said.

My mother tried to defend me. "He's a boy. Let him *be* a boy."

"A handshake," my father explained in a voice struggling to remain smooth, "is how men communicate. How he shakes someone's hand tells the other person *everything* about who our son is."

"He's a *boy*, Colonel," my mother repeated.

"He shakes hands like a girl."

I remember inspecting my hands for overt signs of femininity.

"Let him have fun," my mother said. "Leave him be."

"He can have fun when I'm gone," my father said, his annoyance unabated. "When I'm dead and gone, you can throw a goddamn party."

My mother placed her hands on my father's barrel chest, and like a paper clip to a magnet, she drew him in to her bosom.

"We'll have the biggest party in the whole world when you're gone," my mother said. "We'll invite the entire neighborhood."

And I remember grinning up at my parents' banter, and then a sourness invaded my stomach as my father's hand crept towards my mother's breasts.

"I need you, Leigh," my father said. "You fill me up."

My dad had fought in Korea and retired a colonel. He'd rode in a tank and crossed an ocean in a Victory ship, but by the time we were in fifth grade, after his first stroke, he hardly ever left the house except to go to the doctor's. Even when he improved somewhat, he was in a wheelchair most of the time. (Once in a blue moon, he'd limp around with his cane, and then there were his chaotic "well" periods, which never lasted too long.) He also had an abnormal curvature of the spine that had developed later in life, so getting in the car became painful for my father—and too difficult a task for my mother to pull off. We tried to help her, but bending his body to lower him into the seat made him yell something fierce. One time, after we'd successfully squeezed him in, my mom didn't drive four blocks before he started screaming—and didn't stop all the way to the doctor's.

"It was awful," my mother told us, lighting a Marlboro Light from a match offered by Bobby Haber, who said he always carried a book of matches for just such occasions. "Jesus, Mary, and Joseph, it was awful."

After my father's second stroke, every symptom, every difficulty, every pain became magnified. The only time we tried, post-second stroke, to get him into the car, the colonel screamed so loud, old Mrs. McGraw four doors down called the police to report a pervert. My mother convinced a local doctor to come to the house on a semi-regular basis ("unheard of," she told us) and eventually even resorted to knocking my father out with a couple of Valiums when he required a service he couldn't get anywhere but in a doctor's office or at the hospital, such as an x-ray; it wasn't ideal—the medical professional would have to give him a stimulant to bring him around and my mother would have to sedate him again for the ride home—but it became the only way he could get in the car.

Strokes: that was what my mother called them, but they looked more like battery drains to us, like when a toy winds down. That was my father: wound down. It feels odd, even now, to write "my father." Everyone called him the colonel, even my mother.

When my mother told us the story of how they met, we always thought the only thing missing was a USO band playing Glenn Miller's "In the Mood" in the background. There was an officers' party, and my father, after a few shots of courage, asked my mother for a dance—outside. My mother said my father was shy; he didn't want to ask her in front of his buddies, but we thought that the age difference must have played a part. We only knew the barest of facts. My mother was an Army brat from South Carolina, all of thirteen in 1952 when she met my father. ("I developed early," my mother told us once, as if that explained everything.) Her father was my father's CO. When my parents first became acquainted, the future colonel, who'd recently celebrated his 30th birthday, had just returned to the base from duty overseas. The one time I asked my mother about the age difference, she shrugged. She was good at shrugging. But this much I gleaned from family gatherings, pretending to be interested in the paper plate of potato salad balanced on my lap: my parents had eloped, my father somehow fudging a parental consent form. (Tensions were eased a bit with my maternal grandfather when it was revealed that my mother was not in the family way; I would not come along until she was twenty. And moving back to my father's hometown placated his family who viewed the bride as nothing more than a teenage gold digger—except there wasn't any gold, my mother said, laughing.) Every time I asked my father about the details of their initial meeting, all he would say was that my mother was a sweater girl.

And while we didn't quite know what a "sweater girl" was or what my father meant by the appellation, we all agreed that my mother's breasts were outstanding examples of the form, the likes of which we'd only glimpsed in the magazines that had been destined for Johnny Fingers' trash can.

We were watching in mute indignation one afternoon as Johnny carried a stack to the curb.

"I'm done with these," Johnny Fingers said. "You want 'em?"

We shook our heads, and Johnny lit a cigarette and squinted into the sky.

"Save your soul, these ladies will," he said. "And I'm in the saving business."

"Going down to the Fields tonight?" Bobby asked with the kind of casualness I could never pull off. "Heard there's gonna be a party."

"Gotta get out, babe," Johnny Fingers said. "I'm feelin' it."

Whatever "it" was, we were unaware. (Although he went to the same school as we did and was in our grade, Johnny was a little older than we were.) Johnny Fingers went back into the house he "shared" (his word) with his dad, a construction worker who always seemed to be away on a job, and we waited out by the curb, whistling, Indian wrestling, kicking at pebbles. Chris Lee went home. He knew we were going to liberate the magazines when the time was right, and despite his innate packrat sensibility, his sexual curiosity could never conquer his religious upbringing. Just about the time when the sun surrendered the day, Bobby Haber whispered "Now!" and while Tim-Tim and I both lifted the trash can lid, Bobby reached in, snatched a handful, and we hightailed it back to Tim-Tim's garage. The booty was disappointing: Bobby had only grabbed *pages*, not full magazines—and most of those pages were ripped. We tried in vain to match up tops to bottoms; we had very few full ladies. We hid our anemic haul in the back of Tim-Tim's garage beneath a box of old toys and referenced them as needed. One by one pages disappeared from the stash (I still have some of those pages), and while we deliberated on the culprit (Tim-Tim's dad? bullies from the Lakes?), we were all guilty—even Chris Lee. When he confessed his appropriation to me, he told me that he'd hidden his one single page (just a picture of a model's bottom) beneath an old flower pot in his backyard and, eventually the weather eroded away what little he had to work with onanistically.

Our concern over secondhand pornography deterioration was short lived. Summer was a tantalizing month away, and already the warm days were filled with the songs of the cicadas and the evenings and nights populated with lightning bugs. Chris Lee said that all of God's creatures were tuned to the same frequency and that the early appearance of fireflies and mosquitoes were just God's way of teasing us while we stared at the calendar and counted the remaining days of our sophomore year. Chris said that even crushing ants was a sin, unless the ants had infiltrated the house. When the younger bullies from the Lakes incinerated bugs using pieces of glass, they were breaking God's law, according to saintly Chris Lee.

"Doesn't the Bible also say something like, 'Ye without sin cast the first stone?'?" Bobby Haber asked with a wink.

Chris' mouth dropped open, and Bobby grinned.

"I'm only messin'," Bobby said. "I've killed a few hundred ants, I guess, but I won't kill any more, I promise."

Chris held his stomach. Bobby, Tim-Tim, and I looked at each other but said nothing. Chris' mom was very big into Christianity. She was forever pointing to the many scary portraits of Jesus hanging around her otherwise shambolic house. Her faith was frightening, and her parenting style favored authoritarianism. Nothing was too small to escape her gaze. Once when we were younger and wanted to spend a Saturday afternoon walking around the neighborhood (hiking we called it; we were too young to actually hike in Pennypack Woods by ourselves and too mature to be taken snipe hunting by the older kids), Mrs. Lee drew us a map on the back of a pizza parlor menu, hemming us into an eight block area—a very familiar eight blocks. Chris had a little brother who always seemed to be in diapers no matter what memory from what year I pull up. I don't even remember his name; I just remember him standing in the Lee living room, surrounded by towers of newspapers and Christian magazines, his dirty feet camouflaged by the worn, crusty carpet, wearing nothing but diapers, looking wistfully after us when we came to liberate his brother. Chris was a collector—canceled postage stamps, soda can tabs, dried toads that we found in Pennypack Woods— generally anything that didn't cost money. The precious comic books he collected—only the ones deemed appropriate by his parents— were the generic three-in-a-bag kind sold at the supermarket; Chris bought the few unsanctioned comics he had at neighborhood garage sales with pennies he'd found and saved.

Tim-Tim Butterhook came from a large Dutch family—he was the eighth of twelve. Tim-Tim's parents didn't notice if he went missing at my house for a weekend. We called him Tim-Tim (even some of his siblings did) because his parents initially named him Timothy, somehow forgetting, until they arrived home with the new baby, that they had already named their third child (and second boy) Timothy (who was inexplicably called Junior even though the oldest brother, the first born, has been named after their father; the Butterhooks were clearly nomenclaturally challenged). So the clan's newest addition's name was changed to Thomas, but almost everyone called him Tim-Tim. The double name was fitting since Tim-Tim's weight was edging away from childhood chubbiness into outright fat territory; he was at least fifty pounds heavier than almost anyone in our grade.

Bobby Haber lived with his mom, just the two of them. His mom was the nice, friendly sort of mom who remembered your name but was too busy to remember anything else. Bobby prepared his own meals and signed his own report cards. He said his mom used to party and now she didn't but that she attacked work with the same fervor that she had previously reserved for partying. We didn't much understand or care about either activity. We were always waiting to hear more about the late Big Bill Haber, Bobby's father. Big Bill had ridden a motorcycle into the back of horse trailer that had come to a sudden stop on the highway. The horses made it through okay, although we supposed they'd always be too spooked to ever ride in a horse trailer again. The motorcycle actually came out of the accident relatively intact. Not so Big Bill Haber. The motorcycle was stored in Mrs. Haber's shed. We'd long since outgrown taking turns sitting on it and pretending to be outlaws—except Bobby. Sometimes, he told me, he liked to go out there after his mom went to bed and just sit on the bike. He didn't know why, and I didn't pester him with any questions.

Bobby's dad had been a founding member of the Fields Gang, so named because they claimed as their home turf the fields of tall yellow grass in the southern part of Mondauk Proper, the town just south of our own, Rhawnhurst. The Fields (always capitalized in the *Mondauk Common*, the county's newspaper of record) acted as sort of a border to some of the denser parts of Pennypack Woods. The Fields Gang was notorious, but for what, we were never sure. A remnant exists today as does their original haunt, but across the entire length of the Fields huge electrical towers squat and reach for the skies. What Bobby's dad was most famous for (other than the unfortunate equine incident) was leading an eventually victorious Fields Gang in a rumble against a rival outfit from Paradise Lakes, the trailer park community that abutted Pennypack Creek (better known as the Puddle) in Mondauk Proper. The battle brought about a treaty between the two gangs. Bonnie Bednarz, who'd previously been the Lakes Boys' leader Johnny "Pow" Gunsmoke's "old lady" (in the parlance of Bobby's mom), was "given" to Big Bill in the treaty. Johnny Gunsmoke claimed he was part Pennypack Indian (Bobby's mom always said—"no offense to the dead"—that he'd been so full of horse shit, it turned his blue eyes brown) and so honor meant a lot to him, despite being a notorious junkie and thief. Big Bill had to beat the living hell out of him to help assuage Gunsmoke's wounded honor.

Bobby's dad left the family soon after Bonnie gave birth to his only child, a son. Before he died, Big Bill Haber would stop by once or twice a year. The last time he popped by for a visit ("He smelled like Castrol," Bobby remembered), he gave his son a box of Trojans. Bobby was eight.

I guess I should tell you about Johnny Fingers too. That wasn't his real name, but that was what everybody called him and not because he played piano. Johnny's middle finger was as long as his foot, we swore (but all his fingers were unnaturally elongated). He had an unsettling habit of hooking his middle finger around the top of one our lockers whenever he stopped by to talk; we'd notice his seemingly disembodied digit, a prehensile fugitive from a Peter Lorre film, before we noticed Johnny. Twice he let us sniff it in Tim-Tim's garage following a night spent "fishing," as he called it, with some young chippie in Little City. Little City was the sunken spot in the woods where couples went parking; the cops allowed it as long as the amorously inclined left their parking lights on, making the area look like a little city from the road above. Johnny was so frequent a visitor that he claimed that the cops gave him his own parking spot. But sometimes his fishing expeditions occurred in his own house, which was startling to us. Johnny Fingers was only a few years older than we were, but he knew everybody and everybody knew him. Teachers bummed smokes from Johnny in the school parking lot. The Fields Gang bought liquor and beer for him, and we'd seen him at least twice on the back of a motorcycle, holding onto someone's dirty denim Fields jacket. The list of girls he'd done it with had to be twice as long as Santa's naughty or nice list, but Johnny Fingers never really bragged or even named names—the girls bragged for him. When Johnny walked down the hall, his head bouncing to a tune only he could hear, girls greeted him with a kiss on the lips if there weren't any teachers in sight and sometimes even if there were.

Johnny's father, when he wasn't off on a job, rode with the Fields Gang. He'd ridden with Big Bill Haber and knew every outlaw, Johnny Fingers said, from Philly to the French Quarter. Johnny's dad was thin but had muscular, heavily tattooed arms and wore his jet-black hair swept back, which gave him the appearance of being perpetually in motion. Johnny's father (also a Johnny, but Johnny Bank because of his penchant for knocking over banks in the good ol' days, a habit that earned him a stretch in Waganer) claimed he'd given his son the nickname of Fingers. Little Johnny would often cling to his father's back as they rode around Rhawnhurst and Mondauk Proper and New Hope on a Harley, and the son would make the father proud by giving the finger (an extremely long finger) to every pedestrian and driver. Or at least that's the way I remember the story now.

Memory is a funny thing but never funnier than in childhood. We told each other the same stories over and over and never cried foul if details changed or grew a bit. Bobby, Tim-Tim, Chris, and I were together constantly, in and out of school, and we didn't have too many secrets between us. We knew each other's dirty family laundry. Our birthdays even fell in the same month, November (so Valentine's Day was a holiday of some importance to us).

Although Tim-Tim's garage and Johnny Fingers' basement bedroom (his "den of inequity") were areas of congregation for us, my house was headquarters for the four musketeers. (Johnny Fingers moved between many different crowds.) Our presence was welcomed, not tolerated. My mom referred to us as her boys, and Bobby, Tim-Tim, and Chris were frequent sleepover guests. My father had been sick for a long time. (What had caused the strokes, only my mother and the neurologist knew; we never asked.) Unless it was very hot or very cold, the colonel sat in his wheelchair on the front porch, harassing whomever happened to pass by: the mailman, kids on their way to or from school, deliverymen, neighbors. My father would greet each new victim with a torrent of curse words, some of which we'd never heard before (or since).

"Fucking cod licker" and "cornbeefy little taint," are but two examples of my father's creative cursing. We'd scramble to the old red dictionary my mother kept in the kitchen, but more often than not, the dictionary was a disappointment. Perhaps he learned the words in Korea, we opined. Maybe some of them came from actual Korean curse words. In a bookstore at the mall, Bobby found a Korean-to-English, English-to-Korean dictionary, but it was less help than the old red one.

"Mom," I said, a bit breathless; we'd just run in from the porch. "What's a rectum?"

" 'A pucksucking Chinese algae eating rectum,' " Tim-Tim clarified. He was the most out of breath, but he wanted to get it right.

"Look it up," my mother answered, and paging through the dictionary eventually became another game for us, for her response never changed. But it didn't matter; we just liked being around her. And it wasn't just her breasts, the other guys swore. My mother didn't treat us like kids unless we wanted to be treated that way (like when Chris got scared during a sleepover and wet the bed). She let us sip from her beer and took us to see R-rated movies. She smoked cigarettes and blew rings with her smoke, which Bobby and Tim-Tim would dissipate with their fingers. My mom was notorious for leaving things behind—her keys in the ignition, a burning cigarette in the kitchen when she'd lit a new one in the living room (we were always on alert for abandoned cigarettes), even once her shoes at Wanamaker's after trying on new ones—but it was the lone forgotten bra on the clothesline that drew the most attention; after contemplating it from the porch for the better part of an hour, Bobby and Tim-Tim crossed the yard and stood around it, studying the undergarment up close but never actually touching it. Chris stayed behind on the porch with me; he said the sheer size of the bra frightened him. Tim-Tim told Bobby he thought of my mother when he took a bath, and when Bobby told me, I shrugged.

"You have your mother's shrug," he said, trying to shrug himself. "I can't do it right."

I shrugged again.

"You don't care?" Bobby asked. "About what Tim-Tim's doing in the tub?"

"No," I lied—but I wasn't lying because I was mad; I was lying because although I had a good idea about the kind of thoughts Tim-Tim was having in the tub, I didn't know exactly what he was doing while he was having them—not the mechanics of it anyway. I had yet to start doing it myself—or, rather, I'd started flicking around a bit but nothing ever happened. Nothing worth reporting. I knew biologically what the end result was supposed to be, but I wasn't sure what I needed to do to get there. I was a bit of late bloomer.

My mom looked over everyone's homework. She was especially good with essays; she liked words. Not big words or important words necessarily—just words. She told us that the word "velvet" felt the same in her mouth as the real thing did in her hands. (A trip to the fabric store confirmed this fact for us.) My mother was honest—too honest.

Once when she was in the yard hanging laundry in a pair of short-shorts and a halter top that showed off her flat stomach, we were lollygagging on the tiny back porch, sipping iced tea. Chris and Tim-Tim played Chinese checkers and I read a book while Bobby shot the shit with my mom. Looking up from my paperback, I watched her lean down and whisper in his ear. After she went inside, I went down to the picnic table and sat on the bench next to Bobby.

"What did she whisper to you?" I asked.

Bobby's face was red.

"She told me I could use the downstairs bathroom to take care of it," he answered, gesturing down with his strong cleft chin. "But I can't stand up. Not right now."

Bobby was right: if he stood up, the other guys would see that he had a boner. The front of his shorts looked like a pup tent.

"From my mom?" I asked, but I knew the answer. Sweater girls haunted not only my family but also my friends.

Bobby was my best buddy. He nodded yes and didn't look away.

"What did she mean: 'take care of it'?" I asked.

"You know. Choke the chicken," Bobby said, using the appropriate hand gestures. "Spank the monkey. Flog the bishop."

"Oh, yes, I see," I said, but I didn't.

"You haven't…" Bobby began.

"Oh, of course," I said. "Many, many times. A bunch of times this morning, in fact. Once in church even."

Bobby smiled. "It's not hard to do," he said. "It'll happen for you. I swear it." He was quiet for a few seconds before he said, "You won't end up like him."

"Like him? What—"

"Like your father. Look, when you finally do it, it's like you're filling up whoever you're thinking of. It's like you're filled with stars, and you want to give some of them to the person you're fantasizing about. So you shoot out some liquid stars, almost like you're sharing, you know? You're so filled up, you have to let a little bit out. For the colonel, it's the cuss words. Those and more. Only for him, it's like he's just getting rid of something bad. You know what I mean— that's what he's doing when's he drinking and greasing all the doorknobs or telling the Girl Scout selling cookies to weigh his yarbles. Don't worry about being him. You're not him, pal—and he's not the colonel anymore. Don't confuse your liquid stars with his sour piss."

During the rare times when my father was "well," he'd abandon the wheelchair and take up the bottle. My father was fond of bourbon. My mother would temporarily stop giving him his Coumadin because the doctor told us that mixing it with alcohol would have a dire result. And for the first few days of pretty much every good spell, my mother would join him for a few glasses, usually starting around dinnertime. It was as if she'd forgotten each previous episode. But it never took her long to remember, for after a couple of days, my father would start drinking at noon and after a full week or so, he'd start as soon as he got up. We once saw him dipping his toothbrush, paste and all, into a tumbler of Jim Beam.

And the more my father drank, the more like the colonel of old he became (or at least the colonel we imagined he'd been.) Gone were the made-up profanities and the front porch outbursts—inspections became the order of the day, and without fail, he'd lecture the four of us on honor. But that phase was brief as he increased his alcoholic intake, and soon my father focused all his energy on manipulating the proceedings and people in his house. It always started small and grew in scope. Once he rearranged the contents of all the kitchen cupboards. Another time he removed all the light bulbs. A favorite activity was to switch the toilet seats. We had two bathrooms: the big one upstairs and a powder room downstairs in a corner of the dining room. Somehow the switching of the seats was one his more disconcerting activities. Our bottoms always knew something wasn't quite right, and we'd each emerge from the bathroom with a quizzical look.

When the drinking reached its apex, he'd leave behind prankish methods of exerting his dominance for less subtle endeavors. We came home one night from the movies, the four of us, to find my mother on her hands and knees in the middle of the living room with my father using his cane like a riding crop.

"It's going to take a while before I can think of your mother's breasts again," Tim-Tim said, and we all nodded our heads.

Once my father broke some of my mother's records and peed on the turntable. Another time, he slashed all the tires on the car. (The sedan was so old-looking, we called it, not without affection, the Corsair.) We walked to baseball practice most of that summer as my mother seemed to regard replacing the tires as an act of acceptance of the colonel's behavior. Even after he settled back into the wheelchair and returned to the front porch, trading his precious bourbon for daily doses of Coumadin, the Corsair sat in the garage, its tire smiles slow motion fading in the heat of summer. When my father was on a "tear" (my mother's word), we frequently hung out in Tim-Tim's dank garage in order stay out of the way. And when it was over, my father seemed to have no memory of his extracurricular activities. We could feel my mother's bitter disappointment and anger—emotions mostly directed at herself. Once again, her imagined reincarnation of a past version of the colonel had been nothing but a pipe dream—a realization that was an embarrassing reminder of the present. But she would rally and draft us into duty as she returned the house to its former domestic state.

"Bobby, your mom still have that drill?" she'd ask, and Bobby would run home to get it, and we'd return the toilet seats back to their proper places, each of us taking a turn sitting on them to be sure it wasn't just our imaginations dictating their individual comfort levels. During one of my father's more destructive jags, Bobby carried the drill in his book bag for two weeks, knowing it would soon be needed again.

And when it was all over, when the most recent tear had petered out, at the end of a day of rearranging, my mother would pour each of us a small glass of beer and give any boy who wasn't sleeping over two sticks of gum for the walk home.

+

Bobby Haber's Trojans were on our minds when Kerry Mackenzie transferred to Father Hoskins High. (Chris even nicked a condom from Bobby's dresser.) Bobby said she came from down South. Tim-Tim said the Midwest. Chris Lee thought she was too frightening for words (she was a pretty girl after all) and withheld his opinion on her origin. I thought Kerry Mackenzie came from heaven—and when I said it aloud, everyone, even Chris (via a mute nodding of his head), agreed with me. Regardless of her birthplace, she *did* have an accent—not a heavy one, but one with enough of a lilt to keep us up and on the phone to each other at night.

"I bet her hair smells like a twister," Tim-Tim whispered into the receiver, his Midwest Wizard of Oz fantasy in full flourish.

"She's been witness to great tragedy," Bobby Haber hypothesized.

"Her clothes are very wrinkled," was Chris Lee's opinion, but what Bobby had said was more like the kind of mysteries we were interested in—although it didn't stop us from discussing Kerry Mackenzie's wrinkled school uniform for ten minutes.

I sat on a stool in our dark kitchen and twirled the phone cord.

"What kind of tragedy?" I asked, hoping that it wasn't one that involved a "tragic love," for those kinds of love, we were finding out from the books and plays we read now that we were firmly in high school, rarely, if ever, resulted in the fairy tale endings of the old movies we'd grown fond of watching on late night television.

"She's like Ingrid Bergman," Tim-Tim said. It was something we'd heard him say before. Tim-Tim had a thing for Ingrid Bergman, and he thought every girl had that "Ingrid thing."

"Like one or both of her parents are dead or something?" I asked.

"That's pretty tragic," Bobby said in a strange tone, and I could hear Chris suck in his breath and hang up the extension in the basement. (Chris was sleeping over at my house, and Tim-Tim was at Bobby's.)

I was referring to Ingrid's parents, but it didn't matter. I should have said sorry to Bobby right then and there. If I had, maybe this whole thing wouldn't have happened the way it did, but I didn't know how to say to my best friend, "I'm sorry for forgetting your dad is dead." The phone line remained silent until Chris picked up the basement extension again, and we listened to his asthmatic wheeze.

"That's it then," Bobby Haber said, and I knew right then: despite how exciting the idea seemed, getting involved with Kerry Mackenzie would become a tragedy. "We ask her to come over."

"Over here?" I asked.

"Yes," Bobby answered. I knew his jaw was set like it was whenever it was his turn to sit upon his father's old motorcycle.

Chris Lee's wheezing increased.

"It could be done," Tim-Tim said, "if all the conditions are right." He excelled at biology and chemistry and had a feel for science that none of us possessed. "A reaction rate depends on a single reactant and—"

"You lost me already," I said, feeling flustered.

"It has to be handled just so," Tim-Tim explained.

"I'll handle it," Bobby Haber said.

And that was that. I couldn't sleep that night and neither could Chris. We showered and dressed early, skipped breakfast, and met Bobby and Tim-Tim on the corner. We didn't speak as we walked to school. The only sounds came from the competing respiratory racket of Chris' strangled whistling and Tim-Tim's labored breathing as he struggled to keep pace with his far skinnier pals.

I should tell you: Kerry Mackenzie was not your ordinary girl. In our school, like in most, there was a caste system. The cheerleaders and the girls with rich parents called themselves the Bod Squad. They ruled over the other girls (or attempted to) with sharp tongues and a disregard for others' reputations. The jocks, of course, were the princes among the male population. Some of them could be oppressive and intimidating, but the real bullies weren't jocks, and they had their own little tribe. The few black kids that went to our school paid little heed to the Bod Squad or the jocks, but they kept their eyes open for the bullies. The remaining groups that followed were stereotypical: brains and geeks; hipsters and aspiring hippies; and the final mix of ugly or big girls and the handicapped. Kerry Mackenzie fit into none of these categories and didn't seem to want to. The Bod Squad kept their distance: she was an unknown entity and therefore dangerous. Her hair was on the short side and dyed jet black, and her bangs, which hung down past her eyes, were sometimes hair-sprayed excessively so she could form them into a spiky curtain that was swept to one side. Otherwise, she wasn't defined by a particular hairstyle, and actually at times appeared to have more than one. She wore dark eyeliner, but not in the same way that the Bod Squad wore makeup. (Despite occasional crackdowns, makeup was only passively discouraged by the school). The Bod Squaders always looked to us like they were playing dress-up with their mommies' cosmetics; it never looked quite right on their faces, and their misuse often grotesquely exaggerated their worst features. Kerry Mackenzie wore all that eyeliner, we surmised, because it gave her a mask—like the Lone Ranger. And if you wore a mask, Tim-Tim said, then you could do whatever you wanted to because it was never really you.

But most of all, Kerry Mackenzie was pretty. She had big dimples that came out when she smiled, and they complimented her prominent cheekbones. She possessed an easy laugh and a mouth that wouldn't stop—but she didn't gab or gossip. She discussed. She argued. She debated. She conversed. And she did all these things with *everyone*. Bobby and Tim-Tim saw her sharing a joint with a couple of public school kids behind the Roosevelt Mall. Chris Lee said Kerry spent an entire lunch period talking with Babs Toner, a top Bod Squader—out of earshot of the rest of the herd, of course. We all witnessed her enthusiastically recommending rock'n'roll records to the geeks. Tim-Tim wrote down all the bands Kerry mentioned, and we pooled our money and bought some of their 45s. We sat in my room, huddled together around the record player, wondering what lyrics, what melodies had made her so passionate when she was talking with the geeks. Did she dance around her room in her underwear? Did she copy the lyrics into the back of her notebook? We watched her behavior in school carefully and tried to divine from her public persona her private one.

We had even consulted Johnny Fingers on the matter of Kerry Mackenzie, but the information he freely gave confused us even more. We were without precedent in the matter of romantic love.

"*All* of you are in love with her?" Johnny Fingers asked as he stuffed books into his locker.

We were surprised that Johnny actually had books. Although he attended Father Hoskins High School, we had never seen him in a classroom.

"Chris isn't sure," Bobby said.

"I'm not sure," Chris Lee said.

"Not sure about what?" Johnny Fingers asked, pushing his locker door shut with a single long finger. We trailed after him as he sauntered down the south hall and out towards the gazebo. *Sauntered*, we'd decided, was the best word to describe the way he moved; *glided* was too surreal although not incredibly far off. He walked like he talked: slow but not lazy. He had a crooked smile, and his eyelids drooped when we passed some girls, as if he was half asleep, yet he appeared to see everything. We exchanged glances behind Johnny Fingers' back. His navy blue school tie dangled from his back pocket. His hair, which extended beyond his collar—a Catholic school no-no that somehow didn't apply to him—bounced on his head like he was in a shampoo commercial.

"Not sure if I'm in love with Kerry Mackenzie," Chris finally answered.

"Ah," Johnny Fingers said as he took a pack of cigarettes from his shirt pocket, lit a Marlboro, and offered the pack around. We shook our heads, but I thought Bobby looked tempted.

The gazebo was empty. We gave silent thanks. Because it was technically not on school grounds and was fairly removed from public view, being partially surrounded by the woods, it attracted bullies from as far as the Lakes. It was considered neutral territory, and we heard it was often used as a meeting place. We had never even been near the gazebo before, and we were prepared to run into the woods if necessary.

"Relax, boys," Johnny Fingers said, smiling, and his eyelids fell to half-mast again and his head nodded a little as if he had headphones on and was listening to Kerry Mackenzie's record collection.

"That's the key," Johnny said, exhaling. "Relaxing. Girls don't like to see you all keyed up. Makes 'em think you got an agenda."

"We don't have an agenda," Bobby Haber said.

Chris Lee scribbled into a notebook. He told us later he wanted to collect words of wisdom. Chris told us he wanted to be in the saving business too.

"Do we need an agenda?" Tim-Tim asked. "I mean, would it be better if we had one?"

Johnny Fingers stood up and walked in a circle around Chris, dictating.

"If a girl lets you touch her—just *touch* her, I mean, not finger her," Johnny explained, raising his impossibly long middle finger into the air, "then don't stop: keep one hand gently rubbing her shoulder or her arm or her leg. If you're making out with her, the same rule applies. It loosens them up."

"Massaging them," Bobby Haber said.

"Not massaging them," Johnny Fingers clarified, the skewed smile and creased eyes reappearing. "Just a finger or two, lightly running over their skin, just two fingers tracing a little circle."

"…little…circle," Chris Lee repeated as he memorialized Johnny's pearls of high school seductive wisdom. Afterwards we congratulated Chris for remembering to bring a notebook and a pen. It would have been hard to recall all of Johnny Fingers' remarks; there was a lot on our minds.

"But most of all," Johnny said, slowing his voice down, "girls appreciate a guy who's not afraid. Even if Kerry turns you down—all of you—even if she turns you down cold, word'll get around. You walked up to her and asked her out. People'll know. It'll end up being a positive. Girls talk, right?"

We nodded our heads although we didn't have the first idea *what* they talked about.

"Why do you think they call me Johnny Fingers?" he asked, and at that moment, we believed him, the story of little Johnny giving his middle finger forgotten.

"Kerry, Kerry, Kerry," Johnny said, shaking his head, and we started to panic. Was Johnny Fingers going to demonstrate his tried and true finger technique on Kerry Mackenzie, *our* Kerry Mackenzie?

"Kerry's got a nice rack," Johnny said, his eyelids lower than usual.

We agreed afterwards that we didn't know what shocked us more: Johnny Fingers commenting on Kerry Mackenzie's rack or the way that he said her name, as if he knew her intimately.

"I wouldn't do that," Johnny said when he noticed our distress. "She's fair game, sure, but among gentlemen—well, let's just say gentlemen don't do that."

We exhaled.

"Besides," Johnny Fingers said, "she's got a snaggletooth."

And she did. It was the only flaw on what we thought was her otherwise perfect face. Kerry Mackenzie had big eyes that always looked overly moist. Her straight nose was vaguely European-looking (and it was "cute" according to Chris Lee, who possessed a bulbous honker that attracted bullies of all stripes). Her dimples were distracting. ("I don't know whether to climb a tree or wet myself when they pop up," Bobby Haber said.) Her wit (witnessed from afar) was quick, and her laugh, as I've mentioned, was always within reach, but when she smiled or opened her mouth, we couldn't tear our eyes away from her teeth. One tooth jutted away from the others as if in revolt; it kind of sat on top of the neighboring tooth. Kerry Mackenzie seemed neither self-conscious about her snaggletooth nor aware of the attention it brought. We were fascinated by it.

"It makes her more like us somehow," Tim-Tim said, and we all understood exactly what he meant. It was that small imperfection, that little slight from God, that made her flesh and blood to us. Kerry Mackenzie's snaggletooth made us love her more than we already did.

It was Bobby Haber who would speak for us in the matter of Kerry Mackenzie. Bobby had always been our leader if we'd ever needed one. I was second-in-command. I had brains, which Bobby did too, even if he didn't believe it, but he also had brawn—and one other thing that kept the bullies at bay (even though Bobby avoided them as much as possible anyway): he was Big Bill Haber's kid.

"You're legacy, man," Johnny Fingers told Bobby once. "Wolf and Harry, they'd let you in the Fields, man, on blood alone."

Bobby already had several run-ins with the police. It was a family tradition, it seemed. Although his mom didn't drink anymore, she still enjoyed a good skirmish and had once ended an argument at her front door with Deputy Police Chief Kenny Lynde by grabbing his balls in her fist and pulling upward.

Old Spoonie Ranger, who worked part-time at the library stamping books we were sure he couldn't read and who spent the rest of his day listening to his police scanner, witnessed the Balls in the Sky Incident, as it became known in our circle, sitting on his scooter across the street.

"I ain't never heard no one scream like that," Spoonie told us. "One time, I was openin' boxes at the library, and I cut my finger real bad with the knife, but I didn't scream, no sir, least not as loud as the Deputy Chief."

"She grabbed his actual balls and lifted them *up*?" Chris Lee asked.

Spoonie nodded his head eight or nine times.

"To the sky, I tell ya," he answered, nodding his head eight or nine more times for good measure. "Not his actual testiculars, mind you, but she knew right where they was nestin'. Deputy Chief Lynde came himself to arrest Bobby, but Bonnie wasn't havin' any of it. Took matters into her own hands, so to speak, and the Deputy Chief passed right out, right the hell out."

"On Bobby's porch?" Tim-Tim asked.

Spoonie nodded his head the requisite eight or nine times.

"She was keepin' him up," Spoonie told us. "If she hadn't-a been, he woulda fallen hard and cracked open his melon for sure, yes sir."

We looked at each other.

"Mrs. Haber kept him from hitting his head," I asked, just to be clear, "by holding him up by his...?"

Spoonie nodded his head sixteen times.

"She grabbed his jewels, lifted 'em *up*," Spoonie told us. "And when the Deputy Chief passed out, Mrs. Haber was still holdin' onto 'em. She 'ventually lowered him to the ground by them balls, yes sir. Balls to the sky, then balls to the ground."

Spoonie covered his own balls with his hand.

"I heard that the Deputy Chief can't produce no more of them semen," Spoonie said (only he pronounced it like "sea-men"), and we nodded back. I couldn't speak for Chris Lee, but I had yet to produce any sea-men myself.

The police seemed to target Bobby mainly because he was Big Bill Haber's kid, but Bobby didn't help matters shoplifting. Truancy was another problem, but Bobby ultimately decided he'd rather be in school with us during the day than by himself.

"Bobby's smart," my mom had told us. "He'll wise up and go to college with the rest of you."

"Not if he doesn't stop swiping stuff," I said through a mouthful of peanut butter and strawberry jelly. My mom wiped at the corner of my mouth with a wet paper towel. I wiggled away, not wanting to be babied in front of Tim-Tim and Chris, but I had to force myself not to smear the sandwich all over my cheek. As much as I enjoyed unprecedented freedom, it had little to do with my age. My usually wheelchair-bound father required the kind of care a mother gave a baby—a baby with a longshoreman's vocabulary. Sometimes I secretly wanted that kind of attention again.

From our porch, my father yelled, "I'll doublefuck your lynx!" to a deliveryman, who dropped the package on the walk and instinctively touched his throat, clearly confusing his voice box with a potentially violated wildcat.

But many of my father's words weren't so easily defined.

"Fondle my nads," he told Father Phil when the priest came around for block collection.

"What are nads?" we asked my mom.

We were told to look it up.

What we couldn't look up in the big red dictionary was how to ask Kerry Mackenzie for a date. It was Bobby Haber's time to step up to the plate; he was the self-appointed leadoff hitter. The last bell had rung on Monday, and we were dawdling on the little grassy hill near the school library. Bobby's forehead still bore the bruise from Mrs. Barchenko's tennis shoe. Bobby had tried to steal a half-filled box of Topps baseball cards from the counter of her tiny Loney Street convenience store, which he'd believed to be temporarily untended. He didn't see Mrs. Barchenko sitting down behind the counter, "picking her feet," the police report said. When he lifted up the box, Mrs. Barchenko rapped Bobby in the head with her shoe.

The only reason she didn't press charges, she said, was because they were last year's cards.

"Why even try?" I asked.

Bobby shrugged. It was catching.

"My mom says you're going to go to hell," Chris Lee said.

"She said that?" Bobby asked, looking angry, but sounding anything but.

Chris looked away.

"You're never gonna get into college with a police record," I said.

Bobby started to shrug, then stopped.

"I have to get a job after we graduate," he said. "But I might not even finish high school."

Tim-Tim whistled through his teeth.

"That's just fool talk, Bobby," I said, but I'd always wondered how Bobby would go to college: his mom worked hard, but they never had any money, and Bobby's grades were only so-so.

"What's quitting high school gotta do with stealing?" I asked.

Bobby puffed out his chest. "I'm legacy. Johnny Fingers said so. When you guys go away to college, I'm gonna have to join the Fields," he explained. "Ain't no one else gonna be around."

"Shhh. Here she comes," Tim-Tim said, and indeed, coming out of the library and towards the little hill, was Kerry Mackenzie.

I wish I could remember every detail, every little thing about her that day. Before that afternoon, Kerry Mackenzie had been pretty from afar—and, for us, *all* girls were pretty from afar. It wasn't like we didn't talk to girls or they didn't talk to us, but the ones that did weren't the ones we fantasized about. We desired girls out of our reach.

What I do remember is that Kerry Mackenzie wore what appeared to be an ill-fitting Army green t-shirt with a stretched out neck beneath her white school blouse, which had the top three buttons undone. Her regulation navy blue pleated skirt had been discarded (stuffed, we discovered later, into her book bag, thus solving the mystery of the wrinkled clothes), and she wore the kind of pants that Audrey Hepburn wore in *Sabrina*, the kind where the legs don't reach the ankles but instead halt mid-calf—waders, we decided they were called. Kerry's waders were also an olive drab color. Her eyes were bluer than we'd imagined, and her eyeliner had run a bit. Tiny drops of perspiration crowded her forehead and clung to her bangs and balanced on her upper lip.

Kerry walked straight up our hill, and we stood up and smoothed our trousers.

"What are you guys doing?" Kerry Mackenzie asked, and for a half a heartbeat, I thought Bobby Haber, nascent criminal and (possible) future Fields Gang member, had lost the ability to speak, for the only sounds coming out of his mouth were small noises, like the ones nuns make saying the rosary. Kerry laughed, and we all got a close-up of her snaggletooth.

"Did that happen in an accident," Bobby Haber asked, "or was it something your folks just never got around to fixing?" That was his opening salvo.

I thought I was going to throw up from sheer nerves. Chris Lee actually backed down the hill. Tim-Tim pulled a candy bar from his pocket and nervously ate it in two gulps. Johnny Fingers had told us that girls liked sweet talk, but they knew it was just bullshit—they just wanted to hear it once in a while. Doll face. Baby. Sweetheart. But what they really wanted was honesty. "A girl appreciates a guy who's honest," Johnny had told us. (Chris Lee had written it down.) "But not *too* honest, if you know what I mean," he finished with a wink. We didn't—at least that was what I thought. But Bobby seemed to have taken the lesson to heart, and now that the floodgates had been breached, we were about to see honesty in action.

Kerry Mackenzie opened her mouth wide and flicked a fingernail against the surface of the renegade tooth.

"Want to touch it?" she asked, and we nodded yes, and one by one, we touched her snaggletooth. It was like touching something ancient, a fossil, a link to a different time, certainly a time before Kerry Mackenzie came to Hoskins High. We imagined moments of self-doubt in the mirror, and we pictured Kerry shrugging away any insecurity, embracing her dental disfigurement. Kerry had to take Chris' hand and place his finger on her tooth. We shuddered. Later, Chris told us how warm her hand was.

"It was like her insides had been cooking," he said, and we understood. Kerry Mackenzie was so alive, her blood competed with her skin for attention.

After the tooth touching, introductions were made.

"Do you wanna come hang out with us?" Bobby Haber asked, fulfilling his duty as our leader.

"Sure," Kerry said, "where?"

"My house," I answered, my voice squeaking.

"Chase that puberty, young man," Kerry said.

"Grab it with both hands and make it go *woooo!*" she cried, demonstrating by bringing all ten fingers together and moving her hands up and down. Everyone tried to look elsewhere. She poked Tim-Tim's belly.

"Who you hiding in there, Tim-Tim?" Kerry asked.

The walk to my house seemed endless. Years later, Bobby and I agreed that the walk held portents of what would happen at the party.

First off, Chris Lee threw up, a not uncommon occurrence. Tim-Tim once said that Chris' mother made *him* nervous, and he wasn't alone. We'd long ago assumed that Mrs. Lee's domineering presence must be what kept Chris' stomach in such an uproar. But how much honesty was too much?

"Is he okay?" Kerry Mackenzie asked, genuine concern manifesting itself in the scrunching of her eyebrows—tiny unplucked caterpillars, we would later agree.

"Yeah," Bobby said, his hand on Chris' back. "Bad stomach is all."

Chris wiped his mouth with the tissues he carried for just such occasions.

"Your parents take you to the doctors?" Kerry asked.

Chris nodded. He said later he was afraid to breathe on her.

"What they say? The doctors?"

Chris' facial expression indicated that he didn't know.

Kerry clapped her hands and snapped her fingers at us.

"Hello?" she said. "Do any of you guys see Chris here is sick? Does anyone know what the doctors said?"

Already Kerry Mackenzie was one of us.

"I don't think it's medical so much," Bobby Haber said, and Kerry ran her fingers through Chris' hair. We were jealous, but we relished her sympathy and suddenly wanted to lay everything bare to her: the frightening religious devotion of Mrs. Lee; Big Bill Haber and botched shoplifting attempts; the colonel and his bourbon binges and porch profanity; the odd loneliness that came from being the eighth child in a family of who knows how many this time tomorrow. But for the moment, we held our tongues.

"My parents loved me," Tim-Tim said in our annual phone call a couple of summers ago. "They were Super Catholics—not in the scary way that the Lees were, but in the baby making department, I'm sure they think they made the Pope proud."

"But you spent all your time with us," I said. "And your older brothers made fun of you because—well, because of everything."

"Coke bottle glasses," Tim-Tim said. "That was the main thing."

"Tim-Tim, you were chubby. You were chunky," I said. "You had an awful lot of ear wax."

"I was just trying to give my brothers some credit," he responded.

"I'm not trying to be mean, but they had an awful lot to work with."

"Kerry Mackenzie didn't see any of that," Tim-Tim said. "She was the only girl who touched me until I got into college."

"You started working out by then," I said, "and Kerry Mackenzie never touched you."

"My brothers were always flicking my ears or slapping my fat," Tim-Tim admitted. "Kerry poked my belly. Not to make fun—just because she wanted to. That's touching of a sort."

"You were at my house so much," I said, "I thought you were *my* brother."

The line went silent for a few seconds. Just Tim-Tim's steady breathing. After shedding thirty pounds in his freshman year of college, he became fanatical about working out. We talk each year right around the time when spring ends, as if we were plotting our summer back in Rhawnhurst again—as if we were deciding whether to build a tree house first or go Puddle Jumping instead or maybe take the train to the city—but we hadn't seen each other in a decade.

"Tim-Tim," I whispered into the phone—just like we did the nights leading up to Kerry Mackenzie's first visit to my house—"you still there?"

"You were my brother," Tim-Tim said.

"You were all my brothers," he added before hanging up.

"Yes," I whispered to the humming phone line.

We didn't unburden ourselves to Kerry right away (although Bobby almost did). We thought our troubles hung from our necks on brightly painted signs; surely, someone as worldly as Kerry Mackenzie didn't need to be told, we thought. This was an assumption, of course—Kerry's worldliness—but our world didn't extend much beyond the borders of Rhawnhurst and the surrounding towns of Mondauk County; just an occasional trip to the city. Kerry's voice had an accent that spoke of rivers and bayous and swamps—of places other than where we were.

+

Kerry dug into her pocket and gave Chris her last piece of gum. Chris told us later it was warm like her hand, as if it had been in her pocket for days, slowly roasting against her thigh.

Kerry winked at Chris. "Freshen you right up. That way you don't have to go home and miss out on anything."

"I don't want to go home," Chris said. "If I go home, then I'll have to pray until suppertime."

Kerry looked at each of us.

"Because of the throwing-up," Bobby Haber explained. "Mrs. Lee'll smell it—gum or no— and get piping mad. Like he's been drinking or something. She doesn't know it's—"

I dug my elbow into Bobby's ribs. It was one thing to discuss amongst ourselves the terror of Mrs. Lee, but not in front of Chris— and especially not in front of Kerry Mackenzie. But we all harbored the anger Bobby had just about unleashed.

"Toothpaste," Chris Lee said. "My mom makes me eat toothpaste whenever I upchuck. A lot of it."

We walked in silence for the next couple of blocks, and at a red light, Kerry turned and waved and walked straight into traffic. A light blue sedan swerved and another car honked its horn. Kerry waved again when she reached the other side of the street. We stood frozen on the corner.

When the light turned green, we caught up to Kerry (she'd continued to walk towards my house as if she'd always known where I lived) and she told us Life Lesson No. 1: It doesn't get any easier, it just gets more familiar.

"I'm not sure...I don't think we..." Bobby said.

"My mom..." Kerry began, and we leaned in; we were so anxious for any morsel of personal information. Her light accent hinted of tragedies older than anything the tired town of Rhawnhurst had ever experienced. We longed for a little something to distinguish us (especially Tim-Tim), to make our lives somehow seem different even if they really weren't.

"...moved us around a lot.

"My mom is my best friend," she added proudly. "She tells me all the time."

"Tells you what?" Bobby asked.

"That she's my best friend."

"You move 'round a lot 'cause of your mom's job?" Tim-Tim asked.

Kerry shook her head.

" 'What looks in the beer light like a diamond on the floor, Kerry,' she told me, 'is usually just a peanut shell.' "

"Life Lesson No. 2," Kerry explained. "Meaning, instead of looking, we're watching. And instead of doing, we're looking."

We nodded our heads sagely although we didn't understand a whit. Decades later, Bobby and I were sitting on my back porch watching the lightning bugs and drinking a fair share of the random mix of beers I had in the basement fridge.

He thought Life Lesson No. 2 was a bigger clue to Kerry's character than I'd ever considered. "I think she meant that her mom had dated a whole shit barrel of losers, some of them really bad news," Bobby said. "Think about the scar. Her mom was probably on a desperate search for love—you know the type—and as a result, I bet she brought home some real dregs, exposing her daughter to God knows what. I think the floor of whatever place Kerry and her mother called home was littered with peanut shells." I could barely see his face in the dim glow of the old porch bulb; I hadn't changed it since I'd moved back to Rhawnhurst. In the faint light, Bobby didn't look like an adult with two little girls and a pretty wife, a decent mortgage rate, and a prestigious job with the city. His expensive haircut appeared tussled and windswept; his wrinkles were like the sun lines of late summer. He looked like our Bobby, not somebody's Robert. "I think she was looking for the same thing her mother was," he continued, "even if she didn't know what that was at fifteen."

"They moved away from Rhawnhurst pretty damn quick," I said and drained my beer. I hadn't drunk much since the last night the four of us had been together in my parents' house. I kept beer in the fridge for the rare guest. Even in college, just the smell of the ever-present kegs made me sick to my stomach, but this night, with the summer air still thick, the perspiration on my upper lip signaled a job well done, although I had done nothing more than not throw up when I cracked my first beer with Bobby.

Above his title, his business card read, Robert R. Haber, Esq.

"I don't think her mother ever completely unpacked. I think she was the kind of person who slept with one hand on her suitcase whenever she slept alone, if you know what I mean."

"Fight or flight," I said.

"No," Robert R. Haber said, shaking his head, "just flight."

+

We were a block from my house when Kerry Mackenzie lifted her shirt. A scar ran almost all the way across her otherwise smooth, pale stomach. Tim-Tim told us later that he'd sprouted wood, even though he was sure a terrible story accompanied the scar. Tim-Tim wasn't alone in his assumption—or in his physiological reaction to Kerry's bare belly. We were ashamed of the involuntary nature of our bodies.

"Do you want to touch it?" Kerry asked, and we took turns again—even Chris Lee. It was ridged like a mountain range on a raised-relief map.

Whether it was her snaggletooth or her scar, we realized that there appeared to be no end to touching Kerry Mackenzie. Robert R. Haber and I would later note the ease with which she made herself available to be touched, inviting strange hands to feel her body. Where had she learned that behavior, we wondered. With us, it seemed as if she wanted to share her embarrassments and tragedies; despite our tumescent state, there was nothing sexual in a snaggletooth or a horrific scar.

"Who did this to you, Kerry?" Bobby asked—and though I've never heard him question a witness on the stand, I imagine that when he does, he sounds like he did the day he asked Kerry Mackenzie about her scar. Bobby eventually told me, years later, that Kerry was the reason he chose to study criminal law; there were too many mysteries and not enough bookworm gumshoes, he said.

Kerry ran a finger slowly across the length of her scar, as if she was remembering its cause (or so Bobby suggested the next day).

"Life Lesson No. 3, gents: 'If it smells like horseshit and looks like horseshit, it's probably horseshit,' " she said.

"Horseshit," Bobby Haber pointed out, "can be washed off."

Kerry ran ahead of us again, then turned back around.

"But it takes a while to get rid of the smell," she hollered through her hands. Any smell, she might have added.

There are times when I lie in bed, unable to sleep, and go over lesson plans in my head just to have something to think about other than Kerry Mackenzie. Some nights, the stink of the faraway Puddle, old Pennypack Creek, mixes with the pinecone sap and drifts through my windows. It's a familiar smell, the clash of the rank Puddle and the fertile woods. On humid days, it clung to our clothes and haunted our bed sheets as it does now in my little cottage house, as it does to my students, still encumbered with the familiar regulation navy blue skirts and ties. And beneath it all, I think I can still smell Kerry Mackenzie's cocktail of generous amounts of body splash accented with excessive perspiration.

"That's why you're a teacher, right?" Robert R. Haber asked me, cracking another beer. "You need one?"

He tossed a can, and I caught it lightly like I'd been taught in college, though I rarely pulled the tab back then. I had plenty of acquaintances at the university but no real friends. All my friends were trapped in the snow globe past.

"No, I'm a teacher...I don't know...because..."

"Because you want to enlighten the minds of the youth of Rhawnhurst?" Robert suggested. "Is that why you teach at Hoskins High?"

"Yeah," I said, sipping my beer. "Something like that."

I didn't much care for Mr. Haber's prosecutorial tone.

"No, more like this: you want to find her—and him. Not literally, of course, but you're looking for another Kerry and another Chris. Only this time, you save them. That's right, isn't it?"

"Sounds like you're talking about yourself, counselor."

He was starting to crawl between my epidermis and connective tissue and was beginning to itch, as Tim-Tim was fond of saying.

"Maybe," he laughed softly. "Maybe the reason I know it's true for you is because it's...not unfamiliar to me."

I swallowed the rest of my beer in two gulps.

"Toss me another, alright?"

"Life Lesson No. 4, remember?" Robert R. Haber asked.

" 'The truth ain't waiting to be found if you're already standing in it,' " I recited.

"It's gotta be hard, moving around a lot," Bobby said.

Kerry shrugged.

" 'No attachments.' Lesson No. 5. You get attached, then you always want that one moment to happen over and over, and that's never gonna happen, boys."

She shrugged again, and I caught Bobby's eye: another shrugger. Tim-Tim smiled.

"You'll like his mom," Bobby said. "She's cool."

"Of all the mothers and teachers, she has the best bosom," Tim-Tim said without a hint of embarrassment.

Bobby punched him in the shoulder.

"What?" Tim-Tim asked, looking around. "She does. We all agreed."

Bobby punched his shoulder again—harder.

But Tim-Tim was undeterred by violence, having to deal with the savagery of his older brothers every day. "They might be the best breasts I've ever seen, and I've never actually seen them—not *live and in person*, if you know what I mean."

Bobby cocked his fist again, but Kerry placed her hand on his arm. ("It *was* warm," he told us later.)

"It's okay, Bobby," I said, "I don't mind."

"Why would I lie?" Tim-Tim asked. "She's the sweater girl," he said, by which I thought he meant that my mother was unique and special—something we all believed.

"I kind of missed that whole transition phase," Kerry said, a hint of wistfulness haunting the lilting cadence of her voice. "I went from being 'flat-as-a-board, easy-to-screw' to this." She briefly cupped her breasts, and for a second I forgot how to breathe. "Not exactly Raquel Welch but definitely a sweater girl—in gang parlance."

A sweater girl? We started to understand then that being a sweater girl had to do with how one filled out a sweater, and we tried not to stare, for Kerry was indeed well-endowed. Later, however, we would decide that the term was a moniker reserved for only the most exceptional of women, regardless of cup size.

"I'll pop out your eyes and stutter-hump your skull," my father greeted us from the porch.

"Whoa!" Kerry Mackenzie exclaimed.

"Good afternoon, Colonel," Bobby Haber said.

"Playing pocket ball, are you?" my father asked, his usual grimace now a leering smirk.

"No, sir," Bobby said.

"What's pocket ball?" Chris Lee asked.

"Just some old Army game," I lied.

"It's when you stick your hands in your pockets and play with your balls," Kerry Mackenzie explained.

"Oh," Chris said. He looked like he wanted to throw up again.

"What's wrong with…?" Kerry asked, gesturing towards the colonel.

I shrugged.

"He was out of his chair last night," I said. "Just for a couple of minutes. We were sitting in the living room, and he suddenly got up, grabbed his cane, and started rooting around. Told us he was looking for his sidearm."

"Jesus," Bobby whispered.

"Scat monkey," my father said.

Kerry Mackenzie climbed the steps and stuck her hand out towards my father.

"Pleased to meet you, sir," Kerry said. Surely my father would approve of Kerry's warm, probably firm grip (and her Army green clothes).

"Clitoris, clitoris," my father intoned, as if he were starting a poem.

Chris Lee threw up a little on the lawn.

"Penis breath! O penis breath!" Kerry Mackenzie said.

My father scrunched his face and made like he going to sit up.

"Toe jamb jerker," he said.

"Scrotum sucker," Kerry responded.

My father reached out and shook Kerry's hand.

"He shakes hands like a girl," my father said, gesturing towards me.

I coughed. "We should go 'round back and see—"

"And just leave your dad here?" Kerry asked.

"Life Lesson No. 6," Bobby Haber said. " 'If it's already broken, it's already broken.' "

We sucked in our collective breath. Kerry Mackenzie stood on her tippy-toes to meet Bobby nose to nose. Bobby said later that even her breath smelled sort of familiar.

"No," Kerry said. "Life Lesson No. 6: 'It ain't broken; it's just you in a thousand pieces.' " She smiled and gave Bobby the briefest of Eskimo kisses. "*Memento mori*: remember you are mortal."

"Bruce!" my mother yelled from the backyard.

"Let's go," Bobby said, grinning. "Could get ugly."

"Who's Bruce?" Kerry asked as we hopped over the side of the porch and ran up the driveway.

"Our dog," I said.

"And what's happening?"

"More than likely he's pooping in the Nazis' yard," I answered.

My mom stood in the middle of our backyard wielding a broom. Mr. Federov was on his back porch next door brandishing what looked like a BB rifle made for toddlers.

"I will shoot this dog," Mr. Federov said, except that he had an eastern European accent, so it came out like, "I vill shoot zis dog." My mom said that Mr. Federov was a former Nazi in hiding. (He and his wife were Lithuanian really.) We thought he was just plain scary. When we were younger, the Federovs had two poodles, both dirty white, and if a ball landed in their yard, Mr. Federov released the poodles. One bit Tim-Tim on the finger, but my mom said he didn't need any stitches. Tim-Tim cried harder in front of my mom than in front of us, and my mom held his head to her bosom. When she started to pull away, Tim-Tim cried even harder, and we left the room. When Tim-Tim joined us again in the backyard, his boner pushed at his shorts. (We had just discovered boners and did not know their significance.) The dirty poodles expired during the summer before our final year in Resurrection of Our Lord Elementary School; my mother claimed their sudden disappearance, one after the other, was the result of a Nazi basement experiment gone awry.

Our dog's name was Bruce. He was a mutt, covered in curly tufts of coarse, black hair with odd-colored brown patches, part Chesapeake Bay retriever we were told (although he rarely retrieved), part something else—Affenpinscher probably—he was kind of small, nowhere near as big as a Chessie. (Chris Lee said that Bruce was part German shepherd; Chris was afraid of dogs—especially German shepherds.). The wooden fence separating our yard from the Federovs' was ancient, but my mom said that there was no good reason to repair or replace it now that I was older, and besides, she didn't know whose responsibility it would be, hers or our neighbors, since the fence had been there when she and the colonel moved in. Last year, Mr. Federov threatened my mother with legal action if she didn't mend the large hole near the back of the fence. (Apparently, it *was* our fence.) My mom ignored Mr. Federov. And no matter what Mr. Federov did to cover the hole, Bruce found a way to break through, like the time our (supposedly) Nazi neighbor put plywood against the opening and then placed cement blocks against the plywood. Like a prisoner with a spoon, Bruce nudged at the plywood a little every day—my mom once had to remove a splinter from his nose—until he created a passage. Bruce never did any damage to Mr. Federov's yard or to what he called his garden, which was really just a small patch of tomatoes on the far side of the property; likewise, our dog ignored the plants and flowering shrubs that surrounded the Federovs' back porch and the ivy covered trellises on either side of it. Maybe Bruce peed now and again but mostly he sniffed around and lazed in the sun. (We had a dilapidated shed that gave our yard plenty of shade.) The only times Bruce actually *did* anything in the Federovs' yard was when Mr. Federov would charge out of his house waving a broom. (One time he even appeared with a shovel.) Then Bruce would shit—literally. You've heard the phrase, "Scared the shit out of someone?" Mr. Federov scared the shit out of Bruce. It was like Bruce couldn't move anything except his bowels. Mr. Federov would rush out of his backdoor, broom in hand, and Bruce would sit up, squat, and bear down. Mr. Federov would circle Bruce with the broom, but Bruce would try to waddle out of range, still pooping.

And that was exactly what Bruce was doing as Mr. Federov threatened him with a miniature BB gun: waddling and pooping.

"If your dog does not stop the shitting," Mr. Federov yelled, "I will shoot him, and I will be within my rights."

"The boys'll clean the poop up," my mom said. "They always do."

Bruce whimpered, waddled closer to the fence, and farted.

Mr. Federov raised the BB gun.

"I will do it!"

"It was a fart, for God's sake," my mom said.

Bobby Haber inched closer to the fence. "Please, Mr. Federov."

"If he urinates or makes more little shitting, I will shoot him in the balls!" Mr. Federov yelled, and the little BB gun rose up to his sightline.

I wondered if it was worth mentioning that Bruce was no longer in possession of his balls.

"We should do something," Chris Lee whined.

Then it happened.

Kerry Mackenzie hopped the fence, yanked down her olive drab waders, and peed on Mr. Federov's lawn.

My mom coolly lit a cigarette, and Bobby Haber snatched Bruce through the hole in the fence. Mr. Federov lowered his BB rifle, walked back into his house, and slammed the door.

Kerry finished peeing but remained squatting.

"Go in and get her some t.p.," my mom said, and we all ran in to free the roll from the holder in the downstairs powder room. We tossed it to my mom from the back porch.

We should have turned our heads. Wiping should be a private act, but we couldn't look away. Kerry Mackenzie swiped at her herself twice, waved at us with the damp toilet paper, and hopped back over the fence once she zipped her pants. She'd left the soiled bathroom tissue behind.

And what was the first thing my mom said when Kerry walked into the kitchen?

"You have a snaggletooth," my mother said. Chris Lee sat down hard on a kitchen chair. Bobby took my mom's glass of beer and downed it.

"You want to touch it?" Kerry Mackenzie asked my mother and she did. Without reservation, she ran her finger down the errant tooth. We all touched it again. Kerry told us that flaws weren't bad things. She told us that there were only so many face types out there, and what separated one from the other were what ignorant people called flaws. Life Lesson No. 7.

"White people say black people all look alike. Black people say Chinese people all look alike," Kerry Mackenzie told us, and my mom nodded.

"But we *all* look alike. I can go out right now and find your face," Kerry said to Bobby. "The cheek bones and the strong cleft chin and the ears that stick out a little—I bet I could find three or four people with your face type in Rhawnhurst alone."

Bobby Haber covered his ears with his hands. Kerry lowered them with hers.

"No, Bobby," she said. "That's your flaw. That's what makes you *you*."

We could all smell her sharp scent of Jean Naté and sweat. We were familiar with her brand of after bath splash because my mother used it—but only when she was feeling "frisky," she'd told us. I was still a little jealous over the Eskimo kiss. Was Kerry feeling frisky towards Bobby? I could tell from Chris and Tim-Tim's faces that they were thinking the same thing. We had never even considered that she would actually pick one of us; we didn't feel that we were in competition. Picking Bobby made sense, but, boy, were our instincts off.

"It's all right there," Kerry said. "Life Lesson No. 8: 'What makes you unique is as clear as the nose on your face.'"

"A sweater girl," my mom pronounced, both her hands on her hips, her head nodding in approval. "A real sweater girl."

Kerry fished a pack of cigarettes from her pocket. Chris' eyes grew wide.

"Mom, this is Kerry Mackenzie," I said, somehow proud—of what I wasn't sure. Proud that the girl we all had a crush on had just urinated in my neighbor's yard? My unexplainable pride would continue to confound me.

"Leigh Silver," my mom said, lighting Kerry's cigarette.

"Leigh," Kerry said (and we all gasped at Kerry's instant familiarity), "fine brood you got here."

My mom laughed.

"They're not *all* mine," she said, "but they might as well be."

"I know *exactly* what you mean," Kerry Mackenzie said.

Chris Lee stole a cigarette from her pack and one from my mom's too—not to smoke, God forbid, but to collect.

"He collects what he can't do," Bobby told us once. "And he also collects everything else."

The rest of the week in school was glorious. Kerry Mackenzie hung out with us every day at lunch, and we walked her home after school—sort of. Kerry wouldn't let us walk her *all* the way home—just to the corner of her street. We respected her too much to follow. It wasn't a nice part of town.

Hanging out on the hill by the library, we were in contact with the Hoskins High hippie crowd. If it was raining, they'd be down by the gazebo behind the school, but if the weather was sunny, they'd be crouched behind our hill. It was a risk, to be sure, but no one expected the hippies to be near the library. And to tell the truth, they weren't smoking pot *all* the time—mostly just cigarettes. Although the school had strict rules about smoking—it was a senior privilege and was only allowed in a designated area—the faculty rarely went looking for violators. In spite of being a Roman Catholic institution, the administration could often be lax; the changes implemented in the late '60s as a result of Vatican II still had the elderly pastor and the equally ancient headmaster in states of agitation. The hippies, however, seemed unaware of Church politics; they were a somewhat insular crowd. But whenever Kerry would join us, they all knew her name and she knew all of theirs.

Although we thought of the little hill as ours, plenty of kids congregated on the library lawn, some even on our hill, studying or just checking out the opposite sex. When it was *really* nice out, the lawn was crawling with students, and the air was filled with Frisbees. Kerry said hi to everyone, and because she palled around with us, we became minor celebrities. By the end of the week, kids who'd never even looked in our direction for anything other than answers to a test or a spare pen, waved or stopped by the hill to bitch about a teacher or a test. Only the Bod Squad continued to ignore us completely. (Tim-Tim said they were jealous because Kerry was pretty like a meadow or a sunset, and they were pretty like models in magazines that had been left out in the sun.) So it was no surprise when Johnny Fingers eventually stopped by our hill.

The change in Kerry was palpable—it was as if her body temperature shot up ten degrees. Her face and neck were flushed. Bobby said later he was surprised the entire lawn population couldn't smell the strong scent that rose above the Jean Naté and exited her body in waves.

"Kerry Mackenzie," she said, taking Johnny's outstretched fingers.

"Johnny," he replied. "Johnny Ewell. Everyone 'round here calls me Johnny Fingers."

He released Kerry's hand and wiggled his long fingers in the air. Tim-Tim slumped to the ground. Johnny Fingers looked unfazed.

"What are you doing tonight?" he asked, squinting towards the library. We were stunned. He said he wouldn't, but here he was, asking Kerry out right in front of us—at least that was what we thought he was doing.

"I had a date with Chrissie, but she flunked the Civil War exam— grounded," Johnny Fingers explained. "Brainiac didn't know Jefferson Davis from Thomas Jefferson, so I'm flying solo—on a Friday night."

"We're just hanging out with Leigh," Kerry said, gesturing towards our dejected little group. "Just an intimate little party. Want to join us?"

Johnny Fingers didn't drop his squint, but his mouth twitched as if he was fighting a smile.

"Leigh?" he asked. "As in…?"

"My mom," I said quietly.

Johnny broke his squint.

"Hell, yeah. Your mom has the nicest…sorry."

"It's okay," I said, but I didn't know why. Johnny was a friend but not like Tim-Tim was.

"Life Lesson No. 9: 'A boob is a boob is a boob,' " Kerry Mackenzie said. "*Carpe diem*: seize the day."

Confusion clouded Johnny's face but only for a second. "Yeah, okay…no matter. What time? You guys want some beer or wine or whatever?"

And that was how Johnny Fingers came to be at our house that night.

On my back porch with Robert R. Haber, Esq., the damp summer heat soaking our brows and shirts, we theorized about Johnny's culpability in the events that followed the meeting on the hill.

"He was the catalyst," I argued. "Without Johnny Fingers, none of it would have happened."

Robert spit over the railing.

"That's bullshit and you know it," he said. "We all wanted Kerry. Johnny didn't. He was true to his word."

"Yeah, but—"

"Your mom was an adult. While it may have been poor judgment…"

"And illegal," I said.

"…and possibly crossing the line *if* something had happened, nothing really did as far as we know. Johnny wasn't some little kid anyway. Worst she would have been guilty of probably was corruption of a minor if he'd been our age. But Johnny was eighteen, if I'm not mistaken, so age wouldn't have been an issue. He'd been left back like, what, two, three times?"

"More like four," I lied and kicked at a beer tab. I was certain Robert knew the exact number. Attorneys don't ask questions unless they already know the answers. "Your point?"

"He wasn't dumb," Robert said. "He just didn't care about anything except girls."

"You track him down too?" I asked, half hoping the answer was no. I blamed Johnny Fingers for much of what happened, but I knew, behind my growing beer buzz, that we were all guilty. We had broken Kerry Mackenzie's Life Lesson No. 10.

" 'Hard to walk a straight line if your eyes are closed,' " Robert said.

"Yeah, but we were drinking and we didn't know how to drink, and Kerry—"

"No 'yeah but.' We should have seen it coming—with Chris, I mean. All the throwing up," Robert R. Haber said. "That wasn't from the drinking. His parents—"

"There was a lot on our minds," I said.

My best friend belched in agreement, and we sat in silence afterwards, listening to the crickets and the katydids, watching the lightning bugs and the moths.

When I said that there was a lot on our minds, I was referring to my father—my father *and* Chris Lee. Kerry too, but she was more of a puzzle than a problem. My dad was a problem. Chris was a mess.

The day of Kerry's first appearance at my house—the day of the BB gun and the pee—also turned out to be the start of one of my father's "well" periods.

"I feel fucking great," the colonel announced to my mother, Bobby Haber, and I that night in the kitchen, the wheelchair abandoned on the porch. "Leigh? A shot and a beer please."

We were grateful Kerry had gone home, though we knew we'd end up telling her of the ensuing events anyway. She was that kind of girl. Besides, there was a good chance she'd see plenty over the next week or two.

My mother clapped her hands at my father's request as if she didn't know that this would turn out just like all the other times, and her smile made her look like the woman in the faded wedding photographs she kept in a book stored in the end table cabinet. There wasn't any point in Bobby and I trying to talk her out of it; there never was. The drinks were on the table before my father even sat down—and when he did, my mother perched herself on his lap, and Bobby and I slipped out to the backyard and watched Bruce sniff the patch of grass in the Federovs' yard where earlier Kerry Mackenzie had peed. When we looked back to the house, we could see my mother turn towards the twin windows over the sink, and before she closed the plantation shutters and lowered the wooden blinds, we watched the wedding photograph smile dissolve into a tired and bitter one. The charade was already wearing thin.

Chris Lee was another story. His parents had just announced, two days before, that he'd be spending a large chunk of the summer at the Miracle Christian Summer Camp for Boys. Chris' response was to throw up more often than usual. When he left my house that day to go home for dinner, he stopped at the end of the driveway to vomit, but nothing came up but a thin, red gruel.

We finally confided in Kerry on the little hill while Chris took an exam after school. (He had upchucked during class and missed the test.)

"Life Lesson No. 11," she said. " 'Once in a while, the underdog wins.' "

I exploded.

"Where do you get off? I mean, just where do you get off?" I screamed. "Do you even know what's going on with this kid? Do you know what's going on with my mom? Do you know *anything*? Where did you come from? Where did you learn these *Life* Lessons? From the back of a cereal box? Where do you fucking get off?"

When I finished screaming, I cried and apologized, and when the tears subsided, Tim-Tim bought me a soda, and Bobby and Kerry took turns rubbing my shoulders. At one point I could feel Kerry's boobs against my back; I wasn't completely sure—I'm not even now—that she wasn't doing it on purpose.

So we were dealing with a full slate of situations. My father's drinking had progressed faster than usual. He'd finished off whatever bourbon was in the house, and my mother refused to buy more. By Friday morning he was back in the wheelchair on the front porch. It had been a mercifully short "well" period, although things had escalated quickly. Just the night before, he had stomped around the house, shit-faced, taking my mother's dresses one by one down to the kitchen and burning them in the sink. "You're a fucking *sweater* girl, goddamn it," the colonel yelled. My mother called him "sir" to placate him as she doused the flames, her hair plastered to her forehead. Then he tried to hide Bruce's food and water bowls inside the powder room toilet. But when I got up for school, he had returned to the wheelchair (on his own, my mother told me). The next day or two, we knew, would be crucial: he could have already exhausted himself (he'd been limping something fierce the night before) or he could be recharging his corroded batteries for one last assault on the household.

And to top it off, the cherry on the sundae, the nut in the poop, as Tim-Tim used to say, was the impending arrival, that night, of Johnny Fingers to our get-together. Despite his seemingly sincere assurances, we were convinced Johnny would get beneath Kerry Mackenzie's sweater, metaphorically or otherwise.

"I've never actually seen her wear a sweater," Chris Lee said. He had yet to throw up this particular Friday (or at least we hadn't witnessed it).

"I don't think a sweater has anything to with it," I said.

"But last night your dad said—"

I didn't have a response, but Bobby Haber did.

"I don't think the colonel remembers what a sweater girl is anymore," he said.

My father, still in his chair on the front porch, was oddly silent— no invective screaming, no stringing together of curse words for those wandering down our street. While lighting a cigarette for my mom a year or so before, Bobby had asked her, in a grown-up and matter-of-fact tone of voice, what my father's diagnosis was. My mother had no answer for the future attorney. When he was "well," my father seemed to walk fairly fine at first with only a slight limp. Towards the end of a bourbon-soaked cycle, he'd be bent to one side, sometimes lurching like Frankenstein's monster and frequently bumping his head into walls as his faltering walk became a stagger under the influence. He'd become incontinent and moderately paraphasic and would often have trouble with his vision.

Neither my mother nor any of us knew what this early retreat to the wheelchair signaled. Was it an end to the revelry of late or just a respite before continuing battle on the state of the household? But tonight's success hinged on my father's behavior. Even Bruce was unusually nervous. When my mother tripped going up the stairs with the laundry, our dog mistook the sound for the coming of the colonel and peed in the kitchen in front of all of us.

"Portentous," Robert said some twenty years later on my back porch.

"Pass me another beer, please" I said.

Kerry arrived first. She had a laundry bag tossed over her shoulder.

"In case I stay over," she said, and we all nodded and commented on the marvel of her thought process in loud voices. We stayed over each other's houses all the time without bringing so much as a toothbrush. My mom kept one for each of the boys in the hall closet. But we'd never had a girl stay over.

Bobby kicked my leg.

"Where's she gonna sleep?" he whispered.

I shrugged.

"Kitchen smells like pee," Kerry commented.

"I didn't do it," Chris said in a high voice.

"Bruce," I explained. "He thought he heard my dad. He doesn't like Bruce much. He calls him Becky and once stuck him in a sack because 'he's as useless as a bag of—' "

"Brucie," Kerry said in a baby voice that somehow managed to sound titillating to us.

Bruce bounced over to Kerry at the sound of his name.

"The colonel's back on the front porch, I see," Kerry said as we watched her rub Bruce's belly then reach down briefly to gently cup his tiny penis.

"We don't know what's going on…" Bobby Haber said.

"My mouth went so dry," Robert R. Haber told me.

"…with the colonel," Bobby finished.

Kerry stashed her bag in the corner. (Bruce sniffed it and rubbed up against it, acting out our most secret desires.) She rolled up the sleeves of yet another ill-fitting t-shirt with a stretched neck (black this time) and placed an open box of cookies on the table. Tim-Tim looked around and seeing no opposition, began gobbling. Chris waited until he thought no one was looking and pocketed a macaroon.

"What do you think is in the bag?" Bobby whispered to me. "And don't shrug."

I didn't.

"So, what's first?" she asked as she rolled up the cuffs of her jeans.

We all looked at one another. We'd been so preoccupied, dreading the imminent arrival of Johnny Fingers and the possible reanimation of the colonel that we hadn't even thought of what we'd do when Kerry appeared.

"Parcheesi?" Tim-Tim offered. Tim-Tim loved to play games—all kinds: cards, board games, checkers, chess. There were too many kids in his family for him to be included in every game. With us, he was always included.

"Wiffle ball?" Bobby asked. "There's still a little light left."

"Risk," I suggested. We had a monotonous summer of little league coming soon. I didn't want to spend extra time playing any variation on baseball.

"Monopoly," Tim-Tim mumbled through a mouthful of cookie.

"Poker," Bobby proposed.

"No gambling," Chris Lee reminded us.

"Strip poker?" Johnny Fingers asked, lifting up two six packs of beer, and we all jumped; no one had heard him come in. Johnny's t-shirt was so white, it looked fake. All his wiry muscles were perfectly framed. Even his hair looked slightly longer than usual. He wore a puka shell choker, the pukas also unnaturally white. Between his jet-black hair and the puka shells and t-shirt, Johnny Fingers' skin glowed. Bobby and I agreed later: we both saw Kerry Mackenzie blush.

"No stripping," my mother said as she walked into the kitchen. She had a stack of pizza menus in her hand.

"Leigh," Johnny Fingers said, placing the beer on the table like an offering and bowing slightly. "Couple of the Fields boys helped me out with the malt and hops," he explained. "I hope you don't mind." Although his eyes were looking right at my mother's face, it was like he was somehow staring at her chest at the same time. My mother wore a tight, light purple sweater with no sleeves.

"Been workin' out, Leigh?" Johnny asked, squeezing my mother's bicep. My mother blushed like Kerry had and so did we. Here again: immediate familiarity.

"Hitting the books, Johnny?" my mother asked back.

"Indubitably," Johnny answered.

My mother laughed a silvery laugh, and we looked at one another: just what was happening here?

"Help yourself to the beer, boys."

Bobby pulled Johnny aside. "Let's keep Chris to one bottle, okay?"

"Yeah, sure. You gotta take care of your boy."

"Do you know Kerry, Johnny?" my mother asked. "Kerry Mackenzie?"

Johnny bowed again.

"The only sliver of civility in this irascible bunch," he said.

Kerry grabbed his long fingers with what we knew was a warm, moist palm.

What felt like a lifetime later, Robert R. Haber, attorney-at-law, declared, "There's no way he knew what those words meant. 'Indubitably.' 'Irascible.' "

I suddenly thought of Jefferson Davis. Was Robert testing my memory? If so, I didn't appreciate it.

"But you said he wasn't a complete dummy."

"True. But he only used his intelligence when it came to girls. So he had to have studied before he came over that night. At least the words that began with 'I'."

It was late and we'd drunk most of the beer—the good brands anyway.

"He wanted your mom to think he was as smart as we were," Robert said, "but she already did."

"Whatever happened to Johnny Fingers?" I asked, but the piercing notes of the katydids and the car alarm songs of the mockingbirds were so intense, I didn't hear the answer if there was one. I started thinking about my father's hoagie.

My mom and Kerry had written down everyone's hoagie order. They even ordered one for my father, but he didn't eat it. A recent Ukrainian immigrant who lived on the other side of the street found it in his mailbox upon his return from vacation. How he knew to bring the moldy, soggy hoagie back to our house only served to underscore the terrible events of that Friday night. We were already dressed for the funeral, my mother and I, when the sandwich was returned. (Thank God for language barriers!) The service at Resurrection was the last time I saw Bobby, Tim-Tim, and Chris at the same time, although we didn't speak. Bobby nodded at me once, and I nodded back, but that was it. Kerry Mackenzie was gone. She never returned to school. We weren't even sure which house was hers, so no one knocked for her. Besides—without the group, even a small investigation like finding Kerry's house was too much to handle for any one of us. We were nothing without each other.

+

Kerry was on her knees in the living room in front of the large, low cabinet. We were standing around her, nursing our beers. My mother said we could drink as long everyone stayed over.

"Look at all these albums," she said. "Does the record player work?"

"You bet your sweet behind it does," my mother said. "I've had that since the *White Album* came out. 'While My Guitar Gently Weeps.' '*I look at you all see the love there that's sleeping...*' You can't beat it with a stick. The colonel bought the stereo for me as a birthday present. Put a big bow on it and everything."

"Shouldn't we bring him in?" I asked—not that I was anxious for my father to join us, but, however submerged the man my mother had once mooned over was, he was still my father and it was getting dark.

"He's fine," my mother said, ruffling my hair. "It's nice out still."

She squatted down next to Kerry who thumbed through my mother's records.

"He's quiet tonight," Bobby Haber said.

"Sodomize this, eunuch!" my father yelled from the porch, right on cue.

"What's sodomize mean?" Tim-Tim asked.

"Look it up," my mother said. "Oooh, that's a good one, Kerry. *Jesus Christ Superstar*. Put that one on. Judas gets all the best songs—except for 'I Don't Know How to Love Him.' Only a woman could sing that song."

"Sodomize means plugging someone up the bum," Kerry said.

My mother feigned shock. "Need to let them figure out these things for themselves, hon."

"Yeah, but we don't want them sticking their little peckers in some poor girl's armpit now, do we?" Kerry responded, and we looked at our shoes, chastened and chagrined: Kerry Mackenzie had pronounced our peckers small.

Johnny Fingers popped out of the powder room.

"Someone getting sodomized?" he asked, his grin revealing his perfectly straight teeth, which were astoundingly white despite his incessant smoking.

"You if you don't graduate," my mother said to Johnny. "You're smarter than most of the class."

"The teachers don't like me," Johnny Fingers claimed, his arms outstretched like he was on a cross.

"Nuts to that," my mother said, pushing herself from the floor. "I think you just don't give a shit."

Johnny lowered his arms.

"You're right," he admitted. "I don't."

"Well, start," my mother said, brushing past him. "I gotta shake the dew off my lily pad before I have a smoke."

"I need another beer," Chris Lee said, burping. "This one's almost done."

Of course we saw how deliberately close my mother just was to Johnny Fingers as she passed him, and we noticed how Johnny's expression and body language changed. He became like a cartoon Big Bad Wolf: he licked his lips, let his mouth hang open, and slicked back his hair—he did everything but howl and pop his eyes out of his head. But mostly we watched Kerry Mackenzie watching Johnny Fingers. She was still on the floor, playing records. While Johnny composed himself and returned to his interpretation of cool, Kerry wore no mask: it's still the most direct and naked look I've ever seen one human being give to another—and the other never noticed.

Soon everyone shuffled back into the kitchen. As we arranged ourselves around the Formica tabletop, sipping our beers, we watched the dynamics unfold: my mom subtly flirting with Johnny, Johnny not-so-subtly flirting back, and Kerry Mackenzie smoking two cigarettes for every one Johnny or my mom smoked, never ignoring us, but staring so intently at Johnny's profile, that years later, on my back porch, Robert R. Haber said that at first he'd wondered if Johnny's cheek had split open. Chris' struggle with a fresh bottle of beer provided the only brief comic relief.

"I can't seem to…doesn't want to open…can anyone?…sealed like a tomb…"

Without shifting his gaze away from my mother, Johnny opened it for Chris by banging the cap against the edge of the table.

"Hey, Johnny, wanna see something?" Tim-Tim asked, and Johnny, reluctantly but not rudely, agreed. Bobby Haber pushed me back down in my seat.

"Stay here with Chris," he said.

"What are you doing?"

"We're just gonna show him the hole in the fence," Bobby whispered, but whatever the desired result of the plan—separating Kerry from Johnny or Johnny from my mother—there wasn't much I could do to further our cause with Kerry Mackenzie.

"I was young," my mother told Kerry, "too young."

"But you were in love."

"Oh, yes. Very much so. Or I was then. Or I thought I was. I forget. Sometimes I still could be. Doesn't take much. My father, oh boy, was he ever pissed off. The age difference. They had a fistfight, and the colonel…"

I couldn't believe what I was hearing. I'd never been told any of this. Suddenly, nothing mattered: not Kerry Mackenzie, not Johnny Fingers flirting with my mom, nothing.

Chris belched loudly in my ear.

"Cut it out," I said and punched his arm. Chris acted like I'd stabbed him.

"...so he made me take the test anyway, even though I'd already covered all of it at my old school," Kerry said, tapping ash from her cigarette for emphasis. "Sometimes I feel like I'm never going to learn anything new."

"They don't care, hon," my mother said, her hand on Kerry's upper arm. "All the emphasis is on making sure the school's cumulative GPA is higher than that of the school in the next parish, simply to get diocese subsidies. The parish subsidy isn't enough; they need to make the school more attractive so more parents will move into the parish and help swell the rolls. So they focus on the best and brightest to the detriment of the rest in order to win. It's just typical male bullshit, you know what I mean? The Catholic Church is run by men. It's just the celibates' way of measuring to see who's got the bigger dick."

"And whoever's got the bigger dick gets the bigger hat!"

As the two women in our lives commiserated on the state of womanhood, Chris and I nervously sat forward, laughing at all the wrong times, nodding our heads knowingly at God knows what. (Chris even smiled at the Catholic digs, which would normally have sent his stomach reeling.) But when Johnny Fingers walked back in with Bobby and Tim-Tim, he tipped his chair against the wall, placed one black boot against the back of Chris' chair, and laughed at *all* the right moments, exhaling perfect cones of gray in between. (Chris didn't mind Johnny's boot and, in fact, seemed upset when it was removed.) When it was his turn to hold the table, Johnny embarked on a recitation of a series of extremely dirty jokes. Bobby and I took turns flipping pages in the red dictionary. So much to know, we agreed later that night. My mother seemed to enjoy Johnny's routine—at least she laughed the loudest and longest, possibly purging the stress that had built up over the past few days. When Kerry and my mom decided to walk to the store to get more beer and Johnny went to use the bathroom again, Bobby Haber stood on a chair and ran his finger across the white ceiling, above where Kerry, Johnny, and my mom had been sitting and vigorously smoking.

"It looks stained alright," Bobby reported. "Two—no, three— circular gray stains."

"Those were the funniest jokes," Chris Lee said, and we all agreed even if we didn't understand every biological reference. In a phone call a decade later, Tim-Tim said that it was the only time he remembered Chris *ever* laughing at jokes. And laugh he did. Chris laughed so hard that at one point he fell off his chair. Johnny Fingers handed him another beer as Chris lay on the floor.

"I thought we agreed to go easy with..." Bobby Haber said. I was sure Bobby was going to pop Johnny in the mouth.

"He's among friends," Johnny said, cigarette dangling from his lips. "What's the problem, Haber?"

Bobby snatched Chris' beer away.

"I stole one earlier," Chris said, pulling a bottle from one of his pockets. "Souvenir. I have all your bottle caps too."

"Whatcha building there, Chris?" Johnny Fingers asked. "Museum?"

"The Shit Museum," Chris Lee answered.

None of us had ever heard Chris curse before.

No one spoke for a few minutes—except Chris. He couldn't stop talking—about anything, nothing, everything. But amid all the nonsense he spewed, it was obvious later that he alone saw the big picture; the rest of us only perceived things wallet-sized that night: "So Kerry has a crush on Johnny Fingers, we have a crush on Kerry, and Johnny thinks your mom is a sweater girl."

"You said that?" I asked Johnny. I knew my face was red. Everyone else's cheeks were too. This was not a term to be used frivolously.

"Your mom *is* a sweater girl, man," Johnny Fingers said to me, and the other guys looked away because it was my mom he was talking about. But secretly I think I was proud, although I didn't know why—maybe because someone else besides the four of us (and the colonel of old) had recognized my mother's incomparability— and so I let the moment pass without incident. When my mom and Kerry returned with the six packs, they were leaning on each other, their faces caught up in a joke. As Johnny liberated the beer, his hand brushed my mother's right breast. I wasn't the only one who saw it— Kerry did too—and even though he'd just copped a feel, the corners of my mother's mouth rose mischievously as she smiled at Johnny. (I wasn't feeling so proud now.) With a quiet sound of exasperation that no one seemed to hear but me, Kerry left for the living room and took over the record player; she would be our DJ. My mom put on shorts and gave a pair to Kerry who changed in the powder room. After making double-sure that Bobby, Tim-Tim, and Chris were staying over since they were drinking beer (she'd apparently already asked Kerry to sleep over, adding to our anxiety), my mom sat in the kitchen with Johnny Fingers and smoked and talked. Johnny rubbed two fingers on my mom's thigh.

"What records did Kerry play?" ADA Robert R. Haber asked me on my back porch. "Do you remember all of them?"

"Well, *Jesus Christ Superstar...*"

Robert sipped his beer. "Yeah, the Yvonne Elliman song—two or three times."

"It's like she was trying to communicate with us," I said, as if this were a new idea.

"That's exactly what she was doing. She was broadcasting to an audience of none. Remember how she sang along to certain parts, as if she wanted to emphasize their importance? I always thought that a couple of the lines she sang from 'I Don't Know How to Love Him,' the ones from the verse right after the bridge, were telling: *'So calm, so cool, no lover's fool / Running every show / He scares me so.'* She wasn't singing about herself, not really; she was singing about who she thought she had to be like: her mom—so in love with love that she was frightened of it but not frightened enough to avoid being the metaphorical moth that flew into the very real flame. But hindsight means never having to say you're sorry, mainly because the person you were is already in your rearview mirror. It's flight as absolution."

He squashed a mosquito on his arm.

"Okay, what other records did she play?" he asked.

I was lightheaded. It was hard to concentrate.

"Neil Young. I remember hearing Neil Young."

Robert nodded. "Yeah. Neil Young, 'The Loner' mostly. *'Nothing can free him...'* But don't forget 'Help Me' by Joni Mitchell. That song got played a lot. *I'm in trouble 'cause you're a rambler and a gambler and a sweet talking ladies man.'* Hell, remember the second verse? *I've seen some hot, hot blazes come down to smoke and ash.'* Goddamn portentous song."

He chugged his beer and finished it off.

"Did she play any Laura Nyro?" I asked.

"Nope. Hell, we're almost down to the Schlitz."

"Heart? The one with 'Magic Man?' "

"Didn't come out till '76."

"Oh. 'Sister Golden Hair' maybe."

"Wasn't released until the following summer."

I should know this. I should know Kerry's soundtrack.

My lawyer rooted around the coolers for an acceptable brand of beer. (I call Bobby my lawyer even though he works for the DA's office down in the big city.)

"I can't believe you don't remember your mom's records," he said, barely slurring even after maybe ten cans.

"I remember the old ones. There were a number by Johnny Horton—or was it Johnny Hodges? And, oh, *September of My Years* by Frank, the one with the song that went, *'It was a very good year for small town girls and—'"*

"Right, but there was one song Kerry kept playing over and over."

"Oh shit, yeah, yeah," I said, spilling a little beer on my pants.

"Remember now?"

"No, no…wait—"

" *'You walked into the party like you were walking into the sun.'* "

I jumped and spilled more beer.

"That's it, that's it. Only…only…it's *'yacht'*…*'like you were walking onto a yacht.'* "

Robert scratched his nose. "Really? Yacht?"

"Yeah, the sun part comes later: *'to see the total eclipse of the sun.'* "

"It's coming back to you. This is good. This is real good. Now remember the part of the song Kerry sang every time it came around? I'll give you a—"

" *'I had some dreams there were clouds in my coffee…'* "

" *'Clouds in my coffee.'* "

"What happened to Johnny Fingers, Bobby?" I asked my best friend.

+

Kerry played the Carly Simon record again and again, just the one song. Bobby, Tim-Tim, and I sat in my room listening.

"Something's going on," Tim-Tim said.

"It's a signal," was Bobby's opinion.

"I think I'm going to get sick," I said. Too much beer.

Bobby and Tim-Tim led me down the hall to the bathroom.

"Occupied," Chris Lee said from the other side of the door.

"You alright?" Bobby asked, quietly turning the knob.

"Fit as a fucking fiddle," Chris answered, and we looked at the cracked paint on the bathroom door for answers. Too much was going on for us to look at each other.

"That was our mistake," Robert R. Haber, fantastically wealthy lawyer, said, as I peed from my back porch into the yard. "One of them anyway."

"Seriously, Chris," Bobby said, "you okay? You can stay at my house."

"Or just crash in my room," I said, a proposition that Chris normally found exciting.

"Can you make it to the powder room?" Bobby Haber, our pack master, asked me.

"Might have passed," I said.

"Go anyway; can't hurt," Bobby suggested. "I'll go down with you...just to get some water, okay?"

Bobby lowered his voice. "Tim-Tim, stay here...in case..." He gestured towards the bathroom door. "In case Chris needs one of us for anything."

"Can you bring me back some cookies?" Tim-Tim asked.

"Sure," Bobby said. "Any special kind?"

Tim-Tim said no, and we separated. The next time the three of us would be in the same room at the same time, prior to the funeral (which was the last time we'd *all* be together), would be in my kitchen after the garage had been opened.

Kerry Mackenzie squatted on the living room floor with an array of records spread out before her. She looked pretty in my mom's shorts. They were a little tight on her. Kerry's curves were startling. When Carly finished singing "You're So Vain," Kerry lifted the arm and started it again.

"How's it goin'?" Bobby asked her. "He's not feeling too good," he said, jerking his thumb towards me.

Kerry started to shrug but instead graced me with a compassionate look, one I've recalled a thousand times as stars dead a thousand years refused to shut out their lights and die behind my closed eyes.

"Bad luck," Bobby said. "Lightweight."

"Life Lesson No. 12," Kerry Mackenzie said. " 'There's no such thing as bad luck or good luck—only lies and truth.' "

"Well, a skunked beer'll tip the scale," Bobby said—but tip it how, I wasn't sure. Kerry went back to reading lyric sheets. I made my way towards the powder room. From the kitchen, I heard my mother laugh at a joke that I knew couldn't have been nearly as funny as her laughter made it seem. I imagined Johnny's fingers tracing tiny circles on my mom's thigh.

"I only took my eyes off Kerry for a second, a minute," Mr. Haber testified. "Just to let Bruce out."

Kerry's underwear had been tossed in a corner of the powder room along with a pair of jeans with the cuffs rolled up. I had no idea why Kerry had taken off her underwear, and my mind could barely handle imagining her squatting in our living room without them. The underwear was off-white—not at all the color I expected. Light purple, baby blue maybe. Off-white was too—I'm not sure—too *true*. If Kerry Mackenzie was a color, she'd be off-white, slightly flawed (as had become obvious). I sat on the toilet, contemplating the abandoned undergarment, my nausea long since passed.

I wondered what they felt like. I'd never touched a pair of women's underwear—not even in a store at the mall, not even my mom's in the laundry. I wondered what they'd smell like. It was a consideration that caused my nostrils to flood with Kerry's intoxicating aroma of strong, liberally applied bath products and even stronger sweat.

My father, when I was very young, only told me one thing about sweater girls: "They fill up every little thing," and here I was, sitting on the toilet in the powder room, staring at Kerry Mackenzie's off-white underwear, which appeared far too big for her to fill (having no understanding of female hips). Until tonight, my father's words had done little to aid us in our understanding of what being a sweater girl meant. (The very phrase—*sweater girl*—had taken on a mythic quality, due perhaps to the overstimulated imagination of four pubescent boys, or simply because the idea seemed to be one of those adult mysteries that if solved, would bring us one step closer to maturity.) It was upon the toilet that I began to comprehend the colonel's enigmatic utterance, but as I was already brimming with Kerry, I longed to fill her up with the stars that Bobby had talked about, the stars whose sudden pulsating presence had given to rise to my tumescence.

"I went into the kitchen to grab some cookies for Tim-Tim, but I would have gone in anyway. I was curious what your mom and Johnny were laughing about. Kerry was still fiddling with the records in the living room." Robert squinted into the darkness that surrounded my porch. "Johnny was all over your mom—I mean, they weren't, like, *doing* anything, but it was obvious I'd interrupted *something*. Johnny's face was buried in your mom's neck, and when I walked into the kitchen, he looked up, a little embarrassed maybe, but very little. He was just grinning ear to ear. Your mom looked drunk. She wasn't slurring or anything like that, but her eyes weren't in the same room with her smile, if you know what I mean."

I nodded and rubbed my arms.

Even in the summer, it can get a little chilly in Rhawnhurst late at night when the wind comes off the creek and through the woods, but if I went in to get a sweatshirt, Robert might take it as a signal for him to leave, and I needed to reach the end of the story. I needed to find out what happened to Johnny Fingers and Kerry Mackenzie and my mom and my dad. I needed to hear the story again. There was a chance I wouldn't see Robert for another year or more. (I don't actually know how often he visits.) Maybe one time the story would stay stuck in my head; maybe one day, it wouldn't give my medial temporal cortex the slip or hide behind inconsequential memories— inconsequential because although I could remember my father's ingenious profanity and the color of Kerry's underwear and every single place where Chris Lee threw up, I couldn't remember my mother's face. I could only imagine it from what I've been told by Robert or from what shards have lodged themselves in my hippocampi. I needed to remember the *whole* story, and, more than anything, I needed to see my mother's face in my mind's eye.

"Your mom asked me, 'Let Bruce outside, will ya, Bobby?' and I said, 'Sure, okay,' " Robert told me, not shivering the slightest in the late night breeze, his face not registering the gaseous smell of the Puddle as it infiltrated our clothes and our hair. But there was a slight hitch in his voice when he said, "Kerry wasn't alone more than a couple of minutes maybe."

In the powder room, sitting on the toilet, my pants around my ankles, Kerry Mackenzie's off-white underwear and blue jeans in the corner, I envisioned a little cartoon angel and a cartoon devil on either shoulder, each arguing the relevance of their message above my throbbing middle—only the angel had Bobby Haber's voice and the devil had Johnny Fingers'. I would have heard the rumpus in the hall but for the cartoon voices, which soon changed along with their images. The devil was now an old drunk in a wheelchair with an encyclopedic knowledge of the carnal, and the angel transformed into

Mrs. Lee with her round, pockmarked, almost Asian face, her eyebrows arched as if, somehow beyond the teetering confines of the Lee household, she'd experienced a world outside the Church and knew, just fucking knew, the evils awaiting young boys who dared to consort with wanton women like Mrs. Leigh Silver, tramps-in-training like Kerry Mackenzie or gigolos like Johnny Fingers.

The powder room door burst open like someone had used an M-80. My mother's legs were wrapped around Johnny's hips, his fingers buried in the flesh of my mother's thighs.

And Kerry Mackenzie's off-white underwear…

"You had it around your…?" Robert R. Haber asked.

"Yeah," I answered.

"Did you…?" he continued.

"Right as the door came in," I confessed.

"Jesus," Robert said.

"First time, right?" my lawyer asked.

"Yeah," I admitted, but I was starting to suspect that he knew all of this already; the conversation seemed familiar.

"Explains a lot," my old best friend said, looking around the small back porch.

"I like living alone," I said, swatting at a bug.

"And how long have you been living the solitary life?" Robert asked rhetorically.

"I'm okay," I said.

"You're okay still being a virgin in your thirties? You're okay being celibate?"

"I'm alright." His questions were making me squirm, but it was all true.

"You're still waiting for her," he said.

"Waiting for…?"

"Either one," Robert said. "Either one."

We stopped talking for a while, but the natural noise level in my little backyard seemed to rise in volume until it was impossible not to talk. I don't think either of us could stand another second listening to the sounds of summer.

"Now it's your turn to answer some questions," I said.

"Soon."

+

My mother gasped (in surprise, not horror), and I finished in Kerry Mackenzie's off-white underwear.

"Christ," Johnny Fingers said as he lowered my mother. "She's gonna be pissed."

"I didn't...I'm not...is this Kerry's?...I didn't..."

My mother fumbled with her bra beneath her shirt and patted her hair. Johnny Fingers looked more upset than she did as he too adjusted himself. I didn't move. Kerry Mackenzie's underwear lay crumpled and stained in my lap.

"Light a match," my mother said as if I hadn't been doing what I was doing. She placed her palm on Johnny Fingers' cheek, and it looked like it could go either way. "Two matches," Johnny said as he winked at me, "one for each Kleenex"—and right there, in the last snap of innocent air, it was like none of it mattered: Johnny Fingers trying to romance my mother, a jealous Kerry sending messages by playing the same records over and over, Chris Lee throwing up in the second floor bathroom.

Then Kerry Mackenzie screamed and we all went to hell.

Robert R. Haber walked inside to use the bathroom, and the chirping of the crickets, the Morse code of the katydids, the peeps and croaks of the toads, and the hoots of the owls crowded the space on the porch where he'd been. I stared straight ahead. I knew if I looked in any other direction, I'd break the spell. I'd notice the spider web glistening alongside the old milk box. I'd realize that the shadow in the corner was an abandoned beehive. I'd see yellow embers blink once, twice, before scurrying into the underbrush.

My best friend settled himself back into one of the green wooden chairs left behind by the previous owners. Beneath the flaking paint was a knotty, warped wood. It seemed like the porch was always littered with little green paint chips.

"When did Bruce die?" Robert asked.

"A year or two later—you were there," I said. "You helped dig the grave."

"Yeah, but I didn't remember whether that happened just last year or after the fire. The funny thing is I know I'll forget what you just said, and I'll have to ask again. Damndest thing."

He was teasing me, testing me.

"Bobby—"

"Bruce was a good dog," he continued. "A bit mangy, but a good dog."

"Bobby, it's your—"

"I was always jealous that you had Bruce; I always wanted a dog. But I guess I had one: Bruce. I didn't realize then that you didn't need to own a dog in order for it to be yours too, that you didn't need to keep someone in order for them to become a part of you." Robert sighed. "You weren't the only...we all did."

He studied his palms and played with his wedding band.

"That night, your mom told me to let Bruce outside, so I did, and when I opened the door, he scampered out. I turned back around, and your mom and Johnny Fingers were gone. So I grabbed some cookies for Tim-Tim."

"But you never gave him the cookies," I said.

"No, I didn't," Robert admitted, and I had to admire his timing. He'd gotten so much better at this since the first time we'd done it. But then as a whip-poor-will began its repetitive song, abruptly punctuated by the frightening tremulous, whiny trill of a screech owl, I wasn't so sure: was this the first time and the others just in my head? I pressed on, playing (what I thought) was my part.

"You never even went back upstairs?" I asked, as if he were on the stand.

"No, I never went back upstairs."

"And why was that?"

"It was completely dark out by then, and I remembered that your dad was still on the porch."

"And where was Kerry?"

Robert coughed. "She was on the porch too."

"On the porch?" I asked.

"The front door was open, and she wasn't in the living room and both bathrooms were occupied. At the time, I assumed she'd thought the same thing I did, and she'd gone out to bring the colonel in."

"Kerry Mackenzie was on the front porch?"

"Not exactly *on* the porch," Robert said. "Not by the time I got there."

"Not *exactly*?" I asked. "And where was she?"

"She was...you were there...she was..."

Kerry Mackenzie was on the front lawn, and my father was on top of her. His wheelchair was turned around and on its side, facing the front door, at the bottom of the porch steps. I'd escaped the powder room and had just joined Bobby on the porch. I froze when I saw the figures on the lawn. Bobby must have froze at first too, but when it was my turn to be in shock, he went into motion, sprinting down the steps and tackling my old man. Bobby pinned him easily but seemed unsure of what to do next. My father screamed like I imagined a horse with a broken leg would: high-pitched, pathetic, mindless. Two neighbors pulled Bobby off. The entire neighborhood, it seemed, poured from their homes to watch. Everyone except the Federovs. Their porch light had been on when I came out, but when I regained my senses and looked over during the fracas, it was off.

Tim-Tim was there, and he found an half-empty fifth of Jim Beam near the wheelchair; half of the label was torn off. Kerry couldn't have bought the bourbon, and she and my mother had come back with only beer which couldn't be bought at the State Store. Robert R. Haber and I agreed that had we thought to look in the bushes out front, we'd have found a receipt from the liquor store, which would have told us that the purchase had been made that very night, most likely after the hoagies had been delivered, when those inside the house had been preoccupied with the drama of a confusing love triangle (or was it a love heptagon?). And if we hadn't been so consumed by the goings-on, we would have realized that, with the exception of bringing him his sandwich, no one had checked on my father since God knows when—not even to see if he needed to use the bathroom.

My mom appeared on the porch with Johnny Fingers, her hair all mussed up, and if I could describe the look on Kerry Mackenzie's face, if I could describe the look on my mother's face, I wouldn't have to keep writing this down every couple of years—but I can't. They'd bonded, my mother and Kerry Mackenzie. My mom had found a female companion and confidant; Kerry had found an adult who listened.

"I wonder if things would have been different," Robert said, "if she'd had someone at home who listened to her instead of someone whose idea of parenting was to make up Life Lessons that shouldn't concern a young girl. What if she'd had a mother who didn't treat her like an adult, one who didn't cling to her daughter after every messy breakup, then dismiss her when she's in the way with a pat on the fanny to push her out the door—maybe even letting the latest deadbeat beau have the patting privilege?"

"*We* listened to her," I responded, forgetting what he'd said about Kerry's unheard broadcast. "Besides, that's a lot of conjecture, counselor."

Robert ignored me, and I had to agree with what he wasn't saying out loud this time: we ignored Kerry Mackenzie too in our own way. We didn't even know she was trying to communicate with us, with my mom, with Johnny Fingers, through her song selections. We were too consumed with ourselves and on what we projected on Kerry and the other participants. We heard the songs but never gave a thought to what they might mean to our DJ. We wanted to fill her up with stars, but we never worked out whether or not she wanted or even needed our celestial bodies.

I didn't see Kerry Mackenzie again until maybe twelve years after the incident and the fire, when I had traveled west during the summer to outrace the smell of smoke that had permeated not only my clothes and my hair but every classroom I'd taught in, and every cheap motel I'd left before my professional companion arrived. I'd smell it drifting from the décolletage of women I'd take out only once. It wafted from the wildflowers near my mother's grave like the scent of an old woman, which my mother had most definitely not been when she died shortly after I graduated high school. Robert said my mother had taken on too much; she'd been too full. I think the opposite: I think she had given all she had and there was nothing left with which to fill herself; not even the love of her only child could occupy the empty spaces where her late husband had once strutted, then shambled, where her hopes had withered as her one true love, who'd been a giant in her young eyes, dwindled in a wheelchair, frequently soiled himself, and often only communicated with inventive profanity when things were normal or through bourbon fumes when things were not. Cancer was the only thing left to take her hopes' place, and it did so rapidly until, right before the end, the sweater girl, after endless chemotherapy cycles, underwent a double mastectomy. But she was too full of poison now despite being robbed of what Tim-Tim had called the best breasts he'd ever seen without actually having seen them, and she spent her last days in a hospital bed, seemingly only attached to the world she knew by plastic tubes and a continually beeping machine. "Throw out the sweaters. All of them," were her very last words to me (or the last ones that made any sense). But I am a bad son, for they are packed away in my attic. Their indentations and the lingering perfume that clung to the fabric is all that is left of our original sweater girl.

But there was more than one.

Kerry Mackenzie stood looking at the jukebox, taking her time with her selection. I wasn't sure it was her at first—I was used to thinking I saw Kerry just about everywhere. I'd never realized that what we mark as unique is usually just quite ordinary—just a little left of center perhaps, skewed to taste. It's our perspective that is unique. Like Kerry had told us: we see what we're looking for—if we're actually looking. Most of the time we're watching. And both pale to doing. A Life Lesson for sure—maybe the elusive Life Lesson No. 13.

But it was her. The bar was filling up with blue collar guys just getting off shift and a contingent from the cubicle state: men in suit jackets with their ties pulled down and women in skirts and sneakers. The light in the bar was dim, and the crowd was noisy. The jukebox was loud too. When the song that was playing ended, there was a brief pause before Carly Simon's self-absorbed ex-lover walked into a party like he walking onto a yacht.

"I haven't heard this song in a long time," I said to Kerry Mackenzie's back.

"You could borrow your mom's record," she said without turning around.

"She died," I said, and I thought I Kerry's back stiffened.

"So I'm alone?" she asked.

I didn't have a response. I suppose I didn't understand the question—still don't. She was *my* mother. I was the one who was alone.

"Still talk to Bobby?" she asked.

"We get together once in a while," I said. "He's a lawyer."

"Of course. And Tim-Tim?"

"Owns a gym," I said. "A couple of them. Chris is…"

Kerry nodded her head.

"What about you?"

"I teach," I said. "I'm a teacher. And yourself?"

"Same as always," Kerry answered, and she turned around. She didn't look much different—a few wrinkles around her eyes, and a wariness inside them that I didn't remember being there before, that was about all. I'm not sure I realized until right then, with Carly Simon blasting over a full bar, that I was still in love with her.

"And what's that?"

"Life Lessons," Kerry said. "I give Life Lessons."

I gently laughed and Kerry smiled. I stared at her snaggletooth.

"Do you want to touch it?" she asked.

I shook my head.

"Bring you good luck," she said.

"Yeah, it did last time," I responded, and we both stopped smiling. "I didn't—"

"No worries," Kerry said. "Life Lesson No. 1."

" 'It doesn't get any easier, it just gets more familiar,' " I recited.

But what I didn't tell Kerry was that I'd found that it (the elusive it) gets *less* familiar and becomes more distant at random times, and that the occurrences of these times were rapidly increasing. It's no different today. It's like I'm losing the thread, and I end up staring at a piece of string wrapped around my finger. I can't lose the string and it won't let me go, but I don't know why it's there or what I'm supposed to remember.

"Buy a lady a drink?" Kerry Mackenzie asked.

"My pleasure." I fumbled for my wallet. "What's your poison?"

"Just a beer," Kerry said, lighting a cigarette. "A lager."

"A lager then."

"Thank you."

I started to turn away but stopped.

"Can I…can I ask you something?"

"You think this is the time?"

"No, well, it's not about…it's just…what's Life Lesson No. 13?"

Kerry took a drag. "There isn't a No. 13," she said.

"Why?"

"Bad luck," was her answer.

"But I thought you told us, 'There's no such thing as bad luck or good luck—only lies and truth.' "

"I lied," Kerry said and smiled. I stared at her snaggletooth again. She didn't lie; she was lied to.

"About that beer?"

"Right," I said. "I'll be back in a second."

And although I knew what was going to happen, I still allowed myself to be surprised when I returned to the jukebox with two bottles and found only a smoldering, half-smoked cigarette on the floor. I didn't bother looking for her. I knew she wasn't in the bathroom or in the next room playing pool. She must have had a lot of quarters. When the Carly Simon song ended, it played again, and for the length of time that I sat alone at a table in the corner, drinking the two beers, the only song that played was "You're So Vain." The clientele never seemed to notice. We were special only to ourselves.

In my head, that was the song playing all through the final events of our Friday night party with Kerry Mackenzie and Johnny Fingers. There were sirens to be sure, and the voices surrounding Bobby and I grew from a chorus to a cacophony of competing concerns. But they couldn't contend with my mind's soundtrack. "I Don't Know How to Love Him" would seem like it would be more appropriate, but yet there was Carly with Mick Jagger: *"I bet you think this song is about you / Don't you?—Don't you?—Don't you?"* And we did. We'd each been too preoccupied with our own desires to bother to look at the big picture like Chris had. But it was another definition of "vain" that described the way we felt when everything we knew became unmoored: "unavailing, futile, or useless."

We carried my father back to the porch along with his wheelchair and deposited him in it, but only after trying to see if he could stand on his own on the lawn—he couldn't.

"Or wouldn't," Robert said. "Your dad wasn't stupid."

"No, but—"

"No one put two and two together—at least not out loud. If he could suddenly get out of his chair at the start of a 'well' period or even just to look for his sidearm, he was probably capable of a lot more—like *possibly* walking off the porch in his robe and making his way to the State Store for a bottle of JB. It was only a couple of blocks away. He could have been there and back in about fifteen minutes. No one checked on him anyway."

Robert paused and moved some paint chips around with his shoe.

"There's no doubt he was ill," he said, "but he was also crafty. Just because he couldn't get in a—"

"But how'd he end up on the lawn on top of Kerry? You're not suggesting…"

"I don't think so. Not in the way that you mean. Your father wasn't right in the head, but he was still the colonel. Remember all those lectures on honor? Something tells me that wasn't just lip service. *But…* "

"But what?"

"But even the most honorable of people can be weak willed—as we know from your father's drinking—and open to temptation.

Those things together can lead to misconstruing flirting for an invitation to fuck."

Robert tapped the top of a beer can before opening it; it foamed anyway, and he tried to suck it all up before it overflowed.

"She climbed on his lap, trying to pull even with your mom," he said. "I'm fairly sure of that."

I didn't ask why.

Robert went into trial attorney mode.

"As to what happened next: one theory has the wheelchair rolling off the porch because of the sudden weight change when Kerry climbed aboard and—according to Tim-Tim's measurements—the porch's slight incline. But that theory doesn't hold water because it only makes sense if the wheelchair started rolling abruptly, otherwise Kerry could have easily stopped its progression. I think it's more likely that your dad suddenly found a sweater girl in his lap, and whatever reason he still possessed went right out the window. He became…frisky, handsy.

"I believe that Kerry suffered at the hands of older men, her mother's choice paramours more than likely—a kid didn't inflict whatever injury left that scar. Kerry was trying to compete with your mom, but her method was the result of learned behavior; her mother would want her to be welcoming and friendly with the latest 'uncle' that she brought home, and Kerry, wanting to please her mom, would comply, probably swallowing her fear and repulsion until the first grope or at least until she couldn't take it anymore. When your father tried to…become more familiar, Kerry panicked, and during the ensuing struggle, they went over the edge of the porch. I don't believe the colonel's intention was to assault an underage girl, his history with your mom notwithstanding. I believe he was trying to recapture his sweater girl. Just the night before, he was burning your mother's dresses, as if she'd broken some sort of sweater girl code by wearing them. I think the trip from the porch to the lawn was the result of a series of bad choices and misinterpretations."

For a moment, I couldn't hear the noises of the night or feel the sting of the mosquitoes or smell the rancid Puddle. All I could hear was my own breathing and the thump-thump-thump of my rapidly beating heart. Then—*snap!*—the rest of the world returned, and I was subsumed.

"He still couldn't have gotten in the car by himself," I said, as if discovering this fact for the first time.

"No, he couldn't have done that," Robert R. Haber said quietly. "But I think everyone but the police and the medical examiner knew that."

I sat up. "Even during his 'well' periods, it took him the better part of an afternoon to change the toilet seats, and sometimes even getting him back in his chair could be difficult," I argued to no one. "His back—"

"When I was in law school, I went back and read the reports. In determining the motive, the ME focused on his dementia and other neurological consequences of having two strokes. He didn't investigate whether what happened was physically possible, so he didn't consider the scoliosis to be anything more than an additional contributing factor to his distressed mental state, listed well below alcoholism, episodic ataxia, and memory impairment. The lack of a note wasn't a factor; they concluded that it may have been too difficult, even impossible, for him to write one, or maybe he just forgot. Your father's physical disabilities and cognitive deficits were well documented by various doctors. The inquest was just a formality. All involved tacitly agreed that he had every reason to want to cash in his chips. Obviously that opinion wasn't explicitly expressed in the official reports, but it's there, between the legalese and medical jargon."

I had nothing to say. I had never read the reports. I'm not even sure that I knew there'd been an inquest.

"It was a matter of leaving people alone," Robert said. "Unwatched."

"You can't keep blaming Tim-Tim, Bobby," I said. "Besides, he went around and roused any of the neighbors that weren't already out. It could have traveled fast: twins on our side, row homes across the street, and all those huge sycamores on either side, their uppermost branches reaching across and touching."

"We were responsible for each other. That's all I'm saying."

Then he smiled kindly at me, which made me feel uncomfortable.

"You remember the sycamores—that's good. You didn't last time. You just remembered all the people, not the little details."

Our front lawn was packed with neighbors drawn by the screams. There had never been much excitement on our street, but now it was like we were having a carnival in front of my house. Johnny Fingers sat on the porch railing and smoked a cigarette, taking it all in. When we carried my father to the porch, we expected the crowd to part, but their focus was oddly somewhere else. Once he was back in the wheelchair, my mom combed what little hair my father had using her fingers. I couldn't decide if it was a gesture of intimacy or just part of a performance. Tim-Tim showed Bobby and I the bourbon bottle. We quickly set it aside as if it were too hot to touch.

"I don't know what made me do it, but the next morning when…well, when Mrs. Federov made us go back in the house," Robert said, "I checked the pill bottles, the Coumadin and your mom's Valium."

I was confused. "But why?" A large moth alighted on my leg briefly before joining his brethren around the porch light.

"To see if they were empty."

The moth had purpose; I could not say the same for myself.

"But they weren't."

"No," Robert said. "Coumadin stays in your system for three or four days. What showed up in the coroner's report was consistent with a couple of days' worth of Coumadin. Nothing unusual."

"But you thought something." I was suddenly nervous.

"Turns out premeditation plays second fiddle to sudden opportunity." He shifted in his chair. "I went too far ahead, didn't I, pal? I'm sorry."

It was okay. I was too far behind. You might say I'm stuck there.

"Is Kerry still on the lawn?" Bobby asked, and I shrugged and followed him down the steps and into the crowd.

And that was when we saw the fire.

Over the years there has been some dispute among the neighbors concerning the height of the flames and the extent of the damage. What was certain was that the Federovs' back porch roof had caught fire. Those were the flames we saw from our crowded front lawn. Some people claim the fire climbed higher and that the roof of the Federovs' house was ablaze, but all I remember afterwards were the black streaks, the long singe marks that came to abrupt ends, like fingers reaching for the roof that were cut off before they found their mark.

We ran around to the Federovs' backyard, and there was Chris Lee. He was naked except for his socks. Bruce huddled nearby, shivering, a small pool of blood collecting beneath his left leg where Mr. Federov's BB had punctured his skin.

Bobby shouted in Tim-Tim's face like I imagine him doing now when one of his investigators drops the ball.

"Why'd you leave him alone?" Bobby hollered over and over. "Why'd you leave him alone?"

"I just wondered where you were with the cookies," Tim-Tim said, crumbs still evident on his chin.

"I wasn't gone that long," Robert R. Haber said.

What we never agreed on later was whether my mother and Johnny Fingers were with us in the backyard. None of us recalled Kerry Mackenzie being there. I remember Mr. Federov and the newlyweds from across the street and the woman from around the corner who used to write pulp novels in the '50s plus a couple of kids we went to school with sitting on their bikes.

"Doesn't mean anything that we don't remember her being there," Robert said.

"Not a thing," I agreed. I didn't know whether he was leading me on or not.

"I mean, it's been a long time," Robert said. "We might have forgotten."

"Or maybe we just never knew. There was a lot going on," I said. "Maybe we just didn't see her."

Not notice Kerry Mackenzie? I would think it would take more than a fire for that to happen.

We both remembered Chris Lee dancing naked in the Federovs' backyard. We remembered the little kids in their pajamas, unable to control their giggles, being held against their mothers' stomachs, and we remembered the nurse from around the corner lifting Bruce out of our next-door neighbors' yard.

Chris had set fire to Mr. Federov's garden, the trellises specifically. The details were in the police report, and all three of us still have a copy. I guess Mr. Federov has his too if he's still alive. We stood with him and watched the fire dance across the wooden porch and consume the steps, while other flames scurried to the porch roof; the trellises had only entertained the fire long enough to catch the neighbors' attention. I'm not sure how long we stood there, all of our mouths hanging open. Bobby claimed that the time span, from discovering Kerry and my father on the front lawn to finding Chris naked in the Federovs' backyard, was less than five minutes. I couldn't dispute his assertion, but in my recollection, sirens wailed constantly, although they always seemed miles and miles away.

We were still standing there with Mr. Federov and half the neighborhood, when Mrs. Federov walked out of her house in her nightgown, turned on the hose, and sprayed us with it. Her face was severe-looking, and her head of curlers made her seem like she came from Venus rather than Lithuania.

"You, there," Mrs. Federov said in her sharp Baltic accent to Tim-Tim, who'd just returned, huffing and puffing, from his Paul Revere moment. "Clear the driveway between the houses so the firemen do not trip on a rake or a ball—and move everyone out."

"You," Mrs. Federov said to the nurse holding Bruce, "get that dog to a place that can fix him. Tell them to send me the bill."

"You two," Mrs. Federov said to Bobby and I, "where is your mother?"

Mrs. Federov thought we were brothers.

"I'm not sure, ma'am," Bobby Haber said. "She was out front."

"Get your friend some clothes and get him inside," Mrs. Federov told us. "It will go easier for him if he is not in the nude when the police talk to him."

"He could run away...he could—" Mr. Federov began.

His wife thrust the hose in her husband's hand.

"Shut your mouth," Mrs. Federov said. "Open the other spicket. *Pasiskubinti!*"

Chris Lee didn't resist or even speak when Bobby and I led him into the house. We didn't see his clothes outside, so we dressed him in some of mine.

"We didn't ask him anything, did we?" I wondered.

"No. His possible answers were too frightening to consider."

I didn't tell Robert that I'd been considering them for years, although something told me he already knew that. Whatever the case, it was apparent that tonight neither of us wanted to discuss what Chris' answers might have been—if he even had any.

"At the funeral—I never remembered him being that skinny," Robert said.

"He didn't get skinny overnight."

"Life Lesson No. 4," I added.

Robert finished his beer. "Guess so," he said.

He stood up and stretched, and his shadow appeared to tower over my backyard.

"Best be getting out of here."

"You alright to drive?" I asked.

"Yeah, yeah," Robert said. "No worries."

He popped a mint into his mouth.

"Bobby," I said.

"Yeah?"

"What happened to Johnny Fingers?"

"Another time."

But I wasn't to be denied, and somehow I knew Bobby expected this; he was waiting for me to push back. A melancholy smile crossed his face as he returned to his chair.

"You went back upstairs," I said, "after the police took Chris. Did you see him then? Did you see Johnny Fingers? Did you see my mom?"

"I…yes, I went back upstairs," Robert said.

"And?"

"I didn't Johnny or your mom."

"And what did you do upstairs?" I asked.

"I cried," said Robert R. Haber, Esq., ADA.

Neither of us remembered seeing Kerry Mackenzie the rest of the night, and we weren't surprised when she wasn't in the house the next morning. Bobby and I were there—Tim-Tim too. The police had taken Chris but released him into his parents' custody when Mrs. Federov, over the strong objections of her husband, refused to press charges or even believe that Chris had ignited their garden. Their house was fine; only the porch and its roof sustained significant damage.

"Boys make mistakes," Mrs. Federov said, not looking my mom in the face. "My husband was once a boy. He forgets."

Mrs. Federov attended my father's funeral, but I rarely saw Mr. Federov again. It was like he equated the porch fire with the colonel's death—as if his actions that night had something to do with my father's expiration: reacting poorly to the fire while the colonel breathed his last. Or maybe Mr. Federov was just afraid. He'd shot Bruce with a BB gun, then his porch went up in flames. To make matters worse, he knocked on our front door the following morning to tell us our garage was smoking, not knowing we'd find my father dead inside of it.

Bobby went to college—community college at first, then as his grades improved (and he grew more comfortable in his study habits), he transferred to an out-of-state university.

"If I leave Rhawnhurst—if I leave Mondauk County—then there *isn't* a legacy to fulfill," Bobby explained to me over the phone. "Nobody will know I'm Big Bill Haber's kid."

I stood in the kitchenette of my little apartment and pretended I wasn't crying.

"What about your mom?" I asked.

"She told me that she worked every hour of the day to escape this place, so she was happy at least one of us was getting out."

"It's not that bad here," I said.

" 'It doesn't get any easier, it just gets more familiar,' " Bobby recited.

Life Lesson No. 1. It has many applications.

"*Carpe diem*," Bobby said before he hung up.

"*Memento mori*," I replied to a dead line.

Tim-Tim got a scholarship to a local university. He dropped out before he graduated. He'd become so enamored with weight lifting and working out that to make money in college, he hired himself out as a personal trainer. A degree seemed superfluous by his senior year. He started a gym (T.-T.'s) and was soon in the process of opening another. He bought a house in Warminster. And within a couple of years, he too moved out of Mondauk County.

"I never knew where I fit in," Tim-Tim told me on the phone. "Bobby was the leader, the muscle. You were the brain and Bobby's best friend. Chris—well, Chris was runt of the litter."

"True—the school bullies only let up on him when Bobby was around."

"I was the fat kid," Tim-Tim said. "I was one of twelve at home, and even when I was one of four, I was still the fat kid."

"Not anymore," I said, but I should have told him that I'd always thought of him as the brain of the group—I was *just* Bobby's best friend.

"For any runt anywhere," Tim-Tim explained, "the best self-defense is a strong body and a clear mind."

Sounded like a Life Lesson.

A clear mind was hard to come by the morning after the fire. Our faculties were befouled by smoke exposure and the foreign aftereffects of alcohol, and it seemed impossible to shake the overwhelming sense that our lives were different now, that some test had been administered and we'd failed. We'd failed Chris Lee. We'd failed Kerry Mackenzie. We'd failed each other. We were no better off than my father, lost within his peculiar illness, tethered not so much to a wheelchair or to his profane vocabulary as to a sweater girl—his sweater girl. She filled him up as best she could, but there was no filling up my father. He'd seen war; he'd seen men at their worst and at their best. How could my mother possibly compete? Whatever he held over from his glory days or his time in hell, the colonel lost when he grew ill. Filling up my father became a full-time job for my mother. It's no wonder she was more of a pal to us than a mother in the traditional sense. It's no surprise that Johnny Fingers' heavy cologne and finger massage techniques worked on her. My father wasn't the only one in the house to have given everything he had; he wasn't the only one empty. Even sweater girls fade.

We found him the next day. After we woke, Bobby, Tim-Tim, and I gathered in the kitchen, taking turns having coughing fits. We were groggy from the night's events and anxious too. Anxious for my mother to return to being be our den mother or to being just *a* mother this particular morning. Too much had happened. We weren't sure we wanted to know everything. If my mother, for instance, had found comfort of a carnal sort with Johnny Fingers, we decided at the kitchen table that we didn't want to know. Bobby Haber made scrambled eggs, and we waited for my mother to come down the stairs. Tim-Tim made some joke about his stomach rumbling even after he'd eaten breakfast, and we all heard it, this low rumble, even before Mr. Federov warned us about the smoke coming from our garage, but we chose to ignore it; we didn't need any more excitement, whatever it was. My mom's Marlboro Lights were still on the table, and we each took one, figuring that because she was so drunk last night, there'd be no way she'd notice if three were gone. I don't know why we did this; we were still hacking our brains out. We had yet to open the shutter blinds so the kitchen was dim, but we looked up to where we thought the circles of gray on the otherwise white ceiling were and tried to leave our own mark—it seemed important—and still the rumbling continued. It was only after an understandably cranky Mr. Federov banged on the front door (and we hastily extinguished our cigarettes) that we found the colonel in the garage, through the exhaust fumes, inside the Corsair.

His skin was pink as if my father had been tanning on the front steps for hours. An empty bottle of bourbon was in his lap; it appeared to be the same bottle Tim-Tim had found the night before: Jim Beam with the label half torn off. Only now it was empty. Bobby reached in and switched the Corsair's motor off. Tim-Tim opened the garage door all the way, and the bright, late spring morning sun blinded us—me and Bobby and Tim-Tim and Mr. and Mrs.

Federov—as we stood around the car, momentarily frozen, a blinking, miscast *tableau vivant* whose spell was broken when the coughing began anew.

"It was more like a fucked up Passion Play than anything, one that didn't end with Mary Magdalene finding an *empty* tomb," Robert said. For a moment, he gripped the arms of his chair, as if he might fall overboard at any second.

"Is the Easter story even included in a Passion Play?" I asked. I was pretty drunk myself. My best pal did not sail this particular sea alone.

"You're the teacher. You're still a Catholic," Robert R. Haber said. "I'm a prosecutor."

"What happened to Johnny Fingers?" I asked. "What happened to his finger?"

Mrs. Federov left the garage to call the police back to our neighborhood. Mr. Federov made some comment about watching over us, as if we'd steal my father's pink corpse, but as soon as his wife was gone, he waited about a minute, then left the garage without saying a word.

"He thinks he's next," Bobby said.

"Next to commit—" Tim-Tim started before jumping back.

There was a finger on the garage floor. A long finger.

"There's no way it would have come off that clean," I said over the night noises of my backyard.

"It wasn't a clean cut," Robert explained. "But whatever blood had been on the car had been wiped clean. Then why leave the finger? A warning? Or did the perp just…leave it behind?"

Robert was attempting to lead the witness, but he shouldn't have bothered. The memory was like a weak radio signal that, for the moment, I was unable to tune in, so I kept my mouth shut and tried to focus on what came next.

When Mrs. Federov returned and shooed us back into the house to wait for the police (we were actually thankful to be shooed), we didn't mention the finger to her. We didn't talk about it to each other either. I pretended to cry for Mrs. Federov's sake, but I was too numb to do any such trivial thing.

Bobby went back out to close the garage door. "Police can open it again when they come," I heard him say to Mrs. Federov. "We don't need a repeat of last night's crowd."

I wish I could remember my mother coming down the stairs that morning. I wish I could remember if her face looked tired or slept-in, but I'm unable bring up her face at all.

I coughed into my fist to hide my leaking eyes from my best friend and lawyer. "I don't think I saw her face again until her viewing," I said.

"You didn't go into the room at the viewing," Robert told me. "I was there. You stayed in the vestibule."

"Right," I said.

When she came down, my faceless mother made toast and coffee and lit a cigarette. She opened all of the shutter blinds. Nobody spoke, and she never acknowledged our presence. When the police arrived, my mom took her plate and butter knife and coffee cup to the sink and followed the officers to the garage. Bobby, Tim-Tim, and I stayed put in the kitchen. We stared at the ceiling to see if our attempts at creating our own smoke stains, of leaving our own marks, were successful. But in the harsh morning light slanting through the shutters, the ceiling was revealed to be not that white after all; the circular stains we thought we'd seen had been more than likely just shadows, for there was nothing unique about the indefinite color above. And that was how we felt: indefinite, as in "not clearly defined or determined," as in not guilty but not entirely blameless either. While we were questioned, we didn't once bring up Yvonne Elliman or Carly Simon or Kerry Mackenzie for some reason. We were reunited with Chris Lee at my father's funeral. Chris looked thinner and paler if that was possible. His parents would soon send him "away."

"I got a Christmas card from him twice," Tim-Tim said, sounding out of breath, like he did when we were kids and he would be trying to catch up with us as we ran along the banks of the Puddle chasing frogs; more than likely he'd just finished a workout when I called.

"Did you write back?" I asked.

"No," Tim-Tim answered without a hint of shame (but maybe with just a dab of regret). "I was happy when I got the second card the following year though."

"Was he still in the hospital?"

"No," Tim-Tim said, and I heard a woman's voice in the background asking where he kept the fresh towels. "The return address was from some sort of mental health facility. You hear from him?"

"Once in a while. A phone call maybe. We don't talk about a whole lot."

"Can't be much of a life, that I can tell you," Tim-Tim said, and I wasn't sure if he was talking about Chris or me. "That whole nature versus nurture argument stops at Chris—Chris was made," he said before hanging up.

Tim-Tim was always the most scientific of us, so it made sense that the only way he knew how to escape the fat surrounding his soul (as he put it in one of his brochures) was to use reasoning. But whenever we speak, Tim-Tim never proselytizes. His methods are based on experience, and people who never truly had a weight problem would never understand. (His advertising targets a specific clientele.) But Tim-Tim and I shared a different experience, one that seemed to me, at least, to defy reason.

I rang him back.

"Tim-Tim," I said before he had a chance to speak, "what happened to the finger?"

"I don't know," he answered; Tim-Tim didn't have to ask whose finger. "Bobby said the cops must have lost it."

"But—"

Tim-Tim cleared his throat.

"There was never a single mention of the finger," he said, "not in the police report, not in the *Mondauk Common* or the Philly *Inquirer*, not anywhere."

The woman in the background asked him if he ever put up a tree.

"Maybe it turned out not to be an important part of the investigation," I ventured.

Tim-Tim made a sound of exasperation. "A finger not attached to a body found in the garage where your father supposedly committed suicide—with all his digits attached. I'm no Ellery Queen, but unless the colonel collected fingers—souvenirs from the war, maybe—I'm fairly sure it would be considered a clue."

Nothing defied reasoning for my old friend.

"Merry Christmas," Tim-Tim said; his tone was softer, sadder.

"Merry Christmas," I replied and hung up.

We didn't see Johnny Fingers for a long time after my father died. We heard he quit the public high school he'd transferred to and was riding with the Fields Gang. Bobby said better Johnny than himself, and I agreed. Bobby and I rarely spent time together in what remained of our high school years. We didn't make many new friends either. Tim-Tim joined us on occasion, but it was too painful, too obvious that Chris wasn't there; we were missing a piece. And although I was sorry my father died, he'd really been dead for years. I have very few memories of him that don't involve inspired profanity or household meddling, just the ones I've told you about—that's pretty much it. When my mother passed away a couple of years later, I missed her terribly, we all did. I remember thinking at the funeral that I couldn't recall a time before that night with Kerry and Johnny that she wasn't present and involved in my life, but since the service I couldn't even remember the color of her eyes.

"It's because you don't want to," Tim-Tim said during one of the few times the three of us were together after we graduated high school. "You have to pry those memories loose. Stop being afraid to look through old photo albums. Visit the cemetery for once. Find one of her sweaters."

"He still wouldn't see her," Bobby said. "I even try to remind him of the little things, like the heart-shaped birthmark she had on her thigh."

"Or her prominent philtrum," Tim-Tim added. "She used to it call her pleasure slide because of the way ice cream would sometimes get caught there if she was having a cone."

"Then there was the hint of a drawl," Bobby said, "that would sneak its way back into certain words, like *pe-an* for *pen*, and whenever she caught herself 'slipping down to Greenville,' as she'd put it, she would wrinkle her nose, then smile so wide, you could probably count all of her teeth. But I tell him this, and he just gives me that blank stare of his and—"

"Anybody heard from—"

Bobby and Tim-Tim shook their heads.

After we discovered that Kerry Mackenzie was no longer enrolled at Father Hoskins High, we asked some kids we knew who went to the public school, but they hadn't heard of her, and we figured there was no way anyone would not notice Kerry. One night, Bobby and I walked up and down what we thought was her street. We even knocked for Johnny Fingers once. His father answered the door in a canvas work shirt spotted with drywall dust. His sleeves were rolled up, and his tattoos were indistinct and faded. His legendary black hair was shot through with gray (and speckled with dust). He had that weary look of a man who'd just arrived home after a day that started twelve hours ago.

"Hi, sir. Is Johnny home?" Bobby asked.

Mr. Ewell looked us up and down.

"Yeah, I think so," he said.

"Johnny!" he hollered inside. "Some fellas here to see you.

"You guys wanna come in or…"

"Tell 'em I'll meet 'em on the stoop," Johnny hollered from somewhere inside the house.

Johnny's father lifted one shoulder and briefly grimaced: his version of a shrug, we supposed. "Good to see some of you guys comin' 'round," he said before he abruptly turned and left. The screen door swung shut with a bang. We stood on the steps and waited for Johnny Fingers.

"Did he come to the door?" I asked. I was really fucking hammered. Three sheets to the wind.

"You don't remember?" Robert R. Haber, Assistant District Attorney, asked. "Think. Think really hard."

The screen door opened a couple of inches, and Johnny's face appeared in the crack. "Hey," he said. He looked gaunt, as if he'd been sick for a long time, not exactly the aspect of a Fields Gang member. We could only see part of his face, but I was fairly sure he wasn't wearing his puka shell choker.

"Hey," Bobby said back.

"Hey, kid," Johnny said to me.

"Hey, Johnny," I said in return.

Bobby cleared his throat.

"We were wondering if you wanted to—"

"You know what, guys?" Johnny Fingers said, "I gotta hit the books."

He waited a heartbeat or two before withdrawing his face from the crack. The screen door slammed shut again.

"Haven't seen him since," I said, spitting.

"You sure?" Robert asked.

"Yeah," I said. "Sure as shit."

"Let's go for a ride," he said. "I'll drive."

"You are my lawyer, right?" I asked.

"Fuck, yeah," my lawyer said.

"Then as my lawyer, do you advise me riding in a car with an intoxicated attorney?"

"Fuck, yeah," my lawyer responded. "You have to be able to see your mom's face again, even if only for a little while. Maybe this time—"

I stopped in my tracks and wobbled. "I'm not going to the cemetery."

"That's not where we're heading," Robert said. "We're not going to the cemetery."

And we didn't. We drove for what felt like hours but the ride barely lasted the duration of the Carly Simon song we were listening to.

"They still play 'You're So Vain' on the radio?" I asked.

"CD," Robert said. "I had it all ready. I always do."

The gas station looked the same as it did every time Robert brought me here. Even the intermittent blinking of the big sign hadn't changed. At one time, when the white wasn't gray and the green wasn't permanently splattered with mud, the color scheme must have made it stand out against all the yellows and reds of the other gas stations.

"You say that every time," Robert said, smiling.

"Oh, yeah, right," I said.

Robert helped me out of the car and steadied me as we walked to the little booth that stood between the pumps.

"You guys again?" a voice said. "Reunion time once more, huh?"

Johnny Fingers stepped out of the booth. He wore white and green coveralls and wiped his dirty hands on an even dirtier rag. He hair was short and receding, and he had deep smoker's wrinkles around his eyes.

"Tell him," my lawyer said to Johnny.

"Tell me," I said, although I wasn't sure I really wanted to hear it.

"I tried to stop her," Johnny Fingers said.

"Stop who?" I asked, but I knew. I've always known.

Johnny said her name, but I didn't hear him the first time; I never do.

"Tell him again," Robert said.

"Could the court please ask Mr. Ewell to repeat his previous statement?" my lawyer requested.

"I tried man, I really did," Johnny Fingers said, lifting his oddly shaped hand in the air. "I meant no disrespect at the party. She was a sexy woman, your mom."

He cleared his throat.

"I helped her carry your old man to the garage, and I helped her put him in the car. Swear to God, I had no idea. The colonel yelled like hell and cursed up a storm when we had to bend him some to get him in, but your mom, she said that there was still a commotion outside with fireman and such, so no one would hear him. I thought she meant that we could have used a little help. It didn't matter much though 'cause your dad was pretty shit-faced—which was probably why he let us carry him into the garage without making so much as a peep. He got real quiet as soon as he realized he was behind the wheel; I guess it had been a while since he'd been in the driver's seat. That's when it hit me, that's when I caught on to what your mom was up to, and I tried to stop her. Honest to Christ, I did. But it was like she didn't hear me."

I looked over at Robert, but he was looking at me as Johnny continued.

"She'd given your father a bottle of JB when he was still in the wheelchair—it was just sitting there on the porch, about halfway full—and he started hitting it pretty hard. In the garage, when I knew what your mom had planned, I turned to check on your old man, and the bottle of JB was empty; he was passed out on the wheel. I just kept talking to your mom like I guess cops do to a guy who wants to jump off a building: nice and even, never raising my voice, but never shutting up neither. I don't even know what I was saying, to be honest with you. I leaned against the car, casual-like, thinking at least I would be between her and your dad, and I hooked my middle finger around the door frame. Just a habit, I guess."

Johnny paused to clear his throat again. It felt rehearsed this time, but in a whisper, Robert assured me it was not. It was just familiar. A memory of a memory.

"That's when I kinda realized that she was just standing there, in no particular hurry, listening and staring at me with those big brown eyes of hers. Kind of threw me off my game, if you get me. Now I'm just spewing nonsense, but I'm afraid to stop talking. Then she gave me this sad little smile and started moving towards me, holding my eyes like a vampire would, you know? Her arms were outstretched, and I'm thinking—no offense—I'm thinking that we're gonna pick up where we left off, right? I'm thinking—and WHAM!—she slammed the car door on my finger. She went right around to the passenger side to start the car and roll the down the windows before taking me out to the EMS workers. I don't know what she told them exactly—something to do with me getting my hand caught in some storm cellar doors, I think. That woman could sell ice to an Eskimo who had his tongue stuck to a pole. I guess I was too in shock to say anything about the colonel. I didn't even remember what happened for a couple of days, and by then the detectives had come and gone. No one found my finger."

I looked up to see if the shadows that we'd mistaken for burnt halos on our kitchen ceiling so long ago were still there, but I was standing (teetering) outside of a gas station, rip-roaring drunk, with my best friend and the guy who helped my mother murder my father in the family Corsair. I remembered that the ceiling turned out not to be so white after all; like so much of my life, its color was indefinite; it was impossible to tell the good guys from the bad by the color of their hats.

"For the information, Johnny," I slurred, "I thank you. Saved my ass."

Johnny Fingers gave me a quick nod. "I'll see you next time," he said. "I'm in the saving business."

I stuck out my hand, and Johnny turned his palms upward to show me the grease, but we shook anyway. It felt weird—it always does; Johnny's missing finger unbalances the act of two men shaking hands, a most basic civility.

"*Grab* my hand; don't be a fairy," is what I remember my father saying before the wheelchair and the bourbon benders.

"She was tired of being drained," Johnny said as we walked away. "If you don't mind me sayin'. She had you and the rest of your crew, but your mom was being drained. Why do you think she even *considered* being with me that night?"

I wanted to punch Johnny Fingers in the mouth, but a small part of me knew that this scene was simply a rerun, and I was thankful it was over, so I simply waved good-bye instead. I thought it would get easier, but it just gets more familiar, so I forget. I forget everything, at least for a time. I even forgot about the fate of the finger.

"I took the finger," Robert said to me when we pulled up to my house.

"You have the finger?"

"I said I took it," Robert said.

"You took Johnny Fingers' finger?" I asked. "From my garage?"

Robert walked around the car and helped me out.

"Could use the colonel's wheelchair right about now," he said. I just nodded. I was concentrating hard on not vomiting like Chris Lee used to—the less talk the better.

My lawyer carried me to my bed, took off my shoes, and tucked me in.

"What did you do with it?"

"The finger?"

"Yeah."

Robert looked down at me.

"It's in the Shit Museum," he said.

"Chris?"

"I gave it to him," Robert said—then he shrugged.

"He doesn't have the museum with him—not where he is—but he assured me that everything is somehow secure."

Last I'd heard, Chris Lee was living in a sort of mental health continued care facility. He'd been there for years. I'd always suspected Bobby Haber knew more than he let on. Bobby was always a better shrugger than I was.

"I know as much as you do," he said.

"Did I think out loud?"

"Always do," he answered, smiling kindly.

"Is it safe?" I asked. "The finger."

"Yes, it's safe," he said.

"In Tim-Tim's garage?"

Robert laughed. "It's not a bunch of skin mags. Wherever it is, it's probably mummified or floating in a jar of formaldehyde. Chris would have taken the utmost care to preserve it."

"Did I tell you I saw Kerry Mackenzie—at the jukebox?"

"Yes, you did. Many, many times. I never tire of hearing it though."

It was getting fuzzy already—everything.

It is usually my habit the next morning to write to myself, like I'm doing now, in an effort to get it all down, at least what vestiges remain, but words captured on paper, like the memories that play hide-and-go-seek amongst my neurons, have a way of getting lost. Dissociative amnesia, one doctor told me, but I'm in the process of letting him vanish away into my mental morass.

"Will I see you again?" I asked the familiar figure standing in the darkness of my room.

He leaned over me, and I couldn't tell if it was Bobby Haber or Robert R. Haber, Esq., ADA. I didn't know if it mattered, but it felt like it did—like it mattered a great deal.

"I'm your lawyer, right?" he asked.

"You're my best friend," I said.

"*Carpe diem.*"

"*Memento mori.*"

I'll try, I thought.

And I know, at that moment, the next time Bobby and I see each other, we'll do this all over again, and I won't remember writing this narrative nor will I remember what happened to it. And I know by then I'll have forgotten all the details: Carly Simon and the puka beads and the red dictionary—and the finger. And I know, for tonight at least, as I pass out on my single bed, I'll fall asleep looking at my mother's face, and every empty part of myself will flood and overflow, and, for the length of a drunken sleep, I will be privy to all the secrets of the sweater girl.

-end-

Tear Down the Walls, Louise

Meryl walked into the little garden behind her row home and tossed her spade to the ground. It bounced on the hard dirt, sun glinting off metal, and the temporary stars blinded her for a heartbeat.

"Good morning, Mr. DaCapo."

The old man grunted from his back porch and spit into his patch of yard, which was hidden behind a high wooden fence. Meryl waited until she heard his door close to kneel on the little pads.

Now: the begonias. Little brown crisps crowded the edges of their leaves.

"Damn it," Meryl said.

In Mondauk Proper she'd had a proper garden. Of course, in Mondauk Proper, she'd had a proper single house, too, but she adjusted just fine to the row home in the neighboring town of Rhawnhurst. Even though she'd been the one to move out six and a half years ago and give up the house, there'd been times at night, just moments really, when she formulated plans and hatched schemes as she fought the daylight in her head, but slowly these grew less extravagant, eventually vanishing altogether, except for the one: she wanted to sneak over the low, crumbling wall to see if her garden was still being well-tended; she wanted to see if it had changed. She'd named it Hiboux in honor of the owls, whose nighttime hooting made her think of them as guardians of the garden after dark. Were they still at their posts? Was anybody? She knew she could (probably) just knock on the front door and ask Frederic to let her into the garden, but she planned to steal the bloodroots. The bloodroots were her favorites.

She dug into the hard ground. Nothing she planted ever lasted very long. She tried everything, not just flowers: vegetables too, non-flowering plants, once a small bush. Meryl wiped her forehead with the back of her hand. It wasn't even ten o'clock and already the sun had risen to a place where it could bring hell to her little yard thanks to an almost completely treeless street. She ran a finger over a begonia leaf. Better to take them out now, give the begonias to Louise when she came for their late Saturday lunch.

A drizzle of sweat collected in the alcove of her neck before plunging into her cleavage.

"Damn it."

Meryl adjusted her blouse. It was too hot to wear a bra. Already her underarms were perspiring. She knew she was going to stain yet another blouse.

"Damn it."

It took twenty minutes to unearth the begonias. If she caught a quick nap before her shower, then ran down to Bard's, she'd be back in plenty of time for lunch with Louise. Her breasts and neck and back were slick. Blood pulsed at her temples.

In the garden behind the house in Mondauk Proper, she'd had the most amazing array of flowers: oriental poppies, purple coneflowers, strawberry foxgloves, even delphiniums. Frederic lost interest soon enough (in not just gardening), but after they'd first moved to Mondauk Proper, even before they married, they spent many afternoons, side by side, digging, weeding, sweating. They would sip spiked iced tea and make love on cool sheets afterwards, their sweat commingling then evaporating in the summer heat they'd brought to their bed.

Mr. DaCapo stared from his kitchen window. Meryl looked down. Her breasts were clearly outlined by sweat. (So, for that matter, was her stomach pouch.)

"Mr. DaCapo," Meryl said without looking back up, "I can see you."

She removed her gloves, and each hand squeezed the fingers of the other. They were swollen from the heat, but she'd always had chubby hands.

"Because she's younger?" she'd asked. "You wanted someone younger?"

"No, not younger. Someone—goddamn it, Mel. Someone who wants *more* of what you considered diversions. Someone who wants to sleep late and fuck in the afternoon and eat a good steak and finish a second bottle of wine, even if it's late."

"Does she…even if it's late?"

"Even if it's late," Frederic had said.

She took the straw hat from her head and fanned her face. She'd better get on with it if she wanted to sneak in a nap, but her knees were two knots. Goddamn it. Nothing grew back here, and her calves, her back, her whole body ached more and more each time she knelt before the dead soil.

Mr. DaCapo's unshaven face was pressed against the glass.

"Here, Mr. DaCapo," Meryl said, unbuttoning two buttons and pulling open her blouse. "See them? There you go."

The curtains fluttered. Mr. DaCapo was gone, the impression his nose made against the glass disappearing in short order.

Meryl laughed and collected her gloves and gardening tools and handkerchief. She left her blouse open and smiled to herself. If worse came to worst, she could always seduce Mr. DaCapo, though she'd never been one for older men, especially not now, being a woman of a certain age. But a difference in age wasn't a concern for her neighbor. Once, when he had lost his dentures, Meryl had been on her hands and knees looking under his sofa; she wanted to help. Mr. DaCapo had spoken only three complete sentences since she found him crawling around his front stoop toothless (one of those being "I have to piss," scratching his crotch to reinforce his statement and perhaps indicate from just where this particular elimination would emanate). Nevertheless, as she peered under his sofa, he reached down and copped a feel of Meryl's behind. Full-cupped-hand-press.

"Eh?" Mr. DaCapo said.

When she composed herself and stood back up, his dentures were in his mouth.

"Eh?" Mr. DaCapo said again.

So, in a pinch, there was always Mr. DaCapo. She started to laugh but the sound faded as soon as it hit the humidity. Her mind was already on the light purple blouse she'd wear open-throated to Bard's. Two showers. She would have to take two showers. One now, of course, but she'd have to shower again after she left Bard's; she'd be too flustered not to; she always was.

+

"Drew—get Mrs. Payne half a pound—half was it?—no, get her a whole pound of the imported ham."

Meryl's hands flew to her face, her chubby, chubby hands. They snatched at her sunglasses.

"I'm not…well, I am Payne, but not—"

She forced her hands down. They took her sunglasses with them.

"You need some cheeses too, right?" Mr. Bard asked.

Drew brought over the imported ham. Beneath his apron, he wore a white t-shirt. His arms were—well, Meryl thought of a hundred clichés, all of them true blue, as they used to say when they were kids, all of them seemingly torn from the pages of a bodice ripper novel (the kind of novel she couldn't even look at anymore, but the kind Louise was forever going on about). Meryl liked to pick one cliché per Drew encounter: chiseled from stone. That was today's cliché: chiseled from stone.

"What kind of cheese, Mrs. Payne?" Drew asked, hustling the imported ham back into the case, his eyes never leaving hers. Or maybe it was a trick of the glass. She forced her hands to stay where they were and made sure Mr. Bard had moved on to another customer before she spoke.

"I'm not really…it's my maiden—"

"The cheese?" the boy asked.

Jesus. His eyes were true blue indeed. A chubby hand fluttered by her forehead.

"Scorcher, isn't it?" Meryl laughed. Jesus.

Drew knelt down and stared at her through the glass case. He rarely smiled. Meryl wondered if she could make him laugh. He wiped his cheek on his sleeve and sniffed.

Behind Drew, in the back, a butcher's cleaver, like an archer's arrow, kissed the air and found its mark.

"The Swiss, please," Meryl said. "That looks good. Half a pound? Yes, and a quarter pound of the Havarti too. Oh, and how about a wedge of the Gouda. I could serve it with crackers, something simple; just one guest, so sandwiches and—"

"Drew taking care of you, Mrs. Payne?" Mr. Bard asked.

"Yes, but I'm not—"

"Okay, good, good," he said, walking towards Tiddy Wheelwright. "Try the mustards. Good with wine. Romantic."

God. One of her hands was back in the air. Tiddy Wheelwright. Damn it.

She waved at Mr. Bard: "Thank you. I'll try the mustards." Something for her hand to do.

Drew had his back to her as he sliced the Swiss. Undulating. His muscles undulated. God, that's awful. Undulate. Jesus.

Drew tossed the cheese, stacked on wax paper, on the scale.

"Yes, and how about some…"

"It's a little much," Drew said. "A little over half."

"...salami. Oh, that's okay, dear," Meryl answered.

Dear? Jesus on the cross.

"And half pound on the salami?"

"Meryl," Tiddy Wheelwright said. Tiddy was skinny and old and just about as close to royalty as one could get in Mondauk County.

"Tiddy, how good to see you! Yes, four pounds of the salami, and then I think I'm all done."

She had a headache from the heat. She'd chewed two baby aspirins before settling down for a nap, but she'd been too excited to sleep. Going to Bard's Meats had become the best part of her week.

Something fell and splattered in the back. Meryl flinched.

"Pick it the hell up." The voice was gruff and grouchy, underscored by a young boy's shaky laughter.

Mr. Bard jerked his thumb towards the back.

"New kid's driving Frank crazy," he said. "Paj. The more nervous he gets, the more he laughs—and Frank makes everyone nervous. He's hard on the new kids."

"Paj is not that new," Tiddy said.

"Who is?" Mr. Bard laughed, heading towards the back.

Let them all stay there, Meryl wished. Please.

"How's the scribbling?" Tiddy asked.

"Oh, I haven't...not in a while. Semiretired, I guess," Meryl shouted, keeping Drew in her sight. "Semi," she repeated, lying.

Loudmouth.

Paj laughed when he was nervous, she turned up the volume and lost control of her hands.

Tiddy pulled a tissue from her sleeve. "My niece—well, my great-niece, really—she wants to be a writer. Maybe you could talk to her."

"That would be lovely," Meryl said, trying to control her internal volume knob as best she could.

"You make money writing?" the old woman asked. "Not that it's any of my business, but with my Magdalene, I want her to make a good living."

Before Meryl had a chance to respond, Tiddy snapped her fingers. "I know a nice fellow you should meet. He's a police officer, a detective."

Meryl suppressed an eye-roll.

Mr. Bard came from around the cases. Tiddy's tissue disappeared back up her sleeve.

"I had Paj put the meats in your car, m'lady," Mr. Bard said. "Threw in scraps for Raven."

Tiddy blushed and placed a hand on the butcher's arm.

"M'lady," Tiddy said, nodding her head towards Meryl. "Sounds like one of her books."

The sweat was back between Meryl's breasts and under her arms.

"Don't flirt with your butcher," Tiddy Wheelwright said. "Oh, he'll take his thumb off the scale all right, but the next thing you know your niece's dog is eating filet mignon."

Meryl laughed and watched helplessly as her hands flapped in her peripheral vision.

Flirting?

"No, no. Just picking up some things for a lunch."

Mr. Bard walked Tiddy out arm in arm. Meryl watched him kiss her gently on the lips before helping her into a baby blue Cadillac.

Drew coughed, and she turned before she could set herself. Both hands were touching her face; she willed them down.

"I asked if that was all," Drew said.

His skin was tan, and his eyebrows held the threat of becoming one, a hood for his glacial gaze. He smelled like Marlboros, and there was animal blood smeared across his apron. He couldn't be older than twenty.

"Yes, yes, of course," Meryl said. "Is Mr. Bard…what I mean to say…are Mr. Bard and Tiddy Wheelwright…"

"You want those mustards too?"

"Mustards. Oh, yes. I'd forgotten. Two of each, please."

She pulled her wallet out of her purse with such force that some of its contents, including her many Chapsticks and an assortment of coins and movie ticket stubs, spilled onto the counter. A pen from her bank fell on the floor.

She laughed in Drew's direction: you know how it is.

"I'm just a mess some days," she said.

"I'll get a big bag for the mustards," Drew said.

Meryl tried to fix her hair which she was sure was a mess. In her daydreams (and as she fought back sleep at night), it always worked this way: Mr. Bard steps out, and she and Drew exchange witty and revealing banter. Preludes and prologues.

She turned her head a little to keep an eye on Mr. Bard in the parking lot.

Now: spin the plot wheel, Mel.

Mr. Bard stood on the curb and waved as Tiddy's Cadillac pulled away. The Cadillac jerked forward, shuddered, stopped, then peeled off.

Meryl's mouth hung open, words entangled in her saliva.

Writer's block. Jesus.

Mr. Bard walked back in, shaking his head.

"She's something," he said. "You all set, Mrs. Payne?"

"Yes, but I'm not...I haven't been Mrs.,—"

Mr. Bard stopped Drew as he was coming around the counter.

"I'll take 'em out to the car. Watch the front, okay?"

Meryl tried to catch Drew's expression, but he'd already surrendered the parcels. Her hands were tangled in her hair.

"Gonna be a hot one," Mr. Bard said, holding open the glass door with his back. "All weekend they said. A scorcher. Dog days of August." He shook his head.

"Mmmm," Meryl said.

She lowered her chubby hands, red from the heat. Her body temperature ran naturally high, and she feared she was in danger of becoming a screaming kettle of tea at any moment. Drew was behind the counter, spraying, wiping the glass. She saw her reflection in the glass case: she looked undone. Strands of her hair danced in the air conditioning like broken compass needles; a long nose and a high forehead, both crimson; spotty skin stretched over good bone structure that she had little to do with: a collection of quirks hung on a hereditary skeleton.

Kettle of tea. Really, Mel.

She watched as Drew's legs walked into her reflection, and her reflection was gone, consumed.

All of this took seconds though it felt much longer. It was hard to leave, but she didn't want to be rude to her butcher, who still held the door for her, waiting with her bags.

"August," Meryl said, as she hurried past Mr. Bard and led him out to her car. "Fall soon enough."

+

She stood before the kitchen counter, laughing into her hand. Imported ham? Yes. Cheese? Plenty. Plus: crackers and bread, a deli pickle—and four pounds of salami.

Jesus.

Four pounds.

The salami was surrounded by ten little jars of mustard.

Jesus on a Popsicle stick.

Frederic had said that when she was writing, she left the better part of her mind in the typewriter, and she supposed that he was partially right at least until she finished a book. The books helped pay their bills—that was their purpose. She never looked at them again once she approved the galleys. She never read any of her contemporaries either—except at the beginning and only for research. She used a pen name; her loyal readers wouldn't have cared about her masters in comparative literature. (Her publisher didn't.) And her readers *were* loyal. She even received some distraught fan mail after she retired. Well, not retired. Quit.

What the hell was she going to do with four pounds of salami? She didn't even particularly care for salami. It was more for Louise than her. And the mustards! She never used mustard.

The front door flew open—the doorstop shuddered—then it was slammed shut. Meryl jumped.

"You *have* to read this one," Louise said. She waved a paperback at Meryl as she came into the kitchen. Meryl laughed as she cut the Gouda into smaller wedges. She'd already put out the crackers and sliced the bread.

"And what's so different about this one?"

"Sir Geoffrey—oh, you can tell. He really loves her. He's a prince, the heir to Balatro."

"Balatro?"

"It's made-up, Mel. It doesn't really matter where they are."

"Oh, right."

Meryl sucked stray mustard from her thumb. Mustard. She better get used to it.

"So, anyway: Witney is a commoner, a...a—"

"Wench?" Meryl suggested as she brought the silver tray to the coffee table. Louise followed her to the living room.

"Yes! Wench!"

Louise lowered her voice to a whisper.

"Mel, you should go back to writing. You were so good."

Meryl retreated to the kitchen so Louise could gobble down a fistful of cheese. Louise considered it rude to eat in front of other people—either that or she ate like a ravenous animal. Meryl didn't know. In their decades-long friendship, she'd never seen Louise put food in her mouth. Meryl busied herself with the tea so Louise would have enough time to eat.

"Chamomile?" she called from the kitchen.

"Mmmm," Louise answered, her mouth obviously occupied.

"Chamomile it is," Meryl said to herself and sighed. Now there was a sign that she was on the far side of middle age: a cabinet of just teas, mostly chamomile. Perhaps she could make the Sleepytime variety for Drew before she tucked him into bed. Jesus.

"So Witney's father dies under mysterious circumstances—her mother died years before—and she's sold by the evil Volka to the castle as a slave girl."

Meryl took the kettle from the stovetop before it whistled. Volka. First rule of bodice rippers: at least one villain's name must begin with a V. Easier to identify. If there was more than one villain, the second one gets a less obvious name. Rules of the trade.

"But Geoffrey's father is dying."

"Something going around?"

Louise ignored her and picked cheese from her teeth.

"Geoffrey is deeply upset about his father, and he doesn't get along with his callous younger brother, so he gets drunk and wanders beyond the castle, into the woods—the same woods where Witney grew up."

Meryl served the tea. Louise had eaten almost all of the cheese. She hadn't touched the salami.

"Oh, thank you, Mel. So, he's inebriated and in the woods, and he's not wearing his prince clothes, you know."

"Really? My, my," Meryl said, sipping her tea. She didn't like coffee; chamomile was her hot beverage of choice. One had to have one at her age. Jesus: *but Drew, I was a rebel.* Her mother drank chamomile. It was odd, drinking her mother's tea. They hadn't liked each other much. Can't marry a character in a book, her mother had said, dismissing her daughter with a wave of her tiny hand. Holding out for love, her mother had scoffed. Not the marrying kind, she'd told Meryl's sisters and aunts. Judgment pronounced. Drink your chamomile.

"Soon, the prince was surrounded by his enemies."

"Geoffrey had enemies?" Meryl asked. Just the smell of the tea turned her stomach. The smell of the tea and the smell of the salami.

"Well, not really," Louise said. "But his father did. Lots of them."

"Because," Meryl said, "his father allowed the slave trade to continue. Kept the locals in line and afraid, but the woodsmen, they know the old man is sick. They don't know who Geoffrey is at first, but once they figure it out—he, oh, I don't know, he has the family crest embroidered on the inside of his cape maybe—they decide to kidnap and ransom him for the comely Witney and the other people of the woods enslaved in the castle."

"Mel! You're *so* good at this! Really," Louise said, "You should start writing again. You're why I started reading romances in the first place. You were the best."

"Mmmm," Meryl said. Something stronger. Vodka maybe. Did she still have that bottle under the sink? Or was it in the basement? It had been years since she'd had a drink other than a glass of wine if she couldn't sleep, and she hadn't tied one on since Frederic revealed what she already knew.

Louise stirred her tea, and Meryl took her in: on the top of her head was a knit winter hat—a toilet paper cozy. She wore a heavy sweater with a snowman pattern—the buttons had snowmen on them too—over a blouse buttoned to the neck. Her skirt just about reached the floor. Meryl couldn't see her feet, but she knew they'd be tucked into chunky black boots with rusted silver buckles.

"Louise," Meryl said gently, "it's ninety-five degrees outside today—at least."

"Scorcher," Louise said.

Meryl walked into the kitchen and poured her tea down the drain. There—under the sink: vodka. She spun the cap off. Was it still good? If vodka had an expiration date, it wasn't on the bottle.

"I'm having a vodka and tomato juice, Louise," Meryl yelled from the kitchen. "A Bloody Mary. Just need to find the Tabasco sauce. Would you like one?"

"No, thank you," Louise mumbled around a mouthful of something. Salami hopefully.

"I hope you don't mind if I do."

Meryl settled herself into her chair and sipped her drink. Jesus on the cross. She forced herself not to make a face. No wonder she didn't really drink.

"Louise," Meryl said, "you're dressed for winter."

Louise looked down at her skirt.

"This is what I wear all year round. All purpose."

"I know, Louise. But it's summer and hot as all get-out and you're wearing a sweater and a..." she forced herself not to say cozy, "a wool hat."

"I like my hat," Louise said, touching it gently with her fingers, leaving a small piece of Gouda clinging from a stray thread.

Meryl reached over, liberated the cheese, and wrapped it in a napkin.

"Why are you laughing?" Louise asked.

"Because. Look at you: you're not so dowdy that you couldn't meet a man of your own. A real man. Not Sir Geoffrey of Wherever."

The vodka made her loud (and possibly obnoxious).

"He's not *just* a knight, he's a prince, and—"

Meryl lowered her voice.

"Willie's been gone now, what, five years?"

Louise crossed herself.

"Four. He was sick for a year before that so it may seem like five," she said.

Meryl placed a hand over her throat. How could she be so cavalier about Willie's death? She downed the rest of her drink.

"I'm sorry—I didn't mean..."

Meryl walked back to the kitchen and made another Bloody Mary. She leaned in the doorway.

"I'm talking about men. A man. A man for you," Meryl said. The vodka was better than baby aspirin. One drink and the aches from her morning in the garden-that-was-barely-a-garden were gone.

"You were right about the kidnap part, sort of," Louise said, changing the subject.

"Hmmm?"

"The woodsmen don't kidnap Geoffrey. Well, they do, but he wins them over, and soon he's accepted as one of them. Then a day comes when word reaches him in the woods that his father has died, and his evil brother, Sir John, has taken up the crown. Geoffrey's angry with himself for staying away so long—not because he'd been usurped but because he hadn't been there for his father; he was sure his brother had offered no comfort to the dying man. Still, he's determined to do good. He leads the woodsmen in the overthrow of Volka and the slave traders, forcing Volka to seek refuge in the castle. But still, Geoffrey's heart is heavy. He drowns his sorrow in good, hard work—and planning."

"Do you ever think about men?"

"Men?" Louise asked. She fingered a slice of salami and eyed the bread. Meryl was prepared to duck into the kitchen if it appeared a sandwich was in the making.

"Men. You know: men, opposite sex. Hairy. Taller, usually."

Louise peeled the edge of a salami slice. Meryl tried to will Louise to eat a piece. She'd walk out to the yard if necessary; she'd give her friend all of the privacy to eat salami that she needed.

"I don't like it when you drink," Louise said.

"When I drink," Meryl said. "Which is how often?"

She was getting loud again.

"You don't like *it* or you don't like *me*? You don't like *me* when I drink?"

"I didn't say that. I didn't say I didn't like you. I would never say that."

Louise released the salami and wiped her fingers on her sweater.

"I'm sorry," Louise said.

"Me too," Meryl said as she walked into the living room. "Me too."

Jesus. If she could only be this aggressive with Drew.

"You'd think he'd just storm the castle, wouldn't you?" Louise asked. "Tear down the walls."

"Who?"

"Geoffrey. The prince."

Meryl sat down, kicked off her shoes, and slung her legs over the arm of the chair. She might have to start drinking every afternoon (except when she was with Louise); this wasn't a bad way to pass the hours. Too bad about the salami though. Maybe she could bribe the birds with it: all the salami they could eat, just leave her grass seed alone.

"He doesn't storm the castle?"

"No, silly. You being a writer and all, I figured you know this."

"Hmmm."

"He spies. Geoffrey spies. And *that's* when he meets Witney."

"By a well," Meryl guessed.

"Exactly! See! Oh, it was so romantic, Mel. So, oh, I don't know…"

"Hot?"

"Mel," Louise said in a gentle, scolding tone before she sipped her tea. Only Louise didn't sip tea (or anything), she *slurped*.

"Who wrote this one?" Meryl asked.

"Malory Degas."

Larold Finneran, Ph.D. in Medieval Literature. Meryl sighed. Well, why should Larold get out? Lord knows, the money was good. For her and Larold and a couple of others she knew, there came a day when the offer to write in this hackneyed genre went from tempting to necessary. For Meryl it was the day she realized that tenure was a pipe dream. Medieval and Renaissance-era romance novels were easy to write (historical accuracy was not a requirement), and their trashy paperback covers, which depicted women with barely contained breasts usually clinging to or about to be ravished by impossibly muscled, strong-jawed heroes, made them great supermarket checkout aisle fodder and earned them the epithet bodice rippers. Their work was disposable (and probably set feminism back a step with every book sold), but Meryl found that it didn't take long to develop a loyal following; she just couldn't divert from the tried-and-true formulas. Larold's books were always near hers in airport concessions and in those awful spinning wire racks found in pharmacies and just about any store near a beach.

But *Malory Degas*? God, Larold couldn't resist such an over-the-top pseudonym, could he? The pen name was beyond ironic; it was absurd: an unholy marriage of Sir Thomas Malory, who wrote *Le Morte d'Arthur* by compiling French Vulgate *romances* (wink, wink) and Edgar Degas, whom Larold adored, his favorite painting being *Ballet from 'Robert le Diable,'* a work that depicts a scene from Giacomo Meyerbeer's opera, a Gothic *romance* (stop, you're killing me). But that was what was so, well, *hot* about Larold (Frederic and Michaelis too) way back then, when late night coffee or wine or something stronger turned into passionate polemics, for words were living things to them, open to vivisection, and arguments over semantics and hermeneutics were not only high entertainment but also foreplay. Flex the head and the ass will follow, Larold said. All of them: Larold, Frederic, Michaelis: impossible names, impossible brains, she used to sing to herself. She chose Frederic—or he her, for these were men mired in latent chauvinism; unlike Mr. Bard's natural gallantry, chivalry was an effort to her college suitors. But she didn't care then; to be wanted by such a trio of scholars was intoxicating. It wasn't until later that it occurred to her that she was probably just stoned.

She ran into Larold at the last convention—or the last convention she attended. Recently divorced as well, his "soft belly of the academic" (as they used to call it) was now a potbelly (he definitely shouldn't have worn a tight-fitting turtleneck), but his mind was still there, behind the buttressed defense of a fair maiden's heart, distracted by the sound of a corset hitting a dungeon floor. She hated to admit it to herself (so she didn't, not directly): she chose Frederic over Larold, over Michaelis because Frederic's face matched the beauty of his brain. And for that, she'd deserved him.

"Mel?"

Right.

"You don't think of men...at all?" Meryl asked.

Louise looked down to the fingers twisted in her lap. How old Louise looked! The wrinkles, the bags under her eyes. Meryl ran a finger beneath her own eyes. Did Drew see what she saw in the mirror when he looked at her through the smeared display glass or over the worn Formica counter top: a vulnerable, over-the-hill, overweight (only by ten pounds—water weight), middle aged divorcée heading with alacrity towards frumpy old age?

Louise was staring at her.

"I had a man," Louse said.

Meryl shifted her weight and placed a leg on the floor to keep the chair from falling backwards.

"You did? When? Why didn't you—"

"Willie. I loved Willie. He was my husband, and I had him," Louise said.

"In every way possible," she added, turning red, staring now at the salami.

Meryl shook her head and took a drink.

"No, Louise," she said in her softest voice (but she wondered if shouting would have a better effect). "I mean now. Do you ever think of men *now*? You know: dating. Holding hands. Kissing."

Louise's fingers made for the salami then retreated back to her lap.

"Sex?" Meryl asked.

Poor Louise, thought Meryl: the blush of her skin matched the red in her wool hat.

"Mel," Louise said, her fingers now around her teacup.

Slurp.

"What? 'Mel' what?" Meryl asked, trying not to sound exasperated.

She downed the rest of her Bloody Mary and was back in her chair with a fresh one before her mind had time to leave an ellipsis.

"Sex, Louise. You can sit there and tell me you don't have any sexual feelings?"

"No, I—"

"I'm sure Witney has."

Louise jerked her head up.

"Witney has what?"

"Sexual feelings. I'm sure Witney has sexual feelings," Meryl said. "Urges."

Meryl closed her eyes on the last word. Urges. Jesus Christ.

"Someone inside you..."

"Stop. You're being filthy," Louise said, pulling on a hair on her chin.

"What about pornography? You read these romances..."

Did drinking also make her mean?

"Pornography is a sin, Mel. And they're all so ugly..."

"A-ha! How do you know? How do you know they're all so ugly, Louise? Sneak a peek?"

"...with their fake this and implant that."

Meryl sighed.

Louise leaned down and appeared to be smelling the salami.

"Romance novels are just porn for people who think they're above it," Meryl said.

God, she sounded like Frederic just then: high, mighty, and utterly full of cow excrement.

"Witney," Meryl began again, leaving the chair, "Witney, I'm sure, has thoughts, designs, of a sexual nature."

"Mel, Witney's a—"

"I know, I know: a damsel in distress, a maiden," Meryl said, pacing the length of the area rug. "Bodice rippers."

"She's just—"

"You're afraid to fall. That's what it is, Louise," Meryl said. "You're afraid."

Louise plunged four fingers into the stack of salami.

"You're afraid. But we're fragile creatures, Louise. We're fragile, needy, little creatures, hardy in so many ways but one: love."

"Love," Louise repeated, her eyes fixed on her meat-enclosed fingers.

"God, Louise. Christ on a cracker."

"Mel."

"I'm sorry, Louise, I really am." And she was. She knew better than to say things like that around Louise.

Meryl knelt next to the coffee table and tried to catch her friend's eyes. The room smelled strongly of salami.

"But do you know how alive you'll feel if you allow yourself to fall? Do you know how every ache, every pain, every annoying little thing becomes just that: little? Do you have any idea how *little* we are and how *little* time we have?"

Louise's fingers seemed to be frozen in the salami. Meryl stared at the side of her face, focusing on a stray strand of wool clinging to her friend's cheek. In the kitchen, the old Pennsylvania Dutch clock that worked only when it wanted to, wanted to. The sound reminded Meryl of an errant pirate's footfalls on the plank. *Click. Clock. Click.*

Louise freed her fingers and wiped them on her skirt, then safely knotted them again in her lap. The sunlight had subtly moved, and Meryl and Louise were ensconced in a light draping of shadow.

"You only fall in love once, Mel," Louise said in a slow, measured cadence, each syllable smacking with saliva, a tone for speaking to children who should know better but obviously, painfully, do not.

Louise raised one hand like a princess waving to her subjects.

"Everything else is just faint traces. Wisps. You only fall in love once, and then you're all used up."

Meryl tried to take Louise's hand and capture her fingers, but the wrinkly, bony, brown-spotted appendage flew away. Once Meryl withdrew, it landed with a *plop* in its owner's lap, next to its partner.

"What about us, Louise? People like us? What about all those people who get married after a death, a divorce?"

"Some people can't be alone. They have to—"

Meryl smacked the coffee table. A startled Louise grabbed her hat with both hands. The salami shifted slightly on the serving tray.

"That's it! That's what I'm saying. You *can* fall in love again."

Meryl folded up a piece of salami and popped it into her mouth. Her stomach took no time at all in telling her that room temperature spicy, dry sausage did not go well with Bloody Marys. She thought a couple of crackers would help settle the dispute, and she woofed them down—she didn't want to lose her momentum.

"You know what I did this morning, Louise? You know what I did? I flashed Mr. DaCapo. Right in my backyard. I opened my blouse and flashed my big ol' boobs at him."

Meryl laughed.

"He ran from his window. *Not* the reaction I expected, but it *was* Mr. DaCapo."

"You exposed yourself to—"

"That's what I'm saying," Meryl said around another slice of salami. "You have to let yourself fall. Even if it's only for sex. Okay, maybe not with Mr. DaCapo, but if he cleaned up real nice, new pair of dentures, a shave…he's not *that* old. And neither am I! That's it: we can't cling to the past, we don't dare. And I know, honey, I know—but we have to let go, we have to. We have to fall before we fly."

Jesus. *We have to fall before we fly.* She sounded like one of those inspirational posters they sold at the Roosevelt Mall.

"You still wear your wedding band," Louise said.

Meryl grimaced.

"My hands are fat. My fingers: they're chubby."

"Soap," Louise said, her mouth popping on the p.

Meryl blinked. Did Louise just…? She took a long drink. Well, good for her.

Her stomach settled, she reached over for a piece of cheese— Gouda would be tasty right now. This afternoon drinking was underrated.

"Come on, Louise, have a drink with me. Here, eat some—"

The cheese board was empty.

How did she not notice until now? "Jesus…" She didn't think she'd left her alone that long.

Meryl shook her head, then finished her Bloody Mary. "Doesn't matter," she said, though she hoped Louise didn't end up constipated. "What matters is this: you *can* fall in love again, like I said before. It's time, Louise. It's time for you and for me. Time to tear down the walls. Lower the drawbridge, if you will. People do it all the time. People get remarried or find a partner or *multiple* partners every single day."

"Then they didn't love the first time around."

"Hmmm?"

Louise gathered herself and made to stand. Meryl tried to get off the floor and out of the way, but her legs were heavy and numb and she was buzzed.

"I said: if they found love again, it means they didn't love the first time around. Or, maybe they loved, but their husband or wife didn't. That might be different."

Louise shuffled down to the end of the sofa, walked around the coffee table, and opened the front door. Cheese dropped from her sleeves along the way.

"I'll see you next week, Mel," she said from the front stoop. "I'll let you know what happens to Geoffrey and Witney. You really should write romances again. You were so good at it."

Meryl stared at the dairy product on her floor. "You dropped your cheese…"

The door slammed shut.

She'd never given Louise the begonias.

Meryl's legs still refused to stand up, so she napped on the living room floor, inches from the nearly-pilfered cheese, until the sun was within an inch of ceding the day to the night.

+

Joni Mitchell was still singing.

"Oh, I hate you some, I hate you some, I love you some, oh I love you when I forget about me."

Jesus.

With consciousness came pain. It was clear to Meryl that her head had been used as a tribal drum during the night, and she was convinced, from the rhythmic patterns that were repeated at the same terrifying volume and intensity, that her cranium had been part of a drum circle on steroids. Her lips were raw from kissing and her mouth tasted like college—specifically college mornings, when she'd wake believing that, for the better part of the hours past remembering, she'd housed a dying mouse in her mouth, as it shit and pissed its way to mouse heaven. Red wine threatened to rise further up her throat. She groaned and returned her head to the pillow.

Drew was gone, of course. That was the way these things worked, right? What would Sir Geoffrey have done?

When the latest wave of nausea passed, Meryl piled both pillows to angle her head. She couldn't see it on top of the bureau where she'd left it, but she knew it was there. It had been there the whole time she made crazy, out of control, bodice ripper love with someone young enough to be her son. It had taken almost a half hour to soap the ring from her finger before she drove to Bard's. Christ on a crutch, her fingers *were* fat. It was hard to believe Frederic had once slipped the ring on her finger after they'd picked up their wedding bands at the jewelers, just so she could try it on again as they lounged in front of the fireplace in the house that had recently become *their* house. The ring had slid home, like it knew where it was going, where it belonged. She had cried, just like she had at the jewelers—not because she was so in love (she *was* in love, just not *so* in love maybe), but because the ease with which the ring had met her finger and snuggled up to her knucklebone was perhaps the first time anything in her life had fit just so. Her happiness had a lot to do with Frederic, of course; he was erudite (they all were back then, their entire circle) as well as dashing, never without a suit jacket and a book, always something witty clinging to the precipice of his tongue. It had a lot to do with the house too. It was fairly huge, too big even, but big enough for a family. Frederic feigned interest when the conversation turned to children, and it took a bit before Meryl realized that his interest was laced through with annoyance, but the house held out hope—and so did she, for a little while. But mostly her happiness had to do with the garden.

The garden was hers. It was substantial in both size (a little less than a quarter of an acre including a fountain) and scope (the number of perennial varieties alone was breathtaking). Frederic helped in the beginning and even seemed to enjoy himself, but Hiboux was her baby. As it turned out, it would be her only baby, as Frederic perfected the fine art of feigning. But there came a time when his annoyance won out and he could pretend no longer—about anything. Eventually he even went so far as to occupy another bedroom in the fairly huge, ultimately barren house. At first, it didn't matter to her where Frederic slept, she was that disgusted and disillusioned by everything. Even when he began sleeping in another woman's bed, eventually being so bold as to have this much younger woman, now his wife and the mother of his beautiful little boys, sleep over at *their* house (figuring, Meryl guessed, that it was big enough to conceal an infidelity, even one blatantly maintained), she dealt with it by not dealing with it. It wasn't until later, when the amount of cold, empty space in the king size bed became a black hole where the light she needed to fight the darkness could not escape, that she began to slowly stop pretending too. What she discovered was that a small part of her didn't care that she was being so casually disrespected (it was her fault, she deserved it, this was what she got) or that their home was being treated like a dormitory, where bed-hopping was nearly a sport. But, oh, the rest of her cared a great deal; she had grown into being *so* in love with Frederic. She no longer felt feminine, no longer felt as if she had an identity of her own since hers had been tied up with his for so long. He even questioned whether there was a point in continually "pouring" money into the garden; wouldn't that land be better utilized, he asked; a guesthouse would be nice back there, he told her. But her book sales soon bumped her up into a higher tax bracket, and she was able to finance Hiboux on her own. It was her only solace, the only place where she could find herself; the garden had become the only thing in her life that she could control. Yes, Frederic had the English chair at the university before his last book took off; yes, he was in demand on the lecture circuit; and, oh yes, he had his concubine. But Meryl, at least, had her garden.

And then she didn't. Giving up the house was easy. Giving up Hiboux was hell. But she'd been too tired to fight and had gone for a clean break. She stopped writing. She had enough money to see out her days now—or maybe it was just: no Hiboux equaled no words. Either way, she would never write about romance again; even the trashy sort she'd excelled in was too much to bear. She bought a row home because anything larger would remind her of the dream that had turned out to be nothing but angry smoke. Construction had already begun on a rampart; she would never allow herself to be so exposed again.

God.

She could still feel Drew inside her. If she rolled over, she wondered if she'd land in the wet spot or if it had already dried. (She was fuzzy on how much time had passed.) She couldn't remember the last time her bed had a wet spot. Certainly not since Frederic took his own room in their marriage house.

"Everybody's saying that hell's the hippest way to go," Joni sang.

Sunlight struggled with her curtains and shades in an effort to smack her in the face.

She could never tell Louise about Drew, about tonight. Louise wouldn't understand: her blank stare would (eventually) give way to a dissertation on the love entreaties of fictional knights and ladies of yore, or she'd blush, that grand Christian leveler of all temporal transgressions: every sin was an express ticket to Hell, her blush communicated, and there were no extenuating circumstances. For years, she'd thought Louise blushed because she'd embarrassed her in some way, but this morning she realized that Louise blushed because her friend was embarrassed *for* her.

Or maybe her rattled brain was just making stuff up.

Meryl smacked her lips and mouthed some vowels. She needed a glass of water, but standing up seemed a Guinness feat: she'd fall, maybe even throw up. And she'd lose whatever remained of what Drew had left inside her. Having found no purchase, it would simply slide out and Drew would be gone. It was a tough call. Her tongue felt like it had shriveled up like her Aunt Alma and had grown little dotty spikes. Her lips were dressed in a thin, white film. Her eyes were dry and burned like hot coals. She turned her head to the side as if he were still there. Let what he left stay a little longer. If it wasn't love, it was close, and close was close enough. It was wonderful and terrible, thrilling and terrifying all at the same time—everything she remembered it to be. Considering her previous experience, she was surprised that she hadn't peed the bed out of fear when she woke to find herself naked (though the apprehension would have nothing to do with her lack of raiment). But thus far fear remained just a distant threat.

Still she wondered: could she go back to Bard's? Everything preceding the sex had been discreet. She drove her car past the butcher's three times like a schoolgirl with a crush but never slowed down. She began to believe that the vodka from her lunch with Louise (and the drink she had for courage before she left) had fermented her blood and, just maybe, her common sense. (Oh, that would have looked good in the local papers, wouldn't it? *Local Former Romance Writer Arrested for Driving Under the Influence.*) During her third pass, the lights blinked out in Bard's except for a row at the front. She pulled into the parking lot and watched him clean up. Deliberate were the movements of his body. Insouciant? A little, but determined as well somehow. Before things went to hell, Frederic used to say, "Do a job," every morning as he left her to her writing and went to instruct horny undergraduates. Drew was doing a job. She grew wet in the car.

On an earlier pass, she'd seen a couple of the other guys leave, so he was closing alone. She waited until Drew locked the door and walked towards the bus stop before she called out his name. It sounded—no, *she* sounded—so pathetic, desperate, drunk in the echo of the parking lot. A million insects worshipped at the parking lot lamp, and Drew lit a cigarette. She bummed one. Coughed. He laughed but not unkindly, not at the middle aged woman (*this* side of middle age, sadly) trying to chat up a young buck still adorned with the smell of the meat shop, the scent of the slaughter. At least she made him laugh.

Then there was a bar, McCullough's in the Promised Land of Mondauk Proper (not far but far enough from prying eyes), and she beat Drew at pool. Twice. Her laughter came easy, like rain on a Sunday, and infected the entire tap room: everyone understood, she thought; everyone, liberated by libations, knew just how lonely the sound of a wounded heart beating really was. And hell, why not laugh? No one had told her that that was the *only* thing she could count on: the beat of her own heart (although that too someday would fail her)—certainly not her single-minded mother, who regarded her bright, young daughter's resistance to marrying the first available breadwinner as an anomaly among her betrothed brood of delicate dainties. (Such were Meryl's sisters.) Her mother scoffed at her dreams of one day finding true blue love, for to her mom, marriage was an arrangement, not a fusion of emotions; a crush and a wallet were enough (and a crush wasn't even necessary). Meryl dedicated her first bodice ripper to her mother, who swore, even while she was in hospice care, that she'd never read the worn, well-thumbed paperback that sat on a shelf near her bed.

After Frederic had surrendered the marital bed, Meryl had said to Louise, "You think being married means you'll never feel alone again," a pronouncement that turned out to be more ominous than self-pitying. Willie, Louise's sweet, bewildered Willie, with his Frankenstein monster forehead, his dress shirt pockets stuffed with notes and old receipts and mash letters to Louise, was discovered to have a metastatic brain tumor, and during his tortured, aphasic final year, Louise was most definitely alone. Marriage seemed designed to take the bride back to the altar without warning and leave her there, only there were no flowers, no guests, no wedding dress, no groom, just the setting to act as a reminder of—to paraphrase Led Zeppelin—what was and what will never be again.

She shivered. It was startling how easily she could spook herself.

"He gave me back my smile, but he kept my camera to sell."

Unlike Joni and her paramour, there was no kind of trade with Frederic. He didn't retain the garden as much as she abandoned it.

What made her shaky sometimes was that she surrendered the house and the garden as quickly as Frederic had thrown her over for a college girl—however, Meryl was running away, and he'd been just fucking all the livelong day. But her last thought before passing out in a motel room the night Frederic told her everything was that she couldn't bear to see Hiboux in a stranger's possession. (She was still afraid he would sell the property without her knowing.) Although she never did, the idea that she could maybe visit the garden if she just gave up the house to Frederic made her decision…well, at least easier to swallow (though she never ended up suggesting such a deal). The truth was that she'd hit the ground running and the garden was a casualty to her need for speed.

Going to Bard's last night was the first time she felt like she had somewhere to run to and maybe somewhere to stop, though she wondered if she could ever get far enough away from the memory of the desolate altar. She wondered if she'd ever be able to raze the rampart for Drew. (She was awash in metaphors and ethanol.)

It turned out that she didn't need to worry about any walls. In no time at all, she was opening up at McCullough's. (Now that she thought about it, Drew didn't reveal a single piece of personal information.) She told him about Hiboux (she didn't know why) between blaring jukebox selections she didn't recognize. The bar fête then led to a more private celebration back in her Rhawnhurst row home. They played her CDs and records, and she was surprised how many of her choices met with Drew's approval: Dylan's *Desire*, the Band's *Music from Big Pink*, even Joni's *Blue*. And he was surprised that she also had stuff by the Stones and the Velvet Underground. She remembered thinking: how jealous Mr. DaCapo must be! She also thought how odd it was that she was going to bare her breasts to a stranger for the second time in one day—if it was still Saturday. The Pennsylvania Dutch clock in the kitchen had stopped again. A bottle of wine was uncorked and at the time, the merlot settled nicely with the vodka.

When she took him to bed, he was neither eager and fumbling nor aggressive and competent. He was simply Drew. The alcohol didn't seem to affect his performance, which was measured and careful…deliberate. He didn't make love like she thought a twenty-year-old would. At first, Meryl tried to hold back her moans. She was too drunk to be self-conscious of her stomach or the saddlebags on her thighs, but she feared her moans would reveal just how needy she'd been. But by the end, she enveloped the boy with her legs and gave herself over to him, drowned in his love, swam in his wake— every bodice ripper cliché: she surrendered to them all and understood, at least until she fell asleep (or passed out), why Louise clung to her paperbacks.

When they finished (Drew had come twice), they were too drunk to wallow in the awkwardness Meryl had felt even with Frederic after their swift sessions. She clung to Drew, and he allowed himself to be consumed by her generous flesh. She stayed conscious a little longer than he did, counting the barely discernible stubble on his chin and the tiny, tiny blackheads on his straight nose, feeling for those few moments like the giddy schoolgirl-with-a-crush she'd never allowed herself to be. And what would her mother have thought of what had just happened? (Drew, thank God, had never mentioned his mother.) Joni's voice drifted from the living room. She must have put the CD on repeat. "True blue," she whispered into Drew's ear. She was asleep when he left. She hoped she hadn't snored.

"Oh, will you take me as I am? Will you take me as I am? Will you?"

Meryl fluffed the pillows again. They held just the hint of cold cuts. A little Marlboro. Would there be a note waiting for her on the kitchen table, pinned under an apple or a wine glass? (In her books, it would be a piece of parchment paper beneath a goblet.) If there wasn't a note, then what? Could she ever go back to Bard's? Jesus. What if he bragged? Young men—hell, old men too—bragged about sex. Would Drew boast about bagging that sort of older woman who bought all that salami and mustard?

She had to risk getting out of bed, vomit be damned. She had to know. Each step would be perilous, but she'd never go back to sleep now, not even this hungover. If there was a note, she could go back to Bard's. Maybe not during a busy time when Drew's attention would be on his work (she didn't want to misinterpret his focus for the cold shoulder), but she could go back, and there'd be other rendezvous. If there wasn't a note, she'd have to find another butcher.

The lights were still on in the kitchen, and the room smelled of wine and meat. The bottle of Merlot was nearly empty. Two glasses, both drained, were on the table. Nothing else. The basket of fruit was sitting on a chair (oh, yes, yes, she had moved it so they could arm wrestle); no fruit appeared to be missing.

Meryl slumped into a chair.

No note.

Jesus Christ in a bucket.

She glanced at the sink. Her underwear hung from the faucet. (Oh, right.) They looked exceptionally huge. More disturbing: the cheese board and the serving tray from her lunch with Louise sat on the kitchen counter, fully loaded again, next to two plates. Serving lunch meat to a butcher's apprentice: good, Meryl. What was it? Cold cuts as foreplay? Or had she been trying to feed him like an anxious mother? She winced when she remembered taking out all four pounds of salami for some reason. God, she was out of practice. She could have blown it right there. But she didn't, did she? Drew didn't touch the food. Instead, his hands were on her thighs. His lips were on her throat. His fingers were—

She looked at the cheese board and the serving tray again.

The salami was gone.

+

Monday was sunny. Unbelievably, her head still tangled with a dawdling hangover. It was going to take some time for all that alcohol to exit her system: multiple Bloody Marys and whatever she and Drew had drank at the bar—shots of something and beer too, she thought—plus a good amount of Merlot. Meryl chewed two baby aspirins and decided that if the Pennsylvania Dutch clock in the kitchen started *click-clocking* again, she'd go to Bard's. She made chamomile tea and ate a piece of toast. Joni was still singing; the stereo had been playing since Saturday night. Meryl wondered when the CD would go up in a puff of smoke. Back in bed, she opened the first few books scattered beside her nightstand. Drew had knocked over the piles climbing into her bed, and she hadn't bothered to straighten up. *Lady Chatterley's Lover?*—no, no: too obvious. Joyce Carol Oates? Too, oh she didn't know; maybe too *incisive*. Psychological realism was the last thing she wanted right now. Meryl tossed the books and counted to one hundred until the latest wave of nausea passed.

She woke to banging. *Someone was at her front door!* She ran into a pair of slacks and a blouse. The knocking persisted. *Drew!*

When she descended to the living room, she knew it wasn't her front door bearing the brunt of Drew's insatiability. It came from the back door. Meryl put the water on for more tea (to be hospitable) and looked out of the windows above the sink. The banging had stopped. She watched Mr. DaCapo close her gate and return to his backyard.

"What?...Jesus..."

She opened the back door (she *tore* open the back door—that was how it worked in the bodice rippers: urgency, not subtlety), and the sun smiled smartly: still here, Meryl! How's the head? If you close one eye and squint with the other, Meryl, you can see to the end of the world. You can see all the way to the garden in Mondauk Proper.

She slammed the door shut, and the Pennsylvania Dutch clock burped a few second hand movements before returning to silence.

Her sunglasses. They were at Bard's. She'd left her sunglasses at Bard's Saturday afternoon, left them on the counter maybe. She'd have to go back. Couldn't leave her good sunglasses at the butcher's, now could she?

She changed into her red summer dress, nothing revealing except the color. Before she started the car, she removed her pantyhose.

+

The sunglasses slid around on the dash as she drove. She knew she shouldn't keep them there, but old habits just got older in her experience. When she pulled into the parking lot in front of Bard's, Meryl spit into a tissue and cleaned the lenses. Jesus on a biscuit: the lenses were scratched. No matter. The sunglasses would disguise her. Hide her eyes. She'd only have to worry about her hands.

"Paj—two pounds, alright? Two," Mr. Bard said.

If Drew had bragged...

Deep breath.

What's to stop us, pretty baby, but what is and what should never be?

Meryl waved and held her smile until her eyes could take in the shop: carefree, the smile said. She could be insouciant too, it said. Ah, life, her smile conveyed to the room: ah, life!

"Right with you, Mrs. Payne," Mr. Bard shouted.

She didn't bother trying to correct him.

Two other people bustled behind the counter. Grumpy, broad shouldered Frank wrestled with the big carcasses and uttered only the most necessary of words: next!, how much?, anything else? The skinny kid next to him had dusky skin, an easy smile, and an Indian accent. What was his name? Ravi? No, no. Paj—that was it. He was new at Bard's, but not that new. Then again, Meryl thought, bathing the shop in her casual glow, who was?

(Where had she heard that before?)

Bard's was busy. Housewives three deep in two lines. No one she knew well, thank goodness. A bustling Bard's was exactly what she had wanted to avoid, but she'd lied to herself to get here, so she had to deal with it.

As she took in the scene, her hands, which for some reason had been twisted together at her chest, began to rise and appeared to be on the verge of oscillating near her head. She stared them down.

Frederic had walked into the garden behind their big house, and as she knelt in the dirt, he squinted into the sun and announced (as if she didn't know) that he'd been sleeping with a student—wasn't the first one, either. (She'd sort of guessed that.) Sorry to tell you like this, dear. These things happen. (Sip from his martini.) I'm in love, Mel, really in love. (*That* she didn't know.) It's the greatest feeling in the world. Hope it happens for you one day. I honestly, truly hope it happens for you. (Another martini sip.) So there's that. Should we put the house on the market, or...

Skinny and stark, not a perennial and neglected regardless, their marriage had withered away, ending, ironically, with a liquid send-off:

"Does she...even if it's late?"

"Even if it's late," Frederic had said.

"Is it? Is she?"

"Mel, dear..."

Only two women in front of her. Was she still smiling? Careful: she didn't want Drew to notice her crooked teeth—though, of course, he'd known her intimately, but they'd been drunk and it had been dark—which struck her funny bone hard, since her time with Drew had been anything but gloomy: Meryl thought it had been filled with a most fortunate and fortuitous light.

So: no more smiling. Not right away. And definitely no laughing to herself.

"No, Paj, not the domestic," Mr. Bard said in an insistent but patient tone. "Mrs. Pastorek wants the Krakus."

And there he was: grinning at—no, no, not at her. Drew rested his elbows on the counter and held the widow Tidwell with only his blue eyes, grinding his pelvis against the glass display case—as if to say to Mrs. Tidwell: see what I can do for you? See how I can wake up those parts that you've shut down? As if to say to Meryl Payne:

remember this move? How about this one? Remember how I woke your—

Chop!

Meryl shook her head. Behind the counter: one, two, three—only Mr. Bard, Frank, and Paj.

Mrs. Pastorek ordered more salami, "just in case." Meryl smothered a grin. I would offer you some of mine, she imagined herself explaining to Mrs. Pastorek, but the twenty-year-old boy I took to bed two nights ago absconded early in the morning with all four pounds.

Mrs. Pastorek wobbled on her arthritic legs to the register. Only one person left in front of Meryl: a woman in a housecoat with a shabby perm and an inquisitive look.

And there he was: in the back, leaning against the butcher block, which she could partially see from where she stood. An unlit Marlboro dangled from his puffy lips. He was laughing with Paj. Drew took two fingers—no, *three*—and shoved them into the center of his fist: in and out, in and out, in and out. He squeezed the air at chest level with both hands, then lowered them down to his stomach, as if whatever he'd been squeezing had drooped. Paj giggled and Drew slapped him on the back. Once more: three fingers into his fist. Paj saluted him back in the same manner. Drew sniffed his fingers, then offered them to—

Chop!

Frank came out of the back with some lamb chops.

"…a scorcher, huh?"

Mr. Bard was slicing some Asiago for the woman in front of her.

"Yes," Meryl said, "it is…it's gonna be…"

"Hot," she concluded.

Maybe Drew had Mondays off. She remembered him saying he had to work on Sunday—just before they sang along to most of the first side of *Desire*, both of them huddled in front of her stereo, their breath clashing, emitting fumes that threatened to ignite if exposed to the right amount of friction.

The woman in front of Meryl shook her head, as she took a cough drop out of her housecoat.

"Ohhh. I just don't know. So hard to decide. What's else is good?"

Meryl thought that if Drew was there and he waited on her (and maybe even if he didn't), she'd order four pounds of salami. The smile returned to her face. So did her hands. In the reflection of the meat case, she thought she looked like someone who was in the middle of a fit.

And there he was: she was next!

"What can I get for you, Mrs. Payne?" Drew asked her.

"I'm not…Drew…married…I'm—"

Chop!

The woman in front of her asked about the price of pork chops a second time.

Sinewy: in bed, she'd found Drew to be sinewy—and durable. This one was no pretentious academic, she'd thought at the time, no delicate aesthete. This one had strong roots. Strong with traces of dirt.

Maybe he was out back, loading in Monday's deliveries. She removed her sunglasses. She didn't want to hide. If Drew was here, Meryl wanted him to see her as she was, she decided. If she appeared anxious, so be it. If she appeared brittle, well, maybe she was. She couldn't pretend she was something she was not. It was enough to dig in the dead earth behind her house. If Drew—

"Ooh, and where's the boy with all the muscles?" the old lady who Frank was waiting on asked.

Paj flexed his skinny arm. Mr. Bard laughed. The grumpy meat cutter ignored them both.

"School, Mrs. Friedman. Up in Boston. Drew drove back yesterday," Mr. Bard said. "Classes start next week."

"Ooh, do they? Where does he…?"

Meryl didn't realize until she was peeling out of the parking that she'd dropped her sunglasses in Bard's, but she wasn't going back.

+

"Will you take me as I am?" Joni sang.

Meryl ran through the house, discarding her red summer dress and sensible shoes as she went. When she entered the kitchen, she eyed the bottle of vodka on the counter but decided any imprudent imbibing could wait. She didn't break her stride until she reached the backdoor, which she *ripped* open (subtlety be damned), descending the crumbling steps to the little backyard wearing nothing but her bra and underwear. At the bottom, she sat to pick little pieces of concrete from the soles of her feet, delaying her inspection of the weeds.

Meryl thought she couldn't help but be haunted by her garden in Mondauk Proper: she'd been in such a hurry to buy her house in Rhawnhurst that she'd failed to properly inspect the backyard, which turned out not to be conducive to growing much more than a spotty lawn and crab grass. But for the time being this was what she was stuck with: a hardscrabble garden-that-was-barely-a-garden, where every withered begonia reminded her of a flowering bloodroot. She stood and wiped her face dry, but there was no erasing her bitterness. Thinking that Drew would stick was like believing that the booty from her pipe dream botanical theft would ever take root in her dead little—

Her hands flitted about her face like insects smacking into a street lamp.

It couldn't be, it couldn't be.

Jesus H. Christ.

The garden was aflame in colors: reds and yellows and, yes, there: blues! Purples too. Blue fortunes. Milky bellflowers. Even root beer hyssops.

Who could have…?

Drew?

Meryl knelt in the dirt and cried until she was empty and didn't get up until night returned.

+

"You sleeping?"

"Mel?" Louise asked.

"It's me. Yes, yes. *C'est moi*," Meryl shouted into her phone.

"Are you drinking?"

"I had a glass of wine," Meryl said. "Maybe two."

"You better be careful, Mel. You don't want to end up—"

"What happened to Witney, Louise?" Meryl asked.

"Witney? What time is it?"

"I don't know. My clock is dead."

"Your clock is…?"

"My garden's not though."

"Your garden?"

"Goddamn garden gnomes."

"Mel!"

"I know, I know: *not* alliteration. The g in gnomes is silent."

"What's gotten into—?"

"Witney, Louise. What happened to Witney?"

"Witney? I don't understand." Louise cleared her throat, and it sounded like she still had some pieces of cheese stuck in there.

"In the book. Sir Geoffrey? The Kingdom of Balatro? The dying lord or king or whatever he is—was—is?"

"The King died, remember?" Louise said, her voice now wide-awake and clear. "I told you about Sir Geoffrey being kidnapped?"

"Mmmm hmmm."

"So he's with the woodsmen now, a leader. He spies on the castle, making plans, and that's when he meets Witney by the well. She'd been sitting there contemplating throwing herself in, wondering if it wouldn't be better to 'follow the bucket' than continue being—"

"A slave. A sex slave probably."

"I never said—"

" 'Follow the bucket.' Larold always did have a way with a phrase."

"Larold? Who's Larold?" Louise sounded flustered. "I was telling you about Witney's situation."

"Right. Let's see: she'd been stolen from the woods years before, sold to the castle by Volka with a V, and her people want her back. How'd I do?" She didn't wait for an answer. "Now, Sir Geoffrey's brother—"

"Sir John," Louise said, fully recovered. "Oh, I hate him so much. Their father was a decent man, though, despite the slavery."

"Despite the slavery," Meryl repeated. "Notwithstanding the human trafficking."

"His thinking was…old."

"Antiquated."

"Yes, yes. In the beginning of the book, both John and Geoffrey want to reform the laws of the land, but they—"

"They have to wait for the old man to die."

"Exactly, but Sir Geoffrey loves his father. Sir John didn't even shed a tear when he died. All he was concerned about was getting the crown, which had been his obsession since he was young. Sir John never really wanted reforms; he only said he did to keep Geoffrey close. It turns out he's been secretly working on plans with his lover, the wicked sorceress Countess Olenda, that would enslave the *entire* countryside, including all the people of the woods. Terrible man. He even likes to take this one serving woman down to the dungeon so he can pour hot wax on her. Honestly, did you ever hear of such nonsense?"

Boy, Larold really liked his subplots. Her publisher would have stripped them right out, and she'd have been the recipient of a rather terse memo. It was formula or famine.

"Witney?" Meryl prodded.

"Witney and Geoffrey keep meeting by the well, and she falls in love with him. She believes he's just a spy from the woods. She doesn't know who he *really* is. Witney's under almost constant watch. Her only free moments occur during the changing of the guard, and that's when she meets with Geoffrey. The reason she's so closely watched is because was forced to become engaged to Sir John, who's really King John by this point. John thinks that if he marries a commoner, a slave, he'll earn the respect of the people of the woods and weaken their hearts before he crushes their souls. Witney spies for Geoffrey and finally sneaks him into the castle, but just when he is ready to jump out from behind a curtain and kill his brother, Witney stops him, stays his hand."

"She does?"

"Oh, yes, but she has no love for John. She's even been beaten by him. Really beaten, Mel. But Witney doesn't believe that more violence is the solution. 'This isn't the way,' she tells Geoffrey. 'I know of no other,' he responds. 'I do,' Witney says. 'Only resort to the sword when one has been drawn on you.' She kisses him, and he tells her everything: his true heritage, his dreams of a free Balatro. Then—oh, this is one of the best parts, Mel—he drops to his knees and with a ring that he carved out of wood, he asks if she'll put her hand in his forever, which is the traditional way of proposing in Balatro. Witney, of course, says yes. She tells Geoffrey that violence only begets more violence, and that their love, the love of a girl from the woods, a mere slave, and the son of a king, the true heir in exile, will stand as a shining example of freedom for a lost people; they will become a symbol of hope for the resistance. Witney helps Sir Geoffrey disguise himself as a slave. He starts out as a gong farmer. Do you know what a gong farmer is, Mel?"

"Sure do. They cleaned out the cesspits beneath the garderobes, which were a castle's 'toilets,' " Meryl said. "Gong farmers were frequently up to their knees or higher in waste. It was a bad gig." Her stomach turned a little; the only thing she'd put in her body since dark had been vodka.

"I knew you would—"

"They were shit herders." Regardless of her stomach, Meryl couldn't resist.

"Mel!"

"Come on, finish the story." She couldn't believe she was (drunkenly) absorbed in Larold's convoluted narrative.

"Well, with Witney's help, Geoffrey moves to kitchen duty and quickly rises up in the household hierarchy until he becomes a butler. Oh, Mel, every night they meet beneath the stars and the moon and re-pledge their love. 'As long as there are stars,' Sir Geoffrey tells her, 'our love will never be forgotten. We only have to look skyward.' I'll never forget that, Mel. Never. So beautiful."

"Hmmm."

"Over time, Sir Geoffrey replaces all the key servants with people from the woods. Oh, the scene where the woodsmen clean themselves up before they enter the castle is so funny. Poignant too. Like they're the dirty ones."

"Uh-huh." Meryl imagined an animated Disney song-and-dance number.

"They have to neaten up because slaves that serve in the court or in the royal chambers have to be well-scrubbed and in uniform. But it's the uniforms—"

"—that allow Geoffrey to switch out the staff. John and the Countess just see the getup, not the person wearing it." Meryl wanted to go make another cocktail, but it felt so *good* to be stretched out on the sofa, still in her bra and underwear. She'd never cleaned the dirt off her knees. She'd been so restless before she called Louise, she was sure she'd stained the cushions—and she found that didn't care.

"Okay, so the woodsmen are in place. What's next?" Meryl felt that if she didn't help move things along, Louise would soon be describing the type of fabric used in the making of the uniforms— and it was starting to sound like Larold's trashy paperback romance was filled with just such minutiae.

"They wait until the moment is right and trap the usurper John as he prepares for his bath—swords drawn, the whole thing. But John—he's not stupid. The slave he had draw his bath that night is none other than his betrothed: Witney. John grabs her by the neck and places his fingers on her windpipe and a dagger against her jugular. He's been watching his household, Mel. He knew something wasn't right, and he began to sense a familiar presence. Countess Olenda told him of a vision she had of Witney being raised up by a faceless mob. So he began keeping Witney close during his more vulnerable moments, like when he bathes or uses the garderobe. She's his insurance: if he dies, so does Witney. He even makes her disrobe whenever she attends him so that she can't hide a weapon on her person in case she's guilty of 'chicanery against the crown.' "

"He probably just wanted to see her naked," Meryl said. She'd gotten up and made another Bloody Mary. While in the kitchen, she turned the back porch light on. She could just make out the colors, and she quickly turned it off. "Alright—it's King John. In the bath. With the dagger." She suppressed a giggle. "Please continue, dear."

"John says, 'One step closer and this maid joins me in hell.' Guards loyal to the false king, led by Volka, surround the rebels. Sir Geoffrey rips off his disguise and reveals himself to his brother. Geoffrey explains the plight of the woodsmen, how they're good people and deserving of more than what they've been dealt. 'Everyone is,' Sir Geoffrey tells his brother. 'Everyone deserves the right to love and to be loved. Everyone deserves the right to make their own way and choose their own destiny. All of us, we're like the stars in the heavens and each of us burns brightly.' Even the knights surrounding the rebels murmur in agreement—they haven't been treated too well either, Mel. Volka remains silent. 'We're all stars,' Sir Geoffrey says, and he extends his hand but the gesture is ignored. 'If you take one step closer, my prodigal brother,' John hisses, 'the only star you'll see tonight will be a falling one: the fey Witney.' And Witney, she looks Sir Geoffrey right in the eye and says—"

" 'As long as there are stars,' " Meryl finished.

"*Exactly!* Mel, really. You should—"

"Witney," Meryl said.

"She says, 'As long as there are stars.' Then she pauses, and John nicks her neck with the dagger. 'A sword has been drawn—take him,' Witney says, and on a signal from Geoffrey, one of the woodsmen looses an arrow into the hand holding the dagger. None of the guards lifts a weapon, Volka sneaks away, and Sir Geoffrey runs his blade through his brother. But as John dies, he squeezes Witney's windpipe, and she collapses into Geoffrey's arms."

"So much for no violence," Meryl said.

"They had no choice, Mel, and they followed what they called Witney's Precept: 'Only resort to the sword when one has been drawn on you.' Sir Geoffrey was going to ask John to step down."

"Wouldn't have been as exciting."

"No, I guess not."

"And Witney?"

"She survives."

"Right."

"Just barely. But she never speaks again…"

Sounded like a male fantasy: a hot chick who can't speak. Very Larold.

"…and she requires a lot of care."

If the perennials that mysteriously appeared in her garden somehow survived to the end of the week—and she had a sneaking suspicion that they would—then they were planted by someone with a thumb more verdant than hers.

"And Sir Geoffrey, he becomes king and marries someone younger and in better health," Meryl said. "Someone with an intact windpipe."

"I'm always afraid they're going to end that way, but they don't. You told me, Mel: all the endings are the same."

"How insightful of me."

And how cruel. But Louise didn't see formulas; hers was the kind of heart easily excited by romantic fantasy novels. After Willie died, Meryl was sure Louise would stop reading about true love vanquishing all, but her friend never lost faith. She just wasn't going to look for new opportunities; the love she believed in was either in the past or between the pages of a book. Louise wanted Meryl to return to writing, but for all of her gentle cajoling, she was too retiring to ask her why she stopped churning out silly medieval-themed romances in the first place—though her cheese-filching friend would never call them silly. (Meryl realized that *twice* this past weekend, food she'd purchased at Bard's had been pinched!) Even if Louise did manage to ask, Meryl could never tell her it was because she believed that romance of any kind was predicated on lies—if she did, she would sound like a hypocrite, especially after scenes like the one this past Saturday afternoon: trying to coax Louise out of her cozy and into the arms of a man, calling romance novels porn. But she'd never expected to be handed divorce papers in her garden while Frederic sipped his second martini. The twisty, cold legalese mocked the prose that flew from her typewriter, and she read the Petition for Dissolution of Marriage surrounded by her beloved flowers and shrubbery, which she knew before she finished that she was going to leave behind. It was all tied up in the garden: their marriage had given birth to Hiboux and that was where she'd been checkmated in a game she had never wanted to play. The argot of lawyers shone a light on the lies she was promulgating in the supermarket checkout aisles and pharmacy wire racks. She listened for the hooting of the owls, the guardians of the garden, but she heard nothing but the thoughts flying willy-nilly in her head. So she abandoned Hiboux and left her words behind—and her punishment for doing so was her Sisyphean toiling in the garden-that-was-barely-a-garden. It was a punishment, she felt, that signified that she would never get any of it back—not love and words especially: those things were as dead as her Rhawnhurst soil.

Except now…

She flicked the porch light on and off a couple of times and watched the colors in her garden come and go. When she was finished, she left it off and stared into the darkness. *Were they still there? With every flick of the switch, she'd expected them to be gone as magically as they had appeared. And what else was out there?* She listened to Louise say her name and ask if she'd fallen asleep. *What else was out there?* That was it: she was going; she put on her wireless headset and tucked her cell phone into her bra.

"I'm sorry, dear. I dropped the phone into the sofa cushions. What were you saying about how the books end?"

"I said, I keep thinking one will be different."

"You want to read one that breaks the formula." She was going to add, "and is more realistic," but the fantasy setting was Louise's window dressing of choice. "A book that colors outside of the lines at least a little bit," Meryl said as she hurried down to the basement and grabbed the big flashlight, the one with the handle on the side.

"I wouldn't want anything bad to happen," Louise said with genuine concern.

Meryl exited the basement through the storm doors. They opened with a loud creek, and she emerged in a shower of rust flakes.

"Mel, what was—?"

"Damn cell phone probably. Such lousy reception."

Placated, Louise continued: "I don't want a tragic ending."

"You don't read the books to go to a dark place. You still want a place of many colors." Prescribed colors, but colors nonetheless.

Louise was quiet for a few moments, as if she was digesting Meryl's last statement. Finally she said, "What I mean is that I just keep thinking one will be different. I worry about it. But they always end sort of the same, and I'm relieved when they do."

Oh.

"And this one?" Meryl asked.

Even though she was in her bare feet, as well as in her bra and underwear, she stood on a bucket and clambered over Mr. DaCapo's high wooden fence with the flashlight's handle between her teeth. She tried not to breathe too heavy into the headset.

"As the rightful heir, Geoffrey takes the crown, and the people rejoice. The day arrives where Witney is to become his wife and queen, and in a moving ceremony, she puts her hand in his forever. Together they free all the slaves and vow to protect the people of the woods for as long as they reign. Volka goes to prison for his crimes, a life sentence. Countess Olenda disappears in a puff of smoke, but the woodsmen discover her crystal ball, filled with smoke, in a chest in the dungeon. They place it on a stump just outside the woods and smash it with an axe. The smoke dissipates with a weak little scream."

Meryl crouched on Mr. DaCapo's lawn, just listening to Louise. Once she was sure that her presence hadn't been detected, she turned on the flashlight, focused on the garden, and swallowed a gasp. She was surrounded.

Raspberry wine bee balms. Whirling butterflies. Pretty Lady Susan anemones.

Most of the yard was a garden. Meryl sat on the ground and moved the flashlight's beam from flower to flower and ignored how wet her face had become.

"And when King Geoffrey and Queen Witney die from old age, they pass away together, and every year the people of the woods commemorate that day by forming a large circle around the well and silently pointing to the stars."

Meryl turned the flashlight off. In the dark, she thought, she could be anybody. In the dark, she might even be able reemerge with her history in her pockets (or tucked into her bra) rather than on her shoulders—she couldn't escape who she'd been, but it didn't need to weigh her down—and she silently, tentatively pointed to the stars.

"Could that happen?" she whispered.

"Could what happen, Mel?"

"Not the story. Jesus, not the story. The sticking."

"The sticking?"

"Witney stuck by Geoffrey even though she was putting her own life in danger," Meryl said. "Geoffrey stuck by Witney even after she couldn't speak." Meryl heard the *hoo*-hoo-*hoo hooo-hooo* of a distant owl. "Could that happen?"

She turned the flashlight back on, and the colors returned, as loud as "White Light/White Heat," as vibrant as Beethoven's "Ode to Joy," as powerful as a sucker punch.

"Mel," Louise said, "it's a made-up story. 'Could that happen?' Does it matter? It's made-up. You used to make them up yourself!"

"Hmmm."

"You okay, Mel? Are you still drinking?"

"Tear down the walls, Louise," Meryl said.

"Goodnight, Mel," Louise said before hanging up.

+

On Tuesday morning, Mr. DaCapo knocked on her front door and handed Meryl a bouquet of flowers, fresh earth still clinging to their stems. Next to his recently polished loafers was a large bloodroot in a chipped pot.

"Would you...would you like to come in for a cup of tea, Mr. DaCapo?" Meryl asked.

He did, and Meryl left the front door open for a little while to try and catch the first breeze of fall.

-end-

Second Best Bed

Part of David McNulty knew it was a sickness or at least that he was sick. But who would blame him, he thought. It wasn't like he had a choice. He was as much made as born. And damn it: until now, following Ariel O'Connor to the bathrooms in the National Constitution Center with a rag soaked in chlorine bleach and nail polish remover, he hadn't done anything more than sniff her panties for the better part of an hour during one of the girls' sleepovers at his house.

And there was another thing: *his* house. It *was* his house. He paid the mortgage. His teaching job paid the bills. His wife Rachel still lived there, but that was a matter of time—not the other way around as had been recently suggested again. "The Apostle Paul wrote that love, 'does not rejoice in iniquity, but rejoices in the truth,' " Pastor Josephus said two nights ago as he gave a sermon on 1 Corinthians 13. " 'Bears all things, believes all things, hopes all things, endures all things.' " Well, that part rang true. He felt he had endured and then some. "Love," Pastor Josephus continued, " 'love never fails,' " his stern gaze alighting on David who was trying to be inconspicuous at the back of the tiny church. "Love never fails"—that part was pure unadulterated horse hockey. Love fails all the time, every single day. Love was a sickness worse than his own (or close)—they were related for sure.

(He hated when the Pastor focused on him, even nonverbally, because it made him think. Usually he was easily overlooked; it wasn't that he blended in as much as he was so uninteresting, and it quite often rendered him socially invisible, which was fine with David, especially in church: the last thing he wanted to do was think.)

Rachel had failed. She'd driven him here in his very own padded carriage. She'd driven him to the Remnant Church, which despite having grown up Roman Catholic, he'd taken to like a thirsty fish to shallow water: any port in a storm and all that. And Rachel hated them, the Remnants. She said Pastor Josephus was a charlatan, resurrecting a long dead Seventh-day Adventist offshoot sect.

But David had stopped listening to Rachel the night he discovered her on her hands and knees with Mr. Rogers, the history teacher and varsity basketball coach, pounding away behind her.

Rogering her. That was the phrase, or some variation of it, that Jim Rogers always used in the teacher's lounge while painting a picture of his extra-curricular activities to male faculty members, whether they were interested or not. Jim claimed that he was always giving some young bunny he'd picked up at McCullough's a good Rogering. His sexual braggadocio was odd and discomforting in a Catholic high school, as was his aversion to undershirts, which allowed thatches of chest pair to poke out so that at times he resembled an overstuffed scarecrow, but one who'd been doused in Drakkar Noir. Jim was one of those men who grabbed you hard by the upper arm when he needed to speak to you and didn't let go until he was finished, as if it somehow proved his virility by showing how much stronger he was than poor, poor pitiful you. But as much as David had despised him before being cuckolded (on top of his machismo and tales of bunny hunting, he was a lazy educator), at least Mr. Rogers was a bachelor, completely unattached. "No barnacles on this cock," Jim had announced on more than one occasion. Rachel, on the other hand, had at least two attachments, even if she considered her husband and daughter to be just causing hull drag now—though they apparently hadn't gotten in the way of her being sodomized by a second-rate social studies teacher. But, oh, did she ever stick to David (not *stick with* or *stick by*), and she was proving difficult to dislodge. Rachel, it turned out, was parasitic in nature. He appreciated the irony that he wasn't the only man being sucked dry by Rachel, except all he pulled out of his pants was his wallet. A car lease, credit card payments, Pilates class fees—David paid them all. Pastor Josephus would often remind him of 1 Timothy 5:8 whenever David started to get worked up: "But if anyone does not provide...for those of his household, he has denied the faith and is worse than an unbeliever." It *was* his house.

The panty sniffing incident aside (which had occurred a good while after Rachel's doggy-style display in their marriage bed and shortly after the England trip), David had been a good boy, tempering his rage and his lust by attending Remnant Church functions at least four times a week in addition to the Saturday service. (It kept him from throttling Mr. Rogers at school or anywhere else, but that oft-imagined scenario seemed like the least of his problems now.) He'd gotten involved at the church, overseeing the collection basket, filling in on keyboards one Saturday, even taking the lion's share of the readings on a couple of occasions.

Other than his time in front of a class as an English teacher at Father Hoskins High, which he enjoyed, David was not much of a people person. In fact, there were only four people who moved him, all for different reasons: Rachel, his hump-happy spouse, who moved him now only because he couldn't move her from his house; Amanda, their once-sweet, now sullen adolescent daughter; Pastor Josephus, who looked like Christopher Plummer with prison muscles and sounded like him too during shiver-inducing sermons on the investigative judgment or conditional immortality; and Ariel O'Connor, Amanda's best friend and David's new personal saviour.

Ariel and Amanda had become friends during their sophomore year, when they both served on the crew for Hoskins High's production of *The Tempest*. They were complete opposites in every way. Ariel was a lithe giggle-goddess, and like her namesake in the play, she was whip-smart. His daughter had yet to shed her baby fat, and her face was awash in both freckles and pimples topped off with a red blotchiness. She was awkward around strangers and a mediocre student—except in Theater Arts. There Amanda excelled behind the scenes, painting a Danish castle for a backdrop or sewing pantaloons, occasionally filling in as the prompter—and, once, treading the boards as Anita in *West Side Story*, no longer the understudy. (The original Anita was unavailable for the final show; she'd gotten herself pregnant and had finally told her parents, who were having the situation taken care of immediately—at least that was the scuttlebutt David had heard in the teacher's lounge; the Remnants were soon protesting outside the girl's house.) For one nail-biting performance, David clung to his program as his daughter, in a quavery warble, made her way through the comedic "America" and her sensuous contribution to the "Tonight Quintet" by treating each note and syllable the same way she treated school, her parents, even the news of her father's recent conversion: with palpable boredom and a hint of outright hatred. (The latter helped her, however, when it came to the fury needed for her part of "A Boy Like That/I Have a Love.") Her dancing was clumsy—it was as if she suffered from some sort of vestibular disorder—but it was obvious that she knew the routines. Her non-singing acting scenes were a little better, but she still looked as if she'd rather be anywhere else. Amanda loved the theater, but she wanted to be behind the stage or under it or even above it, anything but on it. She was a facilitator, not a player. (At home, she was a navigator, maneuvering between the sacred and the profane, not a facilitator, which was an impossible job for an adult let alone a teenager, but one Rachel had tried to force upon their daughter unsuccessfully.)

Ariel O'Connor first showed up on David's radar during the England trip, a school-sponsored event for seniors in the AP/Honors program; David was one of the lucky chaperones. (He'd pulled some strings so Amanda could go, foolishly believing the trip would afford them some much needed father-daughter time.) Ariel and Amanda had been friends for almost two years, but since his daughter rarely had a conversation with him or brought friends home to hang out and eat pizza, he'd never met Ariel formally. (The camaraderie of the students on the trip, however, would result in sleepover events at home.) David had seen them together in the halls, goofing off between periods, but he'd never had Ariel O'Connor in one of his classes, and she wasn't in his section for British Literature, a required course for those planning on going to the UK. In England, however, there were no sections, no divisions except one: the adults slept in their own rooms, separate from the students, which he supposed was a given, but it was too bad: David would have liked seeing what Ariel wore to bed (he was already smitten), he would have enjoyed hearing what it sounded like when she peed. He knew his lusting for Ariel—who was only seventeen—was a sin, but somewhere deep inside, he was starting not to care, not even when Pastor Josephus, apropos of nothing since he'd never mentioned Ariel to him, whispered Job 31:1 in his ear: " 'I have made a covenant with my eyes; how then could I gaze at a virgin?' "

While there would eventually be a doctrinal shift concerning virgins, at the time David wanted to retort with Psalm 37:4: "Delight yourself also in the Lord," which he had, "and He shall give you the desires of your heart," but he would do no such thing to the Pastor, who was here in Mondauk County solely to prepare the core of the 144,000 remnants ("the number of those who were sealed," according to Revelation 7) for what was to come. Normally, meditating on the Rapture made his balls tingle, but now they tingled for another reason entirely.

He'd been lucky enough to have his own room on the England trip. Most of the other teacher-chaperones were women, and the one other male teacher suffered from a bronchial ailment that required him to have a humidifier going twenty-four hours a day—all of which was good for David; he needed his space, though he knew that the amount of time he spent masturbating about Ariel was absurd and could have been better spent reading his Bible, the one with the red cover that Pastor Josephus had given to him on his first night at Remnant Church, but the red Bible wasn't as new as Ariel was, and, right or wrong, he thought, beauty wins out every time, even over salvation. And a beauty she was: slender but with enough meat on her bones to give her thighs some definition. (The students didn't have to wear their school uniforms on trips, and Ariel's short skirts drove him to distraction; he always wanted to drop his pen so he could bend down and look up her skirt—the old schoolboy trick— and possibly see the crotch of her panties, which he imagined to be a very warm place.) Because she tended to show a little cleavage, he could tell that she was a full B cup, and since she occasionally went braless, he knew that she had slightly puffy areolas with nipples that became tight little buttons whenever they got hard. Her hair was black like Rachel's, but David ignored the similarity. He doubted very much that Ariel had been butt fucked by one of his colleagues on David's bed, leaving a stain that ruined the sheets.

Ariel was prettier than Rachel in the way that girls are prettier than women. But Ariel was more than just pretty, a word that implied being aesthetically trifling. She was also beautiful, maybe more beautiful than Rachel, who rarely laughed anymore, having once been a dog in front of her husband. The unsullied always trumped the stained.

Rachel was insolent rather than sorry—sorry she got caught maybe, but that was it—and it wore on her looks. Other than some initial blubbering, Rachel's tone had only really changed once: instead of pinballing from indifference to contentiousness, she became conciliatory and coquettish; she even seemed to look, if not younger, than at least lighter, but that was the day after she'd been served with divorce papers, it was the day it became clear to her that he intended to use every possible legal means to keep the house. The change lasted less than an hour when he proved immovable, her face returning to its post-anal countenance, a creased and furrowed choleric look. When he finally asked her why she had broken their marriage covenant, she told him that she took Jim Rogers, unprotected, up her ass because David had become just another boring little man in their boring little town who was content with being little, his dreams having expired when he lost his ambition and willingness to strike out for new territory, both literally (since he seemed okay with living and dying in the borough of Mondauk Proper) or figuratively (since, according to the latest poll in *Cosmopolitan*, her man was dead inside). Well, the joke was on Rachel, because he had dreams (mostly about Ariel now, which had eclipsed the ones where he caused Mr. Rogers grievous harm), he'd struck out for new territory by joining the Remnant Church, and as far as having a particular goal, his ambition was to turn his dreams about the giggle-goddess into lip-smacking, Technicolor reality.

Ariel had cheekbones stolen from da Vinci's *Madonna Litta*, which depicted the Virgin Mary breastfeeding the Christ child, a fitting image, David thought, since not only did he want to kiss Ariel's breasts, but she was also (unknowingly) giving him sustenance—not to mention that she was more than likely still a virgin. Atop one cheekbone, she had a mole, or maybe it was a tumescent freckle, that gave her face Hawthorne's little flaw. Oh, and her eyes—in the light admitted by the stain glass windows surrounding Shakespeare's grave in the chancel of Holy Trinity Church he noticed how her amber-colored eyes had reddish-orange flecks that seemed to relish the opportunity to flare flirtatiously. And her laugh! My God—it could be so conspiratorial. And when he'd given his little speech to the students about Shakespeare's death and she'd whispered her little joke, pitched low but so he could hear it, he was part of the conspiracy—much to Amanda's chagrin.

David told them about the old charnel house, then read the last two lines of Shakespeare's epitaph to the group: " 'Blessed be the man that spares these stones / And cursed be he that moves my bones.' "

Ariel shivered, crossed herself, and moved so close to him that the back of their hands touched more than once.

"No boners for Bill," Ariel whispered. "Poor, poor Bill."

"Eww," Amanda said, disgusted, her arms crossed.

Ariel shrugged. "He doesn't want his bones moved," she whispered again. "It's out of my hands."

"Double eww," Amanda said.

When Ariel had moved to his side and they had their slight bodily contact, David had lowered his clipboard to hide his hard-on, but he couldn't help but wonder if Ariel's silly joke had a double meaning. Was the line about not wanting his bones moved a reference to his marital status—because he was still married, he didn't want her to touch his boner, thus it was out of her hands? Did that mean she had she noticed his arousal?

He knew no one else had. Some of the students (and a couple of the teachers) were practically asleep on their feet. They weren't impressed with Holy Trinity Church or Shakespeare's grave, but Ariel asked lots of questions once they were outside, especially about Shakespeare's will and his puzzling bequeathment to his wife Anne of "my second best bed." The line continued to be a source of debate among Shakespearean scholars, David told his attentive, alluring pupil, while his daughter stood nearby looking increasingly irritated. Without warning Ariel grabbed the upper part of his arm and leaned in close. He could feel one of her boobs pressing up against him. "It's a mystery for the ages," she stage whispered before Amanda dragged her away.

David realized choices were about to be made as he stood in the unusually warm afternoon air and smelled Ariel's woody perfume, which rose from her neck like incense from a thurible. And David was aware, even then, how terrible these choices were, but in retrospect, hugging the wall outside the Constitution Center bathrooms in Philadelphia, deciding a course of action hadn't been as dramatic as he'd imagined. He'd ended up where he was not because he'd fallen backwards into a pool with no visible bottom, but because after his concupiscence wore down his conscience, drop by drop, like Chinese water torture, he'd waded fathom by fathom until he was immersed; in other words, there was no big splash, just a sudden awareness that he was in over his head, absorbed in evil, which is how it appeared on the surface. Isaiah had warned, "Woe to those who call evil good, and good evil," but David thought that also implied that good and evil were two sides of the same sword; all it would take would be a turn of the wrist to reveal his desire for fleshly delights to be a yearning for cleaving and covenanting. Because that was what this was all about, wasn't it? 1 Corinthians 7:14: "The unbelieving wife is sanctified by her husband." It was a matter of degrees: one quick step to the left, one twist of a skinny arm, and a young girl would be saved.

David's conversion had begun with a sign—a sign on the small front lawn of a shoebox-shaped church. The sign was one of those large Going Out of Business numbers complete with a trailer hitch.

THE CHOICE IS YOURS was what the first Remnant Church sign he'd seen had read.

What choice, he'd thought at the time. When he'd stumbled home from some parent-teacher conferences that had ended abruptly due to a fire alarm, he didn't choose to discover his wife, in a position she hadn't adopted since before Amanda was born, being willingly violated by a fellow teacher (who must have ducked out of the meetings early). David believed the choices left to him after that moment were extremely limited. And to add a punch in the face to a kick in the balls, the hirsute individual screwing his wife was the boneheaded and smug Mr. Rogers, the swaggering macho man who turned into a glad-handing, apple-polishing reincarnation of the more famous Mister Rogers whenever he was around the headmaster or the dean, only instead of "Won't You Be My Neighbor?" he blathered an obsequious hymn, his boastfulness replaced by soft-spoken deprecation; he would even wear cardigan sweaters to faculty meetings; all that was missing was his hand up some puppet's ass. Pointing towards John 8:7, Pastor Josephus was always urging David to forgive Rachel and reconcile with her before the Remnant congregation. (Even if reconcilement was in the cards, which it wasn't, David knew it would never be sealed in a Remnant ceremony; he wasn't sure who Rachel hated more: him or the Pastor.) The tenets of the Church then were clear: his only other option was to shun her (divorce was forbidden), but according to the Pastor, that would require him to shun Amanda as well. He cited First Corinthians: if a wife is not consecrated by her husband, their "children would be unclean."

David liked neither option. He wanted three things: to kick the Whore of Babylon out of his house (accompanied by her collection of vibrators); to have their unholy union severed legally (even if doing so meant he was risking being shunned himself); and to gain sole custody of Amanda. Rachel had become a lousy, dangerously narcissistic parent since being buggered by the history teacher. She spent her days shopping at Peddler's Village or antiquing in New Hope, then lunching at Dettera or Karla's, and she spent her nights: who knows where?; Amanda was an afterthought.

But the tramp somehow had a better lawyer than he did. (Maybe she used her anus as an incentive or even as a form of payment.) She refused to sign the divorce papers. She wanted the house and began playing the game well, well enough to leave him playing nothing but catch-up. She filed a counter-affidavit denying that the marriage was irretrievably broken, and because she continued to live in his house, the cohabitation prevented him from suing on the grounds of adultery, which would be difficult to prove in court and expensive anyway. (Their cohabitation was part of a condonation defense—that Rachel's behavior was somehow condoned by their remaining to live in the same house; it was tricky to fight unless he could provide evidence of another "conjugal unkindness," but he didn't think even his harlot of a wife would be so stupid, not if she was serious about keeping the house.)

So what kind of choices did he have left? Leave his wife and home and never see his petulant kid, whom he loved more than he'd previously allowed himself to admit? Pretend it had never happened, pretend he'd never seen Jim Rogers' hairy, spotted ass? Not a chance in hell. "Grow up," Rachel had told him, and *there* was a choice. Of course, she'd said that after initially expressing that she was sorry (many tears), it had never happened before (huge crocodile tears), it would never happen again (boo fucking hoo), Jimmy (*Jimmy!*) had worn a condom (a lie, he was sure), a Magnum (the first dig of many to come as the curtains fell on the obligatory *show* of penitence). So not a lot of choices, no siree Bob, no good ones anyway, and it wasn't easy to maintain clarity either, not when Mr. Rogers was apparently hung like a racehorse.

But what he realized (and maintained through the fever dream of Ariel) was that it was incredibly important to him that he didn't lose Amanda. He held out hope for some kind of relationship with his daughter. Since eighth grade or so, it was as if blood was their only connection. He desperately wanted to change that, but he didn't have a clue how. Of course, the Ariel situation could muck things up even further, but he was going to try to have it all; there was nothing to lose since he had nothing now—nothing except the Remnant Church.

IT'S YAHWEH OR THE HIGHWAY, JOHN 14.6 was what the sign read the next time he passed it. A lapsed Catholic (or as he and Rachel used to joke in better times, a relaxed Catholic), he found the sign funny. (He was also somewhat inebriated at the time.) My way or the highway, he told Rachel that night, and her attitude changed from contemptuous to indignant and she dug in her (stiletto) heels.

On a Friday night that was no different from any other Friday night since the infidelity, he'd been halfway through a bottle of Tullamore Dew (his usual companion after witnessing the Rogering of his wife) when he drove past the sign a third time—and came to a cartoon-like screeching halt.

SLOW DOWN—FEEL THE LOVE was what the sign said, and it spoke to him; it murmured to the Dew in his veins. *What did love feel like? He wanted to know.* When he stumbled into the church, Pastor Josephus was just setting up for the next day's Sabbath service, for the Sabbath (as he would learn) was observed on Saturday (a fundamental Adventist belief). The Pastor didn't speak a word as David made his way to the center of the church, where he stood swaying. The holy man simply embraced him and told David that he was home and that here his pain would be healed. The Pastor called him David son of Catriona, although he didn't remember mentioning his mother's name. Most members didn't call Josephus Pastor; they called him Prophet.

Since then, David had missed only a few Saturday services, and early on he started frequenting the weekday Bible study classes and often attended Friday night Vespers. He even went with a few other members, all wearing Jesus Loves You t-shirts, to proselytize on the Mondauk Common near County Hall. He felt silly and hoped he didn't bump into anyone he knew, but he figured it was just new convert jitters. He'd found a saviour in Jesus of Nazareth. He'd been saved from hairy, spotted asses like Jim Rogers. He'd been saved from the memory of someone else inside his wife. David grew to love Jesus Christ, whom he hardly recognized from his days as a Catholic. Since his rebirth as a Remnant, Jesus was like an imaginary friend made real; He was not only beside him, He filled up his entire being—that is until Ariel O'Connor entered into his heart and ignited a blaze in his loins.

Had she been sent here to save him too or tempt him? David didn't know but as far as Ariel was concerned, he didn't see much difference between sanctification and corruption. It came down to a matter of degrees, as so much would when it came to Ariel: whether he ended up tasting heaven or having his tongue (and everything else) burnt by hell, it suddenly didn't matter a whit, as long as he was led to his fate by this sweet, dark angel, whom he desired to hold tightly in his arms lest she fly away. He was in love with her, and he surrendered his torrid heart to Ariel much the way he'd surrendered his unkempt soul to Jesus. Ariel was now why he got up in the morning, and she was the reason he struggled with his body night after night in the guest bedroom before he finally fell asleep, satisfied and damned.

Rachel didn't know about Ariel; if she ever found out, he would need to tread lightly. But he assumed she would only become aware of her if he actually began a relationship with the giggle-goddess, which would mean he was already proceeding carefully, as there would be Amanda to consider, not to mention the age difference. And if Rachel one day discovered that David had consummated this still-imaginary relationship, it would essentially close off any remaining legal avenues to being rid of her, for if he ever got Rachel in court, she could use recrimination as her defense and counterclaim that he too was being adulterous, which would mean that neither of them could claim the fault of the other in order to get a divorce. The result would be that for the time being, unless circumstances changed, they would be legally stuck together. Other than the house, which she'd decorated and landscaped meticulously, he couldn't figure out why Rachel was working so hard to remain married when it was obvious, at least from where he stood when he opened his bedroom door to find her in flagrante delicto, that it was not very important to her.

In the pre-Ariel days, Rachel's attorney had made some noise about David belonging to a cult, but his lawyer told him that they were just sabre-rattling; regardless, cults had First Amendment protection unless they were causing injury to themselves or to others. (David thought that the Church got a bad rap, mainly due to an earlier incarnation years ago; he'd seen no evidence of thought-reform and there'd been no violence.) The implied threat in her attorney's denigration of the Remnants was that she could make a case to the courts that David needed to be removed from their home for Amanda's sake, for her safety. But Rachel only wanted custody of Amanda because she thought it would help her get the house, never taking into account that her poor and at times nonexistent parenting practices were easier to prove in a court of law than any of her threatened assertions.

All of which was why shunning would be necessary if David did not take the appropriate actions that would lead to a rapprochement with Rachel: the congregation needed to be kept pure, as they were the firstfruits (Revelation 14:4) of the 144,000 remnants who will be raised up in the Rapture when the End of Days comes. Reconcilement was important for more than just the reasons he was originally given, but its ecclesiastical significance was revealed to him, like everything was to the members, in a piecemeal fashion; it could be frustrating, but maybe this was the way the Pastor's gift of prophecy worked, or perhaps there were reasons beyond their understanding that required him to dole out the truth in such a way. Regardless, mending his marriage was an ongoing topic in the Church. They prayed on it and the Pastor laid his hands on him on more than one occasion, but David did nothing and had no plans to—until Ariel came into his life, an event he kept to himself as long as he could.

Although the Pastor stated that Rachel's adulterous actions would lead her to perdition if she did not embrace the Lord, the holy man placed the failure to reconcile squarely on David's tense shoulders: his refusal to return to the marriage bed not only made it more difficult for Rachel to repent, it was also a repudiation of the Word of God. "Hebrews 8:12," he was told again and again. " 'For I will be merciful to their unrighteousness, and their sins I will remember no more.' " Priestholder Jakob told him to always keep in mind Colossians 3:19: "Husbands, love your wives, and do not be bitter toward them." There was no end to scripture verses that applied to his situation. (His head swam with them, mixing uncomfortably with images of Ariel in various states of undress.) The Pastor and the Priestholders and the other members believed that the verses lent spiritual weight to the Remnants' insistence that he let his wife back into his heart, missing the part where she kicked him out of hers. (They continued to labor under the false belief that once the McNultys were reunited, he would bring her into the Remnant fold.) He was reminded that although Rachel was ultimately responsible for her own actions, so was he. He was told that shunning doesn't dissolve the sacred bonds of matrimony, so it would make it next to impossible for him to remarry. "For to do so," Priestholder Jakob said, "would be considered adulterous and bigamous—if Rachel was still alive, that is."

"One cannot go underground without a mate," Pastor Josephus said. " 'A male and his female,' like God said to Noah."

Go underground?

David was asked to examine his life to uncover aspects of his behavior that may have contributed to the marital discord. What could he tell them? Before the shit hit the fan, he'd grown apathetic: teaching was joyless; he'd rather masturbate than sleep with his wife;

and saddest of all, he'd begun to think that he felt the same way about his daughter as she apparently felt about him. It didn't take him long, however, to realize that he loved her as much as he did the day she was born, but it seemed clear that they were both suffering from melancholia in their own unique ways; he just didn't have the vaguest notion on how to respond to Amanda's gloominess and hostility. He also didn't have a clue as to why this ennui had settled upon him, but before Rachel had allowed Mr. Rogers to park the Neighborhood Trolley around back, David had begun to think it had something to do with having almost everything that a middle-class guy could reasonably hope to attain. He had a great house with a decent mortgage rate, and he and Rachel always drove nice cars; he had the job

that he'd gone to college to get, and while it didn't pay a whole lot, it paid more than most parochial school teaching jobs did; he had an intelligent, hot wife who just kept getting hotter (and increasingly temperamental, then dissatisfied, and ultimately unfaithful); and he had an enigmatic daughter (who didn't love or respect him, but at least she was still under his roof, and there was always hope that this was just an overly-long phase). What happened when you believed you had it all, even if it wasn't perfect? He had no idea that Jesus and Ariel both awaited him after his generally idyllic life had become blemished; he had no inkling that there was going to anything more to look forward to especially after his marriage became thoroughly damaged.

Rachel used to be the definition of a good Catholic girl. It had taken him months just to get a hand job after they started dating, and that awkward tug was it until they were married, she told him. He went out and bought a ring the next day and proposed before lunch. He worked hard on becoming a Super Catholic (which wasn't easy) and made sure they sprinted to the altar. He wanted her that bad. Pre-infidelity, Rachel's faith in Catholicism grew shaky in the wake of all the sexual abuse scandals; she spoke disdainfully of Mother Church and the Bishop of Rome. But altar boy diddling was one thing; the Remnant Church, with its shady past and premillennialist beliefs, was another fucking ball of wax altogether. After he became a Remnant and started not only going to services but also attending AA meetings in the basement of the church, the first thing Rachel did was to forbid Amanda from ever attending a Remnant Church function. (As if! Given his non-relationship with his daughter, he thought that dragging her to see the Pastor would go over like a lead balloon.) The second thing Rachel did was lay down the law (she was good for a lay): no proselytizing in the house. She didn't ever want to hear anything about the Church. (Remnants were required to proselytize, starting in the home, and they were required to find or have spouses within the faith.) There was to be no witnessing or laying on of hands, she said. No problem there—David tried to give his testimony to Rachel only once (and wasn't that fun?), and he didn't know how to lay on hands, not in any way that would mean something. Laying on of hands was necessary for someone to receive the Holy Spirit or the Paraclete, as the third person in the Trinity was sometimes called in the Church; he'd been the recipient (more than once) but it hadn't taken enough for him to confer the Spirit upon others yet. It was one of the things in the way of his becoming a Priestholder—that and he had no mate. "144,000 is an even number for a reason," Priestholder Jakob told him; he wanted to ask how that would work since some families had three kids, but he didn't; he just continued tithing as well as making weekly Freewill Offerings equaling an additional five percent of his paycheck, plus he paid fifty dollars for every mortal sin, a Transgression Reparation.

David did his best to ignore Rachel, and he tried not to bring up his faith in the house. (It wasn't as if they spoke anyway, not unless it was completely necessary.) But when the Prophetic Seminars became intensely eschatological in nature, he began giving some serious thought to building a small bunker in the yard underneath the shed, especially after aiding in the construction of a large one beneath the church. It was around then that Rachel, in a prescient moment, added an amendment to her list of Remnant don'ts: there was to be no building of a backyard or basement bunker in advance of the End Times. But it was *his* house, and he could put in a moat if he wanted.

The need to build bunkers was the latest piece of divine direction from Pastor Josephus regarding the necessary preparations for the Apocalypse. He told the congregation that the End Days were nigh. "When the first angel blows his trumpet, the scriptures tell us that hail and rain mixed with blood shall fall from heaven, and so it begins." (It had certainly been raining shit in the McNulty house for some time, David thought, if that was a sign of anything.) Over the next couple of weeks, as Pastor Josephus revealed more of his visions of the Second Coming and presented a lengthy exegesis of Revelation, it became clear to David that God had given mastery of

His Word to the master. He felt sorry for the apostates (the Papists, the Protestants, the infidels), for they did not hear the Prophet's voice; they couldn't even begin to understand the meaning of the word redemption.

Before Ariel materialized and he discovered that there might be more than one way to be saved, the Church was his life, so it didn't take long for him to decide to start excavating in the shed so he could begin building what the Pastor called "your personal ark," even if his inclusion in the 144,000 was far from certain. All because of Rachel. He'd be better off a widower. He kept praying that he'd receive a dispensation from the Pastor or be paired up with another "single" if he truly needed to have a partner—not a mate—to ensure the number was even and that he would be included: perhaps the ninety-year-old spinster in the wheelchair or maybe the autistic girl, the Millers' only child. In church lingo, matchups between two Remnants who were not romantically involved were called "pairings of potential" and couldn't consist of a brother and a sister or a single mother and her child. The word "potential" was taken seriously; anything vaguely incestuous was to be avoided, as were same-sex pairings, so two unrelated grade-schoolers of the opposite sex—frightened half out of their minds with all this talk—or a middle-aged man with an eight-year-old girl: these were permissible pairings of potential.

He was considered a "true single," meaning that he was someone who was already part of a union, but that his spouse was an unbeliever, a hostile; that he was estranged from Rachel (even though they lived in the same house) was just icing on the cake. One of the Priestholders intimated that David could only be paired with another true single, but the Pastor never mentioned such a stipulation (and David was afraid to ask). True or not, he thought that he couldn't be the only true single in the congregation—could he? He wondered what would happen to any unmatchable singles (or true singles) if the Pastor remained intent on only having couples and Church-approved pairings be part of the 144,000. Would they be left here to suffer the tribulations or would the Priestholders take them out back and shoot them before all hell broke loose, mercy sacrifices? Neither answer would surprise him, especially since the Priestholders all appeared to be packing as of late. (He was curious why they needed all that heat if they were going to be raptured; did they expect an assault on the church before the Big Event?) The ever-evolving eschatological rules left him disoriented, and while he still believed in the Pastor's mastery of the Word, he began to struggle with the whole concept of millennialism. When he finally came out the other end, there was still much he couldn't wrap his head around, but he now thought he understood the pairing policy, especially after Ariel appeared. David just wanted to be saved with the other Remnants after the plagues and before their thousand-year reign began. But a thousand years was just a prelude to eternity, and eternity could get mighty lonely.

And that was where Ariel came in—and Pastor Josephus agreed.
I AM ALSO MAKING A LIST AND CHECKING IT TWICE
LOVE,
GOD

Some of the girls on the bus giggled at the latest Remnant sign. David looked to see that Ariel O'Connor wasn't one of them. She wasn't. (His daughter's face was unreadable.) There was an old radio hanging from the back of the bus driver's seat, and "Cry Me a River" poured out of it at a volume so low, it took David almost a full minute to recognize it, but he couldn't figure out who the female singer was. The song had an earthy feel to it, and for an unknown reason, it unsettled him. Ariel's eyes were closed and her lips were moving over the old lyrics like she was muttering a prayer she wanted no one else to hear. God, how he loved her. He wanted to eat her up.

The seniors were on their final class trip. Destination: Philadelphia. Compared to England, this was nothing, David knew, but the City of Brotherly Love was less than an hour from Mondauk County, and there was plenty to see and do there, starting with Edgar Allen Poe's house on Seventh Street where the Hoskins High students listened attentively to an apparently entertaining park ranger during the short tour. David blocked it all out. He too had made a list and was checking it twice. He'd worked it out so that Ariel was on his bus and in his section. Amanda was too—it might have looked suspicious if she wasn't; the girls were practically inseparable, which was going to make this a significantly trickier operation. Ariel called them the Janus Girls, after the Roman deity who was usually depicted as having two faces; he was the god of beginnings and endings, which David thought was fitting. Splitting the Janus Girls could be like trying to split an atom with a pair of scissors—or it could be like trying to crack an apple in his bare hands: challenging but not impossible.

What his plan really depended on was the End Times being right around the fucking corner, but he was sure they were. There were too many signs now. Pastor Josephus had said so himself. David believed there was a significance to the events that led him here, a synchronicity even, and all the signs, taken together, signified a discordance, a calamity, an annihilation: Rachel getting banged in her backdoor by Mr. Rogers (who didn't stop on his hurried way out to put on his shoes like the real Mister Rogers would have if he was an over-cologned lecher); David discovering the Remnant Church and actually being baptized in his new faith (which would have sent his late, severely Catholic mother over the edge); Amanda disappearing down the rabbit hole of adolescence (and who knew how deep that went?); and the biggest, most momentous sign of all: Ariel O'Connor's conspiratorial joke at Holy Trinity Church.

The Remnant Church believed in signs. It believed that the final sign signifying the coming of the End Times would be when the so-called "Christians" who ran the government, the born again liars and the Bible Belt scavengers, passed a law requiring everyone to observe a sacred day of rest—on Sunday. The Remnants, 144,000 in number, would go underground, crouching in root cellars if necessary. Remnants they would truly become. (David didn't see how they were going to reach a membership of 144,000 in time—they were a small congregation—but perhaps this number included good souls from other Adventist churches and maybe even some from the Jewish faith, for although they didn't know Christ, John wrote in Revelation that members from each of the twelve tribes of Israel will be saved; one of the Priestholders said that any believer who recognized Saturday as the Sabbath would go into hiding, but only the 144,000 Remnants, led by the Prophet, would emerge; David assumed the truth was above his pay grade.) Seven deadly plagues were scheduled to follow their going underground, then a great darkness, a sign that that their time to be caught up was imminent, and out of that darkness God was to reveal the date and time of His return to the Remnants. This would be the Parousia, as they called it, the Second Coming of the Lamb of God. "And upon His arrival, the righteous dead will be resurrected and reunited with the righteous living," Pastor Josephus explained, "and angels will carry us unto He who loves us fiercely, and in heaven the righteous will rule for a thousand years while the wicked writhe and scream and beg as Lucifer is loosed upon the earth during the Great Tribulation." This was the culmination of the Pastor's vision.

David felt like he was in a period of tribulation already, as if God had found him unworthy to be caught up. He'd fallen off the wagon during a dark night of the soul when everything crowded his cranium until he thought his skull would crack: his increasingly desperate thoughts on how to be rid of Rachel, and his helplessness as he watched Amanda slip-slip-slipping away; a growing fear of the End Times, and incongruously, a gnawing worry over his monetary woes (he'd been racking up the cardinal sins)—and worst of all, his urgent need to satiate his acute lust and equally severe love for Ariel. So he started drinking again. But he wasn't stumbling out of McCullough's or passing out in the yard this time; it was just a nip here and there, sometimes before second period and again before seventh, it was nothing to worry about—until it was, until he was finishing a fifth of Tullamore Dew every day. It came to a head on the bleakest night in memory when he was convinced that he would literally explode from all the whiskey, rage, and backed up semen that flooded every available space in his wretched body. He somehow managed to drive to the church. (It took him almost five minutes just to find the right key to put into the ignition.) When the Pastor opened the church door, David dropped to his knees, and check in hand, confessed all, including Ariel, and to his surprise, the holy man forgave him for everything. He almost fainted as the pressure left his body. (It didn't help that he was pretty drunk). Although he was certain the abjectness would return, he was also sure that the master, whom the Lord God saw fit to impart certain aspects of His grand finale for mankind, would have the answers or at least tell him where he could find them.

David was humbled and felt blessed when the Pastor invited him into the Sanctum, the room behind the altar. They were told that only the Priestholders could go back there—but apparently the Daughters of God were also allowed to enter the on the nights they were on duty. As the Pastor rested on a wine-colored velvet chair, one Daughter sat on the floor and massaged his feet. The other sat in his lap and rubbed his neck and shoulders. The Pastor was always attended by two Daughters at night after the final function was over. It was a relatively new development. As the visions came fast and furious, illuminating his understanding of the resurrection of the dead and the book of Daniel, the Pastor was plagued by migraines that left him unable to walk without assistance during their duration. The Blessed Service of the Daughters of God was established (by whom, David didn't know) to take care of the Pastor at the end of a long day. The Daughters consisted exclusively of teenage daughters of Remnant members. Participation was completely voluntary, but the parents of those who served were told that they would be among the Chosen who surrounded the Pastor during the Rapture. The Chosen previously only consisted of the Priestholders, so his gift was enough of an honor for parents to offer up their daughters; they vied for the privilege. (A new pair was chosen every day.) Lately, the Pastor was often escorted by two Daughters after school let out, and since he'd begun encouraging parents to homeschool, he was occasionally accompanied by a pair of girls throughout the day. Two was a number of importance in the Bible: two of every animal were put upon the ark, two angels were sent to Sodom, Jesus sent out the Apostles two by two, and so on. The Remnants even ushered in the Sabbath by lighting two candles. When serving, the Daughters wore silk robes and from what David could tell, little or nothing else; they were even barefoot. Around their necks, the Daughters each wore a choker of what appeared to be ruby-red, slightly misshapen rosary beads. They were required to wear the choker at all times, the red symbolizing Mary of Bethany, who anointed Jesus' feet; Mary of Magdala, who was courageous enough to stand by Christ during His crucifixion; and the flow of blood that made the girls women.

The Pastor slept in a small building called the Chamber. It was just behind the church, close enough that when David used to drive by before he joined, he thought it was all one building, when in fact they were separated by an alley so narrow, they often joked that they wouldn't be surprised to discover a fat cat stuck between its walls one day. Some of the Remnants who'd helped build the church's bunker were able to break through the foundation walls in the basement to create a passageway between the two structures, so that the Pastor could retire for the night without having to worry about inclement weather. (The Pastor could access the basement from the Sanctum.) It was considered a big honor by the parents of the Daughters of God when their child was chosen for the Nighttide Tribute: every night one Daughter was allowed to prepare the Pastor for bed, assist him in his ablutions, and sometimes stay with him until he fell asleep. What the Pastor's wife thought of all this, David didn't know. She didn't appear to reside with her husband in the Chamber, but even if she did, the congregation would never find out from the Daughters; they were sworn to secrecy, and the Pastor said that if they broke their oath, they risked eternal damnation for themselves and their families, for they will have sinned against the Prophet. The only time David saw the Pastor's wife was during services. She sat in a chair on the side of the sanctuary and during her husband's sermons, which could last up to an hour or more at times, she'd take down the Pastor's words by hand, her pen flying furiously over white legal pads (to eventually be typed and disseminated for study). He wondered why she didn't use a recorder of some kind, but the Pastor informed them once that his wife's position in the Church—acting as his human Dictaphone, as he put it—was a way to humble her before God. David didn't even know her first name and neither did anyone else, just as no one knew her opinion on the Daughters of God. It seemed to David like the master was surrounding himself with temptation. The Pastor had told a few of them that every night he wrestled with the demon and every night he achieved victory, and indeed he frequently had scratch marks on his face and hands, but there was never any direct reference to the Nighttide Tribute in his statement. No one seemed to find any of this to be strange. The Daughters' parents happily volunteered them to put him to bed. But other than his curiosity about the Pastor's wife, David really didn't give it much thought. Who was he to question the Remnant Prophet? If sometimes things didn't add up, all that meant was that he hadn't opened his heart to the Holy Spirit—he'd lost the key and was behind the door, in Remnant-speak, he was closed. His faith was all he had, the only thing that was his own, so he accepted rather than questioned and prayed to find the key whenever he felt trapped in his own head.

"There have been doctrinal changes," Pastor Josephus said. "They are not widely known yet—just the Priestholders—but I'm telling you, David son of Catriona, because, frankly, I don't want to lose you from the congregation or leave you in the grip of Lucifer during the Rapture." The Daughter in his lap had a look that fluctuated between deer-in-the-headlights terror and pre-coital anticipation; he didn't know whether she was going to bolt or snuggle. "This concerns your earthly wife—and your sprite." David sat up so quickly, the Daughter on the Pastor's lap gave a little gasp, and the great man grabbed her by the wrist with one hand and placed a finger on her lips with the other. The Daughters were not to speak when in service. 1 Corinthians 14:34: "Let your women keep silent in the churches, for they are not permitted to speak." In the Remnant Church, the scripture only applied to the Daughters of God, particularly the next line, "they are to be submissive" by law. Once as David was leaving a late night Prayer Group, he witnessed a mother stomp into the church to retrieve her daughter, who was escorted from the Sanctum by a Priestholder. The girl was already in tears and had a large red mark on her cheek which became redder when the mother, already incensed, noticed that the choker had been removed and proceeded to slap the hell out of her daughter. Her sin? According to the Priestholder who'd been standing guard outside the Chamber—there was always one—she'd screamed during Nighttide Tribute.

The girl in the Pastor's lap adopted a serene and penitential expression that David thought looked rehearsed, but it diffused the situation; the Pastor released her wrist, leaving a bracelet of crimson finger impressions. Her eyes remained wide, darting from David to the basement door to the girl on the floor. He understood then: she'd been picked for Nighttide Tribute and had first time jitters. He risked giving her a little nod, for he too was nervous now, but it just seemed to make things worse. The girl started to squirm but a quick tug of her hair, disguised as a caress, put that to a stop.

David tried to settle back in the chair. The Pastor smiled at him. Sprite was how the holy man referred to Ariel. But he addressed David's wife first. According to Pastor Josephus, Rachel was not attending to her wifely duties. David leaned forward. The Pastor stated that Rachel was guilty of dereliction, citing Ephesians 5:22: "Wives, submit to your husbands, as to the Lord." So, the master said, it was as if they weren't married at all, therefore, he continued, lifting his hand off the Daughter's thigh to bless him: he could dissolve the marriage (spiritually; the legal woes would remain), and he could seal David and Ariel. He didn't want David to miss the big day because he ended up being an odd number, a true single with no mate. He had big plans for David during the Remnants' thousand-year reign; he wanted to ordain him, make him a Priestholder so that he and his spiritual wife could be among the Chosen. David clutched at his chest. He and Ariel would be together for all time in the light of the Lord, while Rachel endured the Great Tribulation alone. He had an erection and hoped it wasn't obvious.

The Pastor continued, saying that David would have to bring Ariel to the church, like Abraham brought his son Isaac to Mount Moriah in order to sacrifice him as God instructed. "Isaac went along willingly, although he did not know what was afoot. He was loyal to his father, but as it is told to us in Genesis 22, Abraham ultimately 'bound Isaac his son, and laid him on the altar,' for loyalty only gets you so far, and you may not even have that. So your Prophet tells you: by whatever means necessary, because time is short. The exact hour has been revealed to me, and the first angel has already raised his lips to the trumpet." He told David that the enormous effort he exerted to keep his house from Rachel was akin to worshipping a false idol, as well as being unnecessary with everything happening so soon: the signs were everywhere. Plus staying in the house, even for the short time that remained, could create a situation: if the Pastor sealed Ariel to David, and then Rachel resumed what was expected of her and made herself available to him, a conflict would arise that would reverse the spiritual annulment—bigamy was a sin and being sealed was no different than being married in the eyes of God. He thought David should move to a motel until it was time to take his sprite down into the bunker. But considering that Rachel could potentially try to prevent David from being with Ariel, the Pastor thought it would be better if Rachel were gone, which is exactly what David had been thinking for the past few weeks. It was something he should do first, he decided. God would forgive him; the Pastor essentially just gave his blessing. Then he would be free and clear to have Ariel as his spirit bride during the End Days and beyond. "Sometimes you need to make a sacrifice," the Pastor said, "to get where you're going—and it's not always about who you brought to Mount Moriah, for God stayed Abraham's hand, and in place of sacrificing Isaac, the first Patriarch made a burnt offering of a 'ram caught in a thicket by its horn.' You are going to bring the girl to the altar, yes, but for love; it's the ewe caught in its own horny skullduggery that needs to be offered up, lest you are again caught in her thicket."

"But my daughter…"

"Don't you worry about Amanda."

The following night he purchased a Buck knife.

The plan developed swiftly. He found out how to make homemade chloroform on the Internet, picking up some additional info from Amanda's old chemistry textbook. Although no Sabbath law had been passed yet, the Pastor told the Remnants the day was fast approaching (he wouldn't reveal the date) and everybody began confessing sins that they'd hidden away for years before the whole congregation. One woman admitted to going on a coke binge and leaving her two-year-old alone for most of a weekend while she had sex with a dealer and an associate in exchange for blow. A man confessed to hitting a pedestrian with his car and not stopping— either then or on the way back when he saw the same man, covered in blood, crawling on the shoulder of the road. Another man confessed that he'd had homosexual encounters in college and still fantasized about them. (His wife looked like she wanted to throw up.) It was all coming to an end; sometimes the excitement and fear made his hands tingle.

He finished his bunker beneath the shed. But as he'd discovered when helping to build the one at the church, he had no construction skills, and he didn't think his bunker was especially fortified. When he was building it, he hoped that the need for bunkers was at least somewhat metaphorical. However, in his heart he knew that none of what Pastor Josephus said would happen was either allegorical or metaphorical, which was why he was so focused on the plan, and when he realized that the seniors' visit to Philadelphia was coming up, things kicked into high gear.

He'd decided that he couldn't handle Rachel until he had Ariel. He'd struggled with the idea of dealing with Rachel at all for a bit because he so wanted her to be in the throes of the tribulations but concluded that dispatching her towards the Final Punishment on the Day of Judgment would actually be more fulfilling. To cut down on the screams, he would chloroform her first and make the sacrifice in the bathtub. He had a bunch of blankets and trash bags so he could wrap her body, put it in the backseat (the trunk was reserved), and go back inside to clean up, using a mixture of hydrogen peroxide, baking soda, and water, which according to Amanda's chemistry textbook, could make even invisible traces of blood undetectable. (It must have been a hell of a class.)

Amanda had already told him that she was going out that night with her cousins, which was fortuitous, although Ariel going missing in Philly might scuttle those plans—unless he sent her a message or two from Ariel's phone; that might assuage his daughter. He'd overheard Amanda tell another girlfriend once that Ariel was boy crazy—oh, and how that had made him swim in jealousy—so he could always write, as Ariel, that she'd met a boy from another school and snuck on his bus. *Can't talk right now ;-)* followed by *Call u later.* He wanted to get it all done in one day and hoped the Rapture occurred before an Amber Alert was issued. Either way, they'd be in the bunker by then. (No one would ever find Rachel. He didn't want Amanda to have to face the horror of having a parent murdered— possibly by the other parent. So he thought that if Rachel and Mr. Rogers were both missing with luggage and some clothes gone…) But Amanda: a storm was coming, and she hadn't been baptized or sealed. None of his plans included saving her. She would be an odd number, outside in the rain of hail and fire and blood. The Pastor had told him not to worry about his daughter, but his kind words didn't make David feel any better or less guilty.

It wasn't that he didn't want Amanda to rejoice in the glory of the Lord and take part in the thousand-year Remnant-Adventist glory, but some of Pastor Josephus' visions, related during regular services and in more detail during his Prophetic Seminars, scared David, especially the ones involving the final battle for heaven between the Remnants and the evildoers that will occur at the end of the millennium. This was truly terrifying stuff and difficult even for him. The Pastor's eschatological sermons were lengthy affairs full of locusts with tails like scorpions and armies whose horses had lion heads that spewed fire, smoke, and sulfur. He couldn't imagine his daughter sitting still long enough to hear the parts about salvation and eternal life at the end. He also didn't think Amanda could handle riding out the Apocalypse in his crude and cramped bunker, especially with her best friend, who would have been sealed to him prior to going underground, and he really didn't see her taking part in a fiercely pitched battle against Lucifer's minions. But honestly, when it came down to it, he didn't think he could handle spending that much time alone with her (or relatively alone); she frightened him anymore; the relationship he'd had with the young woman he helped create was analogous to Dr. Frankenstein and his monster—not that Amanda was monstrous; she was polite and well-spoken, and though her grades didn't reflect any interest in academics, she used to be quite inquisitive when she a little girl, always ready to jump in Vincenzo Pond to get a closer look at a water lily or to eat a whole jalapeño pepper to see what the fuss was about. But Amanda was moody; even as a child, she was given to bouts of despondency, and once she reached adolescence, she became inexplicably spiteful towards David and Rachel, as if she blamed them for her apparent existential crises.

Ultimately, he wasn't up to saving Amanda's soul or forcing her to save herself, not even now with the Rapture and the tribulations around the corner, and truth be told, not even when he first joined the Church and had the zeal of a new convert. For one, he wanted Amanda to make her own choices, plus back then, he would have had to get around Rachel and her laws, and unless his wanton wife was distracted while on all fours, taking the high hard one from an evidently virile faculty member, there was no way Rachel would have let any saving occur. "Over their dead bodies," Pastor Josephus had said, and at the time David knew *that* wasn't happening, although he'd often wished Rachel dead. It only took a few bottles of Tullamore Dew to turn a wish into an obsession and as the song went, "In time you can turn your obsessions into careers." Not exactly scripture, but the truth nonetheless from an appropriately titled song from his college days: "Hurry Down Doomsday (The Bugs are Taking Over)." But now that he had put the bottle(s) down, everything was stripped raw—no more pretense, no more procrastination—just a Buck knife making his front pocket bulge, so that he felt like an over-excited freshman on his first date, erect before he even rings the doorbell.

The Pastor sent a group of "cool-looking" young people (the God Squad) into the community of Mondauk Proper with the intention of inducing a few young souls into converting and "declaring allegiance," as Priestholder Jakob put it. Culled from the Daughters of God (only the prettiest) and the congregation's budding young Priestholders (just the handsomest), the God Squad haunted wherever teens congregated: malls, concerts, even outside of schools if possible, cajoling their peers to come listen to the Prophet, be baptized, and if found worthy, become one of the 144,000. Because the clock was ticking, they were told to be relentless. "Our future lies in the obeisance of our youth," Pastor Josephus had explained, and at first David had wondered what future he was referring to since the end of the world as they knew it was imminent, but the master explained that he was speaking of the importance of swelling their numbers with blossoming souls: they needed more young bodies to be sealed, especially teenage girls whom the Pastor said were the most fertile of all women. Fertility would be crucial during their thousand-year reign, when they would retain their earthly bodies but remain the same age. "We will need to populate heaven," Pastor Josephus had said. When he was drinking, he thought that the Pastor wanted baby factories, but now he had a better understanding, and he'd confessed his cynicism and paid a Transgression Reparation. Regardless, David secretly hoped that Amanda avoided the God Squad.

On this one issue, he sided with the soon-to-be-disappeared sodomite: even during her fish-on-Friday years, Rachel said let Amanda have God on Sundays, if she wanted to go to Mass (which she usually didn't), and on Easter and Christmas when Assumption of Our Lady swelled with parishioners (there were many relaxed Catholics in the town of Mondauk Proper); when she was old enough, she could make her own spiritual decisions. They'd sent her to a Catholic high school because she'd gone to a Catholic elementary school; they thought she'd want to be with her friends who were making the same transition. Also, her tuition was waived because he worked there, a perk that played that played into their decision. He knew that being a teacher in her high school was a source of endless embarrassment for his daughter, but he made sure that she was never in one of his classes. He just wanted to make things comfortable for her. Hard enough having a Jesus freak for a father and an Ass Master for a mother.

They'd been all over Independence Mall, and the last stop on the Philadelphia trip was the National Constitution Center. Newly sober and armed with the Pastor's blessing, his mind was clear, but as the guided tour dragged on, David knew he was running out of time. The tour was going to make them late (they were to be back at school by last bell), and if that happened, the other teachers would hustle the students to the buses as soon as it ended. According to his plan (which was based on nothing but intuition and desired expectation), it had to happen during the Philadelphia school trip—and now it had to happen at the Constitution Center; for whatever reason, he'd hesitated reaching for her at all their other stops (Independence Hall, the Liberty Bell Center, the Benjamin Franklin Museum). His heart was pounding to be free of his rib cage, and he was sweating through his shirt. Old Mrs. Mingol, the algebra teacher, even asked him if she could get him some water and encouraged him to sit. But Mrs. Mingol tended to believe anything that anyone told her (her students had been taking advantage of her guilelessness for years), so it was easy to send her in another direction with just a simple lie.

He should have known that it would be near impossible to stick to a plan in a situation such as this. Even though they began the day following a fairly strict itinerary, anything involving students outside of school was bound to end up being fluid. (They were late getting to the Constitution Center because Debbie D'Angelo had tripped while running and skinned both of her knees on the sidewalk; the Rangers provided first aid. Then, in all the excitement, they lost track of Craig Miller and finally found him surrounded by three teenage tourists who were taking turns feeling his biceps.) David had hoped for a quick tour, as they were cutting it close with time, but no such luck. If they didn't blow the itinerary timetable, the other faculty would let the students wander around the museum for a bit, which is what he needed to happen before they boarded the buses and headed back to the suburbs. It would be his last chance of the day, and who knows how many days were left? He touched the red Bible in his side pocket.

So if the tour didn't go overtime, it was down to was separate-and-seize; he was going to have to improvise in order to take her with a minimum of fuss. ("Take her" sounded much better than "kidnap her.") Everything was coming to a head. It was difficult to tamp down his anxiety and, honestly, it was equally hard to put a lid on his excitement. The anticipation was killing him. The singer of that song, the one that was big when he was in high school, was right: "The waiting is the hardest part."

He'd already stocked the bunker, even put a few issues of *Seventeen*, along with some makeup and tampons, down there. He wished he'd had more time to learn how to build a proper one. He had the necessary shelter-ventilation pump, but Priestholder Jakob's bunker had a periscope-like contraption and the Pastor's bunker beneath the church had a heating and cooling system (which worried David: did that mean that the Apocalypse wasn't as close as he'd been led—or convinced himself—to believe?). He should have asked one his more knowledgeable Remnant brothers for help in the construction, but it didn't matter now. After they were sealed by the Pastor, they would be counted among the 144,000, so he would just have to pray that what he built would shield them from the terror that was going to fall from the skies and scorch the earth, as well as hope that it would be enough to hold and hide Ariel until such time as Jesus came a-calling.

After he'd cleaned the trunk, he'd driven his car to the Old City neighborhood last night, so it was just blocks away from Independence Mall. (Poe's house was the only stop on the trip that wasn't on or around the Mall.) He just hoped that when they discovered Ariel hadn't gotten on the bus (which would probably be right away because of his daughter), they didn't note his absence too, at least for a little while. He was counting on still being easy to overlook, Mrs. Mingol aside, and she more than likely had already forgotten the incident. Before he left the city with his betrothed, he would call the school on his cell—yes, he would say, he'd been hunting Ariel too—which was true. He'd tell them that through the Constitution Center's glass walls, he'd seen Ariel running across the lawn towards a group of students from another school. They headed west on Arch Street, but by the time he reached the pavement, they were gone, and he'd been searching up and down all the cross streets since. No, he didn't know what school. Maybe the Constitution Center or one of the historical sites would have a list of schools and organizations who visited today. Should he come back? He could just take public transportation, he'd tell them, or he could just stay on site and talk to the Philly PD. He knew they'd tell him to do the latter, but whatever his instructions were, they'd never see him again—not in this life or the next. He figured the school would call the police right away, so better to seem like he was on the case or that he was willing to come running back to school via SEPTA—anything to throw off suspicion for a few hours until Amanda went out with her cousins and he could deal with Rachel. Once he and bride were in the bunker, nothing else would matter. But his daughter: had she seen the longing in his eyes when he watched Ariel in the halls of Hoskins High, on the England trip, during sleepovers? It was a possibility he hadn't thought of until now. Was he easy to overlook to his daughter? It seemed that way, or had she been on to him all this time? It was a risk he was going to have to take. A risk for God. A risk for true love. The Rapture couldn't come soon enough.

During the excruciatingly slow tour of the Constitution Center, David took the time to note the location of every guard and figure out the least populated path to an exit. (He would just carry Ariel out like a sick child and exit through the garage.) He also monitored everything Ariel did (all of which was precious, except for her flirtations with a couple of the jocks—that he didn't care for, but he supposed it was to be expected). When the tour was back on the ground floor, in the Grand Hall Lobby, a couple of students asked for permission to go the restrooms, and he walked them to the short hallway where the lavatories were located. He stood back and clocked the traffic in and out of the ladies room and kept track of the length of each visit (taking into account that the hallway was open on the other end), for he realized while standing that taking Ariel in the ladies room was probably his best shot with what precious minutes he might have left. The Constitution Center wasn't crowded at all and at the moment, there appeared to be only one group of students from another school there. He could always pull Ariel into a stall and wait till the bathroom was empty. (He had a couple of Valiums in his shirt pocket that he'd taken from Rachel's stash to make sure Ariel stayed out for a while; he didn't know how long the effects of chloroform lasted.) Depending upon the traffic, the hallway could give him a little cover before he made his way with her to the stairs leading to the garage. He would have to hurry without seeming to be in a rush; he wasn't worried about being seen by strangers (he would just put on the concerned dad face—worried but not worried enough to attract Good Samaritans), and guards he could handle (*"her insulin kit is in the car; we'll be fine"*); he just had to make sure they weren't seen by anyone from Hoskins High.

But he was beginning to despair and kept checking his watch obsessively—there wasn't much time left at all before they needed to leave, and the tour *still* wasn't over. (It had to be the guide's first day; she was repeating the speech on the thirty-nine signers of the Constitution that she'd given in Signers' Hall on the second floor.) Ariel and Amanda remained attached at the hip, as they'd been for most of the trip. It was going to make separate-and-seize that much harder to pull off; it would easier, he thought, to isolate Ariel from the rest of the class, than to divide the Janus Girls. But he'd known all this coming down here, and he was prepared. If it came to it, he had a second rag hidden on his person, but that was only for the worst possible scenario; it made him nauseous to imagine leaving his daughter knocked out in a corner somewhere. But his options—for everything—dwindled with every minute.

And then it happened: the tour ended as he stood keeping one eye on the bathroom hallway and the other on Ariel across the lobby, and after a word from Mr. Bogle, the Assistant Headmaster, the students dispersed, most going to either the Delegates' Café or to the gift shop, which was where he thought he saw Amanda heading—

solo. The Janus Girls had split naturally. It made him want to drop to his knees and thank the Almighty, but he knew there was work to be done.

"I gotta hit the head," Ariel announced to no one in particular, but David knew it was directed at him. "I've been holding it so long, I think I tinkled in my Underoos."

How adorable, David thought. The idea of Ariel soiling her undergarments made him distracted and hard.

He followed her down the hallway towards the bathrooms. The entrance to the café was near the other end of the hall; he could hear the shrieks and guffaws of some of the students. No other teachers or kids were near, but he knew they'd be in and out of the lavatories soon enough. Ariel pushed at the big yellow door with both hands. She turned her head once before disappearing behind the slowly closing door. Had she seen him? Had she turned her head his way? He couldn't be sure. Her eyes seemed to have been smiling in recognition. Maybe she knew. Maybe she knew they were about to be together for the rest of their lives and then some.

A crowd of students from another school suddenly filled the hallway as they left the café on their way back out to the Grand Hall Lobby. He was obliged to step aside and move out of the hall, then smile and shake hands with Fred, a teacher he'd met once and whose last name he'd long forgotten. "Looks like a storm's coming," Fred said as he looked through the glass walls. Fred had no idea.

Once the hallway was clear, David pulled the rag out of the inside pocket of his sport coat and approached the ladies' room door with stealth. (At least he hoped it was with stealth; he didn't want anyone thinking he was one of those perverts like Jim Rogers.) The smell of his homemade chloroform hit his nostrils immediately. If Ariel wasn't alone in the bathroom, David would apologize and play the concerned parent looking for his lost daughter as he stuffed the rag back into his pocket. But during his surveillance of the hallway, he hadn't seen any other women or girls enter the ladies' room in the past few minutes, at least not from his end. The only time he'd taken his eyes off it was when Fred and his students passed through. Girls were usually quick with their business, so there was no reason to think anyone else was in there.

IF YOU'RE FAR FROM GOD IN LIFE, one Remnant Church sign had read, YOU'LL BE FAR FROM GOD IN DEATH.

David approached the yellow door, the rag in hand behind his back, the odor filling up the restroom area—then the door opened and Amanda was standing in the hallway. She looked radiant, beautiful even, two adjectives he hadn't applied to his daughter since she was a toddler. The pimples were mostly gone and the blotchiness had faded. She seemed to have shed most of her baby fat. (When had that happened?) David could see she was developing something of a chest, and her bearing was more adult than adolescent.

"Our future lies in the obeisance of our youth," Amanda said with an impassive, but sorrowful face, as if she were explaining this to a two-year-old. "For the time when the righteous dead are resurrected and reunited with the righteous living is at hand."

How had he not noticed that she was wearing a Jesus Loves You t-shirt?

"I don't...how...where did you hear that?"

Amanda gave him a small, sad smile.

"From the Prophet, Dad."

David returned the smile but it was fake.

"When...?"

No, no!—his daughter was wearing a choker of what appeared to be ruby-red, slightly misshapen rosary beads.

They'd gotten to her. He'd so busy being anything but a father, digging a hole in the ground, preparing to begin his life as a sex offender, that they'd sucked his one and only daughter into this Dungeons and Dragons madness without him noticing. If anyone had tried to tell him, he hadn't been listening. *"Don't you worry about Amanda."* The tone of the Pastor's placation now sounded more prurient than reassuring, as if he'd been smacking his lips when he said it.

Amanda crinkled her nose.

"What's that smell?"

"Nothing, honey," David said, stuffing the rag into his back pocket. "Go join your friends in the café."

He handed her a twenty.

"Get whatever you want."

Amanda took the money. (A good sign.) David watched her womanly figure start to walk down the hall. He was nauseous and felt faint, and he steadied himself against the wall.

Amanda turned.

"Dad?"

He jumped.

"Yeah, hon?"

"Don't fuck her."

She turned back around and continued on her way.

David stared at the yellow door and studied the places where the paint had begun to chip or peel, each spot an attempt to reveal what was beneath it. When he heard footsteps on the other side of the door, he sprinted into the men's room, pushing the door closed behind him.

The bathroom was empty (thank God—or whomever), and as David made his way to the last stall, he tossed the rags into a trashcan. He paused to look back at the gaunt, terrified face in the mirror.

This sickness was his own, he knew. The Church was just a different viral strain, one equally as dangerous as his. And now they'd infected his daughter.

"*Now, you say you're sorry for being so untrue,*" sang a muted, wounded woman from the overheard speakers. It was the same earthy song that had been playing on the bus; he still couldn't figure out the identity of the singer. "*Well, you can cry me a river, cry me a river; I cried a river over you.*"

What he'd almost done had nothing to do with religion, and even though it was true that he'd been wronged, it had nothing do with his marriage either. He created this situation. Nobody made him trip down this road; he was damaged but not by anyone else. This sickness was his own.

Once in the stall, he covered the seat with lengths of toilet paper and pulled down his pants and finished himself in three or four quick jerks, the devil's seed seeping between his fingers; he was crying too hard to see if he got any on his clothes.

This was the second best bed, David concluded. Mystery of the ages solved. This was the second best bed.

Poor Anne. Shakespeare had left her with the knowledge that there was a place where his shame knew no bounds. David had done the same to Amanda.

When he cleaned himself up and dried his tears, he took the red Bible from his side pocket and placed it on the floor beside the toilet with the Buck knife on top of it.

-end-

The 13th Annual Spring House Spelling Bee

John-John Hagarty had really gone and done it this time.

Albert kept his body tight and hoped he didn't give off any odors. He didn't want to offend Anna. He thought about telling Anna he was sorry if he did, but there was a fresh round of screaming from out in the hallway.

Anna clutched at his arm.

"Do you think John-John will…?"

Albert didn't know. John-John Hagarty had always been trouble, a sore spot. But this time, well, Albert thought it was like John-John was trying to go back to where it had all gone wrong: when second grader Joseph Bochdan shot his best friend Henry Cabot (also a second grader) in the face during recess at Assumption of Our Lady Elementary School a few years ago. In the fracas after the shooting, the school bullies (including John-John and his buddy bully chieftain Stevie Rich) were just about the only group not under suspicion or accused of complicity—at first. Their involvement came to light after a fellow student uncovered the truth: Joseph had brought the gun to school to protect himself and his friend from the bullies, and he'd shot Henry by mistake when Stevie charged him.

Stevie Rich and John-John were older than most other kids in the school at the time, having been left back a couple of times. Practical application of basic mathematics and spelling proved elusive. At Assumption, Albert had once been asked to tutor Stevie Rich, but the kid (a bull dressed in Catholic school attire was more like it) stared out the window or carved tattoos into his arm with a paper clip. Albert stopped staying after school to tutor; he didn't want Stevie to get bored and start carving his tutor's arms. None of the nuns ever mentioned Albert's absence.

But the murder of Henry Cabot shook the school and paralyzed the town. Albert had been in eighth grade when it happened, and the paralysis around him didn't begin to subside until he started high school. The murder must have shaken Stevie Rich too, for he stopped being a bully, just *stopped*. Now Albert was a senior; he thought Stevie was a sophomore. At Father Hoskins High, Stevie had once asked him for a light out in the parking lot, but Albert didn't smoke. He didn't feel particularly cool that Stevie Rich, once the most feared kid in Assumption as well as in the town, had singled him out for a favor, but Albert was disappointed nevertheless that he hadn't had any matches. He wanted to see if Stevie remembered his name. Albert started carrying a book of matches every day for the rest of the school year.

"Sounds like firecrackers," Albert said, for lack of something better to say. His head was pressed to the classroom floor behind the far end of the teacher's desk, and, for a couple of seconds, he wondered if Anna had even heard what he'd said, even though she was right beside him in a similar position.

"They're not firecrackers," Anna said.

Stevie Rich's transformation wasn't a *complete* transformation, not yet; he still found himself in quite a few parking lot dust-ups at Hoskins High, but these were genuine fistfights; Stevie wasn't bullying someone weaker. But Stevie's seemingly sincere attempt at transformation had left John-John Hagarty to flail away on his own, something, apparently, John-John wasn't very good at. John-John had been Stevie's right hand man (or left fist, as he liked to call himself). Not that Stevie Rich had been some sort of evil genius, but without Stevie, John-John entangled himself in quite a few cock-ups, including locking himself in Sol's during a robbery attempt. The Ukrainian woman who owned the convenience store found him the next morning, sleeping on the floor surrounded by empty candy wrappers (or so the *Mondauk Common* reported). Albert believed it; John-John Hagarty was easily two hundred pounds. Albert wasn't even sure if John-John actually attended Hoskins High or if he just stopped by for remedial instruction. He saw him in the halls once in a while, glowering at the underclassmen, or out in the gazebo catching a smoke. At Assumption, he'd always been sucking on a pacifier; now a Winston joined it. (Albert remembered John-John smoking when he attended Assumption too, but in grade school, smoking was a significantly more surreptitious activity.)

Albert's legs were cramped. He'd been in this position for the past fifteen minutes or so. Anna too. Albert knew if he stretched his legs a little, his right knee would crack. He didn't want Anna to think he had farted. He also didn't want to be caught looking at her when he shouldn't be, so he stared at the school floor, then at the crack under the door.

"Albert."

It sounded like John-John was down near the science lab now, but there wasn't any sense in taking a chance and running for it. Try as hard as he could to think of it as anything else (and he was trying pretty damn hard), the thing that he could just make out on the hallway floor, illuminated by the fluorescent lights, was no text book but part of someone's head. Despite his limited view through the crack at the bottom of the door, Albert thought it was Greg Stillman's.

"Albert."

"Emollient," Albert said to Anna. "E-m-o-l-l-i-e-n-t. Emollient."

Anna shivered.

"The two Ls," Albert said. "They'll get you every time."

+

It was posted on the bulletin board in the north hallway, behind the big smudged sliding glass door: The 13th Annual Spring House Spelling Bee, to be held April 11th, 7PM in the Spring House Elementary School gymnasium—Qualifying rounds March 8th and 9th, 4:30. Albert had always liked to spell; he'd never thought of competing officially. (Professionally?) Back in Assumption, Sister Edna used to have Albert's class play Spelling Bee Baseball. Albert was terrible at sports, but he loved Spelling Bee Baseball. Sister Edna was the pitcher, and she had words on index cards: words for singles, doubles, triples, and home runs. Each student chose which kind of card he or she wanted, what kind of word the student wanted to spell. Albert always started off with a single, to shake the rust off, but after one or two of those, he'd always ask for a homer. Albert never missed a homer.

Anna liked it when Albert spelled—she had told Albert this at Megan Riley's party. Albert thought Anna was just about the most beautiful girl he'd ever seen in his whole life. He'd known Anna since they were kids (her house was directly behind his) but he had no idea Anna was a big spelling fan—or maybe, Albert thought, she was just a big fan of *his* spelling.

Anna Lafleur had long brown hair that rarely looked brushed. She usually wore it pulled back a little, nothing too severe, so she'd have a messy ponytail. Albert had never before thought of things like how when some girls pulled their hair back tight, it made them look austere. Albert guessed the girls thought it made them look tough, but he could always see where the foundation ended. Anna didn't look tough; there were always a few strands of hair floating in her eyes even when it was pulled back, as if her hairstyle was an afterthought. Albert understood her fashion. Until Megan Riley's party, he had never really cared about how he looked. Oh sure, if his mom bought him a new shirt or slacks for his birthday or Easter, he might stand in front of the mirror for a little bit, practicing his moves, but they never lasted very long, his mirror moves—he didn't have that many.

Anna Lafleur had moves, but like her hairstyle, they appeared tossed together, random, like chewing on the ends of her infrequently worn glasses when she never chewed on her pen caps and doing so only in certain classes that changed without rhyme or reason, as she followed an internal rhythm. There were days when Albert watched Anna chew the ends of her glasses, and he'd have to spend extra time in the bathroom when he got home. But most days, he'd just lay in his bed after school with his headphones on and wonder what she was thinking at that exact moment—did she have any idea how different she was from the rest of the Bod Squad?

In school, the girls wore blue uniforms. The sameness encouraged quiet revolutions. Some girls rolled their socks down. Other tried to hike their skirts up just a bit. Anna did neither: she accessorized—using only a single item.

Wait, Albert thought, for practice: *Accessorize. A-c-c-e-s-s-o-r-i-z-e. Accessorize.*

Anna's one accessory was astonishingly simple: she wore a piece of black cloth around her neck, not even an inch thick. Albert couldn't explain what it did to her face, her neck, her entire being, but it did *something*. It was like those little things he could never explain to anyone about music: how one detail, one inflection, a cluster of notes, could make even the most rote of blues progressions give him a boner.

Boner. B-o-n-e-r. Boner.

Anna's ears were always visible because of the way she wore her hair, and they were small, compact. Albert always felt like he had to whisper around Anna (although clearly no one else did). And what he wanted to whisper into her little ears were snippets of song lyrics (written by him and others) like he whispered to her school picture at night before he fell asleep.

Anna ran with the Bod Squad. The Bod Squad didn't whisper. Every grade in every part of the county had their own version of the Bod Squad; there was no central leadership. The Bod Squad was a growth on his particular class. They were unavoidable and along with the jocks, they ruled the school. Back at Assumption Elementary, they called the shots socially, experimented with make-up and boys, and greeted each other with shrill birdcalls of recognition. At Hoskins High, the Bod Squad grew slightly subtler and was clearly split between the girls who aimed for college and girls whose ambition ended in the backseat in Little City. Not that Albert moralized; he'd thought about being in the backseat before. But some members of the Bod Squad, Albert knew, would *always* be members of the Bod Squad.

When he would see her outside of school, Anna always said hi, even if she never said his name. "That's because Anna Lafleur doesn't *know* your name," Bridget explained around a breath mint. Albert wasn't sure if Bridget was right, but Bridget usually was. Bridget wasn't a member of the Bod Squad. Bridget, as she often said of herself, was wise beyond her years. She was one of the two friends Albert had at Hoskins. He rarely disagreed with her; no need to disturb the only female friendship he had.

He looked at the spelling bee sign-up sheet again. Was there an age limit? It didn't mention one. Weren't spelling bees usually a grade school level competition? The tryouts were at the public elementary school, so maybe, but then why was the sheet posted on a high school bulletin board?

He remembered his father telling him that the spinning of a record was a quiet revolution. His father had said that quiet revolutions were the only important revolutions because they could always get louder, as records do. Revolutions that started loud could only grow into distortion or retreat into an awkward silence. His father told him the Beatles named their 1966 album *Revolver* not only for the pun but because the pun itself was a quiet revolution; the record announced the changing of the guard; it was the prelude to *Sgt. Pepper's Lonely Hearts Club Band,* and upon that record's arrival, nothing would ever be quite the same again.

I read the news today, oh boy…

Albert liked the sound of that: nothing would ever be quite the same again, and after his father died, nothing ever was. Everything showed signs of stagnation (*stagnation—s-t-a-g-n-a-t-i-o-n—stagnation*). Albert knew when he went home after his final class, the curtains would be drawn (they were never open anymore) and the house would be cool and dark. His mother would be asleep on the couch. Clearly, Albert thought, his mother wasn't the same. But what were now permanent were the cushion patterns etched into her cheek when she was roused by Albert practicing his guitar. He used to play without the amp so he wouldn't disturb her. Lately, he decided he didn't care. His mother did—he tuned by ear and his ear was underdeveloped—but only for a couple of days. Now she seemed to accept the tortured notes emanating from his Telecaster as just part of the natural sounds of her day: the mailman rattling the rust-flaked gold mail box, the newspaper hitting the previous day's paper on the porch, birds singing. Albert imagined them all, but he doubted if his mother heard any sound except her own husky breathing. (She'd started smoking again.) His father was dead right: *nothing* was the same—and once everything changed, it stayed put.

Standing at the bulletin board, Albert didn't bother to look around. If the bullies were nearby or the Bod Squad or anyone else, let them see: Albert Ayler Bannerman was going to spell.

+

Bridget popped her gum in his ear. Albert didn't care.

"You're not actually going, are you?" Bridget asked.

Albert opened his locker and exchanged books.

"Yes," he said. "Anna asked me."

"Anna Lafleur asked you," Bridget said. She shook her head. "I don't believe it."

Albert shrugged. Bridget leaned against the lockers.

"You shouldn't go," she said with some finality.

Albert began walking down the hall. Bridget followed, stomping her saddle shoes, and finally caught his arm.

"I'm serious, man," she said, and Albert thought she looked serious. She had dyed her hair black at the start of the school year, and not a single teacher called her on it. (Father Hoskins High School forbade its students to dye their hair.) Make-up was forbidden too. The female teachers made a sport of it, collaring members of the Bod

Squad and forcing them to scrub the offending paint from their good Catholic faces. But it was rare that someone of authority challenged Bridget, so her surreptitious eyeliner had led to smeared swaths of dark eye shadow to compliment the black eyeliner that frequently ran down over her hundreds of freckles. Serious is *exactly* what Bridget Babka looked like, all five feet two, 180 pounds of her.

"So am I," Albert said.

The first bell rang.

"Megan Riley," Bridget said. "I can't fucking believe it."

"I have to go to class…"

"I can't fucking believe it."

"…so I should go…"

"What are you wearing?" she asked.

Albert looked down.

"What I always wear."

"To Megan Riley's party," Bridget said, exasperated. "I can't believe I'm fucking asking this. What are you going to wear to Megan's party?"

"I…I hadn't thought about it."

"Didn't you say it was a costume party?"

"That's what Peggy Runyon said."

"That cooze."

Albert squashed a butterfly that had dared to take flight in his stomach.

"I'll think of something."

Bridget straightened the knot of his tie. Her fingernails were painted black.

"Don't go…no, listen: come over to my house instead. I have a gift certificate left over from my birthday. We'll go to Geeks & Gawds, get some used records or whatever, maybe take the bus to Disc/Connection. My mom's at my aunt's house until next Monday. We could steal some booze, listen to records, stay up all night, whatever."

Bridget spoke into the knot of his tie. Her breath smelled like Wrigley's. Behind the gum, Albert could smell the Salem Light she'd woofed down before school across the street, off school property, but in full view of the Bod Squad, who, publically at least, frowned on smoking cigarettes.

"You could stay over," Bridget suggested.

The second bell rang.

"I'm late," Albert said.

Bridget removed her hands and squinted down the hallway.

Albert pointed to the next door on his left.

"My classroom," he said.

"Megan has bad breath."

"Yes," Albert said, looking up and down the hall. If he got detention, it would cut down on the time he had to prepare himself for the party. He'd heard the bad breath theory before.

"That's how you know, you know?" Bridget said. "Bad breath in the morning? Sure. But during the day? Fucking evil, Albert. Megan, all of them."

"Yeah, but not—"

"Don't...her too...just because you have a little..."

"Her breath doesn't smell," Albert said.

"...crush on Anna Squeaky Clean doesn't mean—"

"It doesn't," Albert said. If he didn't get to class soon, someone would catch them. Bridget didn't care. She said that because she was a circus freak, the big girl, the teachers had given up punishing her. Albert was skinny and tall with a long nose. If he dawdled, he'd be caught for sure.

"She's one of *them*, Albert. She's not one of us."

Albert started to shrug but stopped. *One of us?*

"It doesn't matter," he said. "I have to go to Calculus."

"I'll give you that Who bootleg you wanted, the one with..."

Albert slipped into the classroom before the teacher arrived. The other students ignored him. He spent the class doodling in his copybook, rearranging the letters in Anna Lafleur's name. Spelling wasn't like math. There were no formulas per se. Sure, "i before e except after c," but the key to spelling was *knowing* the actual word.

Albert had eked out: A RUN A FALLEN before Mr. Drinkwater snatched the copybook out from under his pen, glanced at it, and said, "Detention, Mr. Bannerman," before resuming his lecture. Albert didn't pay attention to the snickers or the kicks to his desk or the way his face had sucked all the blood from his body. Mr. Drinkwater was still angry about Mathletes. He was the moderator but when he couldn't make it, like today, he let Miss Amber, the school's newest teacher, take his place. Albert knew he'd never get the girl while in Mathletes so he'd resigned to Miss Amber before he reported for detention. Quiet revolutions. Miss Amber must have sent Mr. Drinkwater a message because he knew before Albert walked in the door. But the teacher would have to learn how to live with his defection. Albert wasn't about to change his mind.

Detention was hell. Mr. Drinkwater wore short sleeve dress shirts, and by the end of the day, fat, golden halos shone from under Mr. Drinkwater's armpits. Finally close enough to experience for himself, Albert realized the hallway scuttlebutt among the Bod Squad—mainly that Mr. Drinkwater effused an odor by the end of the day—was most certainly true. (During Mathletes' practices, the teacher had always been halfway across the room.) During detention, Mr. Drinkwater assigned Albert an essay to fill the hour—an hour, Albert knew, that would be better spent preparing himself for Megan Riley's party. Albert looked down at his paper. He'd finished the last essay question fifteen minutes ago, but there were still ten minutes left on the dirty-white clock. Mr. Drinkwater scribbled at the front desk, sucking on his moustache. Albert ran a finger lightly over his own upper lip. He'd overheard a Bod Squad moustache discussion group once: "It feels nice...tickles sort of." He'd wondered who they knew with moustaches other than teachers.

"Done there, Mr. Bannerman?"

Mr. Drinkwater leaned over Albert's desk. His body odor was like a slap in the face, and he had the hairiest arms Albert had ever seen; Mr. Drinkwater had more hair on his arms than on his head.

"Yes, sir," Albert answered.

"You can go," Mr. Drinkwater said. He raised his upper lip on the last syllable and sniffed his moustache.

Albert gathered his belongings and made for the door. He'd lost an hour. If his mother was off the couch when he arrived home, he'd lose more.

"I played with your dad," Mr. Drinkwater said.

"I'm sorry, sir?" Albert asked. He'd just reached out for the doorknob.

"Your father," Mr. Drinkwater said. The teacher kept his focus on the papers strewn across his desk. "I knew him. Played with him. He was in my band, or I was in his. Those kinds of things mattered back then. I don't know why."

"Yes, sir," Albert said. If his mother was awake, there was a fifty-fifty chance she'd be a slit-eyed zombie fumbling for coffee or fussing with an egg. Sometimes though, she'd temporarily emerge from hibernation and, beneath the puffy cheeks and eyes, Albert could sort of see the mother who used to sing Loretta Lynn songs while she prepared dinner. Not that she sang now, but she would look like a shadow of who she used to be. It was like she was a washed up lounge singer, the clichéd Vegas type—not that Albert had ever been to Vegas. Sometimes when she briefly appeared to be less than a zombie, she wanted to talk, and in a voice that was rusty from neglect, she'd ask him questions about school (although she seemed to be unsure what grade he was in) until she slowly wound down and just stared at his face until he got up and left. Once he'd come home from school late (he'd been trying to read *The Return of the King* while he walked), and he found his widowed mother standing in the archway between the cramped dining room and the kitchen wearing a ruby-red dress with a plunging neckline that revealed plenty of cleavage and slits that seemed to go all the way up the sides of the long skirt. Albert had ignored her and gone to his room. When he'd come down for a snack, she was still in the archway.

"He could play just about anything. But you know that. Brass, guitar, keys, whatever. Your dad played it. He wasn't a virtuoso at any of them, but he tried everything. Said it was all a matter of mathematics."

"Yes, sir," Albert said, doubting Mr. Drinkwater's memory; Albert knew his father had been all about *feel* not formulas.

"Notes and numbers," Mr. Drinkwater added.

"Yes, sir," Albert said. He hoped his mother would still be comatose on the couch when he got home—her usual state in her usual place for the past three years—not only because it would be easier to get around, but also because if she was up, she'd eventually do battle with the ghosts. It was terrible to watch as she dug through boxes of old photographs taken when she was young, before she'd met his father. She'd caress each one, as if trying to release the person she'd been. She didn't talk to the Ghosts of Emily Montgomery Past, but Albert thought he could see the face she'd worn in the photographs floating beneath her bloated, yellow skin.

"About Mathletes, Albert. Mathletes is the kind of organization that looks great on a college application. Mathletes—"

"I'll put it on my college applications."

"Yes, Albert, but you're no longer a member of Mathletes."

"But I was, and I'll make sure to put Mathletes on my college applications."

"Albert, you quit."

"Yes, sir," he said. If his mother was awake, Albert wondered if she would ask him where he was going all dressed up.

"…go."

"I'm sorry, Mr. Drinkwater?"

The teacher cleared his throat and sniffed his moustache.

"I said you're free to go."

Mr. Drinkwater sat back down at his desk and circled something on a piece of paper with a red marker. Albert wondered if it was his college transcript.

The sun was sneaking away when he left the chalk-encrusted air of Hoskins High. Albert didn't bother to excavate his book from his bag for the walk home. He'd ended that practice after Patrick Lessing had borrowed *A Stranger in a Strange Land*—Albert had still been reading it when he'd asked, but he leant it to him anyway; he didn't know why. On the first day, Patrick read it as he walked home, like Albert usually did, but in the rain, which Albert certainly had never done. (Albert trailed a block behind him.) When the paperback was finally returned, it was twice its size. Patrick apologized then jogged over to where Joe Runyon and Chris Auger and Jerry Eves were kicking around a big ball of tin foil. After that, Albert made sure to keep whatever he was reading to himself, which meant no more walking and reading. Sometimes he would take the bus home. (There were very few student passengers.) He only lived about a mile from the school, but for a few minutes of extra reading time, Albert would ride past his stop and continue with his book as the bus turned around at Zook's Circle—a doleful-looking, grease stained half-circle of concrete named in honor of a local man who'd been killed in the Civil War—and eventually got off as it headed back towards school. It was hard to read at home. In bed after lights-out (a phrase of his father's he could never delete from his vocabulary): no problem. But to read for pleasure while his mother molted skin particles on the couch or shambled about the kitchen dangling a Doral from her lips and making instant coffee, was near impossible; the ghosts tethered to his mother rattled their chains like a chorus of Jacob Marleys.

Albert slowed his pace as he neared the corner of his street. His father had told him that musicians, when they first start out, tend to race towards the end of a song, ignoring the tempo. Better to ease up a little, his father had said: look before you leap. There'll be time enough later to plunge into the unknown. His father was right, and even though the bullies had eased off somewhat now that he was an upperclassman, Albert remembered how they lurked in every blind spot, and he recalled every taunt and punch. Albert turned the corner like he always did: craning his neck slightly, like a sideways periscope. The street was empty, just a few leaves scouting the fall.

The couch was empty too when he eased the front door open. The multicolored afghan was crumpled at one end. Albert listened for the ghosts. If she was in the kitchen, he could head for his room. She only went upstairs to her bedroom to change clothes.

"Albert?"

She was in the kitchen, but she must have heard him come in anyway. Shut up, he told himself, shut up.

"Albert, is that you?"

"Yes," he answered.

"Albert, come here."

He tossed his book bag on the dining room table and entered the kitchen.

"I thought we'd have dinner," his mother said. "Together."

This was new—and ill-timed. Albert watched her shuffle to the stove, her back hunched as if she were very cold. The pattern from the couch cushion was tattooed on her right cheek.

"I'm not hungry," he said.

"Nonsense. Everyone needs to eat."

Albert could smell her museum breath.

"I have to get ready," he said.

His mother lit a cigarette and eased herself—lower, lower—into a kitchen chair.

"Don't use his aftershave," she said.

Albert left the kitchen. He hadn't planned on using his father's aftershave. He'd long forgotten the shaving kit his father had given him when he was eight years old.

"No, not right now," his father had said to Albert's mother. "But the time will come, and I wanted him to have my old kit."

"He'll cut himself."

"You won't cut yourself, will you, son?"

Somewhere in the back-back of Albert's head, in a space he'd long forgotten about, his younger self, the one grinning from the dusty family photographs that hung askew in broken frames near the bottom of the stairs, shook his head.

No, Dad, I won't cut myself. I'll just pretend for a while. I'll pretend-shave when you shave.

"Don't give him a razor."

"Even if I did, Albert's smart enough not to use it, right, son?"

Right-e-o, Pops. Right as rain.

"And not a bit wet," his father said.

Albert finished in the bathroom and flushed the toilet again when he heard his mother call up the stairs. In the mirror, the face looking back tightened its jaw. He wanted to touch himself inappropriately (as the nuns would say), but somehow even that seemed juvenile. Albert reached under the sink. Anna Lafleur was right around the next block, in the house behind his, getting ready herself, tying the black cloth around her neck. If he touched himself, he'd think of Anna, and he didn't want to ruin anything. The clasps on the shaving kit were rusty, and the rust flaked off when Albert opened the lid. He closed his eyes as the ghost of his father drifted to his nostrils.

Right as rain, Daddy, and not a bit wet.

+

A piece of Greg Stillman's skull flew past Albert's ear. Albert stood still for a few seconds in the hall, then jerked into action. He grabbed Anna and pulled her backwards into the empty classroom where he'd been practicing; he shut the door and turned off the lights.

"What was that?" Anna screamed. "What was that?"

"Mr. Bojangles."

Albert covered her mouth with his hand. He hoped he hadn't recently sneezed or used his hand for anything unsanitary. Anna smelled like apricots. He could feel her lips struggling against his hand and he barely noticed her kicks and punches.

"Kneel down," he said, and he lowered Anna to the floor. They were behind the far side of the teacher's desk.

"If take I my hand away, you promise not to scream?"

Anna shook her head. She'd just notice the blood splattered across her otherwise white blouse and his shirt. Albert didn't move his hand.

"We're too high up to jump out the window," he said. Through the bottom of the desk, he kept his eyes on the light that spilled under the closed door from the hallway, around whatever blocked its full passage.

He got her to stop shaking. "Now?" he asked. She nodded and removed his hand.

What would Albert Ayler do, his father had always asked.

Anna shifted, and Albert stared at the pale crest of her chest as it pushed against her blouse. He hoped he wouldn't get a boner. This would be a bad time for a boner.

"What would Albert Ayler do?" Albert asked aloud.

"Was that...?" She looked down at her blouse again.

"Whatever he wanted," Albert said, answering his own question.

"What? What?"

Anna made to get up, looking annoyed. Albert pointed to the shadow that now hung near the edge of the remaining light under the door and pulled her down again.

"Albert," Anna whispered.

"Albert Ayler," he whispered back, "would do whatever he wanted.

"Improvise. I-m-p-r-o-v-i-s-e," he added. "Improvise. Make it up."

But the shadow passed them over—for now at least.

+

She was so fucking stoned.

Anna brought her fingers to her face and ran them over her lips. It was like she was frozen without being cold.

And hungry? Jesus, she was fucking hungry. And horny? Ooo-wee, yes, sir. Not that she'd feel much if she did hook up. Numb, numb. Her privates had gone to sleep like her foot did when she sat on it too long.

"I can't feel anything," she'd said to Megan Riley earlier. (A half-hour ago? An hour?)

"No one can," Megan said. "Dog tranquilizers."

She was suddenly filled with an overwhelming urge to tell Megan how much she loved her, but the truth of the matter was that she found Megan barely tolerable, and the impulse passed. The Bod Squad was cute in grade school and maybe even when they were freshman (and Megan and Debbie made everyone get those satin jackets), but what did it fucking matter now: being in the top caste? In college, if she managed to avoid sororities, there'd be no caste system.

The boys had somehow managed to score a keg, and they'd arrived (an hour ago? two?), happy Roman gladiators. But with the beer had come the losers of the Lakes: including squat, bug-eyed Silver Ritchie (that was his real name), the Morrone brothers, and scary John-John Hagarty. Megan once said that you could tell if someone was from Paradise Lakes Trailer Park—they smelled like tuna fish. She said this was because the kids from the Lakes were raised on a diet of Ramen noodles, Hamburger Helper, and Chicken of the Sea—the only things their single mothers could afford to compliment government cheese. But when the keg had been tapped, Megan danced around the Morrone brothers; she even thrust her hips at the one that didn't have a moustache. The jocks slapped themselves on the back, but Anna knew acquisition of the keg had been delegated to John-John and the rest of the Lakes boys.

"Probably just asked their foster parents to buy it for them," Peggy Runyon had said, as she handed out paper cups.

Now (hours or days later) whatever Megan had given her was *really* kicking in and she could give a rat's ass about beer. That the drug probably came to the party with the Lakes crowd was of little consequence, but she was pretty sure none of their parents (or foster parents) had bought it for them.

The kitchen was empty. Almost everyone was outside gathered around the keg. Anna wanted bottled water and maybe a ride home. Despite an increasing numbness, she didn't want to party with the Lakes boys. She wasn't a snob, but beer and designer drugs would certainly lead to darker activities. John-John Hagarty had been arrested twice already (that she knew of). At Hoskins High, the Bod Squad barely nodded in the direction of the few kids from the Lakes who went to Catholic school, but outside of the hallowed halls, the Paradise Lakes crowd knew how to score—booze, pot, pills—and the Bod Squad and their accompanying jocks courted their services, temporarily elevating trailer trash to their level, as Megan had said.

The kitchen wasn't empty.

"Get lost, creep," Anna said, hanging on to the fridge handle. (Seeing someone lurking near the cupboard had startled her more than she wanted to let on—and the little pill she'd swallowed delayed her brain's reaction.)

"I'm not a—I'm a..." the creep said and then moved out of the shadows. He wore a cape.

"...I'm a superhero," the creep finished.

Anna let go of the fridge handle and collapsed in a heap. The superhero reached down, grabbed her by the wrists, and pulled her back up.

"My dad always said to grab by the wrists," the superhero explained, "in case your hands slip."

Anna leaned against the fridge; it was cool against her back.

"Why aren't you outside?" Anna asked, her eyes closed. "The keg's there."

"I was looking for you."

Anna opened one eye.

"You were looking for me?"

The superhero started to fumble with the s-hook that served as a fastener for his cape.

"The costume's throwing you off," he said.

Anna shook her head and gestured for him stop. Little purple trails traced the boy's movements in the air. The last thing she wanted him to do was undress.

"It's me," the superhero said, leaving his cape be. "Albert Bannerman."

"Albert Bannerman," Anna said, trying the name out, then rejecting it.

"Albert *Ayler* Bannerman," Albert said. "My dad admired Albert Ayler, a great jazz improviser. My mom was upset because Ayler isn't a saint's name, but they just didn't tell the priest who baptized me. Something like that."

Anna closed her eyes again. What the fuck was he talking about?

"It's spelled A-y-l-e-r. He had a brother too—Albert did—and he played trumpet in Albert's band but…"

"The Speller!" Anna cried.

"…he couldn't really play all that well."

"Why did you wear a cape?"

"His brother's presence, though, brought a dynamic to Albert's…I thought I heard Peggy say—in the hallway—I thought I heard Peggy say it was a costume party, a masquerade."

Anna covered her mouth with her hands. Somewhere, behind the sweeping purple lines that used her cranium as a thoroughfare, she knew it was a gesture she'd picked up from her mother: an exaggerated, yet reflexive recognition of someone else's faux pas. Anna teetered between admiring her mother, who'd carved out her place in the real estate business after leaving Anna's father, and hating her. (Her father was still around, but his soiled jeans and grimy face were evidence of an occupation far below the financial accomplishments of Anna's mother; Anna visited him on holidays and his birthday and tried to ignore it when he drank beer out of a can for breakfast; but despite everything, he'd always end up making her laugh before she left.) Her mother not only recognized a caste system, but her entire social—and, on occasion, occupational—preferences were chosen with the caste system firmly in the forefront of her mind. Anna wondered how her mother would react if she saw the world not through four hundred dollar sunglasses but through exquisite purple streaks originating from a little purple pill.

"Everyone has a hard time with that one," Albert offered.

"Purple streaks," Anna asked, her eyes following a wriggling example that disappeared into Albert Bannerman's wide nostrils, "or mothers?"

"Ephemeral. I meant the word ephemeral. The one I spelled for you in Mr. Day's class."

"The Speller!" Anna cried. She wondered if it was healthy for Albert to snort all those purple streaks. She searched her face for her nose and was relieved to find it was still there.

Donna and Cheryl skidded into the kitchen in their bare feet and stood in front of Albert.

"Anna, you *have* to—"

"She's like air-humping him!"

"It's the craziest fucking thing!"

"She's *so* high!"

Donna turned on her heels.

"You the pizza guy?"

Albert blushed and stammered.

"No, I—I'm—"

"He's the Speller," Anna said. "He's the best speller in the whole school. In the whole country maybe."

"He's my Speller," she added.

"Fuck," Donna Gaynor said, "you *are* stoned."

"Slumming," Cheryl added.

"Don't let Megan see you slumming," Donna said, "or Peggy."

"Definitely not Peggy"

Anna followed a purple streak that had leaked from Albert Bannerman's eyes as it cascaded to the kitchen tiles.

"Where are your shoes?" Anna asked.

Albert looked down.

"Rachel's so fucked up already," Donna explained. "She started strip poker."

"We lost our shoes," Cheryl said.

"We lost our shoes," Donna repeated. "I'm gonna get me some tonight, baby."

"Slumming."

"Fishing in the Lakes, baby!" Donna said, and she took a running start and skidded to the kitchen doorway. Cheryl twirled and fell.

"My ass, ohh! Help me up, Speller."

Albert reached down and lifted Cheryl by her wrists.

Anna watched as two purple streaks snaked their way into her friends' bottoms. She briefly wondered if she should say something but thought better of it.

Donna grabbed Cheryl's fingers and pulled her out of the kitchen.

"Who is he again?" Cheryl asked on the way out.

"I'm the Speller," Albert said.

"I love the way you spell," Anna declared.

She kicked off her shoes and twirled on the tiles and was quickly back in position after tripped a little bit. She'd been a ballerina for two years when she was little. Her mother pulled her out when the instructor for the third year was Mexican-American. Margaret Barbette-Lafleur would suffer no immigrant instilling her daughter with multicultural flights of nonsense. Bad enough the Ukrainians moving into Mondauk Proper and the Koreans into Rhawnhurst. Mexican ballet. Really.

"I don't even know what that word means," Anna said mid-pirouette, "and I'm a senior too."

"Ephemeral. E-p-h-e-m-e-r-a-l. Ephemeral. Lasting but a day."

Anna froze, her fingers hovering above her head.

"That's what everything is like now," she said, lowering her arms. "We graduate in May, and for the past two years everything's been focused on college: SATs and picking a major and hoping for a good dorm mate. But yet, it feels like everything could go away—will go away—like this."

Anna undulated her right hand in the air as if she were in her father's car when she was very little and the air would ask her hand for a dance, and together they would wave at the whole world, and her father would laugh but her mother would be cross and pull in her arm so she wouldn't lose her initial ring.

The old Peter Lorre film, *The Beast with Five Fingers*, popped into her head.

"Do you like horror movies?" she asked. "I like horror movies."

"Yes, especially the Universal—"

"Do you see the purple streaks?" Anna asked.

"No," Albert answered.

Anna watched the purple streaks navigate the wrinkles on Albert Bannerman's shirt, each streak looking for a comfortable fit, others squirming in narrow folds or losing all sense of themselves in wider drifts of material. Anna swore, once she graduated high school, she'd never worry herself about fitting in. She'd be free of her mother (if not financially, at least socially) and free of the Bod Squad. It had served its purpose. She'd successfully transitioned from child to adolescent with friends, functions to attend, and status. Anna imagined some of the Bod Squaders remaining Bod Squad members for quite a few years more. Donna still wore her Bod Squad jacket when it got cold.

"It isn't a costume party," Anna told the Speller. "It's nowhere near Halloween. Peggy was fucking with you."

"Oh," Albert said.

"I'm sorry. I shouldn't have let that happen." She wasn't losing *all* of her mind.

Albert shrugged.

"I didn't have time to do much more than find something to use as a cape."

"An afghan?"

Albert shrugged again.

"How come we never talked in school?" Anna asked. She still felt somewhat lucid, although some part of her knew that it was temporary.

"We did. In Mr. Day's class, remember? When you asked me—"

"No, I mean before that. We were in Assumption together too, right? So how come we never talked?"

"I was in Mathletes. You didn't know I could spell."

Anna squinted into Albert's face.

"Mathletes?"

"I just quit," Albert said. "To concentrate on spelling."

"Spelling," she repeated. "Of course. Hey, you have an awful lot of wrinkles."

Albert felt his face. Anna laughed.

"Your shirt," she said. "Your shirt is all wrinkled."

Albert looked down and tried to smooth it out. Anna touched his hands.

"You have long fingers."

She turned Albert's hands over. The fingers on his left hand were calloused.

"Whoa," Anna said. "Lot of self-manipulation?"

Albert looked confused, then shook his head and pulled back his hands—reluctantly it seemed.

"I play guitar."

Anna squealed.

"You do? Electric guitar?"

Albert's head switched from shaking to nodding.

"Can you play 'Stairway to Heaven'?"

"Yes," he answered. "I can read music, but I can learn songs just from listening to records too."

"Wow!" Anna said. " '*If there's a bustle in your hedgerow, don't be alarmed now,*' " she sang. "I swear, I live for those moments when I can see another person excel at something. I guess it's because I never did. My dad wanted to buy me a drum kit when I was a little girl, but my mom wouldn't let him. After they divorced, he bought this small kit with Mickey Mouse on the bass drum and set it up in his apartment. Said I could bash away whenever I wanted. Said the downstairs neighbor worked nights, and I was never there in the morning." She paused. "He wasn't drinking so much then."

"Do you still play?"

"I never played the Mickey Mouse drums."

"Why?"

Anna tried to shrug, but her shoulders—in fact, entire parts of her body—were no longer completely under her control.

"I don't really know. I guess I wasn't a little girl anymore. I might have missed my chance to excel."

"My dad's dead."

Anna's eyes looked for tears but couldn't find any.

"How?"

"Cancer."

"Your mom…"

"My mom—"

"…remarry?"

"No," Albert said.

Anna rubbed her eyes. Albert Bannerman's hair was draped in purple streaks.

"I have to go soon," she said. She couldn't stop looking at his hair.

"To go shopping?" Albert asked.

Anna blinked.

"To get some shoes," Albert explained. "Donna said she was going to get some."

Anna laughed, but this time the laugh caught in her throat and fizzled like heartburn. She reached up and parted Albert's hair to one side.

"See, dress you up, give you a new haircut, and you'd be okay. Your face wants a different cut. Bring out your eyes if you wear your hair different."

Anna played with the buttons on his dress shirt.

"And maybe get an iron."

The top button on Albert's shirt was undone. Anna played with the next one down.

"Maybe *I'll* go shopping too," she said. "I could use a little bustle in *my* hedgerow."

Anna felt his toothpaste breath on her forehead and undid the button.

"I bet you're the best speller in the whole town. It's always the quiet ones."

Albert nodded his head. Anna knew if she leaned into him, she'd feel his hard-on (if she wasn't so numb). She undid another button.

"I can't feel anything," Anna confided. This was some good shit, she thought. She wondered if she would know when she had to pee.

"Save me, Albert Ayler Bannerman, save me from…all…this," Anna said, brushing the tip of her nose against the tip of his.

"No one can," she continued, staring at his Adam's apple. "You're my best friend."

She wondered if she could actually do him right in the kitchen.

"Are you the quiet one, Albert? Are you?"

A big S had been drawn on his white undershirt with blue and red magic markers. Anna backed away and watched as her hands rose in the purple of Megan Riley's kitchen to cover her mouth from where, she knew, no laughter would escape.

Albert buttoned his shirt back up.

"I didn't have time to get a real costume," Albert explained, adjusting his afghan. "I had to improvise."

"It's not a costume party," Anna told him again between her fingers.

"I have to go," Albert said, backing towards the door.

Anna lowered her hands.

"That's the door to the yard. Everyone else is back there, by the sliding glass doors. Go through the front. Hardly anyone's in the living room."

"Okay," Albert said.

"Thank you for inviting me," he added as he walked out of the kitchen, his hair, his shirt, his face glowing purple.

Anna shouted after him: "See ya, Speller!"

She leaned against the counter and closed her eyes. Jesus, she was horny. She'd almost come on to the Speller. Horny and numb. Her feet were cold; her fingers felt like they were asleep. Maybe she should just go home. Go home and go to bed and let the purple streaks have their way with her.

When Anna opened her eyes, the purple streaks were gone. The kitchen was outlined in fuzzy strokes of charcoal. The charcoal lines weren't attached to anything; they just buzzed lightly around the outer edges, sputters of gray and black. The Speller had taken the colors with him. Albert Bannerman had stolen all her colors.

One drink's not going kill her. She couldn't go home with the charcoal. Her mother would flip, freak, throw a fit. One drink. One stiff drink. For balance. Something to take away the numbness. A drink with a splash of color. Like cold water on her face. The colors would come back. The charcoal would wash away. Ephemeral. Everything's ephemeral.

+

"I love the way you spell," Anna Lafleur said.

Albert was sorry he wore the cape. He swore he'd heard Peggy Runyon say it was a costume party. His mother would be pissed when she discovered her afghan missing.

Anna blinked then briefly stared at the space next to his head. She kicked off her shoes. She had on thigh high socks and a skirt, and when she twirled, Albert could see flashes of her thighs. He found it hard to breathe. Anna spun, tripped, and bounced lightly off the fridge. Albert wondered if he should be prepared to catch her should she fall again. What if he dropped her? What if he didn't grab her by the wrists this time if she did hit the ground? What if he had to grab her under her arms?

"I don't even know what that word means," Anna Lafleur said.

The girls at the party were dressed to the nines, as his dad used to say when Albert and his mother gussied up for a family gathering or church on Easter Sunday. And not one of the Bod Squaders looked as lovely as Anna Lafleur did dancing in the kitchen. To think—he almost didn't get in the party.

He'd knocked on the front door, and Megan Riley had answered, screamed, and slammed it in his face. Not ready to give up, but not ready to try again, Albert hung around on the walk. After a few minutes, two cars swung into the gravel driveway leading to the garage and jocks in school jackets poured out from a hatchback like they were climbing out of a clown car. School jackets were an odd phenomenon. Faded blue with red letters outlined in gold, freshman parents shelled out the extra bucks for the jackets, which didn't arrive until more than halfway through winter. As sophomores, surviving their first year led almost everyone in Albert's class to wear theirs as early as the second week of school and as late as mid-April sometimes. By junior year, experience equaled confidence and the jackets had mostly disappeared. Albert noted that the only seniors who wore them now were the jocks. He thought that the reason for this was that the jackets were bulky and made the jocks look bigger.

Albert's Aunt Dottie had sent his mother a check for the jacket, but he had never wanted one. The other Mathletes had wanted to buy Mathletes jackets; Albert didn't want one of those either. (He was secretly pleased they didn't have enough for the minimum order, even after including the headmaster, the dean, and both their secretaries; he knew the Mathletes would have been walking bull's-eyes in their jackets.) Albert used the money to buy a sport coat and a shirt for the funeral. (Aunt Dottie was too old to travel; her check was a sympathy gift, an I'm-sorry-your-dad's-dead check that arrived two days after his departing.) The balance he used to purchase a black leather strap for his guitar; his aunt had been very generous.

Megan's party was only the second time he'd worn the shirt, but he had to fish it out of the bottom of the hamper, where it had been since his father's service three years ago; his mother had stopped doing laundry, and Albert had grown superstitious about washing it, although he made an exception for the party.

The second car in the driveway looked like it must have been cool at some point in time, but it had long since lost its splendor (along with most of its paint—the car appeared to be encased in gray primer). The jocks lifted a keg from its trunk and hustled it around the garage. Someone opened the front door and squealed: "They're here!" Albert had long since backed up, neither wanting to hinder the proceedings or be noticed by the jocks before he even gained entry to the party. "*We'll become silhouettes when our bodies finally go,*" the stereo inside warned to ignorant ears before the door slammed shut. Albert knew some kids partied with the punk ethos in mind: better to burn out than fade away. *My my, hey hey.* What Albert thought separated him from the herd and made him different weren't the blackheads clustered on the long bridge of his nose or his insistent boners or his growing guitar prowess—it was that he knew most of these kids had already faded away. That and the way his father had died.

Hey hey, my my. Rock and roll can never die.

But he knew that none of these things made him superior or more tragic. Just alone.

There's more to the picture than meets the eye. Hey hey, my my.

John-John Hagarty emerged from the gray ghost car, its engine still idling. John-John's long trench coat flapped in the breeze, a pink pacifier between his lips. His massive head blocked the glow from the streetlamp. He gave a nod and the engine stopped (Albert held his breath) and three other shadowy figures climbed from the car.

"Poontang!" one of the gray ghosts howled.

Be ignored or be a target: in the hallways at school, in gym class, even in the lavatories or during the walk home—it was one or the other. Albert turned around and inspected a bush on his left.

"Takin' a whizz!" another gray ghost added, clapping Albert on the back before entering the party.

Albert turned to follow and walked into John-John Hagarty's chest.

"Nice cape," John-John said. "Got a light?"

Albert shook his head. He hadn't brought his matchbook.

John-John stuck the cigarette behind his ear and popped the pink pacifier back into his mouth. When he spoke, a little bit of drool escaped and dangled from his chin. "Fuck it then, huh?"

Albert agreed and held the door open for the bully ring leader.

"After you," John-John said, but it sounded like "Fuck you."

Albert walked in, trying not to breathe through his nose. (He'd caught a whiff of John-John in Hoskins' hallways once; he'd smelled like the dying muskrat Albert had found with his dad.) He slipped into the kitchen without incident or much notice, just as the last album ended and someone put on *Toys in the Attic.* Albert was surprised: he didn't expect that CD to be in Megan's collection (he thought she would be strictly a pop music fan), although he supposed someone could have brought it to the party. Oh, the music he could have brought! *"Voices scream / Nothin' seen / Real's the dream."* In the kitchen, he spent a considerable amount of time reading a yellowing newspaper clipping (from seven years ago) that hung on the fridge. It lauded Brownie troop 27's Megan Riley and her accomplishments in raising awareness in Mondauk Proper of the dangers of drunk driving. And now, a few feet from where he'd stood, reading and rereading the Brownie article, Anna Lafleur, whom Albert assumed had amassed quite a collection of press clippings of her own, pirouetted in Megan Riley's mother's kitchen.

"But yet, it feels like everything could go away—will go away— like this," Anna said, stopping to make her hand swim.

Anna's faded buckskin jacket was too small, but she'd left the cuffs unbuttoned. That fetching piece of black cloth encircled her neck. She had her hair in a loose ponytail with a couple of strands falling on either side of her face. His eyes circled the tiny scar on her chin. When she tilted her head back, he could sense her body heat and smell her light perfume, warmed up from dancing, and a pocket of air exploded in his chest. Albert wondered if it was possible to develop an extra lung, for it would take three to breathe all of Anna in and survive the eruptions occurring around his eager heart.

When Donna and her friend had skidded into the kitchen, Albert's lungs deflated. The party would be a microcosm of the school, he'd thought, the same cliques and the same gossip and the same teachers ignoring the same old shit—only this time, the teachers were Megan's absent parents along with their neighbors, who seemed to turn a blind eye to a group of teenagers getting drunk in the Rileys' backyard.

And then he was alone with Anna in the kitchen again. If his extra lung had existed, it would appear to have been absorbed. There wasn't enough air in the kitchen to sustain both of them. If they kissed...

She told him about her Mickey Mouse drums. He told her that his father was dead. Albert thought it was going pretty well for a first date. His head buzzed with four syllable words he wanted to spell for her.

Anna parted his hair. He hoped she didn't see the multiple shaving nics on his neck. The razor in his father's shaving kit hadn't been changed in a while. He'd only shaved three times before; the water in the sink had turned pink.

Anna partially unbuttoned his shirt. (Major boner.)

They rubbed noses. (He was afraid he going to explode in his pants.)

Then she smothered her mouth with her hands.

She was laughing at him. Anna Lafleur was laughing at him.

"I didn't have time to get a real costume," he explained. He knew he shouldn't have drawn a large S on his Hanes undershirt. S for simpleton.

"It's not a costume party," Anna said between her fingers.

He realized that she wasn't really laughing at him, just at something he'd done, and he felt better, relieved even. She told him which way to go out so he could avoid her friends. As he was leaving the kitchen, she called him Speller again. He really liked that. S for Speller.

Albert left the way he came in, quietly humming "Stairway to Heaven." The living room was empty except for Cheryl who held her blouse closed and ran crying into the next room. Albert thought she had a bloody nose. Outside, he wished he'd brought his iPod. He didn't mind walking home—if he walked rather than hopped the bus, he'd be away from his mother that much longer—but if he had some music in his ears, he wouldn't have to listen to reruns of the kitchen conversation in his head, second-guessing himself and picking apart every word he'd said.

"Hey, faggot."

Ignore it.

"Bannerman!"

Keep walking.

"Hey, tough guy."

Albert turned and Bob Goocher shoved his hands into Albert's chest. If any bits of his extra lung had survived, they were gone now. Albert's cheek hit the gravel in Megan Riley's driveway. Bob Goocher removed his school jacket and threw it to the ground. Albert stared at the gold football that had been sewn on the back; at least he didn't appear to be wearing his school ring—another waste of money, he thought, and potentially damaging.

"Think you're a tough guy, Bannerman? Can't take us, so you go after Cheryl?" Bob Goocher asked, leaning down into Albert's face. "Pussy ass faggot."

"Fuck him up, Gooch," a high-pitched voice said. "Beat down, babe."

"Mess with Greg, then try to fuck Cheryl, you jizz-dripping pussy," Bob Goocher said, his breath spicy with hops and barley.

Albert tried to cover his face with one arm and protect his groin with his other hand, all the while looking for an escape route. After a couple of preliminary kicks to his legs, Bob Goocher kicked him in the stomach and then jumped back as if he'd been surprised himself. Albert shut his eyes.

He could hear someone approach him from behind, cutting off that possible getaway path. He assumed the fetal position but kept his arms in place.

"Problem, Gooch?" the voice behind Albert asked through a mouth full of marbles.

"John-John. Hey, no, well, yeah. This little faggot did a snatch-and-dash on Cheryl Hoffman."

"Tell him, Gooch," the high-pitched voice said. "Grab a snatch and run for the hatch."

Albert peeked from beneath his arm. *Snatch-and-dash?*

"That so," John-John Hagarty said. He removed the pacifier from his mouth. Drool dripped from it in long strings.

"Yeah," Gooch replied, but Albert thought he sounded less sure.

"Bannerman?"

"Yeah, him," Gooch answered.

"I was talkin' to Albert," John-John said. He shook off his pacifier, and somehow not a drop of saliva landed on Albert.

"Sorry, John-John," Gooch said, sounding truly sorry.

"Talking to Albert, John-John is," the high-pitched voice said. "Dressing him down. Fuck him up, he will. He. Will. He. Will. Rock. You."

You got mud on your face / You big disgrace.

John-John grabbed Albert by the wrists and pulled him up.

Kickin' your can all over the place.

"Beat it, meat," John-John said, and the kid with the high-pitched voice did just that. Gooch pointed at himself. John-John shook his head.

"Bannerman didn't touch anyone, did you Bannerman?" John-John asked. "He was with me, catchin' a smoke."

"Yeah, no, right," Bob Goocher said. "Wrong guy. I thought he was someone else."

"I don't smoke," Albert said, but no one paid any attention.

"Pick up your jacket, Gooch," John-John said. "Go make sure no one else is hurt."

"Right. Sorry there, Bannerman. Can I bum a smoke?"

"No," John-John answered. "You can't.

"Instead," he said, opening his palm, "here's some more Purples. Take 'em. Pass 'em around to anyone that ain't had one yet—especially the girls." He stuck the pacifier back into his mouth. "You listenin'? Make sure all the girls got one if they didn't the first round. You can't be too sure."

Gooch popped one of the pills and took the rest from John-John's hand. He jumped like he was catching a pass in the air, then sprinted up the walk. A blast of punk rock escaped the house when he opened the front door.

"Phony Beatlemania has bitten the dust..."

Just who was throwing this party anyway, Albert wondered. Even if they were someone else's CDs, Megan was still letting them become her gathering's soundtrack.

John-John lit a cigarette. He slid the pacifier to one side of his mouth while he smoked.

"Dolorous," Albert said. "D-o-l-o-r-o-u-s. Dolorous."

"Fuckin' rulin' class motherfuckers," John-John growled.

"Thank you," Albert said, looking up at John-John's face. His head sat on his shoulders like a boulder balanced on a mountain—a boulder with a pink pacifier, a mountain draped in a black trench coat.

"I didn't touch Cheryl. I was in the kitchen talking to..."

John-John ground out the cigarette with his boot.

"They don't know," he said. "They don't have a clue what's comin'."

"...Anna Lafleur, but I had..."

"When the garbage men rise up," John-John said, "the stink will reach their perfumed toilet seats and scorch every braided pussy."

"...to leave. I came as superhero, but..."

John-John walked towards the front door.

"Gonna get me some chicken."

"...no one else was in costume."

John-John opened the door, and his frame blocked the light from the house. Albert thought his outline glowed like the picture of the angry angel banishing Adam and Eve from the Garden of Eden in the *New Catholic Picture Bible* he'd had as a kid.

"Who is like God?" Archangel Michael had asked.

"Baby, baby drove up in a Cadillac," the stereo declared. *"I said, Jesus Christ! Where did you get that Cadillac?'"*

John-John entered the house and slammed the door shut.

+

"...it's like a heartbeat. Like a heartbeat just starting to realize its job. There's just a pull, a tug."

His dad laughed and ran his hand down his stubble.

"He was a god, son. He heard the music in his head, then brought it to us."

"Who is like God?" Albert asked.

His dad laughed again.

"Miles was, pal. Miles was."

There'd still been light in the sky when they'd left the library, but the shortcut through the woods had turned out to be a long cut—his father was so deep into the story of Robert Johnson that he'd lost the path. Albert wanted to hold his father's hand, but he didn't think he should at his age. His dad didn't look concerned; he kept profiling what he called the True Giants of Music. Albert was glad his father had moved on to Charlie Parker and Miles Davis. The story of Robert Johnson's deal with Lucifer was too scary to hear now that it was almost dark.

"Just follow the sound of the Puddle, son," his father said. "When we find the Puddle, we'll find our way home. Your mother's gonna have a bird, I can tell you. But if we come out near Rhawnhurst, we'll grab some Maryland beauties at the Crab Lady for dinner. What do you say?"

They were as far north as Rhawnhurst? Albert concentrated as hard as he could so he'd hear the roar of the Puddle, but the Puddle rarely roared. Pennypack Creek was going down a little more each year, his father had told him, hence its Puddle nickname. Not fit for swimming. Barely fit for fish let alone fishing. Albert thought that last one was funny.

His father's voice, caught up in his own stories, covered up the crunch of long-dead leaves beneath their sneakers. It would also cover up the crunch of anyone following them, Albert thought. Pennypack Woods grew louder as the light withdrew. Lingering cicadas whirred like threshing machines from the trees and flying insects buzzed by on important sorties.

"It wasn't that Elvis sounded like a black man as much as he sounded like no one else, really," Albert's father said, placing his hand on his son's chest.

Albert had heard the story of Elvis before. He knew his line.

"Who is like Elvis, Dad?" he asked.

His father placed two fingers on Albert's lips. They smelled like burnt coal from his cigarettes.

Then Albert heard it too: water dancing on stones. The Puddle!

"This way," his father said, and Albert again resisted the urge to take his father's hand.

"We'll keep our eyes peeled for—"

It didn't sound like a scream—not any scream Albert had ever heard before. He felt himself release a few drops of pee into his underwear, as he watched his father reach into his pocket and pull out his Swiss Army knife.

"I'm only going to use the spoon," his father said in a cheery voice. "Give me your hand, son," and Albert was glad to feel the roughness of his father's palm, the gentle grip of the massive thumb. Albert hoped his palm wasn't too sweaty.

The source of the scream that wasn't a scream screamed again, and together, to Albert's surprise, he and his father plunged through the underbrush *towards* the noise, creating their own brand of commotion. Albert hoped his father still had the Swiss Army knife in his other hand.

And then they saw it and it them: the muskrat was curled up at the base of the tree near the banks of the Puddle. Its tail was gone as was one of its arms. It was almost too dark to see, but Albert was sure the ground was stained red. Albert stepped back but kept a grip on his father's calloused hand.

"Something attacked it. It tried to crawl away, but the brush is thin here and thorny," his father said, looking around. "It was trapped, but whatever attacked him didn't finish him off, just left him here."

Albert stared down at the muskrat. The muskrat stared back, its eyes huge, the screaming coming not just from its throat but also from a puncture in its belly, if that were possible.

His father knelt before him.

"Turn your head, son. Here: let go of my hand. Turn your head. I'm gonna…I'm gonna help him out, take him out of his misery, okay? No one should suffer like this, not even an animal. Everyone *feels*, Albert, everything feels. And everything's ephemeral. Remember what that means? Yes? Now, I want you to turn away and tell me the best joke you've ever heard, and when I'm finished, we'll follow the Puddle outta here. Not a knock-knock joke, okay? A real joke. A story joke."

Albert turned around, and after he tamped down the panic that threatened to take hold as he looked into the dark woods, he tried to remember that he loved to tell jokes and cleared his throat.

"Larry Lobster and Sam Clam are best friends," he began. "They play jazz in the same combo. One day, a fishing boat comes by, and they both get caught and die. Larry goes to heaven and joins the choir, and Sam goes to hell and opens a dance club."

The muskrat screamed some more and his father whispered to it.

"God notices Larry dragging his tail around and asks him why he's so sad. 'I miss Sam Clam,' Larry Lobster says, and God takes pity on the crustacean. The Almighty tells him he can go down to hell and visit Sam Clam, but he has to return in twenty-four hours and he can't forget to bring back his halo, his wings, and his harp. 'Nothing from heaven can stay down in hell,' God tells Larry Lobster."

A plunge.

A piercing scream that suddenly expires.

Albert sped up.

"So Larry goes down into hell, and Sam is overjoyed to see him and invites Larry to sit in with the house band at his dance club. They play and party the day away. Larry Lobster is having so much fun, he almost forgets the time. 'I have to go, Sam. It was so great to see you again,' Larry says. 'I missed you too, old friend,' Sam the Clam tells the lobster. Larry rushes back to heaven, but when he returns, God stops by. 'Straighten your halo, Lawrence,' God says. 'And dust off those wings,' God says. Larry does as he's told, but then God gets really mad. 'Where is your harp, Larry Lobster?' God demands." Albert sang the punch line. "Larry blushes and says, *'I left my harp in Sam Clam's disco.'*"

A splash.

Albert tried not to think of the ripples emanating from the spot where the muskrat hit the water.

"Did I mess it up?"

His father wiped his hands on his corduroys and reached for him. Albert's little hand trembled inside his father's large, steady one.

"No, no. That was good, son. I dub you Story Joke Master." His father's voice quavered, then steadied itself. There were crimson streaks on his pants. "You just need to remember how the song goes. It'll be even funnier then. Tony Bennett recorded it in 1962 and—"

"Did he feel it? When you…"

"He didn't feel anything, son. He didn't have anything left to feel."

Albert was quiet.

"When you become your own man—it doesn't happen at any particular age, but you'll know when it does—you might make a different decision than I did if facing a similar situation. That's what sons do: they learn from the mistakes of their fathers'."

+

A Bruce Springsteen song kept playing over and over in his head:
The dogs on Main Street howl 'cause they understand
If I could take one moment into my hand
He'd always felt that his moment would come, but he assumed it would happen at the annual talent show once he finally got up the guts up to play guitar in public, not at a spelling bee in an elementary school. At least it would be far from the prying eyes of the predators of Hoskins High. Anna Lafleur, however, was nothing like the rest of the Bod Squad and their male counterparts. She existed for moments like the 13th Annual Spring House Spelling Bee; she lived for a chance to watch someone excel. Anna had worn many faces over the years— but they were all sort of the same girl to Albert. Variations on a note. Sharped maybe, in the eighth grade. Flatted, perhaps, freshman year

of high school. Augmented? Sure, yeah, probably. Diminished? Rarely. While she was still a mystery of sorts, now that they'd had their moment in Megan's kitchen, she was no longer an unsolvable one; now that Anna Lafleur *was* Anna Lafleur, she ceased to be all things and became just one—the sum of the equation, the root of the verb, the key center. All this from a girl who lived around the corner.

"Half-day, Albert," Raoul said.

Albert turned his head.

"Today?"

Raoul (chess club, Latin club, computer club, Mathletes) shook his head. Tiny pieces of dandruff fell from Raoul's severely combed, greasy looking hair and settled on his shoulders.

"Friday."

Albert squinted. The bell rang, and the hallway grew crowded.

"For the Bee?"

Steve White (varsity basketball; varsity football) hip checked Raoul into the lockers. Chris Auger (varsity basketball team manager) chuckled and put his arm over Steve's shoulder. Chris Auger was always chewing gum. He was the Man with the Plan—that was what the jocks called him. Albert despised nicknames; the only nickname he'd been graced with at Assumption or Hoskins had been Batcherman—as in "rub out a batch."

Raoul adjusted his glasses. He didn't even look at Chris or Steve.

"The half-day is for…are you even listening to me, Albert," Raoul said in his intensely concerned voice.

Albert watched Chris Auger rub Steve White's shoulders and pat his back.

"Why do you let them do that to you?" Albert asked.

"They do it to you too," Raoul said, sounding defensive. "You don't do anything about it."

"I guess not," Albert said.

"Dungeons and Dragons Friday afternoon?"

Greg Stillman (varsity basketball; track and field) ran up behind Chris and Steve and put a hand on each one's shoulder to briefly lift himself off the ground.

"Mr. Bojangles," Chris Auger said by way of a greeting to Greg.

Another nickname.

Greg Stillman executed a tap dance and took a deep bow. Greg was tall and skinny, and his head was like a dodge ball balanced on a bean pole—a muscular bean pole.

"I can't," Albert said. "I'm spelling. Qualifying rounds."

Raoul fiddled with the pens and pencils in his pocket.

"Suit yourself."

Chris applauded Greg "Mr. Bojangles" Stillman's impromptu dance performance. Steve leaned against the wall and shuttled a toothpick from one side of his mouth to the other. Megan Riley and Peggy Runyon pretended not to watch. Megan applied lip-gloss to her already damp-looking mouth.

"Hey, did you quit Mathletes?" Raoul asked. He sometimes came late; the chess club met at the same time and they too were preparing for a competition.

"Dork," Raoul added without waiting for an answer. "Only quitters quit."

A spitball landed on Raoul's glasses. Albert glanced behind him. Steve White shook his head, mulled over his toothpick, and looked at the ground. Chris Auger shoved his hands deep into the pockets of his team jacket and grinned at Steve. Greg Stillman covered his mouth in mock horror.

"Don't let them bother you, Albert," Raoul said.

The second spitball exploded on Raoul's cheek.

"If I had a changeling spell…" Raoul began.

The crowd in the hallway parted and it grew very quiet. Greg Stillman tossed his straw. Albert backed up against the lockers. Raoul licked his fingers and slicked back his hair. Steve White buttoned the top button of his dress shirt and fixed his tie.

But it wasn't Mr. Bogle, the Assistant Headmaster and Disciplinarian. It was someone infinitely more frightening. John-John Hagarty wore his signature long, black trench coat, and a pale yellow pacifier sprouted from his lips. He was unhurried, and his Doc Martens boots—banned in Father Hoskins High—stomped with such force, the lockers rattled. He looked straight ahead, as if deep in thought, but Albert found his expressionless face chilling and he thought his eyes appeared to be empty, but waiting to be filled—with what, he didn't know. Or maybe that was the way John-John wanted to look. It was more than just his size and his well-known juvenile criminal record that kept even joker jocks like Greg, Chris, and Steve from messing with him; it was his bearing and his reputation as well, although the jocks tended to treat the Lakes boys with deference anyway due to their unpredictability and apparent lack of concern for their own well-being.

The hallway soon turned noisy again—John-John may have been feared, but he was in a different league from Mr. Bogle—and Raoul poked a skinny finger into Albert's chest.

"Quitting Mathletes will look very bad on your transcript," he said. "Don't do it."

"It'll be on there no matter what," Albert replied, his eyes still on John-John. "It's not gonna say—"

John-John stopped in the middle of the hallway. He looked like he was going to sneeze. Megan and Peggy turned their heads, as if expecting a tidal spray.

"Some party, ay, John-John?" Greg Stillman asked. "That Gooch, man, he's so fucking crazy. When he drank that…"

John-John discarded his pacifier—girls squealed and jumped out of the way when it hit the floor—and he sucked in some snot.

"…shit, right? Did I tell you, Chris, this fucking guy—"

John-John hacked a green loogie in Greg Stillman's face. Greg clawed at his lips, nose, and cheeks with both hands. Steve White and Chris Auger stared at the floor.

"What the fuck, John-John?" Greg screamed.

"You're going to be first," John-John said. He took a fresh pacifier from his pocket and everybody jumped. "It'll be a head shot."

Raoul whispered in Albert's ear: "Should I thank him?"

"I don't think so."

John-John looked at Albert and Raoul.

"Fuck you," he said before continuing on his way.

"Well, I'm outta here before Greg decides it's my fault," said Raoul, leaving to follow John-John down the hall. "Mr. John-John, sir," Albert heard Raoul call. Albert walked the opposite way. He liked Raoul, even if he had never graduated beyond *Star Trek* and *D&D*, but the only music he listened to was homemade burns of science-fiction television show themes.

Though Albert had only started guitar lessons the year before his father died, he knew music separated him from most everyone in school. He wasn't aware of many musicians at Hoskins High and of the few he knew about, not one subscribed to his father's theories on music, what it was and what it meant. He knew a few kids took guitar or piano lessons, but only at their parents' behest; there was a junior who pounded on the drums, but he rarely played anymore, he said, because he wasn't feeling it; some students played brass instruments in the school band and marched at football games in shiny suits, performing with gusto, as if the music director had said, "Once more with feeling." But his father had taught him that music *was* feeling. It broke down along genre lines, sure, his father had said, but it was more complicated than the Beatles versus Motown or grunge versus hip-hop. He said now that Albert had entered high school, he might find that cliques were defined, in part, by musical genres, and he was right: there were punks and metal heads and squeaky clean country pop fans. Deadheads. Club kids. Albert's father had told him that the reason teenagers did this was because the music made them feel a certain way—ebullient or sad, angry or horny, scared or tough, which they'd already been experiencing; music just gave them a voice—and they sought out other kids who felt the same way, sometimes just to be comforted that someone else felt similarly. Social media didn't necessarily make it easier; everybody seemed to be revealing their every thought online, he said, but no one was really saying anything. Teens had to fight to be heard above all the noise, and they subconsciously searched for outlets where they could express their innermost feelings—and music was a natural release. Albert was aware that it was this knowledge that made him different.

Father Dave, in Modern Religion class, had told them that parents and elected officials too often blamed movies, television, or music for any horrific act perpetrated by a teenager without ever looking in the mirror. Father Dave argued that the reason why these excuses didn't extend to adults was because it was so much bull. Mr. Drinkwater said that today's teens either felt nothing at all or far too much; either way, they were part of Generation Complain. Albert wished he could bring his headphones to Mr. Drinkwater's class.

The area in front of the bulletin board was empty. Albert looked at his watch. He was supposed to be in Health learning about chlamydia and gonorrhea. *Gonorrhea. G-o-n-o-r-r-h-e-a. Gonorrhea.* He didn't have time for Mr. Garbowski's awkward fumblings and well-intentioned, but oft-ignored advice (if the cafeteria chatter was to be believed) regarding the genital area; Albert needed time to just *spell*. He had to keep his mind occupied, for all day the questions crowded his brain: would she come to the Qualifying rounds on Friday, would she actually come to the 13th Annual Spring House Spelling Bee on the eleventh of April? His father had told him that he would know when he'd mastered the guitar when he could play without thinking—for thinking often got in the way of actually feeling.

(Thinking, however, was never to be confused with acting, his father said.) Albert thought if he worked on mastering spelling in the little time that he had, maybe he'd be able to ignore the way the stirring in his trousers matched the butterflies in his stomach.

Albert knew without really knowing that distracting himself with music was exactly what his father had done that day in March three years ago. Not with spelling—Albert didn't recall his father being particularly enamored with spelling—but he'd used *something*. "Distract the mind," his father had said, "so nothing is in the way, no stray thoughts. Music isn't about thinking or numbers or anything *but* playing, son. Distract the mind and just do, just be.

"Maybe distract is the wrong word—occupy is better," his father said. "Fill in every space; let your mind chew on something while the rest of you immerses in *feeling*. Don't worry: when it comes time to act, you'll be ready. You can open the gate and access the cognitive part of your brain anytime you need to. You'll know when the time for thinking is over. You've put the hours in; you've thought it through and studied hard. Now you need to let go and play the chords, write the first chapter, bring the brush to the canvas or the bat to the ball."

It had happened like this: Albert came home from school one day, and his father was gone. His clothes too. Even his books. Everything but his scent. Nobody said very much to Albert other than a few weak lies, and he had no idea what had really happened to his father. It was Aunt Ethel who told him at the viewing. His mother just sat in the front row and smoked cigarettes, tapping the ash onto the carpet. Men in black suits with creased foreheads quietly implored her to extinguish and cease and desist. His mother just stared straight ahead at the closed casket.

"It wasn't pretty. It's a good thing you weren't there," Aunt Ethel told him. Albert felt guilty. He hadn't been there.

"Your mother found him," his aunt said. Albert stared at the scuffs on his shoes. Aunt Ethel smelled like cough medicine. "Terrible, terrible thing."

Albert walked up to the front row and looked at his mother, but his mother had left; only her shell remained. Her eyes were like John-John's, only his mother's eyes didn't look like they were waiting to be filled. They looked like they'd been drained.

"He felt too much, your father," Aunt Ethel continued when he returned. "Too much the dreamer. Too much the thinker."

Albert played with the buttons on his new sport coat. He didn't want to say it aloud—at least not to Aunt Ethel—but Albert thought that his father might have dispensed with thinking altogether; he might have gotten past it so there was nothing left but feeling. It must have been too much; it must have been a particularly bad feeling.

"Your mother doesn't need another dreamer, Albert," Aunt Ethel said.

Perhaps his father had hummed a Charlie Parker riff or recited a few Bob Dylan lyrics—something from *Blood on the Tracks* ("The sound of a man who can't *stop* feeling," he'd told Albert)—or maybe he'd gone over one of his lists. His father had been overly fond of lists. Not lists of chores or goals or party guests. Albert's father wrote and maintained and updated lists of his favorite things, crossing out some entries with such violence that the pen ripped through the paper. Favorite Coltrane solos, the greatest one-off singles, his top ten pre-World War II blues songs. Maybe he'd repeatedly recited one of these lists to himself, between the bars in his head, until he was sure, absolutely sure, that he was no longer thinking—just feeling. A quiet revolution. Only it didn't end quietly, did it? It ended with bang and a stain. Thinking was never to be confused with acting.

In the aftermath, his mother surrendered, retreating to the safety of the couch. Albert was left to figure out how to move forward; he had nowhere to retreat to and nothing to surrender. But one thing he was sure of was that his father had rescued himself from too many wretched feelings like he'd rescued the muskrat. The muskrat had needed assistance to cross over, but Albert's father hadn't needed anyone's help; he'd taken matters into his own hands. Now his name was rarely mentioned. Even his records had been in boxes when Albert came home from school that day, the first step in an unsuccessful attempt to wipe his father from the family's collective memory. While he didn't know what had happened when he walked in the door, just seeing all of his dad's records boxed up, probably in no discernible order, was enough of a clue until Aunt Ethel told him what his mother would not. His father's feelings had caught up with him, and after a lifetime of striving to experience rather than ponder, his emotional immune system had been compromised. He'd become overwhelmed, Albert believed, to the point where every hurt was a wound and every expression of love, a reminder of a moment lost— he could spin a 45 again and again and never retrieve what was.

The problem with the Sam the Clam joke—and Albert had gone over this often in the years since the death of the muskrat—was this: Albert hadn't known the melody of "I Left My Heart in San Francisco." As far as he knew, he had never even heard the song before. His father had assured him that the joke had come across— and served its purpose. Its rhythm helped him to feel rather than think, which might have gotten in the way or made him lose his nerve while he oversaw the muskrat's final revolution; he needed to picture the animal's racing heartbeat and be able to follow it as it wound down. The joke, he said, had also brought him out of his head (or back to Earth, as Albert's mother would say) simply because but because Albert hadn't remembered the song. He was supposed to sing the punch line, "*I left my harp in Sam Clam's disco,*" to the tune of Tony Bennett's signature song's chorus.

Despite being an old joke, Albert's father said it hadn't worn out its welcome; it hadn't become clichéd. To become clichéd meant that a joke, a record, a conceit became universal (as much as the insular and snobbish few who understood the silent *whoosh* of the quiet revolution wished it to be otherwise). It ended up being beyond familiar and ceasing to have any impact. A cliché was loud, his father said, and one didn't have many choices once loud was the adjective.

In Albert's *New Catholic Picture Bible*, there was an illustration next to each little story. The book also had black and white photographs (haphazardly tinted green) of Biblical landmarks (or equivalents). Albert had once insisted to his third grade religion class that the photograph of the tomb in the back of his *New Catholic Picture Bible* was actually a snapshot of Jesus' tomb. He was roundly laughed at, although, looking back, Albert wondered if the kids even knew *why* they were laughing.

Up in the mornin' and out to school
The teacher is teachin' the Golden Rule

It was Albert's conclusion, one he'd come to years later, that his social position in elementary school, which would carry over to Hoskins High, had been pre-ordained, that some evolutionary element had separated out the horde, and the laughter of his classmates was merely instinctive behavior, an early manifestation of recognizing the weak and the wounded.

Workin' your fingers right down to the bone
And the guy behind you won't leave you alone

In the *New Catholic Picture Bible* there was a whole series of small chapters detailing Samuel's choosing of Saul as the king of Israel and Saul's pride and impatience. Albert's father said that King Saul was probably loud. Time and again, Saul disobeyed the God of Israel and tried to assassinate David, his chosen successor. Cursed by Samuel, Saul lived the remainder of his life in constant strife and crippling anger, and overrun by the Philistines in battle, Saul took his own sword and fell upon it.

Hail! Hail! Rock'n'roll
Deliver me from the days of old

"Was that a quiet revolution?" Albert had asked his father, and his father had laughed.

"He asked his armor-bearer first," his father explained, "but it was too heavy a burden for the servant. Saul had been pierced by many arrows. He didn't want to die at the hands of his enemies. So, I guess you could say Saul dialed it down in the end, yes. Of course, you could call him a coward too for killing himself, but rather than go out with a blaze of glory and be torn apart by his sworn enemies, he made quiet the new loud."

"I don't know if I understand it all," Albert admitted.

His father laughed again.

"You will, son. Unfortunately, you will."

The illustration accompanying the story of Saul's death in the *New Catholic Picture Bible* was terrifying. As a servant watched from the right, Saul, his mouth open, his face stretched unnaturally, fell upon a sword he'd propped up against a stone. Disturbingly, his armor, in the picture, was arrow-free.

Maybe Saul had asked his armor-bearer knowing he'd decline, so that there'd be a record of his deed. Albert's father had left a record as well—an actual record instead of a note. He'd put the 45 on the turntable and set the arm to play the single repeatedly. Albert had naturally expected Miles Davis or Coltrane. (They'd been his father's favorites, but Albert didn't think they'd released many 45s.) Or even Lennon, Muddy Waters, Johnny Cash.

At the viewing, when she'd told Albert about the record, Aunt Ethel shook her head and scrunched her lips as if she'd stuck her nose up a dog's ass.

"Some nonsense."

"But what nonsense?" Albert asked. He'd grown anxious, and it had taken all the quiet he could muster to keep down the loud.

"Egyptian nonsense."

"Egyptian non—?"

"I can't even say it."

"Say *what?*" Albert asked. Droplets of sweat crowded together on his upper lip.

"My Carl—God rest his soul—your uncle—he wouldn't even say the name of that Eddie Cantor song."

"Uncle Carl wouldn't—?"

"Don't say it."

"From the musical?"

"Albert, I'm warning you…"

" 'Makin' Whoopee?' "

"Jesus, Mary, and sweet, sweet Joseph," Aunt Ethel stage whispered, crossing herself before pulling a tissue from her cleavage. Her many gold bracelets rattled like a tambourine rolling down the stairs. Heads turned but Albert paid little attention, and his aunt stared them down. The funeral home piped in a never-ending dirge that seemed to consist of the same few organ notes repeated ad nauseum. Albert thought that if there was ever to be a *second* resurrection, it should happen now, his father popping the lid to demand that someone change the music.

"Just what do they teach you in Catholic school?" Aunt Ethel asked, stuffing the used tissue up her sleeve. "Trash talk?"

"My dad's song was a dirty song?"

Aunt Ethel sniffed.

"Floors are dirty," she said. "Songs are filthy."

"And you're sure it was a 45? Not a whole side of an LP?" He'd begun to wonder if his aunt knew the difference.

"Teenybopper nonsense," she said.

Albert believed that that could mean just about anything post-Eddie Cantor to his aunt.

She wheezed to cover the sound of her passing gas. Albert tried not to breathe through his nose.

"Shouldn't you be up front with your mother?" Aunt Ethel asked.

"She doesn't need me there," Albert said.

Aunt Ethel sighed.

"That, dear, dear nephew, is too true. Too true."

She patted Albert's leg and smoothed his tie before picking up a prayer card and pretending to study it with great interest.

"You're going to find out sooner or later from one of your cousins," Aunt Ethel said without looking up. "And you are old enough. Boys always are."

"Old enough for what?" Albert wanted to rip the prayer card from his aunt's chubby, brown-spotted hands.

She looked pained. "It was another song about...you know. It's a Fonzie."

Albert stuck the end of his tie in his mouth to keep from screaming. His best friend in the whole world—his father—was dead. His mother was gone, full press retreat. And he was about to go to jail for shoving a prayer card past Aunt Ethel's heavily lipsticked lips in the hopes that she'd swallow it.

As if she'd heard his thoughts, she laid the memorial card aside and leaned in; Albert held his breath again.

"The Egyptians. The Philistines. One of those. Another song about—" Aunt Ethel whispered. "Bully, indeed. I'm sure you know *just* what it's about."

And Albert did (sort of), but more importantly, he now knew the song.

Sometimes a quiet revolution is louder than expected.

Albert refocused his eyes on the school bulletin board. He blinked and read the notice. Raoul was right: Friday was going to be a half-day. This couldn't have worked out better, he thought. It gave him plenty of time to go over the really tricky words before the Qualifying rounds began. Never know when antediluvian or prospicience would pop up. When Albert turned around, the hallway was empty. Behind closed doors, in stuffy rectangular-shaped rooms, chalk scraped on slate, bored shoes scuffed the chairs in front of them, teachers droned themselves droopy in the stuffy heat— unaware of the emergence of a future spelling star in their very midst. Mathletes? No one even came to see the Mathletes compete! And he'd probably never play guitar in front of anyone if he was honest with himself. (His father had said that the greats would have played whether or not anyone ever watched, but they came alive in front of an audience, so musical greatness wasn't on Albert's horizon.) But to spell, to take the order and rhythms of math and eliminate the formulas, would enable Albert, through an everyday endeavor that confounded almost every non-teaching adult he knew, to rise above and save himself from mediocrity. He'd become the Boy Who Could Spell—the Speller, as Anna called him.

Anna! Albert clutched at his chest. It was as if the front gate of the fence he'd erected around his heart to protect himself from loving and losing again (one parent in the ground, the other on the couch) had swung open, revealing a passage thought lost amid the sameness and inertia. Of course he'd save Anna Lafleur too. He'd saved her once before, at the party, when she'd asked him. He stayed awake all that night thinking of how he should have gone back in, gotten her out of there, rescued her (seeing purple streaks was surely a sign of distress), and done it right in front of all the jocks and the Bod Squaders and the Lakes kids. A quiet revolution required more than just volume control; it demanded revolt. *Revolution.* R-e-v-o-l-u-t-i-o-n. *Revolution.* An overthrow of the establishment—in this case, the caste system at Hoskins High. It only took one (or hopefully two) to bring about its downfall, not by standing up to its adherents but by ignoring them. He couldn't let Anna sink into the sameness, not now that he'd felt the rusty hinges of his own previously camouflaged gate sing and moan.

When faced with being overwhelmed by the enemy of cancer, when forced to confront the idea of suffering and deteriorating in front of his family, of becoming a burden, Albert's father chose one of the loudest songs from his 45 collection. After years of turning the quiet into the unavoidable, his father went with Sam the Sham and the Pharaohs as his farewell. He'd stuck the single on the turntable and wedged the big kitchen knife in the chipped handle beneath the lip of the sink—a decorative handle that opened no drawer—and sometime, Albert imagined, between *"let's not be L-7"* and *"come and learn to dance,"* his father fell onto the knife. Once impaled, according to Aunt Ethel, the upper half of his body bent forward, and he ended up staring into the gaping maw of the garbage disposal.

His father had felt everything—he'd even gone out with a grand gesture of hypersensitivity; no sleeping pills or running the car in the garage for his father. Albert was ready to feel—and he'd make sure everyone else felt this change. Especially Anna Lafleur. He'd rescue her like she'd rescued him. He wished he had the nerve to ditch the rest of the school day to focus on spelling. The only way he'd win the bee was if he could spell without thinking, and the only way he'd rescue Anna Lafleur was if he won the bee. He'd show her it was okay to *feel.* He'd show her it was okay to love him, that he was worth loving back. And he'd reveal to everyone else his true identity. Before the two of them turned their backs on the Bod Squad and the jocks and their artificial superiority, he'd make sure they saw him for who he was, even if it killed him (and killed everyone else to look). Wooly Bully. They'd see. He was the Speller.

+

"Yeah, but how do you spell it?" Megan Riley whispered.

"Oh, I'm—"

"Meg, back off," Anna Lafleur whispered back.

Anna was sitting behind him. Albert was sweating. Anna leaned her face against his back.

"But, Albert, how *do* you spell it."

"Ephemeral?"

"Fem," Megan Riley whispered.

Albert watched Mr. Day's head nod as he read *Newsweek*.

"Yeah," Anna mumbled into Albert's back. "Ephemeral."

"Faggot," Greg Stillman said as he fake-coughed into his fist. Megan giggled.

"Problem, Miss Riley?" Mr. Day asked from his desk, now fully alert.

Megan shook her head.

"I was asking Albert for a pencil. Mine broke."

Albert watched Megan snap the point from her pencil under her desk.

Mr. Day's fingers picked at a razor cut on his throat.

"Well, Mr. Bannerman," Mr. Day asked, "do you have a writing implement for the pencil-poor Miss Riley?"

Albert dug into his book bag.

"Pen or pencil. It doesn't matter," the teacher said absently as he continued to aggravate his shaving nick. "It's just that you can erase with a—"

"Pencil-dick," Greg Stillman said as he fake-sneezed into his hands.

"Mr. Stillman," Mr. Day said, staring at the blood on his finger, "see me after class."

"You're dead, Bannerman," Greg Stillman whispered.

Albert bent lower to better rummage in his bag, which was alongside his desk. If he turned his head just the slightest bit to the left, he could see Anna Lafleur's legs. They looked muscular, smooth, and his eyes followed along their surfaces until her thighs disappeared into the dark mystery of her skirt. He was careful not to let his eyes linger too long.

"E-p-h-e-m-e-r-a-l," Albert whispered. He liberated a pencil from the bottom of his book bag and handed it to Megan, who winked, produced a pen, and began coloring the eraser.

"Eyes on your blue books," Mr. Day said. "Complete silence."

"Thank you," Anna Lafleur whispered. And Albert tried to suck in as much of her bubble gum breath as his lungs could hold.

+

"You almost got caught," Raoul said. He was terrified of getting caught, which was odd, because he never broke a rule. "What were you thinking, Albert? What were you doing?"

"Spelling," Albert said. He couldn't erase Anna Lafleur's legs from his brain. The partial view of her thighs had made concentrating during the test almost impossible.

"You better keep your head in the game, Albert," Raoul said. "If you get caught helping someone else cheat, they'll kick you out of Mathletes before you have a chance to quit."

"Mathletes," Albert repeated. His chest hurt.

"How do you know if you're having a heart attack?" he asked.

Raoul laughed.

"When you're sitting with Jesus and looking down on us kicking butt at the Mathletes state finals."

Albert's face muscles formed a facsimile of a smile. Raoul grinned back and entered the classroom across the hall. Albert looked at the number on the door in front of him. Was this his—?

Greg Stillman burped in his ear.

"Hey, dead man," he said.

Bob Goocher pushed Albert into the doorframe. Chris Auger patted Albert's shoulder.

"How ya doin', buddy?" he said without looking at Albert's face. A toothpick was planted in the corner of Chris' mouth.

Greg placed himself in front of Albert. Chris wiped his hand on his trousers dramatically.

"Bannerman, Dead-er-man," Greg said. "Same difference."

Chris stage whispered into Greg's ear.

"Skinny boy," he said, gesturing to Albert, "let it go. Throw it back. Too small."

"Leave him alone," Anna Lafleur said, appearing out of nowhere it seemed. Albert felt light-headed: her jugular notch visible where her collar was modestly open, the tiny scar on her chin. The loose ponytail. The black cloth choker.

Megan Riley pushed past Albert and Greg and Chris.

"Her Speller," she teased but not in a nice tone.

Greg swung a fist at Albert and stopped an inch or two from his face.

"Psych," Greg said. Chris laughed and pulled him into the classroom by his collar. Greg flashed Albert two middle fingers on his way in.

Soon Albert stood alone in the doorway. Everyone was in their seats, talking, so Albert found his desk (and was careful not to trip over Steve White's extended leg). He wasn't even sure what class he was in. History with Mr. Peitzman? Albert wondered if Anna liked music. Maybe they could hop some buses and trek through the used music stores on Saturday. Stop for hoagies (no onions!) and iced teas at the ITO if they found themselves in the neighboring town of Rhawnhurst, eat their lunch across the street in Solly Playground. (Ending up in Rhawnhurst was a distinct possibility since there was an excellent little record shop there.) But afterwards: where to go? To head to Anna's house seemed daunting. What if he had to go to the bathroom—more than just peeing? Maybe he could try to go at the Italian Takeout before they left Rhawnhurst, just in case. If they went back to his house, he'd have to explain his mother on the couch—and God forbid if she was actually up. But he had a working turntable in addition to a CD player in his room. What was cooler than vinyl? If he told Anna his mother was under the weather, nothing contagious, just a touch of something, the tail end, then they could go upstairs and listen to music uninhibited. He could play her the songs his father told him had changed his life and—

"...Bannerman?"

Albert sat up straight.

"Eyes up here," Mr. Peitzman said.

Red-faced, Albert did as he was told. In this class, Anna sat in the row to his left, one seat up. God knows where his eyes had been.

"*Wehrmacht?*" Mr. Peitzman asked. "Anyone?"

"Weltschmerz. W-e-l-t-s-c-h-m-e-r-z. Weltschmerz," Albert said.

The class tittered; Albert strained his ears for applause.

"Mr. Bannerman," Mr. Peitzman began, "while we find—and I'm sure I speak for everyone—your melancholy and world-weariness 'caused by comparison of the actual state of the world with an ideal state' lamentable, I was: a) looking for some thoughts on the relationship between the SS and the *Wehrmacht*, particularly in the final stages of the war; b) not asking you to spell *Wehrmacht*, let alone *Weltschmerz*, and c)—this one is most important, Mr. Bannerman, so do pay attention—I didn't call on you."

"I thought...I—" Albert stammered.

"What you thought and the reality of our time together here," Mr. Peitzman explained, "are quite mutually exclusive, Mr. Bannerman..."

Snickering punctuated with the occasional giggle.

"...and perhaps this explains the source of your *Weltschmerz*."

Albert looked down and closed his eyes.

"Dickweed," Greg Stillman hissed, covering his mouth afterwards like a little girl.

"Mr. Stillman: would you care to answer the question?" Mr. Peitzman asked. Greg studied the cover of his closed textbook. "No? Of course not. How about Mr. Auger? And, please, Mr. Auger: excise any spelling exercises from your answer."

Laughter.

In Albert's head, Albert Ayler was leading his brother and the rest of his quintet through tumultuous storms, waves lapping at the brass, split second decisions determining their survival or immersion.

"Asswipe. A-s-s-w-i-p-e. Asswipe," Greg whispered beneath Chris Auger's answer.

More laughter. Albert wanted to lift his head to see if Anna Lafleur's voice had joined the others, but he didn't dare.

"Stillman—I'll see you after," Mr. Peitzman said.

"I'm already staying after," Greg whined. "For Mr. Day."

"Good, then I'll see you after school *tomorrow*."

Greg slumped in his seat. Chris patted his shoulders.

Albert kept his head low and when the bell rang, he took his time so he'd be the last to exit. A smoker, Mr. Peitzman had been the first out the door. Albert stood in the hallway, expecting an ambush—and if one came, he thought, he deserved it. He hadn't been paying attention to the room; he'd forgotten where the one was.

Music, his father had taught him, came down to timing. Even those that played with time (like Albert's namesake) understood its rigidness, had memorized its monolithic smoothness, and when they took flight, they were aware of where the one was, the downbeat. Kids who started bands in high school invariably sped up every song, his father said. It wasn't until they were somewhat older or had formal training that most young musicians began to respect time. Albert knew his timing was poor. His internal metronome appeared to be swinging on hyperdrive or struggling through molasses. Especially when it came to Anna Lafleur. He'd ignored girls thus far (even if he didn't want to). Crushes weren't real, he knew, although they always seemed like it at the time. Crushes faded like a pop song: good beat, nice melody, but at its gooey, nougat center was utter vacuousness. Anna Lafleur was no crush. She was the real thing. If he didn't adhere to the beat, if he couldn't tame his own rhythm, he'd lose Anna before he ever had her: he'd run past her or be forever a desk's length away.

"Hey, Speller!" Anna called.

Albert turned, and Anna waved to him from a gaggle of Bod Squaders.

Prior to Anna, his heart, Albert discovered, had only known the simplest of tempos. He'd ignored more complicated rhythms. His mother knew only the slow steady buzz of her cheek imperceptibly rubbing itself raw against the patterns of the couch. His father, he imagined, had known intricacies beyond Albert's comprehension. He knew that he wasn't as rhythm-deficient as his mother, but he wasn't as knowledgeable and experienced as his dad had been, so navigating these new Anna-inspired tempos was daunting.

"…yeah, but they can get a keg," Megan Riley said as he slowly approached the girls. "And: killer weed."

"Some historians believe," Albert said to Anna Lafleur from halfway across the crowded school hallway, "that World War II actually started in 1931 when Japan annexed Manchuria."

He didn't think it was the best conversation opener, but they'd been discussing World War II in class, so it was the first thing that had popped into his head.

"Got yourself a paparazzo there, Anna," Megan said, "just with a dictionary instead of a camera."

Albert forced himself not to spell paparazzo.

"Gotta boot. Chem lab," Megan said to the Bod Squad. "Tonight—seven, okay? I can't be too hammered for school tomorrow. Got Houseman first thing on Thursdays. Discussing

Virginia Woolf with a hangover is a real bitch." She departed in an overly-perfumed swirl.

When he was sure Megan was no longer in the hallway, Albert sidled up to Anna and said, "My dad told me that."

Anna rooted around in her purse.

"Told you what?" she asked, without looking up, her face pinched.

"About Manchuria. He was mostly into music, but he knew a lot about a—"

"Found it," Anna said, holding up a tube of lip balm.

Albert looked away while she applied it. He didn't want to focus on her mouth for too long.

Anna smacked her lips together. "What were you saying?"

"Manchuria. And my dad," Albert answered. "He said that—"

"Megan said seven, right?" Anna asked.

Albert nodded. "Yes. She had to go boot something up in the chemistry lab."

Anna laughed. " 'Gotta boot' means gotta go."

Albert nodded again.

"I'll make a note of that," he said. "I don't know much slang."

"Seven, huh?"

"Yes, seven," Albert said.

Anna blew upward and her breath pushed the stray strands of hair out of her eyes.

"I hate these parties anymore. Especially on a school night."

"Yes," Albert agreed even though he'd never been to a high school party.

"I'll just stay over at Megan's, but the next day drags even if you only had one beer 'cause they run so late. And all the boys show off. I'm just so ready for college. I mean, I know there're parties at college, but there's no Megan Riley." Anna giggled. "At least I hope not."

"I don't know what school Megan is—"

"Listen to me." She shook her head.

"Megan's been my friend since forever, but you know how some people seem to stop moving even though they're supposedly really busy with a bunch of shit? That's Megan. I'm not ready to stop moving."

"In music, when the band stops for longer than a beat or two, it's called a pregnant pause."

Anna blew at her stray strands again.

"Pregnant, huh?" She raised her eyebrows knowingly.

"Yes. A rest is really a rhythmic silence because the music does not end at—"

"You tired of parties?" she asked.

"I've never been to a—"

"Slumming, Anna?" Peggy Runyon asked. Peggy's fist was balled on her hip, and her body leaned to the right. Two anxious looking young girls stood on either side of her.

Anna ignored Peggy's question.

"Thanks again, Speller," Anna said.

"Give your books to the frosh," Peggy said. "They'll carry 'em right into class for you."

One of the young girls approached Anna with her arms outstretched, then curtsied.

"No thanks," Anna said, flashing a forced smile. "I can manage."

"Suit yourself," Peggy said. "Gotta train 'em somehow."

Anna rolled her eyes. "Right."

"Run along," Peggy said to the young girls with a wave of her hand. "Freshmen. They were the hot shit Bod Squad at Assumption, but eighth grade is *so* not high school. If we don't take 'em in hand, they'll never rule the school when their time comes. They'll never be queen bees, just sad, little drones with bad hair and love handles."

Meet the new boss / Same as the old boss, Albert thought.

Peggy waved a hand in the air, and Albert watched it hang there for a silent beat. Anna squinted down the hallway.

"Let's go," Peggy said, defeated. "We'll be late."

Anna took a step, then turned towards Albert.

"You want to come?" she asked.

"To Chemistry? I have—"

Anna's face was suddenly two inches from his. Albert's eyes drifted to the scar on her chin. He wanted to know the story behind it: had she fallen when she was two and cut her chin on an open drawer or was she born with the scar, some slight imperfection that occurred in her mother's belly, a mark to separate her from the rest of the beautiful people who shunned and hid away the awkward, the ugly, the unsure, the different?

"No, silly. To Megan's party tonight."

"Please," Peggy said. "With the charity work already."

"Me? I wasn't…I don't really know Megan and—"

"Seven, right? I'll see you there, Speller," Anna said.

"It's a masquerade, geek," Peggy told him. "Hide your face."

Albert watched Anna walk down the hall with Peggy and was surprised when she was swallowed by the rest of the student body.

+

The truth, of course, was that she felt everything but remembered nothing. Everyone else took care of reminding her: sly asides, courtesy inquiries in the hallway. Her head didn't throb as much as her middle did. Her legs were bruised. But as she started remembering, she mostly just felt fear.

Her focus for the day had been to avoid him. She didn't even know if he went to Hoskins or just attended special classes on certain days. She wouldn't have even known who it was if Megan and Peggy, before Brit Lit, hadn't greeted her by substituting his last name for hers.

Some girls looked at her like she had masturbated with the big crucifix that hung in the vestibule. Others merely snickered. And the boys! Some winked. Most gawked and pointed. Two brothers asked her to hang out in their basement after school. Now a big girl she didn't know was following her. And him too. The monster. Not one from the movies. A real one.

Greg and Chris passed her in the hall, and Greg stuck his tongue between two fingers and wiggled it at her.

Fuck Greg Stillman. She wished his head would explode like the guy in *Scanners*. As she'd pieced together the events of Megan's party during the school day, she knew Greg had been in the audience for her forced deflowering. Cheering. Mocking her screams. And as she overheard in gym class, taking his turn sniffing her torn underwear, which may or may not have been soiled by one or more audience member later.

Two freshmen girls stage whispered about the existence of digital photographs. Someone else said it was all over the Internet.

"Nobody else 'did it,' " Cheryl told her. "They just watched. Boys and tits, right?"

At first, when she came to in an unfamiliar bedroom, she just stared at a cowboy lampshade; she later thought the decorative cover ironic, for not one cowboy in a white hat, like the one pictured on the lampshade, had come to her rescue. There was a reason she disliked westerns—being attacked by a vampire was more believable than being saved by a hero. She was naked and everything but the socks she still wore was torn. Her underwear was missing. When she finally found the energy to get up (her brain had been screaming *escape, escape, escape,* but her body had felt held down by weights), she had no problem finding clothes; it turned out to be Meagan's little brother's room, but he wasn't that little (lampshade notwithstanding) for she quickly found some clothes that sort of fit her. The hallway was empty, and she stole to the bathroom, approaching the mirror with trepidation. Her black cloth choker was gone. There were huge hickeys on her neck (to match the bite marks she'd already discovered on her breasts). She had a purple bruise on her right cheek with a cut running down the center. What the fuck had happened? She was exhausted and shaking. It was a good thing she'd told her mother she was staying at Megan's. She looked like she'd been hit by a Mack truck driven by the Whore of Babylon. The face of her watch was cracked, but the device still ticked; if the time was to be believed, her mother would have left for work already (and Megan for school). She could steal home and grab her uniform and books after taking a long, hot shower, applying massive amounts of concealer to her cheek, and fashioning a new black choker; anything to feel like the Anna of yesterday. The way she looked, concealer or not, no one was going to hassle her about being late for school.

But at Hoskins High, things continued to get worse. Megan and Peggy went from being waitress-friendly in the morning to adopting a policy of total avoidance as the day wore on. And wore on it did: a slow churning of light and dust motes and school bells. There wasn't enough water in all of the school's water fountains to irrigate the dry desert of her mouth. She'd thought about making a run for it but decided she was safer—somewhat—in school, surrounded by authority figures, than outside of it.

She was standing in front of the fourth floor bulletin board near the northern stairwell, where it was usually less populated, pretending to read the various notices, when the big girl caught up to her. That's what she was now: quarry. Walking wounded. Still, better the big girl than the monster.

"He thinks you wanted him to compete," the big girl said. Her voice arrived on a breeze of spearmint gum. Anna stared back at the big girl's reflection in the sliding glass bulletin board doors until she was sure her tracker was alone. When she turned around, she thought the monster was still there, in the shadows at the end of the well-lit hallway where no shadows should be. Anna was sure it was him. A trickle of sweat ran down the side of her face. Where was Mr. Bogle when you needed him?

"Who?" she asked the big girl. Anna thought it was better to deal with whatever this was (she was sort of trapped anyway) than be alone while he befouled his nest of shadows, watching and waiting.

The girl in front of her was huge—big boned, her grandmother would have called her—with hundreds of freckles and dyed black hair that she'd obviously cut herself.

"You know who. He signed up because he thinks you like the way he spells. All because of yesterday. And now he thinks you're gonna go to the public grade school and watch him spell during the Qualifying rounds."

The smell of the big girl's gum, now carrying hints of egg salad, made Anna nauseous. She turned back to the bulletin board. Let the monster come now, she thought. She'd throw up on his shoes.

"I don't know what you're talking about," Anna said to the girl standing behind her.

"You know what: you're all full of shit. Every single one of you: elitist shitbags," the big girl said. "Do you even know his name? Do you? Do you even know my name? I'm in every single one of your classes."

Anna turned around again.

"I'm not like they are," she cried, her walls destroyed. If she had been like them, she wasn't now. "I'm not. They—"

"What's my name?" the big girl asked.

Anna didn't want to play games anymore, but if that was the monster breathing strenuously in shadows of his own making, then maybe he'd stay there if she wasn't alone. Perhaps if she engaged this girl, she could follow her to a more populated area of the school.

"Bridget," Anna said. "Babka. Bridget Babka."

"Good girl," Bridget said.

Anna blinked and the hallway grew darker; they were now surrounded by shadows. Bridget didn't seem to notice. The smell of recently smoked cigarettes overpowered Bridget's spearmint gum-egg salad breath. Anna's temple throbbed, and she peed a little in her underwear.

"You gonna show up Friday or what?" Bridget asked.

Blink. The shadows were closer. Her heart thumped so rapidly, she thought it would burst, revealing whoever had replaced who she'd been. The proof of blood wouldn't only be on the sheets in Megan's brother's room; her newly emerged self, violently dragged into womanhood, was baptized in it. Anna knew just who dragged the shadows forward. She was afraid the creature was drawn to her, as the pain between her legs intensified, as if he could smell the wound he'd created.

"Show up where?" Anna asked, panicked.

"Don't fuck with me," Bridget said, "and don't fuck with him. He signed up for this stupid thing because of you. He quit Mathletes because of you. He—"

"Hey," said a deep voice emanating from within the shadows that now had them penned in.

"Jesus," Bridget said over her shoulder to the owner of the voice. "You smell like a shit from a dead horse's ass."

"Beat it," the monster said.

"Beat this." Bridget turned to the side and gave him the finger. She stood between Anna and the monster, her face watching theirs, before she shook her head and started down the hallway.

"You're all the fucking same, Lafleur," Bridget said as she walked away. "He's spelling because of you."

Anna wanted to say *don't go, stay, we'll cut…we'll cut, we'll blow the rest of the day off, get cappuccinos, just waste the afternoon away anywhere but here, anywhere but right fucking here*, but Bridget was gone. Anna could see her bulky frame walking out of the edge of the shadows, towards the light at the south end of the hall. *You'd see, Bridget. You'd see that I'm not the same, not anymore. A part of me has been taken and everybody watched. I'm so different, Bridget, that I don't just want to spit on the person in the mirror, I want to break the glass and hope the shards mortally wound her, because I don't know who that fucking ugly whore is and I want her dead. If I was as awful as the rest of them, I'm truly sorry, and you have every right to rejoice at my fall, but please come back. Please.*

"Hey," the monster said again.

Anna willed her feet to move, her mouth to scream—anything. Nothing.

"You wanna to go to the coffee shop after school?" John-John Hagarty asked, his hands entwined and twisting in front of his huge skull belt buckle. John-John's trench coat fluttered as he spoke, as if the sides were giant wings. He smelled strongly of cigarettes smoked in a windowless room.

"To get some pie?" John-John added. "And some coffee?"

Anna opened her mouth to say *fuck you* or scream for help or *drop dead, loser*, but nothing came out. She was empty. Just thoughts. Pieces of air. Despite her earlier mental threat to vomit on his shoes, she choked back the urge when she caught a whiff of his Marlboro breath because she was afraid that once she started, she wouldn't be able to stop. Anna wished for the purple streaks. She wished she could have followed the purple streaks when they'd left Megan's kitchen last night with…with whomever.

"Coffee," John-John repeated, "or tea. Chicks like tea."

Anna walked away, through the shadows, careful to not bump into any walls, and headed towards the light that illuminated the doors leading to the southern stairwell. Either John-John would let her go or he wouldn't. Release, she knew, wasn't his style, but she couldn't just stand there like a damaged kitten in the headlights. Of course, he could always just follow her (as he would the rest of her life). Maybe she *would* ask Bridget if she wanted to cut, assuming she could find her. She'd never spoken to Bridget Babka in their four years at Hoskins High; she thought they'd even gone to grade school together, but she didn't remember if they talked there either.

Anna believed her own personal darkness had pursued her from the moment she discovered her ripped clothes in Megan's brother's room. And now storm clouds or black sheets of rain or an angry God blocked the light, and she stumbled. *Fuck fuck FUCK.* She jumped back up immediately, expecting to feel his blistering breath on her neck, but if he was near, he kept his presence a secret. She wanted to run, but it was too dark *(it's only dark in your mind)* and she fought the urge, making her way at a blind snail's crawl, feeling along the walls. *There—that movement: was that him? No, no—over there!* She struggled against a new urge to stand still and get what was coming to her. *See, there—how the darkness shifts? Smell the ashtray musk as he moves past?* When she reached the stairwell, Anna's fear broke free, and she descended two steps at a time, the ache in her middle now a devil baby digging its way to freedom, the bile in her stomach, excess demon sperm.

The third floor was a ghost town. Where were all of the fucking students? Where the hell were all the teachers? According to her determinedly ticking watch, school should still be in session, but the classrooms were dark and empty. Was this all in her head? *(Like the enveloping shadows?)* If she concentrated, she felt she could faintly hear chalk on blackboards, and just below the hum of the fluorescents overhead (the few that were on), she caught the droning of teachers and the tinkling laughter of girls, but it all seemed very far away, maybe because the version of her that she'd known had been ripped out of this world—not by consent, though she thought more and more, it was probably deserved: she'd allowed herself to become one of *them*. But at this moment, she felt like she didn't deserve any more than what she'd already received, and she didn't want to become any further removed from what she knew. Near the north end of the hall, where it was fairly dim, an open classroom spilled a weak, fluorescent glow on the scuffed marble floor. Anna sprinted towards this new light. A teacher, a janitor: anybody to make sure she left the school in one—

"Speller?"

"My name is Albert Ayler Bannerman," he said. "Would you like to come watch me spell tomorrow?"

+

He'd never been this popular, but he hadn't really cared before either. Not that he didn't have friends; he did. And not that popularity at a school that barely tolerated his presence meant jack-spit. (He'd been left back more than once, so he was older than the rest of them, and he now split his time between Hoskins' well-scrubbed walls and the oily trade school in Rhawnhurst with its floors littered with wood and metal shavings.) But the party: sure, his boys supplied the keg and the drugs, and the jocks accorded him the respect he didn't even know existed before he'd taken over Stevie's crew, but the important event of the night had nothing to do with ass-kissers or dog tranquilizers: he'd gotten laid at the party, and that, ladies and gents, John-John announced to his crusty windshield (for he couldn't tell his boys), had never, ever happened before.

Yeah, there'd been that blowjob from Whore Lenore, but Whore Lenore had blown just about every guy in the Lakes. It felt good in the beginning, but John-John couldn't shake the images of Lenore going down on Stevie Rich's old man for drugs or her pleasuring some of the junkies that littered the Lakes, plus it was hard to ignore the number of times she'd been busted for climbing into a john's car up on the Strip—these things ruined the experience for him. He'd spent most of the act wondering how much come clung to her stomach walls. Plus, Lenore was his cousin—a second cousin, he thought—and the family tree served to further remove him from the source of his pleasure and the pleasure itself. He'd pulled his pants back up before she even swallowed, and he had to resist an urge to punch her in the mouth and knock out the tweaker's remaining teeth.

And there'd been Mikey. Mikey was two years John-John's junior, but in Paradise Lakes, age meant shit after the sixth or seventh grade. Mikey was Tommy Two-Fingers' little brother, and he'd been the only participant in the unfortunate (but fucking hilarious) firecracker incident who thought to run back and grab the two digits recently separated from their brethren by the lit firecracker Stevie Rich had handed Tommy. Jesus, Stevie could always be counted on for shit like that back in the day. 'Course those times were long gone. From all accounts (John-John hadn't spoken to him since he left the Lakes), Stevie was playing football and hitting the books, aiming on graduating and hoping to get into the community college. It was a stunning betrayal. He moved out of the Lakes and into his aunt's place in the Heights without saying a word—he didn't even tell his old man, not that they had exactly gotten along. So far as John-John knew, Stevie hadn't spoke to his dad since he left, but Frannie was forever scheming, trying to get Stevie to send him some of his aunt's money: shit like, Grammy fell again, her trailer needed fixing, he couldn't forget his own people, etc. The few times John-John saw him riding by in his aunt's car, Stevie didn't stop, he just lifted his hand in greeting—the fucker would wave!

The old Stevie Rich would have had a fit if he'd known about what had happened with Mikey. Jesus, John-John would be dead if *anyone* knew, even now. They'd beat him (all of them, 'cause it would take that many) until he left the Lakes, an outcast. Mikey: they'd boil his skinny ass alive and feed it to him for lunch. The incident had happened a couple of years back, during the fall. With Stevie recently gone, there wasn't anyone around much in the mornings; even Chloe and them went back to school, at least for a little while, for show.

Tommy and Mikey's dad was a real hard-ass, a construction supervisor and a straight arrow who'd use a piece of pipe to keep his sons in line. When Child Services sent someone to his door (the school had contacted them because the boys were frequently bruised and had more than the average number of broken bones), he hit the guy with the pipe. No one ever came back. He had a garage, an actual brick and mortar garage, behind his trailer, but besides housing a rake, a hand mower, a few two-by-fours, and a cracked green garden hose that everyone—*everyone*—at one time or another mistook for a coiled snake while they were high, the garage was empty. Pretty much the only times he went in were to retrieve the mower and the rake whenever he puttered in the little patch of grass in front of their trailer. Stevie and the rest of the crew used it for everything from a crash pad to a hideout. They even once tried to use it as a shooting range rather than going to the dump where anyone could see them, but the volume of the first shot sent everyone scurrying; it took days before the ringing left John-John's ears. Occasionally, some of the boys had sex on top of the coiled garden hose. One time John-John shot a cat behind the garage and laughed and whooped it up with everyone else, but he came back alone that night and buried it. He sat next to the grave and tried to cry, but no tears came, and after a while, he left and got high. Whatever it had been, he never felt it again and shooting cats became kind of a hobby.

When that fall arrived (he was getting hard just thinking about it), John-John had no intention of returning to school. But until the truant officer dragged his ass back, it was just him and Mikey. Mikey was always sick. John-John didn't remember what was wrong with the kid. He played stickball and baseball when he was well enough, so his arms and legs were okay, and he wasn't sickly as in sniffles and sneezing or constant coughing. Tommy Two-Fingers had told them once that it was genetic, but that sounded too much like something to do with genitals and no one ever asked again. Whatever the reason, Mikey didn't go to school very often, which gave John-John someone to hang around with occasionally. So late one morning he and Mikey were standing in the garage, taking turns peeing on the water bugs that scurried across the gray concrete. John-John had tried many times to remember how it happened, how it began, but he couldn't. One minute they were hosing down some insects, the next Mikey was wacking him off, both of them standing right there in the nearly-empty garage. He remembered Mikey wiping his hand on his jeans afterwards and the way the sun blinded him when Mikey raised the garage door to leave. They'd always climbed in and out through the side window, and John-John recalled being surprised when one of the tiny garage's four walls lifted off the ground. When Mikey closed the door and went back inside the trailer, John-John went home to his and spent a good hour trying to get his cock up again, but nothing worked. He thought of tracking down Whore Lenore, but the idea seemed to make the physical situation even worse. He spent the rest of the day trying to shoot birds in the tall yellow grass of the utility company fields abutting the woods. Guns were real; his huge hands tingled when he shot them. Before Mikey, guns were the *only* things that made him feel.

Guns were easy to get—easier than sex and easier now that Stevie Rich had defected. Stevie's dad, Frannie Tidwell, had been pretty damned pissed when it happened, and everyone avoided him, even the strung out teenage girls he regularly banged. What seemed to have him the most out of sorts wasn't that he'd lost the public face of what he called his youth outreach program, but that Stevie was living high on the hog with his widowed aunt, whose husband (Frannie's brother) had died on 9/11; Frannie felt he had a right to a large chunk of the Victim Compensation Fund payment. Otherwise, Frannie could give two shits that Stevie had left; they never really had a father-son relationship anyway; Stevie was raised by his grandmother. The parties at Frannie's trailer eventually resumed, as did the cooking and distribution. In addition to handing out samples to high school and trade school students, John-John found himself point man in a few of Frannie's heist schemes. (Frannie rarely left his trailer.) But their crew had been like a snake without a head (all rattle, no bite) after Stevie became a citizen. So buoyed by Frannie's confidence in him, John-John took over as leader (under Frannie), and his size kept anyone from challenging him. But John-John didn't possess much of a head for heists—at least not one that made provisions for getting back out after breaking in. He did a little time for Frannie in the juvenile detention center after the botched job at Sol's. (He only got a few months because he didn't actually steal anything.) When he got out, Frannie gave him a gun—not gave him a gun for a job, but *gave* him a gun to *have*. And not just any gun: a semi-automatic pistol. John-John had kept his mouth shut in juvie. Frannie rewarded shut mouths. John-John spent the rest of the day at the dump shooting rats. He'd been temporarily issued a gun for jobs in the past, and when he filled the leadership vacuum, he had no problem getting loaners from Frannie just to fuck around with when he wasn't pulling his pud. But he'd never had his own gun before— and after he kicked the shit out of two Fields Gang members, both at least twenty years his senior, for slinging out of Seventh Heaven, a strip joint that was considered to be in the Lakes crew's territory, Frannie gave him another one just like the first.

There'd been other girls, but they'd all been junkies: they never remembered that John-John had been unable to penetrate them—or maybe they just didn't care. John-John's reputation remained intact. No one ever suspected that he was a virgin. The problem with the girls was all the talking: that was what did him in. John-John was convinced of it. All the sex talk, all the dirty talk distracted him. Failing to fuck, he just wanted them to wack him off while he was standing, but they could never shut the hell up. Bunch of tweakers. He never worried that he was gay; he never thought of guys besides Mikey, and even with him, he only thought about his small hands around his enormous cock. He'd see Mikey around, and it was weird at first, but after a while, the Mikey with the small hands in his daydreams and the real Mikey, playing cards on the trailer steps or watching baseball with his old man on the black and white they'd dragged out to the front yard, were miles apart, barely related.

Most of the other guys had steady pieces of ass, if not outright girlfriends. Girlfriends tended to talk of leaving Paradise Lakes someday, and while the Lakes sucked dick, John-John thought the rest of Mondauk Proper was even worse: church carnivals and dog parades and cops everywhere. (He should be used to cops by now— he'd been arrested four times and they were always cruising into the Lakes—but just the sight of their uniforms made him see red.) Between the trailer park and his experiences outside of it, John-John felt he'd seen it all—whores and wives and strippers and pass-arounds—until he saw Anna Lafleur.

John-John knew the Bod Squad—intimately, in some cases, even if those cases were vicariously. The Bod Squad called it fishing: hooking up with the Lakes boys, drinking their beer, smoking their weed, and finishing them off in the back seat of one of the many cars in permanent states of repair dotting the landscape of the trailer park. Anna was different. She didn't pretend to be some princess of Mondauk like her bitch friends did, and she didn't act like she was slumming when she said hi if they passed in the halls; it struck him as something she did naturally—and just as naturally, he'd grunt a reply. Sometimes she looked a little wary when saw him, but that never stopped her from being herself. Sweet was a word he'd heard tossed around in regards to certain girls, but he never truly understood what it meant until Anna. When he'd dropped some change in Rex's (he'd followed her there and was relieved when she bought Q-tips and not Trojans), Anna, who stood behind him in line, knelt down and handed him the coins.

"All of them landed heads up, John," she said. "That has to count for something."

He nodded, left his purchases on the counter, and exited the store. He'd never *felt* so much in his whole fucking life.

She was telling him he was going to get lucky.

The party at Megan Riley's house was just another exercise in reverse-slumming: the jocks invited the boys from the Lakes, knowing they'd be able to get a keg as well as provide other party favors, and in return, the Lakes boys could break off a piece with the Bod Squaders, if the girls were into it—and why wouldn't they be after taking a dog tranquilizer, synthetic ketamine being the night's sample? John-John looked at it as a job with benefits for his crew, but a job nonetheless (samples always led to sales)—until he saw Anna Lafleur. If she'd been at other parties, he'd never run into her. He didn't think he'd ever seen her outside of Hoskins High other than the time he followed her into Rex's Pharmacy. She'd certainly never ventured into Paradise Lakes. John-John wondered if she ever partied, and now, it was obvious she did—and not very well. He'd popped his head into the kitchen looking for Tommy, and there was Anna, standing in the middle of the room, having a conversation with nobody. Then—bam—that Cheryl bitch was all over him, wanting some of "that killer weed, man." John-John hadn't been holding any "killer weed, man," but figuring his chances with Anna were in the familiar strip of land between slim and none and feeling a slight buzz from the line he'd just done, he pushed Cheryl into the first floor powder room. She giggled. John-John pulled it out. Cheryl giggled some more and made a gesture like she was smoking a joint. John-John ripped her blouse open and squeezed her tits. Cheryl continued to giggle, but the little hiccups were spaced further apart. John-John grabbed her by the hair and forced her to her knees. When he couldn't get it up, he smacked her in the nose.

And who was going to challenge him if Cheryl ran to her jock buddies? John-John Hagarty had made a career out of being a bully; it was the only thing he was good at. (Burglary obviously wasn't his calling.) But the Hoskins douchebags tried to pin it on Albert Bannerman, who seemed more surprised that John-John knew his name than the fact that the jocks were seconds away from making him a permanent part of the gravel driveway for supposedly assaulting Cheryl. From years of administering beatings indiscriminately, John-John knew that some kids were natural targets. Bannerman was one of those, even if you ignored his afghan blanket cape. For an asshole like Bob Goocher, who'd never been in a real fight his entire life, Bannerman was easy pickings. But John-John had zero respect for this crowd of towel-snappers who generally wouldn't even nod in his direction at the mall or in school, but who pumped his hand and slapped his back whenever they needed brew or weed— like that wanna-be Chris Auger or the biggest jagoff of the bunch, Greg Stillman—so rescuing Bannerman wasn't charity as much as it was a way of preventing a natural target from getting his ass handed to him by pond scum like Gooch. Being a bully was something you earned, not something that was gifted to you because you could throw a football. He'd been one so long, he knew the bullying instinct inside and out; it was like a secret power, one these coddled asswipes did not possess.

In retrospect, he'd been angry when he hooked up with Anna Lafleur. He was angry about his inattentive cock in his dalliance with Cheryl, annoyed about rescuing Bannerman, pissed that the glad-handing jocks dared to act like tough guys and bully Albert because he was lower on their goddamn social food chain, and fucking furious that he actually gave a shit. But something else was surging through his muscle and fat and swelling his noggin, something not caused by drug or drink. Bannerman had set it off, but John-John suspected that this mysterious feeling had always been there, at least since he first noticed Anna. Whatever it was, whatever it signified, John-John knew he up to the task. Bannerman may have worn a cape like a superhero in the comic books he and Stevie used to heist from Rex's, but it was John-John who did the rescuing; it made him feel like Travis Bickle—only bigger.

John-John was leaving the powder room after taking a celebratory piss when Anna, clinging to the walls, made her way out of the kitchen. His timing was perfect for once. Anna stumbled into him and clung to his trench coat. For a few seconds he was as exhilarated as he was scared. Then her eyes fluttered and she let go of him, and when he bent forward to catch her, she laughed in his face. (He almost fainted from the sweet-sour smell of her breath; it smelled like home, and John-John hadn't smelled a home, a true home, in years.) Then there it was: that mysterious feeling coming to the surface, as John-John vacillated between wanting to save her from all of it—not just the Bod Squad and the jocks, but her seemingly preordained future of sororities and frat boys, suburban townhouses, and dead-end jobs that shrunk the soul and pinned it to a point on a map—and wanting to be saved, wanting her to expunge the record of his life as he melted enough to lower his defenses and open up his blackened heart (temporarily at least). He just needed to get the ball rolling.

It didn't take long. They found an empty bedroom that had a lamp with a cowboy lampshade. At first he was concerned when she wanted to talk, to really talk, she told him, but eventually he loosened up and actually listened. Everyone was fake, but the Speller was real, she said. (He was instantly jealous of whoever the fuck this Speller character was and wanted to do him grave harm.) The Speller had calluses on his fingers, Anna said, that was how hard he spelled. She told him about the purple streaks and how they'd been stolen by the Speller, along with every other color, and how that was just about the saddest goddamn thing she ever did see, but everything's ephemeral. That's what he was trying teach her, the Speller, that everything's ephemeral, she said. John-John had never heard the word ephemeral before and it made him uncomfortable, but at the same time it also felt true and appropriate somehow. Anna said in a wistful voice that she wished the Speller would at least bring one color back. She told him that if she squeezed her eyes real tight and then peeked out, she thought she could see the color green going past her, on its way to important verdant business. *Verdant?* John-John nodded his head politely at whatever she said, and when he realized that his nodding was neither required nor expected, he stopped. Drug talk. *Christ.* But he knew how to handle it. At least she wasn't a chattering meth head. But he was peaking himself, and when Anna Lafleur stopped to take a breath, he kissed her, and when she acted surprised, shocked— disgusted—he hit her but good and held her down and tore off her clothes and pushed her legs all the way back and fucked her until there was nothing left, until neither one of them would ever be the same.

She screamed a lot, of course, and that brought the hero out in some of the jocks—he heard their battle cries and stomping sneakers as they ran to the room—but John-John didn't pay them any attention, and they didn't try to stop him. They crowded the doorway, yelling encouragement and imitating Anna's moans and other involuntary noises. (He didn't like the mimicry, but he was too far gone to do anything about it.) When he came, they cheered and applauded, but when he slid his dick out (wiping it on the bedspread), they were gone. John-John wasn't sure they were ever really there, but it didn't matter either way.

Afterwards, he lay next to Anna, trying hard not to squirm or fidget. The bed was too small; his feet dangled over the edge. The pillows were too soft; his head sunk right to the mattress. His pants were still below his knees, and his trench coat was still on. He wanted Anna to understand that he'd been trying to save both of them tonight: he'd torn everything down so they could build it back up together, far from prying eyes. What he'd done had been their salvation; nothing could get between them now: he was no longer trailer park trash and she was no longer a Catholic schoolgirl virgin. (He knew he was her first.) He tried to hug her, cuddle, but he bloodied her nose with his elbow and decided that maybe he'd follow-up in school the next day. Sex wasn't enough. He'd gotten laid, he'd lost his virginity, and he was happy about that—but he wanted more. He wanted to be *really* inside Anna Lafleur; he wanted Anna inside of him. For a brief moment that night, driving back to the Lakes, John-John understood cannibalism. Fucking just wasn't enough.

He had to erase all previous experiences from his mind. *Real* girls, not hophead sluts, liked to be courted and taken places. They liked to sip tea and eat what Stevie's Grammy called "petting fours." The bitches in the Lakes just knew how to get on all fours. Anna Lafleur was high class but didn't know it. Yeah, she'd cried when he fucked her, but she'd been a virgin, so maybe it hurt. He was a big guy.

In the morning, he dressed himself as sharp as he could within the strict limits of the Hoskins High dress code. He wore his trench coat (teachers had long ago stopped asking him to take it off in class) with the shoulder holster he had his boys "pick up" for him underneath. He wanted to show off his two guns to Anna. He holstered one pistol and stuck the other inside his coat, putting all the extra clips he had in the pockets. He borrowed a double sawbuck from Frannie (who bitched and moaned like it was a million fucking dollars) and combed his hair back with gel. He'd forgotten to shower in all the excitement, but this wasn't going to be a sex date. This was going to be a real date. They'd have the rest of their lives to fuck. Today, he just wanted to hold her hand and feel her breath on his face. Today, John-John just wanted to be as close to Anna Lafleur as he could without eating her. He'd let her touch the handles of his guns; she'd introduce him to some exotic tea. And the rest, ladies and gents, would be fucking history. Together, they'd level the world. Together, they'd feel *everything*, and the world—well, the world would feel them right back.

+

He'd found an empty room to practice in on the third floor. Room 304. But his worries constantly affected his exercises. Did she jot down the time? It was going to be a half-day tomorrow: would she get lost in whatever activity she engaged in during her free hours and lose track of time? What if she decided that she had her fill of spelling? The last one made his stomach acidy.

My name is Albert Ayler Bannerman, he'd start—not that she didn't know who he was now, but since they'd discussed the origin of his middle name in Megan Riley's kitchen, Albert thought it might be a good idea to reference that conversation. Jog her memory—just in case. He'd never *felt* so much before. He went over every detail of their meeting repeatedly. Anna seemed entranced by his name although she insisted on calling him Speller (with and without the definite article), as if he was a superhero. He didn't mind Speller. It wasn't a nickname; it was a title. A man is what he does, his father had said.

Albert wanted to shut the door to block out the noises of the other classes taking place, but if a teacher found him alone in a closed classroom, it could look funny. Of course, talking to himself and extending his hand to grasp an imaginary one was fairly odd behavior as well. Albert figured his social status (or complete lack of one) would cover him as far as the adults were concerned: oh, it was just Albert being Albert. He shook his head. Feeling was hard work—harder than learning scales or doing calculus or spelling gamopetalous.

Gamopetalous. G-a-m-o-p-e-t-a-l-o-u-s. Gamopetalous.

When he wasn't consumed with worry, this was what played in the back-back of his head, the scene spooling out, rewinding, and starting again and again: he's on a stage and he's spelling. He's whipping through words. The other contestants are just that: contestants. He has no competition on the stage. The lights are in his eyes, so the gym floor is completely dark, just a cloud of nervous shuffles and muffled coughs. He knows she's out there—maybe even in the front row, maybe hanging near the back wall—and as the last word is spelled (it's always "solipsism"), the gym lights come on, and there, in between Bridget and Raoul, applauding so fervently he fears for her skin, Anna Lafleur beams, astounded, proud, the massive fluorescents reflecting off the tiny scar on her chin, as if to point out to Albert Ayler Bannerman: see, she's flawed, she's real, she's real.

Okay, relax.

Viscera. V-i-s-c-e-r-a. Viscera.

Improvisation was a dead art, his father had said, and Albert agreed and wished he could be extemporaneous occasionally and not so rigid when it came to his chosen mode of expression, but Albert didn't want to leave anything to chance. Casual is as casual goes, his father had said. Casual as in "happening by chance" is good if you were playing in Albert Ayler's quintet but not so great if you were participating in a spelling bee. Casual as in "done without much thought, effort, or concern," well, he didn't know when that would be a valid approach. If he could apply his father's maxim to more than area of his life, he wasn't sure casual was the best kind of attitude for him to adopt as he proceeded with Anna. He couldn't be cavalier; that would go over like a lead balloon. He dare not rely on luck; there was too much at stake. But Anna was going to require some improvisation—he was in unknown territory with a virgin heart for a compass—so he had to leave room for things "happening by chance." Spelling, however, was an art that did not lend itself to improvisation. If even one or two of the tingling lines pulsing along his spine, his skull, his private area, even his eyes, were real, he needed to be prepared and not color outside of the lines. He hated letting his father down, but it was time for him to be his own man and make his own mark with the tools available using the appropriate methods. He knew the melody to "I Left My Heart in San Francisco" now. He planned to spell with panache.

Abattoir. A-b-a-t-t-o-i-r. Abattoir.

Albert supposed that Mathletes didn't improvise either, with the team's reliance on formulas. But English was built from so many different languages—German, French, and Latin for starters—that the Mathletes' playbook would never work at a spelling bee. So there was *some* measure of danger in spelling, an inch or two of tightrope.

Begin again.

Arrhythmia. A-r-r-h-y-t-h-m-i-a. Arrhyth—

Footsteps in the hallway. There wasn't much time left, Albert thought.

Interregnum. I-n-t-e-r-r-e-g-n-u-m. Interregnum.

He stepped into the hall and closed his eyes, wishing everyone away for a few more minutes.

Occlude. O-c-c-l-u-d-e. Occlude.

When he opened his eyes, there she was!—somewhat distressed but nonetheless intoxicating.

"My name is Albert Ayler Bannerman," Albert said, just like he practiced, but he didn't think she heard him.

"Speller?"

Speller!

He stared at the floor, suddenly flushed.

"My name is Albert Ayler Bannerman," he began again, even though she remembered his alter ego. "Would you like to come watch me spell tomorrow?"

He looked up. Expectation caused his entire body to throb.

"Albert," Anna said.

He blinked once. Twice.

"So you'll come?" he asked.

"I know you're not going to understand all of this," she began, speaking in a quick whisper, "but I did something I shouldn't have done last night, and I think I need to go home right now, but I need you to walk me there. Can you do that?"

"Okay," Albert said. He'd find time to practice later. Anna came first.

He leaned forward to kiss her, closing his eyes like in the movies.

"Albert," Anna said, "something bad is going to happen. We need to—"

They both started when they heard it, and he opened his eyes reluctantly.

The sound of the first shot was almost hidden beneath the ringing of the school bell; the screaming that followed and the subsequent shots were not.

"It's John-John Hagarty, Albert," she said.

He felt his lips with his fingers. Had she kissed him?

"Did you hear me?"

Her voice penetrated his interior monologue. "John-John?" he asked. Something unexplainable stained his thoughts.

Improvidence. I-m-p-r-o-v-i-d-e-n-c-e. Improvidence.

He was having a hard time putting what they'd heard in context. "But last night he stopped Gooch from—"

"Yes—last night—something happened last night. Megan Riley had a party. Her parents were out of town and her brother was staying at a friend's. Everyone was drunk or stoned..."

"I was there, remember?" Albert said. "I was a superhero."

"...and something happened...I can't...I didn't...you were there?"

"Dead man Bannerman," Greg Stillman said, leaning by the doorway, tapping his fingers on the frame, his toothy grin staking out a large area of real estate on his long face, which showed no concern about the commotion happening down the hall. "Time to pay the piper, Bannerman, and the bill's past due. Collection time begins with the last bell, and I'm—"

Greg Stillman's forehead broke into many pieces. One eye exploded with the forehead; the other looked upward to where his forehead used to be.

Albert pulled Anna into Room 304, closed the door, and shut off the lights.

Thinking was never to be confused with acting, his father had said.

"What was that?" she screamed. "What was that?"

"Mr. Bojangles."

It must have been the wrong answer. She continued screaming. He covered her mouth, and at first she fought him like a trapped animal, but she stopped when she started trembling.

"Kneel down." He lowered Anna to the floor behind the far side of the teacher's desk.

"If I take my hand away, do you promise not to scream?"

No—she'd noticed her bloody blouse.

"We're up too high to jump out the window," he said, not helping matters. Her eyes were so wide that it looked painful, and her trembling was starting to look like convulsing, so he spelled for her until she stopped shaking. It took a while, but he knew a lot of words.

"Now?"

Yes, but her eyes were no less wide.

She smelled like apricots. When he removed his hand from her mouth, he fought an urge to smell his palm. He hoped he didn't have bad breath.

Malodorous. M-a-l-o-d-o-r-o-u-s. Malodorous.

He caught himself watching her chest strain against her blouse and willed himself to look away and not get an erection. He thought a boner now might send the wrong message.

"Albert."

He was pretty sure the object he could see through the crack under the door was a large piece of Greg Stillman's head. Judging by the cacophony of shattering glass, John-John was down by the science lab.

More urgently: "Albert."

He didn't know what to say; he was bad in social situations, and he'd never been in a situation like this one. "Emollient. E-m-o-l-l-i-e-n-t. Emollient." Spelling had worked before, but she just stared at him and a tremor seemed to go through her body. "The two Ls," he explained. "They'll get you every time." But that didn't seem to make anything better.

Other than the sounds of running overhead, all was quiet for a little bit. Both of his legs were asleep, almost completely numb.

"Albert, I have to tell you some—"

From the classroom diagonal to theirs, Ms. Sokolov, the Social Justice teacher, yelled in her Russian accent, "No! No! Not the children! Please not—" Rapid bursts ended Ms. Sokolov's plea and some of her students' wails.

"What would Albert Ayler do?"

"Was that...?"

"Whatever he wanted."

"What? What?"

Her face balanced irritation and anger, and she started to get off the floor. How her shapely legs weren't victims of intense pins and needles, he didn't know. But he saw the shadow whose presence had sucked all but a small portion of the light that came in under the door, and he pulled her down.

She whispered his name, and he whispered to himself, "Albert Ayler would do whatever he wanted."

He didn't take his eyes off the shadow.

"Improvise," he told himself with determination. "I-m-p-r-o-v-i-s-e. Improvise.

"Make it up," he added, and he heard the doubt creep into his voice. The truth was that he'd never improvised before. But for Anna...

The shadow departed. He rested his hot forehead against the cool floor. When he looked over, Anna was doing the same.

"Do you think John-John will...?"

"Sussultatory. S-u-s-s-u-l-t-a-t-o-r-y. Sussultatory," Albert spelled, for he had no answer.

"I have to tell you something."

She spoke quickly into his ear, making him shiver; she was so close, he could feel her body heat. "He was stalking me all day, and he followed me into the girls' bathroom. No one else was in there. I started to yell for help, but he choked me with one hand and grabbed my boob—hard—with the other."

Albert blushed.

Something exploded from the direction of the science lab.

She pulled back her collar and showed him the ligature marks.

"I'm hitting him in the face, scratching the hand around my neck until he was bleeding, but nothing seemed to register. He told me that together we'd crack the world or something like that. Wanted me to touch his guns. That's when I started really freaking out."

Boudoir. B-o-u-d-o-i-r. Boudoir.

He didn't know what spelling would do against such evil, but that was where improvisation would come into play, he hoped.

Iniquitous. I-n-i-q-u-i-t-o-u-s. Iniquitous.

One book he'd read on jazz improvisation stated, "The characteristics of the style make for swift decisions, enabling the music to move along without interruption." With the imminent threat he believed they were facing, he couldn't afford even a semiquaver rest, which meant he had to better than good.

Were those approaching sirens he heard just below the latest barrage?

Anna continued, her lips so close to his ears that her breath tickled the little hairs inside. "The hand around my neck pinned me against the wall and applied just enough pressure so I didn't pass out. He pulled out his...like he was handing to me, and I reached down and squeezed his balls until he let go of my neck. He had such a confused look on his face, my fear went into overdrive. I ducked under his arm, but he grabbed my hair, and when I tried to turn and bite him, I watched the confusion on his face clear up real quick. You're in Ms. Shue's Brit Lit class, right?"

She remembered him from class!

Something else exploded down the hall.

"You remember in our text book that reproduction of the Blake engraving, 'Satan,' the one where you can see up his nose and his mouth is hanging open and his eyes are rolled up inside his head? That's what he looked like—except for the eyes; his were dead. He reached inside his jacket with his other hand and put it around a gun, and I ran so hard, he tore the hair right out of my—"

They listened to a fresh round of gunfire and some cries and shouts were silenced.

"Sounds like firecrackers."

"They're not firecrackers," she said.

Right as rain and not a bit wet.

"Arcanum. A-r-c-a-n-u-m. Arcanum," Albert spelled as his ears picked up an approaching sound. Heavy footsteps in the hall.

Albert blinked. The shadow was back. Smoke began coming in from under the door, even though it sounded like there was a curtain of rain in the hallway following a third explosion. There were a lot of chemicals in the science lab.

He raised his head slightly to peer over the desk. The doorknob turned. He ducked back down. No sense in placing his head back on the floor. He didn't want to give the shadow his back.

Following his lead, Anna started to lift her head, but before he could stop her, Albert heard the classroom door begin to open, and she pressed her face against his chest, wrapping her arms around him.

"We're trapped," she moaned.

Like the muskrat, he thought: *it tried to crawl away, but the brush is thin here and thorny.*

"Oh God, oh God, don't let him see my face," Anna said into his chest, her nose dangerously close to his armpit.

He held her head firmly but gently, using his hand to cover any exposed area of her face.

The heavy footsteps crossed the room, and Albert lowered his head upon Anna's (*distract the mind, his father had said*), hoping to inhale the smell of her shampoo and the scent of apricots. If they were to be cut down by a vicious strain of scholastic fate, he wanted those fragrances filling his head when it happened, but all at once the air was filled with a most rancid odor.

I-m-p-r-o-v-i-s-e.

The smell came not from Albert's underarms, as he feared, but from the heavily scuffed black Doc Martens planted about a foot from where they knelt. Albert looked up. John-John grinned back. There was a smoking gun in his hand.

"Do you know who I am?" he asked.

Albert nodded his head.

"No, do you *really* know who I am?" John-John asked.

Albert didn't, but decided it was best not to answer.

"I'm your archenemy. I'm the archvillain," John-John said. "I'm the evildoer who's goin' to fuck your skull after I shoot you in the brain."

Anna moaned into Albert's armpit. Albert was surprised John-John remembered his pathetic attempt at a superhero costume.

What would Albert Ayler do?

"How do you spell mousetrap?" Albert asked. His spoke softly, hoping John-John didn't think he was testing him; he just thought it was an appropriate opening. "C-a-t."

John-John opened his mouth and a roar came tearing out his throat; he sounded like a lion on fire. It rattled the chalkboard and the teacher's desk. Anna squeezed him even tighter and dug her nails into his back. Albert didn't think John-John was doing a big cat impersonation in reaction to his joke, and the wave of fetid breath that followed the roar smelled for all the world like what Albert imagined a pile of dead cats would smell like. But he was using what he had. The jazz book stated that among the factors "chiefly responsible for the outcome" of an improvisation were intuition, intellect, and emotion. He didn't have his guitar, but he was still the Story Joke Master. A good one could buy them time and a long one might even act as a distraction, Albert thought—if they survived long enough for him to work up to one.

His father had said that quiet revolutions were the only important revolutions because they could always get louder.

"There's the one where the professor was correcting essay papers," Albert said at a normal volume (in a voice which he willed not to quaver), as if he were sharing a joke with a friend, "and he found the sentence, 'The girl tumbled down the stairs and lay prostitute at the bottom.' "

"Prostitute," John-John said.

At least he was listening.

Albert smelled urine. He hoped it wasn't his own, but he didn't want Anna to feel awkward about wetting herself either. "Sorry about the pee," he whispered to her.

"So the professor writes in the margin of the paper," Albert continued, " 'My dear sir, you must learn to distinguish between a fallen woman and one who has merely slipped.' "

It wasn't the sound of heavy rain in the hallway; it was the echoes of endless screaming. The room was filling up with smoke. The school was on fire. They'd already begun to cough, but not John-John.

"Who you got there?" he asked.

Anna stiffened up and sobbed; her nails had already ripped into the back of his dress shirt.

"Eileen McDonald," Albert lied.

"Head of the Chess Club and the Young Readers' Circle," Albert added. "Both."

John-John lit a cigarette.

"The geek gets the girl," John-John said through an exhale. "Goddamn good thing too."

John-John squashed the cigarette with his boot. "Gotta quit," he said.

Albert kept his counsel to himself. He was sure Anna could smell his sweat now. His back was slick. Anna was a kind soul: she didn't mention the smell. She just shivered.

"Goddamn good thing," John-John repeated. "You a virgin?"

Albert nodded. Not the kind of thing he wanted to admit in front of Anna but better the truth in this situation, he thought, than a lie that could trip him up later.

"Nothin' to be ashamed of. I was too. Not anymore. Just last night. Hard to believe, right? Guy like me?"

Albert had the Sam the Clam joke lined up, but he thought it was best not to interrupt at the moment.

John-John leaned against the teacher's desk. Sirens approached through the noise of the screaming.

"Love, man. Hits you hard, huh? Never knew. Shit, I don't know if I would have ever fucked if I'd known about all the other shit that went with it. I just wanted to get laid; I didn't want all the rest of—"

John-John spit.

"Goddamn, it's hot."

Albert nodded his head. It was.

Maybe this body odor and peeing would become some sort of private joke between him and Anna, Albert thought—not a joke though, but an experience (like stabbing a muskrat) an experience that bound them together, a literal sticky situation.

He'd already decided that he wasn't falling on his sword (which in this case would mean provoking John-John, a sort of backward suicide-by-cop). He wouldn't leave Anna to be ravaged by the monster no matter how bad it got. He'd learned from his father's mistake.

Let's not be L-7
Come and learn to dance
Wooly bully...

The sirens were in the parking lot—many sirens. The sprinkler system finally kicked on, and they were soaked instantly.

"Well—gotta go," John-John said. "Good luck with Eileen, man. I really mean it."

"Thank you," Albert said, and he meant it too.

"Might want to look away now," John-John said. "Gotta stop feelin'."

"Of course," Albert said. "Everything's ephemeral." He turned his head and the sound rang in his ears for a week.

+

The last word wasn't "solipsism" and neither Bridget nor Raoul were in the audience at Spring House Elementary School. There wasn't really an audience at all. There weren't many teachers either. Albert wondered if a lot of them had quit after what the *Mondauk Common* had called "The Hoskins High Hagarty Massacre." (Most other papers didn't add John-John's last name, and the *Common* dropped it after receiving a deluge of angry letters to the editor, according to the local news.) Two teachers had gone down along with seven students (which included three starters on the varsity football team)—not counting the shooter himself. Two more students died later from burns sustained in the fire. One girl killed herself out of grief for her fallen classmates (or so the *Common* reported), but Albert remembered her as always looking depressed, like she'd just finished a crying jag, so maybe she just needed an excuse to end her pain. (*Wooly bully.*)

He'd done just fine with "precipitous," but he'd almost stumbled with "wiseacre," of all words. He righted himself at the last second, fully expecting to hear the usual cacophony of giggles rise behind him, but none came. His fellow contestants, his competitors, were too serious to giggle, too scared. Maybe it was the Hoskins High Massacre, but Albert knew from Mathletes that even the lowest level tournament caused some of his former teammates to vomit before the competition began. His current combatants also had to deal with their age, when every emotion was easily accessible. (There was a lot of crying.) The next oldest after Albert was a seventh grader, and he never made it past the first round. ("Harbinger" brought him down.) A fifth grader, a little girl who showed zero signs of stage fright (unless pulling on her pigtails between her turns at the mic counted), proved to be quite formidable.

The committee responsible for the 13ᵗʰ Annual Spring House Spelling Bee had initially rejected his application due to his age, but after the Hoskins High Massacre, nobody said no to Albert. Even his mother shifted a little: she still slept on the couch most of the day while Albert was in school, but when he came home, there was always a snack waiting for him and instructions on how to prepare dinner. Albert's role in the Hoskins High Massacre, once it became known (he'd never told her), made it possible for his mother to sleep in her bedroom again—as if she recognized her son's refusal to follow King Saul's example in the face of overwhelming odds—and she'd retire there when Albert got home from school. For the week after the shooting, classes were canceled, and for those few days, it was like summertime: he and his mother hid in the darker recesses of the house and greeted each other the few times they crossed paths. The first couple of days after school resumed, she awkwardly tried to make conversation while Albert ate his snack, but he didn't have anything to say, and his mother had even less. Once she left a newspaper clipping on how Mondauk students were coping; Albert cut out the picture of Anna Lafleur (he'd never seen that one before) and threw the rest out without reading past the headline. His mother eventually stopped trying to engage him, but she continued to leave little notes on how many minutes he should nuke his noodles in the microwave and other culinary directions. She'd go to bed; he'd play his guitar. Albert thought it was a good arrangement.

Anna didn't come to the competition, even though she lived for those moments when she could see someone else excel. The dates for the Qualifying rounds and the Bee itself had changed three times, as teachers and the Faith Board argued whether children could spell after such a tragic event. Anna probably lost track of all the changes, and seeing how she'd moved away (down south someone said, but Albert couldn't imagine her pale skin in the Sun Belt), there'd be no way for her to know the final date.

He'd asked the counselor they brought into the school if he knew when Anna was coming back, but the counselor didn't know a thing—about anything. Post-traumatic this and stress-induced that. When the For Sale sign went up on the front lawn of the house directly behind his, Anna's house, Albert stopped going to his scheduled appointments. No one said a word.

He knew that she'd broken her leg when they started to finally leave Room 304, but it was probably healed by now—she'd slipped in the mess made by John-John Hagarty's brains and the water from the sprinklers. Anna hit the floor hard, flailing in the pools of bloody water and expired gray matter, her right leg twisted in an odd direction. On the way down, she smacked her chin on the teacher's desk, and Albert wondered if she would have a new scar on her chin. He tried to help her up, grab her by the wrists, but Anna floundered and opened her mouth like she wanted to scream, but nothing really came out. The police and firemen would be on their floor soon, so Albert took what might be his last chance; he didn't think she'd heard him in the hallway before the shooting began.

"My name is Albert Ayler Bannerman," he'd repeated. "Would you like to come watch me spell tomorrow?"

And that was when Anna screamed.

So now it was down to just him and the pigtailed fifth-grader. His last word was "ephemeral," and Albert's brain registered that the skin around his mouth turned upward, but he was too focused to truly enjoy the moment; involuntary facial movements had no bearing on the outcome and did not reflect how he truly felt at that moment, something he would be unable to articulate even if he wanted to, and he didn't—not without her.

When Anna heard he'd won, she'd come back to Mondauk Proper. His victory would be something they both could feel, after trying not to feel anything since their time in Room 304. (At least that was what Albert assumed she was doing while she was away.) And when she came, he'd be ready. He'd tell her the joke, the one about Sam Clam's disco. He'd play her *Revolver* and *Sgt. Pepper's* and tell her about quiet revolutions. He'd even written her a song on his guitar, though he didn't think he'd be able to sing it to her. But there'd be time, he knew, there'd be time to do everything.

"Enduring. E-n-d-u-r-i-n-g. Enduring," Albert spelled.

When Anna heard he'd won, she'd come, and together, they'd do and feel everything.

-end-

Damn Right You'll Rise Again

Julie and the John (Part 1)
7:30 p.m.

It was raining cats and dogs in Mondauk County, and Julie huddled against the Sunoco wall. Tonight had been a bust. Two blowjobs and a cheap half and half she'd agreed to only because she was too tired to haggle; the last guy had taken nearly forty minutes to get off, and she thought her jaw was going to drop right out of her head. Because of the rain, she'd worn her jeans instead of the standard miniskirt, which was a no-no; with a miniskirt (and no underwear), she could just climb in a car and hop in someone's lap; jeans required more of an effort, but the rain was cold. She nervously turned her Claddagh ring round and round her finger, its heart facing out (of course). True love was something for television and the occasional movie. The man who'd given her the ring didn't love her, although he said he did. He'd told her every Irish lass should have one. Yet this was the same man that she was, at the moment, very afraid of, or at least she was afraid of his minions. Mr. Foster didn't come down to the Strip, which was what this portion of Bethlehem Pike was called. The Strip didn't have fancy restaurants or flashy casinos, just some strip malls and gas stations, very rough bars and very cheap rooms, and lots of hookers and drugs. Hookers and drugs went together like peanut butter and jelly. Prostitutes and dealers shared a lot of the same customers. However needle junkies didn't fuck a whole lot (unless they needed a fix) and she didn't do tweakers (meth mouth freaked her out more than trucker ass), which may have accounted for her poor showing this evening—that and it was pouring. Julie's underwear felt damp, not an unusual occurrence in her line of work, but this wasn't come, it was just rain. She kept turning the ring. Even though it was only seven-something, she wasn't on track to have enough money to turn into Tic-Tac; she could tell early when she was going to make her goal and when she wasn't. Tic-Tac was short and stocky and had crossed eyes; he was Julie's handler, and he was as scary as he looked and quick with a beating; sometimes he'd even punch her in the face, which made working even harder and which in turn meant more beatings. She didn't want to return to that vicious cycle again. Last time, it had cost her a tooth. (Thank God not one of her front ones.)

" '*The problem is all inside your head,*' *she said to me,*" the tinny overhead speakers sang. " '*The answer is easy if you take it logically.*' "

Going home was not an option. She'd left when she was fifteen and started hooking when she was sixteen. That was five years ago. Twenty-one was almost too old for Mr. Foster's train, and she knew what happened to girls who grew past their sell-by dates: they were either found behind a dumpster or farmed out to a ghetto in the city. So she worked hard and took on extra shifts. Her parents lived in Warminster, just a town or two to the west, but a world away. She needed money to get out of here, away from Mr. Foster and Mondauk County, but she would never ask her parents. She thought she'd like to work in the fashion industry. She kept up with the latest fashions in all the magazines they sold in the convenience stores. They wouldn't know it to look at her, she thought, but she could design fashions. She was always drawing on the back of diner napkins. Once she was clean, once she was out of the life, she'd come back for Jenny. That was always the plan.

" '*There must be fifty ways to leave your lover,*' " the stranger sang. " '*Fifty ways to leave your lover.*' "

She didn't like the way he looked. Baseball cap *and* a sweatshirt hood pulled over the cap. Real undercover-like shit, but he didn't move like a cop. More like a nervous kid, which he certainly wasn't. In his 40s or 50s, maybe even in his 60s, going by the quick glimpse of his hands that she got before he shoved them into the pockets of his hoodie. He had a suspicious looking '70s moustache, like the kind Eric Roberts had sported in *Star 80*, and long sideburns. But fuck it, she needed the cash.

"Like your singing, mister. Lookin' for a date?"

The man laughed.

"One of Foster's girls?"

She nodded.

He looked up to the sky.

"Want to just split a room?"

She squinted at him.

"What for?" she asked.

"Doesn't have to be sex. Doesn't have to be much of anything. Just to get out of the rain."

She paused. She'd encountered weirdoes like this before, guys who just wanted to cuddle and call her baby like she was their daughter while their hard-ons poked into her bottom. She feared those freaks more than the ones who wanted to tie her up. At least she knew where she was when she was bound and gagged. Playing daddy and daughter...foreign territory until their cocks came out. But what the fuck, a buck was a buck, and it was cold in the rain.

"You got money?"

"For the room? Yeah."

"For me."

He smiled and for an instant he looked familiar, then it was gone.

"Sure. But I got something extra too, something even better than money, little one." With two fingers he slid a bag of white powder out of his inside pocket. "If you're game."

He'd used his left hand, and Julie saw the white skin around his ring finger where a wedding band used to sit. Divorced, cheating, widowed. Not that she cared but the cheaters were usually the fastest, divorced guys the angriest and, at times, the most violent, and the widowers most apt to have trouble getting it up. Whatever the case was with this guy, it wouldn't matter once was fucked up.

He stuck a piece of gum in his mouth while she mulled it over.

"I'm Julie. What's your name?"

He looked at his pack of gum and offered her a piece.

"You can call me Big Red."

"Uh-oh."

But she was kidding. Julie turn down some free smack *and* money for whatever daddy brokenhearted wanted to do with her body? After mainlining, she wouldn't care anyway.

"Hub Motel?" She gestured down the street.

"Rub-a-dub-dub, three-men-in-a-tub," he said, and she laughed, her voice cutting through the rain.

"You're a real riot, you know that?" she said.

"Oh, the riot has yet to begin, little girl of mine."

The Weary Detective (Part 1)
7:45 p.m.

His partner had told him that there was a fine line between being the most decorated and the most defecated upon dick on the force, and when the chief, the DA, *and* the mayor called him into a meeting one evening, Feargal understood what he meant. The headline on the front of the *Mondauk Common* the next morning was: "Detective Feargal Finnerty to Head Up the Red Ribbon Task Force." That was nine months ago, and the most they'd turned up was a bunch of strung out hookers, who'd already turned the whole thing into an urban legend, and some frightened johns, who didn't know shit. The perp didn't strike during a full moon. He didn't write letters to newspapers or leave behind a Joker card. He didn't seem to prefer brunettes or blondes or redheads or white girls or black girls or Asian girls. The perp did prefer hookers (hence was more than likely male), but not exclusively. He didn't dump their bodies; they were all left at the scene. No security cameras caught his face, no ATMs; none of the traffic cameras caught the same vehicle arriving or leaving each killing ground. One denizen of TJ's Lounge had claimed to see a man in a baseball cap and a hooded sweatshirt cruising the Strip on foot and later hanging out near the No Tell Motel the night a body was found there. However, the potential witness was drunk off his ass (as he'd been the night in question) and kept changing the color of the hoodie, but it was the only possible description they had and they dutifully called in a sketch artist. They'd added extra patrols along the Strip and over at Paradise Lakes Trailer Park (another place favored by working girls). They'd even gone so far as to send two female undercover officers (wired and dressed like street prostitutes) to walk the Strip, but that was a bust. Feargal did leave his one male undercover cop out there; he was less conspicuous than his female counterparts had been, mainly because he just had to blend in with the scumbags that populated the Strip and its dive bars and back alleys; the female officers had been tasked with impersonating hookers, a group that knew its own and could smell a cop a mile off.

Feargal always believed that his best investigative tool was his gut. If he could feel something in his gut, it was usually worth following up. But his gut required stimuli, and they had really nothing to go on since there were never any witnesses, and the killer left no fingerprints, no semen, no hair, no blood (other than the deceased's). The only thing he left was a red ribbon tied around the victims' right wrists. (They weren't even sure if they were looking for one person or more, but Feargal was sure that this was the work of a loner; two or more guys always cruising the Strip together would stand out—call it a gut feeling.) The Red Ribbon Killer was a handy sobriquet bestowed by the *Mondauk Common* and soon picked up by the *Philadelphia Inquirer* and every other major newspaper on the east coast. But the cases had only one thing in common besides the red ribbons and the predilection for hookers and that was himself and the Red Ribbon Task Force. They had almost no clues, a pissed off mayor, Chief Hagen breathing down their necks, but his crew could take a licking and keep on ticking. They worked each case with diligence and obsessive attention to detail.

Nevertheless, Feargal was fucking tired. It had been a rough year. Another school shooting. Increased organized crime activity. Increased drug trafficking out of the Lakes. Gay bashing in New Hope, of all places, a town with a heavy gay population. New Hope was also a major biker hangout, had been for years, and everyone co-existed peacefully. Now the Fields Gang, notorious local bikers, had come to the defense of the gay community, issuing death threats to the families of the accused bashers.

Then there was his brother. Always a handful, Feargal's younger brother had gone and done it this time. Feargal had pulled the case, but he could only do so much. His brother had been on the job; he knew how things worked. He had to know it was only a matter of time before Feargal figured it out. And he had. For now his brother could play the grieving boyfriend, but his girl's brake line had been cut and neighbors said the happy couple had been having fights, loud ones. Her bags were packed for a vacation to Florida. His brother fingered a biker, said he was always bothering her, stalking her, but the guy had a matching plane ticket. So the girlfriend was splitting with the biker? His brother denied it, said there was no rift between him and his girlfriend. But his brother was usually so drunk or high, Feargal didn't think he'd know the truth if it smacked him in the teeth. Some days it was so bad, Feargal was sure his brother wouldn't notice if everyone around him up and disappeared.

So far, the biker was taking the fall. Feargal had buried both plane tickets deep in evidence, feeling so guilty, he almost threw up right there. He'd never done anything remotely like that before; he wasn't that kind of cop—or so he'd thought. The biker had extensive automobile knowledge (but so did Feargal's brother) and a record a dirty mile long, rife with juicy stuff like harassment, b&e, assault with a deadly weapon, plus restraining orders from two different women. Most unlucky for him, he was also a suspect in a case involving motor vehicle sabotage. The biker looked good for it. Unless someone uncovered the tickets or called the airline to follow up on the biker's claims (a very distinct possibility if his public defender was halfway decent), his brother would walk. But Feargal knew he was guilty; he could feel these things in his bones, in his balls even.

"Um, Detective?"

"Yeah?" He cleared his throat. "Yes?"

"Desk sergeant said you'd want to see this first."

"Yes? Speak, lad, speak."

"Someone fitting the description—baseball cap, hooded sweatshirt—was seen tonight at the Hub Motel, just a little while ago."

"Our guy already did one in the Hub. He's not a repeat customer."

"Desk sergeant thought you'd want to see this first."

Feargal snatched the paper from the officer's hand.

"Before it goes in his report. I get it, I get it. Okay, get lost, kid, before I send you out there."

The troops loved him. He was always good for a round. Always willing to cover someone's ass if he could. The brass seemed to like him too. Being born in Ireland had made him very popular in a town chock full of citizens that claimed to be of Irish descent. Many nights he'd tucked away a few Tullamore Dews in McCullough's with the tap room's regulars and its owner, Zooey McCullough—as well as with Chief Cutter Hagen. Why then he'd pulled this crap assignment was beyond him. Yes, he and his partner, Paulie Masconi, had an unusually high closure rate, but this was some down and dirty shit, no doubt about it. Fuck, in one case, the red ribbon perp severed the hooker's head and left it by the motel door so that when the police entered, they kicked it across the room. This was one twisted motherhumper. Usually he just slit their throats. Sometimes carved their faces. It also appeared from all the forensics that the ribbons were placed on the women's wrists before their necks were cut, and the blood patterns suggested that there was rarely any struggle. So there was a possibility that he knew his victims, law-abiding citizens and prostitutes alike; he may have been a repeat customer of the working girls.

"Costigan—you're riding with me."

"Where's Paulie?"

"Aw, eating his way through the Italian Peninsula. The guy's gotta couple of years till he hangs 'em up, but he's accrued a lot of vacation time, and now he's finally using some. Actually, I think he was ordered to." Feargal laughed. "Hey, be good, son, and maybe one day *you'll* be my next partner."

Aidan Costigan grinned. "I don't know, boss. I saw what you did to the last guy. The boys say you almost turned a guinea into a mick."

Feargal gave the younger detective a weak smile. It had occurred to him that he needed to check on his brother, but he couldn't while riding with Costigan. Besides, his brother would just think he was investigating him.

This was some complicated shit. It occurred to him (not for the first time) that maybe he should consider hanging up his spurs too. In a couple of years, he'd be eligible for early retirement. Reduced benefits, but—

"Where we goin', boss?" Costigan asked.

"The beautiful and malodorous Hub Motel on the Strip. Promise to steer clear of the vibrating beds?"

"Ay ay, sir."

"Good lad. Let's haul ass. I don't want to be standing out in the rain getting my balls wet any longer than I have to."

Rum Toddy (Part 1)
8:00 p.m.

"Motherfucking lock!" Adeline screamed. "John! John, open this fucking door right now! John!"

Adeline leaned against her front door and gave it a little kick with the back of her foot. She was going to get drenched, umbrella or not, and probably catch her death; it had been raining cats and dogs for the past couple of hours. Adeline kicked the door again but without much force. She was too old for this. House falling down around their ears. Separate beds. Raising a toddler. She wasn't too old to be a grandmother, but she was too old to raise her granddaughter, that was for sure. But what choice did she have? Her daughter brought the one-year-old baby to the house two years ago then left minutes later in a black Escalade driven by some hard-looking guido with crossed eyes who was at least twenty-five to thirty years her senior; Adeline didn't know if he was her boyfriend or her pimp. It had been the first time she'd seen her daughter in four years. She had grown up pretty, but she had grown up hard. So many scars and her hair was stringy and greasy-looking with a bad dye job. Mascara had run down her face, but she wasn't crying when Adeline came to the door. (She'd called shortly before arriving to make sure John wasn't home.) "This is Jenny," she said, handing her over. "She's my daughter. Jenny, say hello to your Grammy." The girl just stared at her, never noticing that her mother had taken off, leaving behind a plastic bag of diapers, a filthy bottle, and a baby. And that was it. After pitching a spittle-flying fit, John could give a shit. Years ago he'd become apathetic and sneaky, speaking to her only when absolutely necessary and then only in grunts. He carried 'round his Bible for cover (didn't that beat all?), but he was always on the Internet looking at pornography, always watching (dirty) movies in the basement. She caught him once with his pants down around his ankles, staring at the computer in the den, but he didn't see her, thank God. He even had his own PO Box for magazines that arrived in brown paper wrapping, which he took out to the shed. She knew what he was doing out there. He was sinning. Before God and the world, he was sinning. And when He rises again, He will judge the righteous and the dead and the sick porno freaks like her husband John.

She tried the key again and jiggled it just right this time and the front door of her house squeaked open. No John, unless he was playing with himself in the shed. But through the kitchen windows, she could see the shed lights were off. The basement lights were off too. Out again—he was out again, prowling around, probably strip clubs or worse, whatever that was.

"Gram?"

The voice was small and muffled, and when Adeline climbed the stairs, her gout making the journey difficult, she could hear Jenny behind her bedroom door. Adeline tried the knob—locked, of course. That bastard. Couldn't wait until she came home from work, which she did the same time every damn night.

"Just a sec, hon."

Adeline paused to fix her perpetually messy hair in the hallway mirror. Short, all white, tousled. Typical old lady hair. No matter what she did, it always looked like she just rolled out of bed. And her face! The prednisone had given her chipmunk cheeks and acne on her shoulders and forehead. She needed to call Doris for a teeth cleaning. And her weight! She would get her weight under control— she could stand to lose thirty pounds or so—just as soon as she started this new diet everyone was talking about. Then she'd be the one going out mysteriously every other night and John could watch Jenny.

The skeleton key was on the ledge above the bathroom door, and within seconds the dark-haired love child of her junkie daughter came out squealing and hugged her leg.

"Grammy, Grammy, Grammy."

"There, there. Let Grammy make you some cheese and crackers. Would you like that? Stay up late with Grammy?"

The little girl nodded. She was beautiful but haunted. Jenny had coffee-colored skin but white features. God knows what this child had seen living with her daughter and her many "boyfriends"—the drugs, the depravity. She would have been only a baby then, but babies watch and they can be damaged by what they take in even if they don't understand what's happening. Anything that had damaged her daughter she'd brought on herself, Adeline was sure. Even so, she wished she'd had a conversation with her when she'd turned up with Jenny, but she knew that her stranger of a granddaughter wasn't being dropped off at Grammy's for a visit. Adeline hadn't seen her daughter since.

Downstairs, Adeline fixed some cheese and crackers and sliced up an orange as well. She turned on the television and *Rear Window* was playing—one of her favorites. You didn't know who the killer was until Jimmy Stewart did. And when Raymond Burr turned to look right at you! Phew! She was glad to see Jenny was playing with her blocks and Legos, munching on cheese, and ignoring Hitchcock.

Adeline looked at the clock. That motherfucker wasn't coming home tonight, she knew it. Fine, then. He could go to hell—he was already headed that way anyway.

It was Friday. She was going to have herself a little drinkie-poo. Just one or two to take the edge off. A rum toddy! Just the thing. Half a tablespoon of powdered sugar dissolved in two teaspoons of water, stir, add two ounces of dark rum and an ice cube, stir again, and serve with a twist of lime. Oh boy, was she ever ready: old-fashioned glass, sugar, lime, knife...

Her good knife was gone again. That shit bag. What was he up to with her good knife? Last time it mysteriously reappeared, John didn't say a word. The time before that, she caught him rinsing it off in the sink after it had been missing for a few days, and as she berated and grilled him, he just stared at her in that way of his before walking past her to catch the end of the ball game, his right leg thrown over the arm of his chair as if nothing in the world was amiss. But before the last out was called, he disappeared into the shed with his Bible. Well, she'll be damned if he'll get away with whatever he was doing. No siree. No way José. She did a shot of rum—for comfort—and then went to watch the rest of *Rear Window* with her granddaughter nearby. She freshened her toddy whenever the spirit struck her.

The Dental Hygienist (Part 1)
8:15 p.m.

Will she touch me without her gloves?

Daniel had unusually white and straight teeth for someone his age. He took excellent care of his teeth. They were the only bones one could see, and he appreciated that fact and treated them accordingly (even if they were only extensions of bones, as he'd recently learned).

Will she touch me without her gloves? Skin to skin. Will she?

Leah was Daniel's dental hygienist and had been since the dowdy fossil he had before either died or retired. Leah was the reason why his quarterly appointments were like holy days of observation. One of the dentists in the practice always annoyingly stopped in during a cleaning and last time one of them told Daniel that he had a cavity (unbelievable!), but he had no interest in formally seeing a dentist—at least not anytime soon. He'd get around to it. Sometimes, like today, he made an extra appointment when he couldn't wait any longer to see her. What did the office care? This was a business. They didn't keep evening hours for the working stiffs just to be nice.

Leah was super skinny but Daniel got the idea it wasn't because she tried to be. Oh, she most likely watched her weight just like every other woman, but it was probably just the way she was built. She had a lack of self-consciousness that was refreshing, but she was also capable of a deep blush that seemed to originate from her toes. Leah's teeth were perfect of course, stunningly white, offset by her dark brown hair and equally dark brown eyes. And her eyes were huge. Overall, a stunner. Just so pretty, it had been hard to talk to her during the first couple of visits. (Even after he found his voice, it was always hard to talk when she was working on him—the curse of the chatty dental hygienist's patient.)

Leah could talk a blue streak, but not the kind that women usually did, which made you want to look for a sharp instrument. She remembered every detail of their last conversation even three months later. The past few visits, it had been movies. Leah liked chick flicks (deep blush and a roll of the eyes). "Typical, right?" No, no, he assured her. He watched them sometimes too. And he did. Watching a chick flick was like doing homework. Sometimes easy, sometimes hard, but over in ninety minutes. He did enjoy certain romantic comedies and shared these titles with Leah. And she confided in him sometimes—though perhaps confided wasn't quite the right word, but once during a rare afternoon appointment, she told him about a girls' party she went to where instead of Tupperware, the guests were invited to peruse a variety of sex toys. They laughed so hard, one of the dentists popped his head in to see how everything was going. Daniel guessed the blue-haired set in the waiting room didn't want to hear about the Jackhammer or the Pocket Rocket. Leah was never dirty though, never out of line, just blunt in her own unusual, casual way. She got out of him that he was single, and he already knew that there was someone in her life. That annoyed Daniel, but he didn't let it show. Cool as a cucumber.

When she took her gloves off tonight, he noticed the Claddagh ring on her finger, the heart turned in. She'd worn gloves during almost the entire visit. Sometimes she would pat his arm or touch his hand conspiratorially, but always with her gloves. It was frustrating beyond all thought. It kept him up at night. (Though he was usually up at night working.) Each visit he prayed that she would touch him, flesh on flesh, as if this single act would keep him from doing something he would regret later, or maybe it would have the opposite effect. Either way, he wouldn't be able to come back. Still, the Claddagh ring really pissed him off. Leah wasn't even Irish—she was Jewish. The motherfucker she was dating had to be a mick. That was the only explanation. Another plastic paddy. The town was full of them. Daniel hoped his agitation wasn't showing; he hoped he was still smiling. He hoped he would remember to stop.

"Oh," Leah said, noticing his interest in her ring, "Stephen gave it to me—a long time ago. My wedding ring, a stone fell out, so it's at the jeweler's. This old thing is just a placeholder. Should have seen my mother's face when she noticed it last week."

(She was married?)

Then she laughed and Daniel could feel the pendulum swing inside himself; it was the same feeling he always had right before he was about to do something risky. But it was already in motion and there's no racing time. So be it. He was such a poon hound.

Julie and the John (Part 2)
8:30 p.m.

In room 207, she draped a red scarf over the lamp. Big Red kept his hood and cap on but had taken off his boots before he entered the room, as if wet boots could possibly ruin the badly worn carpet. She started to take off her sleeveless shirt, but he told her to stop. He tied her off instead and this was some good shit. She usually avoided needles, but it was so fucking good mainlining. Much better than snorting, she thought. He'd shot up too (at least she thought he did). They climbed into the bed, and Julie stared at the blinking Hub Motel sign through the rain-splattered windows.

"You know how many guys I got off here?" she asked, feeling sort of comfortable with him. She wasn't supposed to talk about stuff like that unless the client wanted to hear it.

He laughed. "No. How many?"

"More than you could count, that's for damn sure."

"The $64,000 question," he said. "Why do you hook?"

" 'Cause I like meeting new people."

"No, come on, seriously."

"For the money."

They were both quiet for a while.

"Do you mind if I play some music?"

"None of that rap shit I hope?"

"Jeez—racist much? No, it's way cooler than that."

She pulled a little CD player from her purse.

"It's got tiny speakers and everything.

"I can't afford an iPod," she added wistfully. "Besides, I don't have a computer."

"Your little hoodrat friend makes me sick, but after I get sick I just get sad."

"This is good," Big Red said above the guitars. "Who is it?"

"The Hold Steady."

"Hold Steady, yeah. Cool."

She thought he said cool like every old man did, like it was a word from a foreign language he just learned for a trip to another country—hers.

"Hey, can I ask you something without you gettin' all mad?"

"Sure." She giggled. She was so stoned, she didn't think it mattered *what* he asked her.

Big Red propped his head up with one hand and leaned on his elbow.

"Julie, have you heard the Good News?"

"No, Big Red, I can honestly say I haven't." She giggled again. Big Red was a gas and an easy john. No hair pulling or butt fucking or salad tossing. No nothing.

"I'm talkin' 'bout Jesus, Julie. Jesus Christ, our Lord and Saviour."

The leader singer of the Hold Steady confessed: "*I've been dusted in the dark up in Penetration Park. I've been plastered.*"

Julie let out a guffaw and then covered her mouth. The last thing she'd thought Big Red would ask about was *Jesus!*

"I'm serious here. Jesus is no laughing matter. 'Every kingdom divided against itself is brought to desolation.' Matthew 12:25. I just want to bring you out of the darkness and into the light, Julie."

Julie flipped on her stomach, bared her neck, and wiggled her jeans down a bit so Big Red could see her tattoos. They were homemade, done with a Bic pen tube, a paperclip, and ink made using ashes from burnt wood and a little bit of vodka, if she remembered right. She'd loved Charlemagne, the boy who did them. Charlemagne was into Jesus too just like Big Red, but with a conviction she didn't hear in Big Red's voice. She always thought there was a light shining down on Charlemagne, for she felt such warmth just being near him. He had a large head of curly hair and almost black skin. (His mother was black.) Julie had fallen for him when they were both living on the streets and in shelters, not soon after she'd left home. Then Charlemagne got a job and split a pad with three other guys. He wanted to open his own tattoo and piercing parlor. She'd stay over and fall asleep on his naked stomach. She had just starting hooking full-time, and she was now one of Foster's girls—which was good and bad. Mr. Foster had a reputation for protecting his property, but he and his men could be indiscriminately violent. Julie had seen them take one girl and drag her by the hair into a car, punching her in the pussy before she got in. Mr. Foster usually made the girls live together in shitty efficiency apartments, four or five to a room. But that was because he thought they would run. They were part of his train, they called it, and Julie knew that many of them were not there of their own free will. Although Julie had gone into service after she'd been caught "hooking without permission" by one of Mr. Foster's men, she was at least given three options: go with him to meet the boss; continue to sell her ass on the streets without a license, as it were, and suffer the consequences; or go back home, which she would never do. Being one of Foster's girls, one of the regulars (which that she was on the street not the train), she was given a room—and charged rent. It was just a sofa bed and a small TV with a tiny bathroom, but it was roof over her head. She could entertain johns there, if she wished, but she didn't; she wanted a space of her own.

Charlemagne had done his share of hustling and he was tolerant of her occupation, but he seemed to spend all of his free time trying to get her to work at McDonald's with him. But other than that minor awkwardness, things were looking good with Charlemagne, really good—until Mr. Foster laid down the law through one of his flunkies: she wasn't to fuck any niggers. And that was that; she had to go. She didn't dare disobey. Julie didn't want anything to happen to Charlemagne. She thought for sure she'd be sent to live in one of those little rooms. (She wasn't.) But it turned out that Charlemagne had given her something far more substantial than tattoos.

The tattooing had happened shortly before she'd been told to leave. Charlemagne had halfway converted her (which was progress since she considered herself a severely lapsed Catholic), and she wanted a tattoo and didn't care much what it was, so Charlemagne went to work. On her neck, in little letters, it read, "Jesus Lived and Died For All Your Sins."

On her lower back, right above her butt, it read, "Damn Right He'll Rise Again."

"I ain't ever been with your little hoodrat friend..."

She did disobey the law eventually—and did so for a year. Something precious and beyond belief lived in Charlemagne's apartment, the only good she'd ever put out into the world after taking in all its bad. But after she got caught sneaking over there one night, she never saw Charlemagne again.

Big Red issued a low whistle as he read her tattoos.

"That's some message there, sweetie."

"Some crazy john, he went ape shit when he saw it. Said I was the beginning of the end or the end before the beginning. I forget exactly."

"Sounds crazy, alright."

She used to wonder why Charlemagne never looked for her if he had just been worked over and run off by the goon squad, but when she closed her eyes after a long night turning tricks, she knew that Mr. Foster had disappeared Charlemagne and his friends like he had so many other people (allegedly).

"He was right about one thing," Julie said.

"What's that?"

Big Red was breathing heavy.

"He did rise again."

"Jesus?"

She looked over her shoulder at Big Red, who was staring at her partially exposed behind.

"Now, who you tryin' convince with that Jesus stuff, mister? You tryin' to convince yourself?"

There was a silence.

"Yes, I am."

"Good to know, Big Red. So what's it's gonna be?"

She nervously spun her Claddagh ring. This was always the worst part besides actually doing it: waiting to find out what was chosen from the menu.

"Can I kiss your ass?" His breathing was *really* heavy now.

"It's your dime. No freebies. Meter's been running since we shut the door, and I'm not the one keeping time, okay."

"Okay."

She pulled her jeans down to her knees.

"I have a kid, you know," Julie said. "Her name is Jenny."

The Weary Detective (Part 2)
8:45 p.m.

The way to catch a creep like this, a serial creep, was to think like him—that much Feargal had picked up from the movies. But there was some truth to it. If he could get into this guy's head, stay one move ahead, he'd bag himself a movie-of-the-week, or at least a trashy true crime paperback.

He'd been dating a nice woman for a little while now. Meryl was a divorcée with a green thumb, a writer from up in Rhawnhurst. A nice woman. Not like his usual sloppy bar pickups. She was his age for one. That was new. Since his own divorce, he preferred them straight out of college only not that smart. The hardest thing about heading up the Red Ribbon Task Force was that he thought about the bastard morning, noon, and night, and that often made intimacy with Meryl somewhat dicey. She wondered if something was wrong, if he needed Viagra (a question she asked delicately), if he was happy. And there were no answers. Even though she knew about the task force, she rarely asked about the investigation and he couldn't very well say to her: you see, babe, I'm mentally pretending to be this psychotic motherfucker who preys on young women between the ages of seventeen and twenty-six, mainly prostitutes, and who ties a red ribbon around their wrists before slicing their throats with so much force that one woman's head was dangling by tendrils—oh, and who sometimes fucks them while they are still alive but for sure after they're dead and maybe even while they're dying, but always with a condom. He might even wear two and he takes them with him. Jeez, almost forgot, honey: lodged up inside one victim's privates was a Ziploc bag with 2 Thessalonians 2:3 scratched onto a piece of recently flayed skin—and none of the victims they'd recovered thus far was missing a piece of flesh. Now, Meryl, honey, if you're still feeling randy, maybe you can help me pretend too.

Feargal spit out the window.

"I think there's a fine for that, boss," Costigan said.

The kid was trying to needle him about his reputation for being such a straight arrow. If he only knew what he'd done for his brother, Feargal thought. "You drive, boyo, let me worry about the oral projectiles."

What did they think they were going to find at the Hub Motel? Some babbling night manager half in the bag with a description that would now no longer match their own fuzzy one? Some of Foster's girls working their johns, their handlers not far off, others just taking a load off after walking the Strip for hours? (As the sun came up, the girls could be seen gathering at the Hub or one of the other trucker motels along the Strip or walking back across the bridge from Spring House, which was as far as they would go; they never hit Warminster—these were street hookers, not escorts.) They could send the muscle packing and round up some sex workers (to use the politically correct phrase of the day) and run down the warnings, show them their stupid sketch. Maybe Costigan would get enough glimpses to help him toss one off before he hit the hay tonight.

"Boss, you ever want to drive, just give me the say so."

"I'm not your boss, Costigan. Not really. I'm just a temporarily raised icon representing good police work and the perpetual spinning of wheels. How's that? Now keep your eyes on the road. It's raining cats and dogs out there."

"You think this manager, you think he saw our guy?"

"No."

It was hard to argue against his own pessimism. He'd obscured evidence that could possibly pin Lorraine Melfi's murder on his brother. He'd let one killer go free, and subsequently he couldn't catch another one. If he hadn't been raised in an Irish Catholic household, he'd call that karma. But Feargal was pleased as hell that not long after the incident, his brother had cleaned up, left the booze and the dope, even the smoking, behind. (Not that getting straight and sober was worth a young woman's life.) He was a runner now. Good thing too. Those plane tickets surface or the airline is contacted, his brother would have a lot of running to do. Feargal, however, was chasing his own ass with the red ribbon investigation. Zero DNA evidence, not even under the victims' nails. (In one case, where there appeared to be have been a struggle, he'd cut off the girl's fingertips with a pair of garden shears—as if he carried them for just such occasions.) No hairs or fibers that told them anything. No shoe or sneaker prints, not even from the nights when it rained.

The investigation was not bereft of irony: while the general public read the *Mondauk Common* for titillating tidbits on the hunt for the Red Ribbon Killer (boosting circulation), the perp's main quarries were prostitutes, a class of people the readership of the *Common* could give two shits about otherwise. And the girls wouldn't stop working the Strip. He and Paulie had even gone up to Anchor Hop to see Foster, who of course claimed zero knowledge or interest in prostitution, but Feargal hoped the message got through: pull the girls off the Strip, at least for a little while. But that never happened.

The Strip ran along Bethlehem Pike from the bridge into Spring House then east until the road turned south, running alongside the Heights. One side of the Strip was within the boundaries of Mondauk Proper, the other within Rhawnhurst's. Chief Hagen had swept through the turf wars (both boroughs were part of Mondauk

County anyway) and established the task force, which had jurisdiction in all six of the county's towns. Feargal, as head of the task force, made sure there was a heavy police presence on the Strip—especially since Foster had ignored them—but since they had nothing more than a generic description of the perp, he could be any john at any number of decrepit places. Even the sketch they had could be anybody—hell, if his Uncle Murray donned a ball cap and a hooded sweatshirt, he'd fit the description, but Feargal expected that they weren't hunting a seventy-two-year old with gout.

The worst of it was this: he'd looked for red ribbons the few times he'd been at his brother's apartment since Lorraine's death.

It was hopeless.

Costigan farted.

"Sorry, boss."

Fucking hopeless.

Over the hiss and chatter of the police radio, he heard Meryl's infectious laugh in his head. It often began as an embarrassed chuckle that ended up becoming an irrepressible guffaw. As it grew, she'd cover her mouth as if she could contain it, but soon her head would be thrown back and her eyes would fill with tears, as if caught up in some sort of brief mad ecstasy. Her hand would return to her mouth again, but the cat had already ripped its way out of the bag. As her laughter subsided, Meryl would dab her eyes and catch her breath. But she was always caught unawares at the next outbreak, as if it had never happened before, even if it was in reaction to a joke in a movie she'd seen too many times to count but was open enough to watch as if it were new. She allowed herself to be surprised even in familiar territory.

"Step on it, Costigan. I just now got a feeling about this."

Meryl had read him an Emily Dickinson poem once, " 'Hope' is the thing with feathers," so why couldn't this be the call? He'd been tarred and feathered before, God knows. Maybe he was due for a different kind of plumage.

Rum Toddy (Part 2)
9:00 p.m.

Rear Window was over and now she was stuck with some popcorn movie with Roy Scheider and a shark. At least it had Robert Shaw—

now there was a real man. He didn't brook no bullshit. She'd seen *The Sting.* One tough motherfucker in that one.

Adeline looked at her granddaughter, who was still immersed in her Legos and blocks and the Lincoln Logs Gram had unearthed in a closet during a commercial break. It was past Jenny's bedtime, but Adeline figured what the hell; if she having fun, let her be. She told Jenny the Lincoln Logs had been Julie's, "your mommy's," but the girl barely nodded. She rarely spoke, and when she did, it was usually only in moments of extreme terror. Adeline wondered if Jenny even remembered her mother. She accepted life here with Gram and the frequently absent Grampa. Adeline snorted and tossed back the dregs of her third toddy. If you knew how mommy was selling her coochie for a high, she thought, you'd never want to meet her again anyway.

Adeline herself had long ago stopped waiting for Julie to return for good and clean up her act. But there was nothing more she could do. John acted as if Julie were dead; there seemed to have been no grieving process for John. Yeah, he went around carrying his little Bible most of the time, but Adeline suspected that there were dirty pictures pasted inside. It wasn't like Julie and John ever got along that well, there was none of that father-daughter bonding, except maybe when Julie was very little and he used to make her those bracelets out of dollar bills. So Julie was gone and Jenny was here and they had started all over again with the damn toys and the special food and the baby clothes. Adeline wanted to adopt Jenny legally, but John would never even listen. He would just make a sour noise with his mouth and go out to the shed with his Bible.

Shitballs!

She'd jiggled the handle of the recliner—the chair hadn't been right for years—and when she pushed down, the chair tilted and she just about toppled to the floor.

"Gram?" Jenny asked.

"Gram's alright, darling, Gram's okay," she answered, but she wasn't okay: she'd done something to her back when she stopped her fall and it had reawakened that ancient pain that she thought was long gone. *Goddamn you, John.* How many times had she asked him to fix her friggin' chair? She climbed out of the rickety thing and headed down to the basement to look for some tools. She'd fix the freakin' chair herself.

But the basement had no tools of any kind besides a rusty wrench and a screwdriver that smelled like someone had thrown up on it. She climbed back up the stairs and paused in the kitchen, pressing on her lower back, as if that would do anything. John's shed was lit by the back porch light. Did she dare? The shed was John's territory. He had electricity out there and everything. Adeline made herself another rum toddy. Well, why not? It was her house too—including the stinkin' shed.

There was a set of keys, she knew, in John's nightstand (she'd been snooping), and a couple of them had looked small enough for a padlock. Usually he took the keys with him but sometimes he forgot. She went upstairs to his room (her back protesting every step), and there they were—next to his Bible. His precious goddamn Bible. But as much as she wanted to open it and see what was really inside, there were streaks of what appeared to be lubricant across the cover, and she wasn't about to touch it without gloves. She stuck the keys in the pocket of her housecoat and hurried back down.

"Jenny, hon, you stay put for Gram."

Like there was anything that was going to take this girl's attention away from her Legos and Lincoln Logs.

It was still raining pretty heavy, and Adeline grabbed an umbrella on her way out. She almost fell down the porch steps. One toddy too many, perhaps.

John had built the storage shed himself. It was made of wood, and he'd put up siding and a shingled roof. It had a set of double doors secured with not one but two padlocks. She went to the back and peered through the only window, but it was too high and too narrow—not to mention that it was too dark—to see anything. She didn't know what she was looking for anyway—maybe John lurking around in the dark. The thought scared her; lately *John* was scaring her. She tried different keys until she found two that did the trick. She flicked on the overhead fluorescent lights and blinked. *Jesus H. Christ.* In one the corner of the shed was a pile of body parts. It was horrific, and she started to retch until she realized that there wasn't a smell. They weren't body parts: they were mannequin parts. Torsos, arms, legs. *What the fuck are you into, John?* The mannequin parts looked like they'd been rescued from dumpsters. They were scuffed and bruised and all female. *What are you doing with all the dummies, John?* This was like his inexplicable need to get a tattoo at his age: his old Army nickname, in big red letters (he had red hair) with a pierced, bloody heart in the center. She hadn't asked any questions. She never saw him naked anymore anyway. At least it was on the upper part of his arm, so no one saw it except him and his mannequins.

The rest of the shed was immaculate. There was a stool and a small wooden workbench. Nearby was a shelf that held a box of trash bags, a small pair of gardening shears, and a spray bottle of weed killer. But it was the two big metal cabinets with long drawers that caught Adeline's attention. That was where the tools had to be. But, of course, the drawers were all locked. Adeline tried the other little keys until she discovered the right one, which had been difficult because her hands had started shaking. She'd noticed that the torso closest to her had had its breasts crudely removed—not that John necessarily had to be the "plastic surgeon," but just knowing that he'd kept the remains, for lack of a better word, was beyond unsettling. She tried to refocus: she was here for tools to fix her chair. The first drawer had nothing but a couple of boxes of nails and some chains links. The next drawer had a box of syringes. Was John diabetic? No, she thought through her rum toddy haze, he wasn't. Had he become diabetic and just not told her? Though she'd never known John to suffer in silence, that had to be it. Why the hell else would he need a box of syringes?

The rain pounded on the wooden shingles of the roof. The third drawer was a mess, stuffed to the gills, and when Adeline pulled on a strand of red ribbon, the drawer exploded like a piñata. Women's underwear and brassieres—lots of them—and more ribbons: spools of them, all different colors. These were young girls' underwear, nothing Adeline could have squeezed into. There were blood stains on some of them, but she didn't think they were from spotting. At the back of the drawer were two almost depleted rolls of Christmas wrapping paper. (She couldn't remember John *ever* wrapping a present, and his gift giving days were long over.) She sniffed one of the panties. It had definitely been worn by a female. So at least John wasn't parading around the shed in Victoria's Secret.

Tucked into the corner of the drawer was his wedding band.

That's it! Enough with this nonsense. If John was catting around on her, she'd show him what the cat could bring home. She could have any man she wanted, even at her age (if she ditched the house coat, used eye cream, and did something about her hair and the brown spots on her hands). That young fellow in accounting. Adeline saw the way he looked at her, like he was undressing her right in the office, his desk shielding his hard-on. She'd show John, she'd sure as hell show him.

She wrapped a red ribbon around her fist—and then she knew. The underwear. The bloody underwear. The red ribbons. Maybe even the syringes.

Jesus motherfucking Christ. She crossed herself. The Red Ribbon Killer. He was on the news again last night. (He was on the news almost every night, and she'd even seen a CNN piece on the investigation.) John was already out. The news showed the police sketch again, which was lacking in specifics; it could be any man in a ball cap. The newswoman said that the task force was receiving assistance from the FBI. Detective Feargal Finnerty spoke at a press conference held by Mayor Greene. "The noose is tightening," he said. It was a matter of time. Her first thought had been: all this nonsense for a bunch of hookers, but she knew that was bullshit. Her daughter was a hooker. For all the ill she thought of Julie, she didn't want her to end up at the mercy of the Red Ribbon Killer.

Particularly if that killer was her own father, she now thought. Hadn't he done enough to that girl?

Adeline grabbed a trash bag and filled it with underwear and ribbons and wrapping paper and his box of syringes—plus four tubes of K-Y Personal Lubricant she'd found in the fourth drawer. (There was a fifth, almost empty tube in there too, but she left it where it was.) For good measure, she tossed in a couple of mannequin arms.

She'd take care of John's ass but good. Detective Finnerty was an old friend from their pinochle days. She bet Feargal would just love a big ol' bag of evidence dropped on his doorstep. And she could do this. She could bring down the Red Ribbon Killer.

The Dental Hygienist (Part 2)
9:15 p.m.

Leah hadn't touched him with her bare hands. It was a huge disappointment. But maybe one he could fix later. He lacked nothing in the way of confidence.

The session had gone a full hour, due mostly to their gabbing about Kate Winslet and Jennifer Connelly. Daniel had recommended the film *Little Children* during his last visit. It wasn't exactly a romantic comedy (it wasn't a comedy at all), but to his surprise Leah had watched it. She wasn't thrilled that the movie was so dark, but she was nevertheless swept up in the affair between the man dubbed the Prom King and Winslet's reluctant housewife. And while it was no *Love Actually* or *When Harry Met Sally*, Daniel thought it was a good recommendation, for the world was a dark place. The loner guy didn't always end up with the comely girl, and if he did, sometimes it was because he was keeping his Betty or Veronica in a pit like Buffalo Bill in *The Silence of the Lambs*, a decidedly different kind of love story. He was sure Leah would shudder at the thought. (But in *The Princess Bride*, her favorite movie, Buttercup was held against her will by Prince Humperdinck, ostensibly for love. Whatever the reason, Humperdinck was more like Buffalo Bill than Leah would care to admit.) But as much as he knew that more often than not, the world was harsh and ugly, he also knew that the darkness was just a pathway to the light, a thought easier to believe while in Leah's presence. Previously he'd thought it was too early to bring his faith into their conversations. Politics and religion could be so divisive, and timing was everything.

But the truth was he was ready to pull out all the stops. It was funny: Leah wasn't even his type, but he was in love, the real deal. How long this love would last would depend on Leah. But husband or no, he had to give it a shot. There was no crime in trying.

He pulled his raincoat on slowly in the waiting room. Then while he was making another appointment, Leah appeared at his side and handed him a bag of free toothbrushes and floss. He knew she gave these to every patient, but tonight it felt as if it were something she was doing just for him.

"Raining cats and dogs out there," he said.

"Yeah and my car's busted, can you believe it?"

Her breath smelled great.

"What happened?"

"Someone vandalized it last night. Took out the spark plugs, my husband said. Cut a hose or something. Maybe two. Who would do that?"

NOW. NOW. NOW. *NOW!*

"Do you want a ride home? You mentioned you lived in Warminster. I'm actually going that way to visit my grandmother."

Leah looked at Doris the receptionist, who'd been pretending that she wasn't listening. "I take the bus," the old biddy said without looking up from her paperwork.

"My husband—he's works late," Leah explained. "Or else he'd pick me up."

"Well, this works out perfect then. I don't have much of a ride, but it'll get us where we're going. It's a rental actually. Some car trouble of my own."

"I was just going to call a cab."

"A cab from here to Warminster? What's that going to run you? Forty bucks, maybe, plus tip. I'm free."

"I don't want to be any trouble. I don't want to make you late for your grandmother's."

"It's no trouble, really. I'm happy to do it. Look, with all the craziness out there today, who can you trust? Red Ribbon Killer, gang violence out of the Lakes. You know me—or at least you know me a little. I'm like you. Just a normal human being skating by '*on the thin ice of modern life.*' "

He knew she liked Pink Floyd.

" '*All in all it was all just bricks in the wall,*' " she sang in response and laughed.

Doris rolled her eyes.

"Okay, I will accept your offer, kind sir," Leah said, "but here's the thing: I still have to clean up, do some quick stuff on the computer. I might be half an hour, maybe a little longer."

"I'll read magazines. As long as Doris doesn't mind me hanging around, I'll just chill out here."

"Doris is working late tonight, so I'm sure she won't mind some company before the place clears out."

Doris hit her stapler extra hard.

"My grandmother stays up all night—she never sleeps, I swear—so it's fine. Take your time."

"I feel like I'm putting you out or taking advantage of you somehow. You have to let me give you gas money at least."

"Taking advantage of me I can handle, and my company is paying for the rental, so while your offer is appreciated, it's not necessary." He gave her his best smile—at least he hoped it was his best. He couldn't blow this. "Go—do your cleanup or whatever. I'll be sitting here reading a year-old issue of *Field and Stream*." And avoiding Doris' judgmental gaze. It was a good thing that he had a face no one seemed to remember. Nevertheless, if it was still pouring, he'd have to come back to take Doris home. He couldn't let her take the bus in weather like this.

"Okay, mister," Leah said playfully. "I'll be as quick as I can.

"And, Daniel," she added, "thank you."

She was quite welcome. So welcome in fact, Daniel didn't know how he would be able to sit still for half an hour or more, but he was glad to be off the streets for a night.

Being somebody else always required infinite patience, especially if he was doing it without masks or disguises or fake accents. Just some poor slob's identity that worked because the unfortunate fellow was missing. All he needed was an adjusted driver's license, a wallet full of plastic, and a plausible backstory. He found that the trick was to wake up in the morning thinking he was this person because that was the time when he was most vulnerable. If he could do that, he could pull it off anywhere at any time. However, it was equally important to never forget the mission to which he was tasked, because although he didn't want to blow his cover, he also didn't want to become *too* comfortable in somebody else's shoes (literally). Being comfortable could easily lead to being dilatory and torpid, and he had to be quicker than that and more aware, for Daniel was undercover. Deep undercover. He'd never be able to explain his job to anyone, not now anyway—it sounded like a movie role. But he could tell Leah. He could reveal to her his real name, his true identity, his true purpose. His job. He could tell her he wasn't Daniel.

Rum Toddy (Part 3)
9:30 p.m.

I can't be alone, Adeline thought. She hadn't been alone since she married John when she was eighteen, and that was a long tootin' time ago.

I can't be alone.

She'd called the police three times and hung up each time. She'd called the Red Ribbon Killer hotline twice. Same thing. Even though she'd blocked her number, it didn't stop her from worrying that her calls could be traced.

I can't be alone.

It wasn't that she thought her husband didn't do the horrible things that the Red Ribbon Killer did. He was perfectly capable. Always sneaking around the house. That quick, often violent temper of his. (She still bore the scar on her forehead from when he threw a lamp at her because she burned his fish sticks.) All the pornography. Always in that shed doing God knows what. (God knew.) It was just that she couldn't imagine life alone. Oh, she'd have Jenny. Thanks to Julie, she'd always have Jenny, but it wasn't the same, even if she and John slept in separate beds, even if he was frequently absent and barely communicated with her.

I can't be alone.

She carried the trash bag full of girls' underwear, ribbons, syringes, and wrapping paper down to the basement and dumped the whole mess, including the tubes of lubricant and the mannequin limbs, into the laundry sink.

She'd burn it. She would burn every last bit of it. John would be mighty pissed when he came home and discovered his stash missing, but once she told him that she'd burned it, he'd understand. He'd understand the choices that had been before her and that she'd made the right decision—for both of them. For what remained of their marriage and good name. For their granddaughter. Maybe there'd be counseling, if there was counseling for this sort of thing. Maybe they'd go see Father Dave.

Adeline hunted around the basement until she found the lighter fluid with the barbecue stuff. This was the right thing to do. This was the right choice. (All those young girls.) There was no way she wanted to die alone. (Everybody dies alone.) This was the only choice. Flame on and it was all gone. No DNA, no fingerprints, no evidence period. Everything: gone.

Adeline put the lighter fluid down. She hadn't heard Jenny make a sound since she'd descended into the basement. While her granddaughter wasn't much of a talker, she figured that most kids make *some* noise when they're playing with piles of wooden and plastic pieces. Julie used to.

"Jenny? Hon?" she called upstairs.

Silence.

No pitter-patter of little feet. No crashing of blocks or Lincoln Logs.

"Jenny!"

Silence.

Goddamn it. Just when things were about to get hot.

Adeline climbed the stairs carefully. Her back was going to be the death of her, not John.

"Jenny!"

Jenny lay still on the dining room rug. Adeline knew she wasn't asleep.

"Jenny!"

The girl was breathing but barely. Her face was blue. Adeline grabbed the phone. She was suddenly sober.

"Did you swallow something? Did you? What did you swallow?"

She couldn't wait for the EMTs. Adeline tried to remember the Heimlich maneuver, and she hoisted Jenny up and plunged her fists into her little stomach.

A red Lego piece shot from Jenny's mouth and landed under the radiator.

Tears were everywhere now, Jenny's and Adeline's. Adeline hugged Jenny tight and although she loved her granddaughter, it was her daughter she cried for. Her lost Julie. The Julie who would never be right. The Julie who used to make Mother's Day cards by pasting macaroni on construction paper. The Julie who had sex for money and spent the money on dope. The Julie who had dropped a half-black kid on their doorstep and said adios. The Julie who would cuddle up next to her mother whenever it thundered. The Julie who got an A+ on her history test in the fourth grade, her last year of good grades. The Julie who she would never be able to save with something as simple as the Heimlich maneuver and would probably never be able to save at all.

I can't be alone.

"Do you want to help me, Jenny? You want to help Gram?"

Jenny sniffled and nodded her head. Despite the hour and the Lego incident, she didn't look at bit tired. She was going to end up a night owl like her Gram.

"Okay, put your rain slicker on. There's some silly stuff in the basement and you're gonna help Gram take it out to Grampa's shed. Think you can do that? We're just gonna put it all away, nice and neat, and then lock it up."

God, what was Jenny going to make of the pile of mannequin parts? She shook her head. She had to stop worrying about what she couldn't control and start taking care of what little she could. Heck, Jenny would probably end up wanting to play with the arms and hands.

"Our little secret, okay, Jenny? Just our little secret."

But he would know his wife had been in there and had opened the drawers. More importantly though, Adeline thought, he would know that she *knew*, and that might be enough.

Julie and the John (Part 3)
9:45 p.m.

"That's all you wanna do?"

It was all he wanted to do. She was still on her stomach.

He'd kissed her bottom passionately, but did nothing more. He didn't try to stick a finger in there or anything else. He didn't even wack off. He'd just kissed her bottom a few times and asked for her underwear, a request she denied.

"That was nice," she said, and she wasn't lying. She was stoned, so it felt like it was happening on a different plane of existence, but a nice plane, one filled with feather pillows and clean bathrooms. Plus, it was still early; she had a long night ahead of her, especially in the rain, so Big Red kissing her cute Irish ass was an easy way to start.

Big Red sat in the room's sole chair, his right leg thrown over the arm of the chair. He looked the picture of contentment, she thought, as he'd just blown his load, except that rocked back and forth in his seat, not manically like he'd forgotten to take his meds, but like he was anticipating something. Sex? She didn't think so—he could have just taken her anally but didn't. (It cost extra anyway and going bareback wasn't negotiable, so it wasn't as popular with the Strip crowd.) No, she thought he was done for the night sexually. He'd taken off the hoodie—he just had a t-shirt on beneath it—but had pulled the bill of his ball cap low over the top half of his face. Regardless, in the glare of the neon motel sign, it was obvious that his moustache and sideburns were fake.

"My kid's half-black," Julie said. "Or quarter-black. Something like that."

She'd begged Mr. Foster not to make her get an abortion, sobbing on her hands and knees, fully prepared to be shot in the back of the head or worse. She knew she was in dangerous territory. After they discovered that Sherise was hiding a pregnancy, two men tied her, naked, to a support column, so that she was in a kneeling position, and Ox, this goon who weighed over three hundred pounds easy, repeatedly kicked her in the stomach and didn't stop until Mr.

Foster saw blood coming from her pussy. Sherise's torture wasn't the only horror story she'd heard. Andi was allowed to remain pregnant and was even taken off the Strip when she started to show. For the remaining months, Mr. Foster didn't charge her rent for her room, and he always made sure she never wanted for groceries. But things turned south when Mr. Foster "insisted" that a physician that worked for him be her obstetrician. The doctor—if he really was one—did nothing more than show up periodically to give her the once-over. No ultrasounds. No blood tests. Just baggies of prenatal vitamins. Andi told her that she thought that the delivery took place in a basement, but she couldn't be sure because they immediately sedated her—and within twenty-four hours of giving birth, her little girl was taken from her, sold, it was said, to the highest bidder at one of Mr. Foster's private online auctions, where men bid to purchase children.

But a ray of whatever light shined down on Charlemagne must have followed her the night she pleaded for the life of her unborn child, because after standing her up and slapping her around, Mr. Foster said she could carry the baby to term if she "agreed" to work his pregnancy fetish customers, right up until the end. She was so relieved, she dropped to the floor again and started kissing Mr. Foster's shoes, and he kicked her in the face. Two days later, Tic-Tac threw a plastic card on her bed and told her she was now on Medicaid. "It's all been taken care of," he said. She gingerly touched the bruise that covered most of one side of her face and thought: *it was worth it; my baby won't be born in a basement.*

Her only communication with Charlemagne was through her friend Violeta. (Tic-Tac made the two of them go on outcalls together if a client wanted two girls, so they knew each other intimately and Julie trusted her.) Violeta would update Charlemagne on Julie's progression. The only thing she asked Violeta to keep from him was what Julie had to do to keep the baby. After Jenny was born, she was again brought before Mr. Foster and again she begged (though she didn't know what for what exactly, but being called on the carpet was never a good thing in her profession). However, it didn't matter what she said; it had already been decided. Mr. Foster nodded at Tic-Tac who took the baby out of her arms. She screamed. Tic-Tac shifted the baby to one side and punched her in the nose. "Take it to the nigger's," Mr. Foster told his flunky. Even with blood coming out of her nose, Julie smiled (and quickly suppressed it): if she couldn't have Jenny, at least Charlemagne could. "In exchange for my largesse," Mr. Foster said, "you will start working the private parties." This she did without complaint. (She didn't want to upset the apple cart.) The private parties were gang bangs, where she could end up with a cock in her pussy, another one in her ass, and a third in her mouth, all at the same time, but she took their come, and thanked Charlemagne's God that Jenny was with her father, even when she was being choked out or pissed on. Violeta kept her up-to-date. Charlemagne was into being a dad, she said, and his friends took turns watching Jenny when he had a shift at McDonald's. Finally her friend said that she thought the coast was clear. (Until then, they'd believed his apartment was being watched.) Soon Julie began sneaking over to Charlemagne's, marveling every time at their beautiful daughter. His roommates would take off, and for an hour or two, it would be like they were a real family. She was careful never to stay long and to space her appearances. During her secret visits, she got to play peek-a-boo with Jenny and change her diapers and be within the circle of Charlemagne's light once more. This went on for a year—and she started to get sloppy, staying longer, even sleeping over every so often. It was blissful. Meanwhile she was taken off the private parties, which made her spirit feel even lighter. She often found herself humming a song that was on the radio when she was little: *"It's a beautiful day / Sky falls, you feel like / It's a beautiful day / Don't let it—"*

Then it was all over. She didn't know how Mr. Foster found out (maybe they'd never stopped watching the apartment), but Violeta came running to her one night—Charlemagne and Jenny and the roommates were gone and had been for days from what she could tell: their door was wide open and there was a pizza on the kitchen table with a couple of slices missing; the pizza was moldy and rancid. Their clothes and video games were still there (the baby's stuff too), but there were no signs of anyone (and with the exception of Jenny, there never would be). Julie wanted to slit her wrists—it was her fault. She'd been stupid somehow and gotten caught; sloppy or not, she knew there were times when she had to cool it, so she hadn't been there in a week. She couldn't even try to call Charlemagne; Foster's girls were only allowed to have burner phones, and she'd used up her minutes already. In the middle of the conversation, Tic-Tac knocked Violeta out cold (they never heard him come in), and Julie was taken to Mr. Foster a third time, but he walked out as soon as she was escorted in. Ox was there, and being alone with him and

Tic-Tac, she started to pee herself until an older woman with sad, hollowed eyes came out from behind Ox, carrying Jenny. If Tic-Tac hadn't been holding her arm, Julie would have run up and snatched her baby, but she didn't need to: the woman handed Jenny over, turned, and walked away into a corner of the room like a zombie. "Mr. Foster says you have twenty-four hours to get rid of it," Tic-Tac said into her ear, "and he doesn't care how. But if it's found in your room or holed up with another 'friend,' then Ox here will bury it alive. It's not yours anymore, understood? You broke the no nigger rule. Get rid of it." Despite his tough words, they were obviously squeamish about killing a baby or they would have already (and perhaps the child auction business was temporarily on hold), and that gave her hope, made her bold. She yanked away from Tic-Tac's grip and was promptly punched in the gut so hard, she dropped the baby. "If you can't manage it, then you tell me where to take it, or I'll take you where you wanna drop it off, but you have twenty-four hours to get it done, starting now. So get a move on, the clock's ticking. Busy bees, busy bodies." So she gave Jenny to her mom. Though the last thing she wanted was for her daughter to grow up in the house where she had, what choice did she have? But she'd be done hooking in a year, she'd thought then, and come back for Jenny. But smack had turned that year into two, and now it wasn't so easy to get out. Sometimes she wondered if she ever would.

She realized Big Red had asked her a question. It was so easy to get lost in her head when she was high, and this was some primo dope.

"I'm sorry, what did you—?"

"Where is she?"

"With my parents. Until I get my shit together, they'll take care of her—though they didn't exactly do a bang up job with me."

"Why? What happened?"

"My mom was okay, a little overbearing. It was my dad. Always in my room. Always wanting to tuck me in—starting when I was in fifth grade. Would walk in on me when I was going to the bathroom; he'd installed a knob that wouldn't lock. When I was sick, he always took my temperature anally—even after I started high school. He said it was the best way. He also wanted to see my breasts, and he would cup and squeeze them, he said, so he'd know what size bra to get. He'd go and buy these Victoria's Secret bras and panties; I could barely fill them out, but he wanted me to model them anyway. I knew it was weird—really weird—but every little girl craves attention from their dad. But then it went further—a lot further. My mom knew. She had to know. Decided to ignore it, I guess. She drank a lot. I eventually made him stop."

"How?"

"I bit his dick."

"I bet he was mad."

"God, I don't remember; I just remember that it worked. I left so long ago. Six years or something like that. They probably wouldn't even recognize me. The only time I saw my mom since I left was when I dropped off—"

"Yes?"

"How'd you know I had a daughter? You asked 'Where is *she?*' "

"Lucky guess."

She couldn't read his tone. "Something going on here I should know about?"

"Did you love him? Your father? Sounds like he loved you."

She pulled her jeans up—that was a messed up thing to say, and it made her feel uncomfortable—but he stopped her, gently. She could sense the force behind his hands.

"Leave 'em down, Julie."

"How do you know my name?"

"You told me, remember? At the Sunoco."

"No, no, I didn't—or maybe I did. Fuck! What the hell is going on?"

"I have to go, Julie. Back out into the rain. Do you want a toot before I hit the road?"

With her jeans still down around her knees, she did a line off the dirty night table even though snorting smack was starting to do little for her anymore. Using a needle once in a while as a treat was okay. She didn't relish the idea of spiking it all the livelong day. But it seemed as if she was heading in that direction.

He threw a dime bag on the bed.

"I'm going to leave you a taste, okay, and here's a clean syringe."

"You have a tattoo too. I can see it peeking out from your t-shirt. What is it?"

"Just my name, Big Red," he answered, lifting his sleeve to reveal the ink on the upper part of his arm, "plus the Sacred Heart. Not much to see."

"We both have tattoos." But she was staring at the dime bag.

"Yes, we do."

"We're family!"

"Yes, we are."

When he turned around to put his hooded sweatshirt and boots back on, she noticed the knife in what appeared to be a homemade sheath attached to his belt.

He was talking to himself: " 'As arrows are in the hand of a mighty man; so are children of the youth. Happy is the man that hath his quiver full of them.' Psalms 127:4-5."

As he spoke, Julie lay on her stomach and pretended to nod out. Big Red leaned over her and wrapped something around her right wrist.

The Weary Detective (Part 3)
10:00 p.m.

The office of the Hub Motel smelled like sour milk.

The night manager had ID'd the guy from their sketch. He was relatively sober and very helpful. The proprietor was a different ball of wax altogether. He'd shown up minutes after they arrived. (The detectives already knew from their conversation with the manager that he hadn't called his boss, which meant their presence had been noted by Foster's men, who'd then rustled up the owner.) The short, odd-looking man who ran into the office also smelled like sour milk but mixed with jalapeños. His body odor made Feargal's eyes water. The proprietor launched into a tirade, spewing legal terms he'd obviously learned from TV shows, but basically he wasn't playing ball without a warrant. When he ran out of gas, Feargal and Costigan tried to explain to him that they had probable cause and could do whatever the hell they wanted; they were just being polite in asking.

The proprietor's demeanor changed then, and not for the better. He grew sullen and stalled for time by suddenly developing a hearing problem after Costigan said they wanted to go room by room. But the owner's confidence had withered and had been replaced by discomfort.

Feargal massaged his throbbing temples. The fact was they couldn't do whatever they wanted and they didn't have probable cause—they didn't even have reasonable suspicion—but the proprietor didn't know that. ("Probable cause" was more than likely just another term he'd learned from TV without knowing the definition—but it did seem to rattle him, which was the point. They weren't trying to pull a fast one; if they were, anything they found would be deemed inadmissible.) The law was pretty clear. They needed a warrant to search an occupied room unless there were exigent circumstances. All they could do was knock on each door and speak to the occupants (unless they were invited in). The owner's permission didn't give them authority to search occupied rooms— but it did for unoccupied ones, no warrants necessary. And that was what they needed: consent from the proprietor to enter and search the unoccupied rooms, which were the ones that truly concerned them. If the perp had been here, chances were he was long gone now; too much time had passed. But a victim or an important piece of evidence could lie behind one of the doors. Feargal just wanted easy access.

"If we don't get permission from this gentleman here, do we just kick the doors in?"

"No difference to me, Aidan. You feelin' up to it?"

"Fit as a fucking fiddle, boss."

Feargal stepped inside the proprietor's personal space.

"We know you get kickbacks from Foster, which means if there's any illegal activity going on in your motel, you know about it. You may not know specifics, but you're not being paid to turn your head for nothing. So we find anything, we're gonna take you in too, understand?"

Feargal stepped back. The proprietor, who had long stringy hair that was thinning in the front and balding in the back, tossed him the master keys and sucked on a strand of hair.

"Now stay put. Don't leave this fucking office, either of you, until myself or Detective Costigan tells you to. Do you follow?"

The proprietor stuck more hair in his mouth.

The detectives approached each door with care, and whenever they entered an unoccupied room, they kept their hands on their guns until they ascertained nobody unexpected was in there. They had the register, but they couldn't make heads or tails of it. "So room by room it is," Costigan said with more enthusiasm than Feargal could muster.

First room: empty and nothing of interest.

Second one: empty and nothing of interest except a quart spray bottle of bed bug and flea killer.

A hooker answered the door of room 103, and they could see her colleague atop a hairy, extremely overweight man who moaned like he had a stomach ache.

A junkie came to the next door, and when they showed their badges, his companion, a skinny woman in her underwear, ran into the bathroom where she immediately started flushing the toilet. Feargal thought the guy was going to do a jig when they left after asking only a few (non narcotic-related) questions. Costigan raised his eyebrows, but the vice squad ran through here on a regular basis, and Feargal wasn't about to get distracted

After knocking on the door of 105, they let themselves in to find a couple of college age students sleeping off an early beer blast.

Considering the activities occurring within, a lot of guests had their curtains wide open (but not the junkies). They witnessed an old woman crying at the end of her bed, a hooker on her knees blowing two guys who seemed to be enjoying each other's company more than hers, and another prostitute who was engaged in the old dildo-in-the-john's-ass game. She was smoking a cigarette and looking bored. When she lifted her hand to wave at the detectives, the pink dildo jiggled in the guy's butt like it was planted in a bowl of Jell-O. The remaining two rooms on the ground level were unoccupied and held nothing in the way of evidence.

The second floor offered more of the same. Overall, there weren't many unoccupied rooms; the Hub did a brisk business, with many guests taking advantage of the optional hourly rate, which meant that if an occupied room had been empty when the possible bad boy was here, any evidence would most likely have been destroyed or contaminated by the various shenanigans. Besides, their guy left his bodies where he did them and never used the same location twice; his kind didn't usually break their patterns, and there was no way he just stopped in for some shut eye; they'd seen no signs of tampering to any of the windows or doors.

The feeling of being fluffed with hope that Feargal briefly had on the way here was now plucked.

"Only a few more left," Costigan said, and Feargal nodded. Good thing this fleabag motel only had two floors, he thought. The weariness was creeping back, as an investigation without end loomed ahead. The thought made the pain in Feargal's temples reach excruciating levels.

Room 207.

"Police department!" Costigan barked. They waited a reasonable amount of time. "We're coming in!"

The girl was lying on her stomach and her jeans were pulled down to her knees. Both detectives drew their guns. Costigan checked the bathroom and it was empty. A red scarf was draped over the lamp, which was switched off. A small CD player played music at a personal level.

"When you gonna let somebody in? You might get hurt just a little bit."

"Jesus, boss," the younger detective said. He clumsily felt her neck for a pulse, then whispered, "Nothing." His hands were shaking. Feargal would have to double-check Costigan's work before the night was through, but he didn't mind; Aidan was a good kid, and for many, their first time was rough.

"Never seen a dead body before, Costigan?"

Feargal had seen one too many, especially with the task force. But the red ribbon investigation was becoming an exercise in futility. They toiled on an endless highway with dead-end side roads littered with the corpses of young women. Maybe the thing with feathers was the seabird from another poem Meryl had read to him: "Instead of the cross, the Albatross / About my neck was hung." The smell of death didn't even faze him much anymore. It was the main reason he was thinking of hanging up his spurs early—that and being an accomplice after the fact in his brother's murder of Lorraine Melfi. Feargal sighed. And now this girl. Dirty blonde hair, slender body, some bruising on the bare skin that he could see. She was in her early twenties, he estimated. If she was working the Strip, the Hub in particular, then she was one of Foster's girls.

"Should I call this in, boss?"

"Don't call me boss, Costigan," he replied absently.

Around the girl's right wrist was a rope or a ribbon; it was hard to tell because of the way her body was positioned. The beam from Costigan's flashlight danced on the walls and furniture. The only other light in the room came from the motel's neon sign, which was visible through the partially opened curtains, but it only illuminated part of the room. Feargal left it the way it was; he didn't want to disturb the mood of the crime scene. This was how he worked best: when the scene was left exactly as it had been found. Too often some uniforms would tramp over evidence or turn on lights and turn down stereos. He liked to stand in every room, particularly the killing room, and soak in every detail and nuance before the techs arrived. He felt this helped him to listen to what the scene could tell him. Paulie, busting his chops, said he was eavesdropping on ghosts. He couldn't remember his ATM pin number, but he had something akin to a photographic memory while on the job, which unfortunately meant that he carried those impressions with him, at least until the case was solved, and if it wasn't…he knew from experience that they weren't going anywhere. Although he never spoke to Meryl about the things he'd seen or the job in general, she would often tap his head and say, "It's pretty crowded up there." Paulie called the whole thing Irish voodoo but stayed out his way when Feargal was in the zone.

"When you gonna let somebody in?"

The girl's bare ass shone in the light from the Hub Motel sign. There was a tattoo on the bottom of her back.

" 'Damn Right He'll Rise Again,' " Costigan read.

Feargal let out a low whistle. So much for Irish voodoo.

"What is it, boss—sorry. Is it a clue?"

The kid sounded like he was in an episode of *Scooby-Doo*.

"No, it's not a…it's Julie McIntyre."

Costigan stared at the register. "Julie McIntyre?"

"That's my name," the corpse said, "don't wear it out."

The deceased rolled over, and Feargal could see track marks on her bare arms. He could also see her shaved privates and wished he couldn't. But he knew from his days in vice that she would get dressed faster if he didn't ask. She was still a pretty girl but a hardness had set in, and he knew from years on the force that once it did, it rarely dissipated or softened.

"Feargal! What are you doing here? Am I busted? I swear I was just crashing out."

"We thought you were dead, miss," Costigan said, looking chagrined as he flashed his badge. Feargal was relieved but knew that when Paulie heard about this, Aidan would be in for a hard time. He looked like he knew it too. "Your pallor—"

"Some detectives," Julie responded, lighting a cigarette. She clicked off the CD player with her toes before pulling up her jeans.

"Aren't these non-smoking rooms?" Costigan asked, trying to find steady ground.

"At the Hub? This whole place could go up at any moment. There's probably someone cooking up a batch in the next room."

"Julie," Feargal began, "what's on your wrist?"

Julie looked and smiled, then ripped it off. It was a bracelet made of twenties. A shadow of malevolence passed over her face

"It's nothing," she said. "Just something someone gave me."

"But you looked surprised. Who gave it to you, Julie? Did a john give it to you? Were you working tonight? You're not in any trouble if you answer yes."

"No, Feargal, I told you: I was just crashing." She exhaled in his direction on purpose. "Whoa, but that was a shitload of questions."

"Here's another: do you think someone slipped it on your wrist while you sleeping?"

Julie shrugged.

She didn't want him to know that she was a prostitute. Feargal nodded at Costigan, who turned on the lights and produced the sketch of the suspect from inside his jacket. It had been folded in half, and the crease ran across the suspect's face.

"You still go over the house?" Julie asked, ignoring Costigan.

Feargal shook his head.

"Not for a while now. Different lives, different circles." Feargal paused. He thought he knew the answer, but he asked anyway. "You?"

She shook her head. "Just the once…and only her…when I dropped off…"

Her kid. Jesus. How could he have forgotten?

"You and my dad were pretty close back then, right?" she asked. "Pinochle, beer, and loud classic rock."

"We were all friends. I don't think your dad was close to anyone."

She stubbed her cigarette out on the night stand.

"I should have talked to you back then."

"You did. Remember, we talked about throwing a screwball when you started playing—"

"That's not what I meant."

Feargal knew what she meant.

He remembered the skittish preteen always sitting on the stairs, watching them drink and play cards when he went over to John and Adeline's—only at the time, he thought she was just intensely shy, not scared, even though all it took sometimes was saying hi to send her to running to her room. But for whatever reason, Julie eventually took to him, and soon she would scamper down the steps whenever he arrived, skirting the other adults, often already in her pajamas, and he'd pretend to lose the hand-slap game or to be scared when she put her little plastic spider on his leg, and he'd always slip her pretzels while he played cards with the grown-ups. When she spoke, little Julie always had a lot to say, and Feargal paid attention to every word—not only because no one else did, but because the opinionated, clever girl that surfaced whenever she was comfortable (which wasn't often) reminded him of his sisters, a brace of kind, funny women who, he was sure, woke up talking. The kid never warmed to anyone else at these gatherings; if anything, she became shyer, suspicious even, as she progressed through grade school, and she started clinging to Uncle Feargal longer than was necessary when she had to go to bed.

Around the time he got his detective's shield, the tone of the McIntyre house changed. John started acting strange—often he was extremely hostile, at other times he would become silent in an unsettling way—and he grew secretive. Adeline's alcohol intake increased, and she was frequently blotto when he arrived. Most disturbing, Julie's pajamas became inappropriate nighties. Feargal ended up being the only member of the crowd that still went over there on Friday nights. Everyone else stayed away. He didn't know why he kept going. Misplaced loyalty perhaps. They didn't even play cards anymore. Adeline boozed it up and John crept around his own house like Dwight Fyre in the *Frankenstein* movies. Julie was always out, sometimes not coming in until way past curfew, and when she was there, she rarely emerged from her room. The talkative little girl had become a brooding, gloomy teen who showed signs of cutting herself. In retrospect, her demeanor was too saturnine to be passed off as just a pubescent phase, but that was exactly what he thought at the time. It didn't occur to him until later that the reason he still went over there was to check on Julie—and keep tabs on John. During her sophomore year at Hoskins High, Julie stopped talking—to anyone—then soon ran away.

And he still kept going to the McIntyres' place but not as often; he would only stop by every couple of weeks. On the drive over, he'd always ask himself: why? He didn't feel sorry for them. At first John was petulant and indignant when Julie ran away (Feargal thought he acted like something had been taken from him), but then he just grew apathetic. Adeline spouted crocodile tears that soon dried up after her fourth or fifth highball or toddy. The last time he was there, she was drunk but lucid, and she begged Feargal to look for Julie, and he did, but she must have been keeping low or else she'd left Mondauk

County altogether; maybe she'd gone down to Philly. By the time he finally found her, it was a year later and she was already one of Foster's girls. (He never bothered to tell her parents that he'd located their daughter and not because she was a hooker, but because he was convinced by then that the McIntyres were poisonous; if Julie wanted to return to their house, Feargal would drive her there himself, but he'd be damned if he'd let them know where she was—and if Julie wanted out of the life, he'd make that happen and find her a safe place to stay, away from Foster *and* her parents.) He didn't approach her; as much as he wanted to talk her into getting off the streets, he felt that his presence might unsettle her, but he didn't know why. It was while watching her try on different faces as she worked the Strip that he realized that what he'd thought was just shyness back then was actually a manifestation of fear. It made him sick to his stomach; it had been so obvious. It was fear that drove the painfully bashful little girl to clutch his leg at bedtime; it was fear that made the talkative munchkin hide under the table during their cards games, nibbling nervously on pretzels; it was fear that set the stage for the moody preteen and the teenage cutter—and he hadn't picked up on any of it until it was too late. That was also when he realized why he didn't approach her: he wouldn't just be a (possibly) pleasant face from an odd past, he'd be a pleasant face that had failed her.

And why had little Julie been so scared anyway?

He stared at the girl on the motel bed, as if the answer was hidden just below the cheap makeup and street grime. When she looked away, he decided to take another run at her. "Julie, did you have a john here tonight? You can be honest with me. We're not looking to bust you."

"So you know."

"Yes, but that's not what we're here for, darling. We're not interested in Foster either. I'm not judging you, and if you *ever* want to talk, I'll make sure I'm available to you. That's a promise. But right now, we're looking for someone. Were you entertaining a client or clients in this room tonight?"

Julie lit another cigarette. Costigan made a face, and she stuck her pierced tongue out at him. "I might have, yeah," she admitted, two jets of smoke issuing from her nostrils. She now looked back at Feargal in a way that made him slightly uncomfortable. She lifted a single finger: one john.

"Okay. Might you recognize the guy in this sketch? I know it's fuzzy, but it's the best we could do."

Julie snatched the sketch from Costigan's fingers.

"This guy?"

She laughed until Feargal wondered if she would ever stop.

"This guy?"

"Yeah, Julie, that guy."

She nodded her head.

"Yeah, he was here tonight. He's the one who gave me the money bracelet. He thought I'd nodded out or something and put it on my wrist. I know my jeans were pulled down some, but he didn't want to do anything, not really. Got me high though. He also left me a little present, but I didn't push off again until after he left. Pretty easy date. Kept me out of the rain, but if I want to make goal, I need to pound the pavement pretty hard the rest of the night."

"This guy? Are you sure, Julie?" Feargal pressed. "This guy in the sketch? Why are you so sure?"

Julie gave him that look again.

"Because it's my father."

Feargal stared past Costigan at the rain-splattered windows and the blinking Hub Motel sign outside. It made sense on a certain level even if his heart didn't want it too. He didn't feel it in his gut, not yet anyway, but his brain was making connections. Did he know it was his daughter? He had to. She was older and harder-looking but easily recognizable. Was John McIntyre the Red Ribbon Killer? Doubtful. The killer, according to the criminal profiler from the FBI, the killer was diligent and meticulous (which suggested a need for control); he was also most likely highly intelligent. Feargal had never known John to be any of these things. The profiler also said that based on the evidence, their guy chose his victims with careful forethought. The murders were ritualistic in nature. Randomness would go against his fastidiousness. The only evidence of forethought he'd ever seen in John was his crude blueprint for what appeared to be a shed with a basement or a bomb shelter. But that didn't mean that John couldn't be guilty of other crimes, crimes against a child, and Feargal was more than happy to investigate. If there was anything there, he'd nail his ass to the wall. Once he had him cold, he'd hand his investigation over to the sex crimes unit. He'd probably take a little heat from Lieutenant Fowler or the chief. It wasn't that he wanted to use the task force's limited budget working a guy who was more than likely not the perp, but this was a chance at redemption: for failing Julie, for not doing right by Lorraine's memory. Of course, Julie was probably still a little high, but he'd rarely seen a more positive identification. So the Red Ribbon Task Force just got a new suspect, and Feargal would have an opportunity to help put John McIntyre behind bars. Julie would have to testify, but there was time enough to work on that.

There are some things in this world, he thought, scarier than little plastic spiders.

"What was it you were playing there?" Feargal asked.

"The Magic Numbers," Julie answered, and she held up the CD cover. "I stay up with all the new bands. Blow this kid over at Disc/Connection and he hooks me up with promos."

He squinted at her. She was trying to shock him, but it was too late. A gratuitous act of fellatio was nothing compared to what he and Paulie had seen.

Julie blushed. "I'm just pulling your leg. The kid at Disc/Connection just likes me is all. I may be a whore but not in real life."

He patted her leg.

"We might need you to come in and answer a few questions. Like I said, you're in no trouble. This will be about someone else's trouble. It'll be *his* trouble. It won't be pleasant, Julie, but I know you can handle it."

She nervously turned her Claddagh ring round and round her finger.

"I knew I should have talked to you back then."

"I wish you would have, Julie, I really do. I wish I'd figured it out."

Now both of them stared out the windows.

"Feargal?"

"Yeah, darling?"

"Do you think each of us is like a raindrop, and we only get one moment to shine? Like some of us get to dazzle light through a window, while others just slide into mud. Do you think that's true, Feargal?"

"I can't rightly say. But I don't believe you've fallen as far you think you have; maybe you just tripped, which means there's a really good chance that your moment just hasn't come yet. But when this is over, I know a good place where you can stay a little bit and get clean, and you won't have to worry about the bill. When you're out, I'll help you find a place that hopefully can be a new home, okay? But first you have to get off the streets for good. Don't worry about Foster; I'll take care of that situation. I know a good organization that can help you find a job, and your past won't be a problem. And once you're settled, I believe there's a little girl who'll be very happy to see you. She might be shy at first, but I think you can understand that. So when you're ready—sooner rather than later, I hope—you get a hold of me, okay? Here's my card. Cell number's on the front, and I wrote my home number on the back. Day or night, Julie. You'll call me soon, right?"

She sniffled and nodded her head. He wished he believed her.

Feargal kissed her forehead and ushered Costigan out. As Feargal was leaving, he stopped and bent down as if he was picking something off the floor.

"Someone must have dropped this," he said. He'd gone to the bank earlier to deposit his check (he didn't trust direct deposit), but he liked to have some walking around cash and to have some money at the house. But he hadn't been home yet.

As he handed her a bank envelope full of twenties and fifties, he said, "Hey, maybe this will help you make goal, so you can stay off the Strip the rest of the night." He was pretty sure it would. "Listen to me, Julie: don't buy dope with this. Just hand it over to whatever goon collects the money. Then go back to your room and rest, maybe order yourself a pizza."

Her hand closed around the envelope, encasing his fingers for a moment.

"Thank you, Uncle Feargal."

He shook his head and resisted an urge to ruffle her hair.

"Just found it on the floor, kid. I was detecting."

"Right."

She smiled and it was nice to see. It looked out of place in this filthy dump.

"Talk soon?"

She nodded, and he shut the door behind him.

The rain hit him instantly and Feargal lifted his face.

"What happened in there, boss?"

"We got a bad guy, Aidan. We got ourselves a genuine flesh and blood bad guy. We're wearing feathers, pal, lots and lots of feathers.

"And Costigan?" The rain was washing away the stale smell of resignation and ruin that permeated the Hub Motel.

"Boss?"

"It's the carotid artery, pal, but I'll leave it out of my report at least. And, look, just grin and bear it back at the station. Everyone reacts differently to their first dead body. Some guys vomit. Avelino passed out. Donaghey vomited *on* the body. So don't be so nervous. If nothing else, I can pretty much guarantee you that most corpses won't sit up and light a Marlboro."

"I just…thank you." Costigan looked crestfallen.

Feargal squeezed the younger man's shoulder and gestured outward through the rain with the other. "Feathers, Costigan. Feathers."

The Dental Hygienist (Part 3)
10:15 p.m.

While he waited for Leah, Daniel read the *Mondauk Common*. There was another piece on the Red Ribbon Killer investigation and the futile efforts of the police. Made him sick. What a joke! The Red Ribbon Killer. Such a wussy name. Why not the Interior Decorator Killer? Of all the cool nicknames—the Zodiac Killer, the Son of Sam, Jack the Ripper—the Red Ribbon Killer didn't make the Top Forty. It didn't even chart. The Rapture Killer. That would be closer to the mark. He Who Raises. That would work, but it might be too blasphemous. But anything was better than the Red Ribbon Killer. He'd kicked it upstairs, but his complaints never received a response. When he'd taken on this assignment, when he began this search, he felt as if he'd been charged with a sacred duty. After years of training, he knew the routine: become someone else, insinuate himself with a chosen few, and make sure he'd be able to follow the signs later. (Clues weren't enough.)

"I'm sorry it took so long," Leah said, as she rushed into the waiting room, looking cute in her raincoat. "I hope that was okay."

"Not a problem at all." He lowered his voice. "Not with Doris to keep me company." Leah giggled conspiratorially. "Time just flew," he lied with a wink. "Bye Doris. See you later."

The old woman never looked up as they left. "Good night. Lock the door."

The rain came down with such force, it smacked the pavement like little explosions. He opened the car door for her and then jogged around to his side. This was going to be so different for him.

He shivered—whether in anticipation or because he was soaked, he didn't know.

"Warminster, right?"

"Right. 7608 Hawthorne. It's that first development past Street Road and 263. Well, actually, it's a little further back, not really in the development, per se, but I'll show you. Thank you so much for this. It's really coming down."

"I'll take Bethlehem across the bridge and pick up Street Road after we breeze through Spring House. Is that okay?"

"Sure. I can show you some back routes from there."

"I know some of my own."

They drove in awkward silence for an eternity until Daniel flipped on the radio.

"License, registration, I ain't got none, but I got a clear conscience 'bout the things that I done."

"Good song, hmmm?" he asked.

"Oh yeah. I love the Boss."

"Good, good."

"Mister state trooper, please don't stop me, please don't stop me, please don't stop me."

"Do you ever think about what happens after you die?" he asked. "I mean, I don't know what your personal beliefs are, but I always wonder about that. It's like the rain. Each drop has its own path down, then it evaporates back up. But the rain sort of evaporates together, whereas we usually go by ourselves."

Leah twisted in her seat and clutched her purse.

"Maybe you got a kid, maybe you got a pretty wife. The only thing that I got's been botherin' me my whole life."

"That's a beautiful analogy, Daniel. I always hope that I'll join my family and friends in—"

"That's my point. How will we *know*? How will we recognize each other? I mean, will we just know that this soul is Aunt Suzy and this soul is that hooker Jamie? Or will we all be just evaporated raindrops, indistinct and indiscernible? Could there be a way for us to find one another? Some signal, some sign, something that will distinguish us from the other evaporated raindrops? These are the questions I struggled with for a long time."

"*Mister state trooper, please don't stop me, please don't stop me, please don't stop me.*"

"You want to turn here."

"I'm going to cut through the woods. I know the back roads of Pennypack like the back of my hand."

She gently poked his shoulder, and something akin to electricity traveled from there down to his toes and back again. No, it wasn't skin to skin, but she wasn't wearing any gloves.

"Ah, you were one of those guys who went neckin' in Little City when you were a kid."

"Not really. The woods to me is just another place to think, Leah. Especially after dark. No one's really around. Gives me time to work on the sign. That's what I always need: a place to reflect before I act—a motel room, an alleyway, even a dorm room once."

"The sign?"

"*Hey, somebody out there, listen to my last prayer. Hi, ho, silver oh, deliver me from nowhere.*"

"I'll show you."

Daniel took a side street and about half a block down, turned into Pennypack Woods, pulling the car over to the spot he'd picked out after sabotaging Leah's car. It was a small picnic area off the road, small enough not to warrant any lights. The sign they passed on their way in read, "Picnic Area Closed Sunrise to Sunset." The only light came from the moon and the sparkle of the rain on the windshield.

He turned in his seat towards her. Without warning, she touched his hand with hers. *Skin to skin!* What little doubt he had was erased in an instant. He could feel her energy pouring into him, just like it did every time he raised someone up, but this was more intense. He could smell her so clearly: the sweat on her skin from a day's hard work, the soap she used to scrub her hands, even the end-of-day scent of her underwear. He was ready now. He'd already ditched the license and wallet. His own car was parked not ten feet away.

"Daniel, you're sweet. But I'm married. Happily married. I like being friends with you. I like seeing you when you come in the office, but we can't go out on a date or go parking or anything like that. Just friends, okay? Buddies."

"Buddies," he repeated, and the ribbon was out and around her right wrist and tied off before she appeared to realize it.

" 'Whatsoever ye shall bind on earth—' "

"What's this, Daniel? I can't accept any gifts. I can't…it's…it's a ribbon."

"A red ribbon. So I can find you in heaven when I die. So we can find each other. I'll be wearing one when I transition too. Then when the Rapture comes, we'll rise again. Together. All of us. We'll rise again."

"Daniel, I don't understand. I don't—"

"*Memento mori.*"

He slit her throat in one swift motion. She clutched her neck, and the blood squirted out from between her fingers. She reached for the door handle, but her hand was too slick, and soon she stopped gurgling and slumped forward against the dash, her blood pooling on the floor.

Daniel wiped the steering wheel and the door handles and the radio buttons and the windshield wiper knob. He wiped the windows and the dashboard and many other unnecessary things. He used a Dustbuster to collect any hair or other particles, but he was wearing a wig, so he felt pretty secure. But better safe than sent up the river.

There wasn't any time left to ravage Leah, but since she'd touched him skin to skin, that was enough, that would count as a marriage in heaven. The red ribbon bound them together so they could find each other again but consummation was equally important; it made it real. He tried to quote Matthew 18:18 to Leah, but she interrupted him; they almost always did. " 'Whatsoever ye shall bind on earth shall be bound in heaven.' " If Leah had listened, it would have better explained what was happening, and then she would have seen with clear eyes.

The rain intensified, and Daniel hurried to his car. Inside, he changed his clothes and threw the bloody ones in a trash bag, then double-bagged it and ran out again to put it in the trunk. (There were a couple of old apartment buildings in town with trash incinerators that he frequented at night.) He put on his hooded sweatshirt and ball cap, pulling the hood over the cap. Then he remembered Doris. He hated killing for reasons other than raising up those chosen and bound. But like the guy whose identity he'd assumed (and just discarded), they all had their part to play—except Doris. She was just a loose end. Sure, he was so average-looking, with no distinguishing facial features, that he could blend in anywhere, and he'd been disguised to boot, but a loose end left loose is the hangman's eager noose. He'd have to change again, but he kept spare clothes in the car for just that reason. He'd also have to park a couple of blocks away from the dentist's office; his previous vehicle was currently occupied. And if Doris had already hopped the bus? He'd committed her address to memory after his very first appointment with Leah.

The rain continued steadily as he sat in his car. He thought of his daughter Amanda and his ex-wife and wondered if he'd ever see them again before it was his time—and his time was coming soon. The wind picked up and the rain pelted the car from a new angle. He should be gone by now, he knew, but sometimes he needed a moment after a raising.

Open your fist.

He'd slipped the Claddagh ring from Leah's finger, and it sat in his palm, glistening from the rain. The girl he'd raise next—she would be the last. That girl, a prostitute, also had a Claddagh ring. It was no coincidence. He'd realized that the whore was the beginning of the end when he'd read her tattoos—they'd given him the answers he needed to conceive the sign and begin his quest—and soon she'd be the end before the beginning. That God would bestow such a precious gift upon him while he sinning in a motel room that smelled of desperation and sour milk humbled him and made him resolute. Now he just needed to raise up the tattooed whore. (Then and only then could he a tie a ribbon around his own wrist and open his veins to the Lord.) Of course, the only raising he was capable of was the transition from life to death following a binding (all divinely mandated)—only the Creator was capable to truly raising a soul; Daniel just raised them to a station in death that ensured their eventual elevation.

The resurrection of the dead was the key, he knew. Because the women's deaths had been unnatural by design, making them martyrs of a sort, they'd be among the righteous dead called forth during the Rapture, as was written in Revelation 20:4: "I saw the souls of them that were beheaded for the witness of Jesus…and they lived with Christ a thousand years." He lamented that he didn't have time to remove Leah's head, but there was rarely time for decapitation; it took so darn long. There was no doubt that he had done his duty: he'd bound the women to him and raised them to what would soon be an exalted position when the Lord begins the end. It was all there in 1 Corinthians 15: "It is sown in dishonor; it is raised in glory: it is sown in weakness; it is raised in power." Those words were tattooed on his chest. Tattooed on his penis in tiny letters was the first line from Revelation 20:6: "Blessed and holy is he that hath part in the first resurrection." He'd maintained an erection during the entire inking, never uttering a peep, and the next night he dispatched the tattoo artist, the corpulent Captain Gary, by tearing off his member and stuffing it down his throat; the Captain had seen the message and he'd touched what God had meant only for the women chosen to receive the sign of the red ribbon to touch. At least Captain Gary had worn gloves the entire time; skin to skin was only an experience he shared with the raised once they were bound together.

He clutched Leah's Claddagh ring. He'd find Leah in heaven too. Just like he'd find the twenty-seven other women he'd released. In heaven they would be reunited and they'd laugh and celebrate and leave behind their worldly desires and conflicts.

For now, nestled in their graves, their souls slept, the red ribbons long removed but burned into their spirits, visible only to him, and they awaited the sound of the angels' trumpets.

And they'd rise again.

Oh yes, they'd rise again.

-end-

The Boxing Mirror

"I saw the Good son
On the arms of a Princess
His beginning froze
Under the weight of the sea"

"What was your wife like?"

"She was…she *is* beautiful. Not in the model kind of way, more like the girl next door, I suppose. She has a lack of regard for her looks; physical beauty isn't that important to her—just look at me. She rarely puts on makeup and never needs to. Her eyebrows are always a little unruly, but her skin is soft-looking even from a distance and her hair is as black as a raven's feather. She's the kind of woman you could easily overlook because she's unassuming and earnest. Laura is always poking her nose where it doesn't belong. It's why we don't have kids. Did you know that? Not that I'm in any hurry, although I always looked forward to being a dad someday. But Laura, she had other ideas, ones that didn't leave time or room for having children. So be it. And when she started working for various human rights organizations, finally landing at the Boston Anti-Trafficking Coalition, when she decided to rescue this one particular girl, the one that had written the letter, there was no going back. There was just time for this one kid, this one teenage girl in Philly who'd been forced to work on her back since age twelve. Oh, it was a mess. Drugs, heroin primarily; her keepers, her…pimps had a steady supply, so participation was probably involuntary. She slept in a dirty room with five other girls and had to have all kinds of sex with a slew of people, even get pissed on, to earn money for her keepers. The kid got a letter out to one of the coalitions somehow, and Laura decided to come to Philadelphia. I don't know what she was planning on doing when she got here. She always hated Philly; it's where she grew up. Bad memories, I suppose, but she didn't ever talk about them. Laura had to come here a few times a year, working with a Philadelphia area anti-trafficking group that was tied-in with hers, the same group that contacted her about this girl's letter. I've never been down here before now, not even for a fight. I'm from Boston; that's where we live. But you probably know that. So Laura left for Philadelphia and never came back. At first, I didn't think anything was amiss when she didn't call me; she always had blinders on when she first she dove into a project, but I never heard from her at all. Nothing. There's no way she…how many more questions do I have to answer, detective?"

"It won't be long, I promise. You're doing well. What did you do next?

+

Follow the money. The one person James had met who'd actually listened to him had told him that. Finnerty was a police detective from the Philly suburbs whom he'd met while nursing a beer in Sugar Mom's, a dark bar in the Old City section of Philadelphia. They got to talking and Detective Finnerty said that if Laura had been kidnapped, one of the coalitions or James himself would have heard from the kidnappers already. And if, God forbid, she was dead, Finnerty said that without a body, Laura was just a name on a missing-person report to an overworked police department. Finnerty advised him to hire a private dick but said that if he was determined to go it alone (which he cautioned against doing), then he should follow the money, for there was a good chance that Laura's nosing about had either gotten in the way of business or made somebody think it would.

Finnerty's advice gave him direction. He had traveled down to Philadelphia with Laura's laptop and not much else, hoping against hope for a clue, some sign of her. It had been almost two months since she left, and the trail was probably cold. But after spending weeks in Boston planted next to the telephone with his cell always charged and in his hand, he'd started to come undone until he decided to go look for Laura on his own. He'd spent the first two weeks familiarizing himself with the City of Brotherly Love, asking questions, poking around. He didn't have much to work with; he'd never read the letter himself, and now it was gone, presumably with his wife. The girl, Laura's girl, was Chinese or Chinese-American, and her parents lived in Chinatown, so he spent a lot of time in that section of the city, but there was a language barrier and he didn't know the girl's full name; all he had was Mei, and he wasn't sure if that was a first or last name. (For all he knew, that may have been an alias used by the Philly Coalition, who gave him as little information as possible.) He thought that if he tried to find Mei, he'd find Laura. He didn't have any other plan. The only photograph he had of Mei (which Laura had inexplicably left behind) was a small snapshot of her in happier days when she was much younger; in the blurry background he thought he could make out another child's hand holding a pinwheel. Then he met Finnerty, and he'd left Sugar Mom's with a renewed purpose and a better plan of action: follow the money. He hit the streets with a vengeance, sometimes using his physique to intimidate when necessary. Other times, he'd just stare someone down as he used to do before each bout.

His perseverance paid off. An irritated, stick-thin old man he'd chatted up in Lun Chung Grocery mentioned the Broadway Club. The man spoke English with an effort, and the more James tried to understand, the angrier the old man got until he began to shout. James didn't want to attract any more attention in Chinatown than he already had, so to speed things up, he cornered a stock boy who told him the Broadway was at Thirteenth and Moyamensing in South Philly. So he made his way there, surveilling the Broadway from the Quattro Bar and Grill across the street. According to the papers, the Broadway was a social club and a reputed Mob hangout. He did his research and soon recognized several of the clientele from photographs he'd found online. The Broadway's notoriety didn't look all that reputed.

The Quattro had its share of shady-looking guys with flashy jewelry, and he was able to strike up conversations with a few connected guys; he looked shady himself. The made men who came into the bar generally only talked to each other. He eavesdropped a little but was careful to seem disinterested without being rude. Then came the night he overheard one of them mention the train and another one tell him to shut his lips. "The little pieces belong to our friend up north. Carmine don't approve, but the old man, he says that's the way it is, so that's that." James didn't think they were talking about the El. Even though his research made it seem as if the Philadelphia branch of *La Cosa Nostra* had only a minor interest in prostitution, James felt he was on the right track, even if he was just guessing at the meaning of their jargon. One night when the wiseguys remained across the street, he showed the young girl's photo to the contacts he'd made among the Mob associates, but they were no help—except for one squirrelly fellow who stared too long at the picture before he eventually said, "Looks like one of Foster's girls," but would say no more. Foster didn't sound Italian but perhaps the family name had been changed at Ellis Island à la *Godfather Part II* (or maybe he needed to stop using movies as reference works, James thought). So he continued asking around South Philly, now including Foster's name when he brought out the photograph, but other than one old woman who furtively pointed north, all he encountered were averted eyes and hurried denials of familiarity. No one wanted to talk about anything that could possibly be Mafia-related. Finally he met a low level soldier from Jersey's DeCavalcante crime family outside the First Ward, a private after-hours club at Tenth and Morris. The guy seemed to be hanging outside the place almost every night, so James joined him a few times until the soldier, Joey, took him for a connected guy. "Just hangin' around South Philly till some heat blows over back home," he explained, "and the old man told mine he'd guarantee my safety while I was here." He often sounded disaffected, and one night he told James, "Your guy up north here, I mean no offense, but he went from shylock to skipper like that, and look at me. Runs the train 'cause the old man gave his blessing and New York backed it up; no one can muscle in. Up Elizabeth, we were cut out and just look at me. I used to have a piece of that. That was something." Turned out that once the guy got wound up, he couldn't start stop talking. (James thought the DeCavalcantes better hope the Feds never pick Joey up.) Information kept coming until James had enough to quit South Philly, where he was beginning to attract some attention, and follow the train—the train of girls (some local, many not) that ran through Chinatown and West Philly and Kensington out into the suburbs north of the city. It hadn't been difficult to find the train once he'd identified a few of its regular riders, but when the track appeared to end in the town of Rhawnhurst in Mondauk County, it became a ghost train.

+

"Did you find the whore?"

"I don't know if I would go so far as to call Mei a…prostitute. I mean, she wasn't on the train or wherever she was because she wanted to be, detective."

"I take it back. Poor choice of words, it appears. Were you able to locate this girl?"

"No. When I heard about the train, I thought I had a chance. But I still had just about nothing to go on as far as the young girl was concerned."

"You were grasping at straws."

James thought he heard someone stifle a congested laugh or maybe it was just an odd cough, but he couldn't see anyone else in the room. He couldn't see much of anything for that matter; there was a bright light that seemed to be aimed directly into his eyes. The detective stood on the edge of the light, preventing James from getting a good look at him. Not that it made a difference really. He'd watched enough cop shows to know that because he was the husband, he was automatically a suspect. But the process was time consuming; the clock was ticking and James felt every stroke. Still, the important thing was that the authorities, Philly PD, knew the story now—or at least the parts he told them.

"That's about right. I just had the photograph, which didn't help much 'cause it was all wrinkled like she'd been hiding it in various pockets for years. I guess you have it now. She must have included it in her letter."

"Did the Coalition—either one—hand the letter over to the FBI?"

"Wouldn't you know that already? Wouldn't they share that kind of information with you?" He waited for a response, but the only sound was the hum of the light. He sighed. "I don't know what the coalitions' protocol is. But, no, Laura didn't give it to anybody. Maybe she should have, but when she gets a bug up her—"

"And you've read this letter? I only ask because you seem to be familiar with many of its details."

"Laura just gave me the highlights. That's it."

"I need you to be truthful, Mr. Miller. It's very important that we know everything we're dealing with here. Mark Twain wrote that, 'If you tell the truth, you don't have to remember anything.' "

"Jesus, I didn't read Mei's letter, okay? As far as the coalitions go, they weren't very helpful with me, like I said, so I don't know what they did or didn't—Mark Twain? Look, you and I, we're on the same team. I got no reason to lie. And I'll tell you this: the girl's a blind alley as far as finding Laura."

"Just sucking for air. Yes?"

"I mean, the girl is important as far as what drove Laura to Philadelphia. In the letter—what Laura told me anyway—this Mei wrote that she wanted to get free, get clean, shower off their gunk, go to school, and study writing. That was the part that got to Laura: the girl still had dreams despite everything. The Philly group had requested her help because of her expertise in these matters. The Boston Coalition cautioned her against attempting an extraction solo rather than working with law enforcement. They weren't sure it was the best idea to go walking into the lion's den without some kind of protection, but Laura was sure. That's the kind of person she is. Fearless but smart: Laura believed stealth would be better in this situation than going in with an army. But Mei could be halfway to Timbuktu by now, especially if they know we're looking for her. They could have even killed her."

"They could have killed you but they didn't. Now why do you think that is, Mr. Miller? What game is afoot?"

"Game? I assume I'm on their radar, but I don't have a clue about what they're up to. I think I've hit a wall. I got to Foster's house. Now where do I go from there? Those guys have probably gone to ground already. But I'm sure you'll get further than I did, if you haven't already. What I'm saying is that I couldn't find Mei, but I stumbled on the train. Turns out perverts who like underage girls are a lot easier to find and track. I don't have any proof but—"

"None? No connection between your wife and this train?"

"Just a gut feeling that Laura had discovered it and that was what got her in trouble—with these guys or somebody else. I thought if I found the train, I'd find Laura. But I've hit a dead end, it seems. Follow the train, detective. You should have enough from me to find it."

"So once she got to Philadelphia, you don't know if your wife was in contact with—"

"I have no fucking idea what she did when she got here. What have I been saying? Laura went missing. *Poof*—into thin air. It's not like she left clues behind. I think something happened to her, something bad. I think she was vanished."

"Whatsoever do you mean?"

"I don't remember. I'm so goddamn tired. I just want to lay my head down and go to sleep."

"Completely understandable. You took a hell of a punch."

"Where's Laura? Did you find Laura?"

+

The only evidence he discovered of the train in Rhawnhurst was a service that operated out of a frequently empty yoga studio. The night he dropped by, the desk was manned by a scantily clad young girl, barely sixteen he figured, with track marks and hollowed eyes. When he inquired after Foster, the girl's frail fingers darted beneath the counter, presumably hitting a button, because somewhere below his feet, he heard a muffled buzzer, followed by the sound of heavy footsteps climbing a set of stairs. It was far too early for things to get out of hand; he didn't want to announce his presence anymore than he already had, so he left. He'd learned early in his boxing days that it was not just advantageous to know your opponent inside and out before climbing into the ring, it was absolutely necessary. So he kept poking around.

Three people he encountered in various corner bars in Rhawnhurst called Foster *Mr.* Foster (they weren't the last), and two of them said they thought he lived in the northwestern part of the county, while the third claimed he lived among the people in a row home in the Heights section of Mondauk Proper, the town just to the south. So James moved to Rhawnhurst and rented a room in a boarding house by the train tracks. He knew he would be easy pickings if anyone wanted to find him, but he needed a home base now that he believed he was close—moving from motel to motel was a waste of time—so taking the room seemed like a good idea, and he knew it was an even better one when he saw the full-length mirror hanging on the back of the closet door.

+

Even in high school he'd been an out-fighter, a light middleweight, and by the time he decided to go pro, his amateur record was forty-two and seven. No one had ever turned his lights off, and not one of the decisions in his loss column was unanimous. He was slippery and knew when to create space to land successive jabs, and he also knew when to close the gap to capitalize on an opponent's mistake. Nobody could catch him. Jack Rabbit James they called him when he was an amateur boxer, Irish Jimmy or Coinín, Gaelic for rabbit, when he went pro. He was extremely disciplined, and his weight never exceeded 175. In truth, boxing was the only thing he was good at. After high school, his amateur career at gotten a late start as he spent almost five years trying on different jobs before accepting his calling. His face had seen better days, but it was nowhere near as bad as some of his opponents' mugs, even after the matches he lost. During his short professional career, he fought about four times a year, trying to build a decent record and cultivate a reputation. In the end, when he met Laura, his pro record was twelve and five, and he'd only been knocked out once. His manager wanted to move him up to cruiserweight with an eye on eventually contending as a heavyweight, but the smell of Laura's hair and the clear blue eyes that looked out from beneath those errant bangs made him choose otherwise. What this bright woman, who held an MS in psychology, saw in this unworldly pugilist, he never knew. But she looked right past the scars and the permanent bump on his nose, and he quit boxing before their second date.

+

Rear foot a half-step behind the lead foot, legs shoulder-width apart: the upright stance. Pure muscle memory. Feet pointed inward about fifteen degrees. Right heel off the ground. Jab. Jab. Right cross. Jab. Left hook. Tap the cheek to remind yourself to keep your hands up. Tuck your chin. Lift the lead leg and push with the rear leg: forward motion. Jab. Jab. Left hook. Straight right. Lift the rear leg and push with the lead leg: rearward motion. Feint. Jab to the head. Duck. Cuff. Fade. Bob and weave. Parry. Rotate the body so that incoming punches slip by. It's all about distance, leverage, and timing. Right hook. Jab to the body. Protect the chin with the right hand. Low guard. Mixed guard. Tap the cheek. Overhand right. Bolo punch. Rear foot a half-step behind the lead foot, legs shoulder-width apart. Jab. Jab. Right cross. Jab. Left hook. Jab. Jab. Uppercut.

+

James stepped back from the mirror. Sweat ran down his naked torso in rivulets. The band of his underwear was soaked. Good to stay in practice; good to stay in shape. He was getting closer. It was almost time for striking instead of chasing.

That morning he'd found Foster. Every a.m., a couple of newspapers were tossed on the front stoop of the boarding house. As was his habit, James woke early to go for a run, and when he came back, he took the local paper, the *Mondauk Common*, up to his room as he usually did, nodding first to the skeleton-thin man who waited in a cobwebby corner by the wall of mail boxes for James to bring the paper back down. That morning, as he sipped his coffee and opened the *Common*, there below the fold: a photograph of a man descending court house steps. (He appeared, in the somewhat fuzzy picture, to have white hair). He was accompanied by a round-faced man, who was identified in the caption as his lawyer. The attorney's face was turned to the side and his mouth was open, as if talking to the reporters that James imagined lined their path, while a slight smile played on the white-haired man's lips. *Foster Evades RICO Charges; Grand Jury Declines to Indict.* Foster. *Mr.* Foster. Mr. Foster of Anchor Hop, Mondauk County, according to the paper. James quickly scanned the article, then consulted his map. Anchor Hop was to the northwest, near Neshaminy Creek. He flipped open Laura's laptop. It was a rich man's town, sheltered by Pennypack Woods on one side and the Neshaminy on the other. Not densely populated. Houses generally starting at $450,000, and those were shacks. From his research, James already knew of Foster's "alleged" Mob affiliation. Now he had a face and a place.

He cruised through the folders and photos on Laura's laptop in what had become part of his daily routine, as if revisiting them would offer a clue to her whereabouts that he'd missed before. He was ready to box the mirror again, let loose a few jabs of bottled aggression; he just needed to loosen his muscles and tendons first. But in Laura's laptop, when he selected "show hidden files and folders," which he'd never thought to do before, he discovered a folder named "Philly Suburbs Relocation." In it was a file named "F." He opened it.

+

Dear Mr. Foster,

I used to think that you wouldn't remember me. Being just one of how many young girls in your stable, how could you? But I think you do. You have me to thank for the scar on your right hand from where I bit you, almost down to the bone. Does that help jolt your memory? I was young and hungry and had just run away from home for no discernible reason other than I wanted to show my father that I was as strong as he was. And I was wrong. He never stopped looking for me; he continued long after I had given up hope of ever being found, let alone of waking up alive on any given morning. During the five years that I was in your "employ," I must have fucked or blown or worse over a hundred men, some old enough to be my grandfather. I was beaten when I refused to do anal and starved when I wouldn't swallow. I was forced to take narcotics until I was strung out. I was told I was one of Foster's girls and Foster's girls never left his "train" alive. Trash bags, in pieces, we were told. But even though you were already on your way to being a capo, it wasn't just *your* train back then, was it? Before you became sole conductor, you had to lend us out to be abused in New Jersey and New York, for which I am sure you received a piece. I heard that when a client in Jersey lit Lucy on fire for his amusement, you were compensated for lost potential earnings.

You were my father figure, you white-haired God, and we feared you, and you fucked us too. You fucked me until I bit your hand. Then you stopped speaking to me, and it was simultaneously like being denied the voice of God and being able to hear my own voice for the first time in years. I was told by my handler that my days were numbered and in the single digits at that. Soon my father's people (he's a judge, you remember) found me and broke me out, and I left behind all my friends, all the other beaten and burnt and violated underage girls.

I begged my father not to bring charges. I was ashamed and terrified of what I imagined your retribution would be. (It was said that you were protected from on high—by which I don't mean your boss.) My father honored my request without question. (When I initially returned, he was as afraid of me as I still was of you.) The authorities stood down (which had an unfortunate side effect: there would be no attempted rescue of my friends). Besides, the testimony of one young girl wasn't going to bring you down, just some of your flunkies. I was no threat to the human trafficking aspect of your operation. But I swore I would someday help find and set free as many of the girls on the train as possible, as well as children in similar situations elsewhere—which is what I do now. None of the anti-trafficking groups are looking to take on the Mob—although if charges come about because of the work we're involved in, so be it, but we are more concerned with extracting the girls (and boys) than doing the job of the Organized Crime Task Force. I'm not trying to catch you, Mr. Foster; I'm trying to free what you've caught.

Thus, so far, I have left you alone. The group I currently work for is networked with the Polaris Project and the NHTRC, and I've developed a close relationship with a like-minded group in Philadelphia, so I'm able to stay involved with trafficking matters in the area; at times, when my help is requested, I work closely with the city or county police (and occasionally the FBI). Nothing from any case that I have worked has blown your way. But winds have a tendency to shift. Now, Mr. Foster, I need you to find and release (if she's in your stable and I believe she is) a young Chinese-American girl named Jiao Dongmei—beautiful winter plum. Her parents have spared no expense as far as private investigators go to no avail, and they are not wealthy people. Local authorities appear to have exhausted their efforts. The Philadelphia Rescue and Restore Coalition are letting me spearhead the effort to free Jiao, and I've kept the mission off the radar—for now. This isn't about you or your regime; it's about the girl. But the Feds are sniffing around, still trying to build their RICO case, and with them comes considerable heat, some of which, I am sure, you are already experiencing; I have no doubt even the slightest tick in degrees would be unwelcome.

Recent information has come to our attention that Jiao Dongmei was seen in one of your brothels in the Badlands, and there was another sighting of her in West Oak Lane. That's convincing enough for me, Mr. Foster. I know the local circuit well, and it appears that nothing has changed.

Any information leading to the recovery of young Jiao Dongmei—alive—would be dealt with in a most discrete manner, far from the prying eyes of law enforcement. It would be less costly to lose one girl than to have the entire train shut down, even for a little while. This is a chance at redemption, however momentary, Mr. Foster, for me and for you.

I pray you will make the right decision,

Laura Katherine Miller, née Colville

+

It had taken a good workout in front of the mirror to erase the image of his wife fucking or sucking off a hundred guys. The thought, however, that Laura hadn't trusted him enough to tell him about this simultaneously destructive and formative part of her past sat hard in his stomach, where it was trapped after spreading like a disease through his body. He almost removed his wedding band in the shower, but in the end he figured everyone had secrets (he certainly had his share), and they usually had them for good reasons—Laura obviously did. (He could only claim self-preservation.) Most of the time those secrets were best left buried. It went without saying that this explained Laura's stubborn insistence that she toil for human rights groups rather than finish her doctorate and go into practice for herself or maybe teach or conduct research at a university.

Still—a hundred cocks or more?

He pushed the thought back through the ropes where hopefully, without negative emotions to stoke it, it would wither and die. He cleared his mind of all except the basics.

Rear foot a half-step behind the lead foot, legs shoulder-width apart.

He needed the absolute concentration he'd always been able to attain before stepping into the ring if he was to find his wife. Without a doubt it was this Mr. Foster that held Laura against her will. The letter sealed it for James. If the boxing mirror taught him anything it was that the enemy never disappeared; he was always right in front of you, waiting for an opportunity.

Jab. Jab. An out-fighter's weapons of choice: lightning fast jabs, short, straight blows thrown from the guard position without hesitation, for hesitation telegraphs intent {maintain the gap}, but speed is not power and each jab requires a slight clockwise rotation of the hips and torso {add a half-step for more power} while the glove rotates ninety degrees, becoming horizontal upon landing: the snap. Speed is not power; power is force, and force is acceleration times mass.

There was strategy and there was muscle memory, but boxing began with and built upon some basic theories, which his first trainer, Father McAuliffe, a retired seminary professor, had told him he should mentally visualize until each exercise and the nuance of every maneuver became a mantra—repeated throughout the day until the practice became "praying without ceasing." It was Father Mac who stressed the use of the boxing mirror to "see without looking."

Jab. Jab. As the punch is completed, the lead shoulder is brought up to guard the chin while the rear hand protects the jaw {angular head movements} but as this maneuver leaves an opening for a counterpunch, after impact the jab hand quickly resumes a guard position, the body moving laterally rather than backwards {tap your cheek}, for every defensive move must set up a fresh attack.

Irish Jimmy was an out-fighter, so he'd maintained his distance thus far, using long-range jabs to chip away at the layers between him and Foster. He just had to remember the goal was bringing Laura home not laying Foster out. A win by decision, every out-fighter knew, was a win by any other name; sometimes it was better to wear down opponents and out-think them rather than always go for the less-than-reliable knockout punch.

One-two combination.

So Mei was Jiao Dongmei. While he'd never succeeded in finding her, she had led him to where he had to go.

He had the directions to Anchor Hop; he had the resolve. Now he just needed to climb into the ring.

He removed Laura's hard drive and smashed it with a hammer, disposing of the pieces down the sewer.

+

"And how did you find Mr. Foster's house once you were in town?"

"God, you're still here? I'm so fucking exhausted. I think I dozed off for a second there. You're probably used to it, but this room has a very musty smell."

"I'll repeat the question."

"I heard you, I heard you. Once I got to Anchor Hop, it wasn't that difficult. I took a day or so to get the lay of the land, then I just started asking for info at the post office and at mom and pop shops. Who would know better, I thought. But no clerks or proprietors would speak to me, but finally a few locals who'd overheard me took me aside and pointed me in the right direction, probably because my busted face makes me look like one of Foster's thugs, even though I'm obviously Irish-looking. The big, dark blue house on the bluffs, they said, the one that overlooks the Neshaminy—which seems more like a small river rather than a creek. Probably a good place to get rid of bodies in a hurry. Swift current. The house is just a few miles south of the watershed, where the body of a badly decomposed man was discovered last summer by a couple of hikers. Otherwise, it's a peaceful, fairly uneventful town. Foster's place is pretty secured, with the bluffs towering over the shore on one side and Pennypack Woods surrounding the rest of the property, from the fire road to the top edge of the cliffs. The fire road is the only passage to the house—unless you take my way or decide to muscle through Pennypack, which is especially dense for miles in pretty much any direction. The other capos in the Philly Mob have unassuming houses; one even lives in a row home in South Philly. But not Foster. His house, it's called Ravenwood. Very Poe, right? 'The Raven'? I looked it up. 'Darkness there, and nothing more.' "

"You're quoting Poe to me?"

"That's for the Mark Twain. But it's appropriate, no?"

"All very interesting, Mr. Miller, this travelogue and recitation, however—"

"I figured there was no time like the present, and after casing the area, I parked my car about a half mile away and hopped a couple of fences to reach the shoreline. It was a hell of a climb up the bluffs. Couple of scary moments, I can tell you. When I reached the top, I crossed an enormous yard, passing a fancy pool filled with leaves, and made my way to a stone porch. I peeked through the windows into what appeared to be a sunroom. All the lights were out in that part of the house. The sun had just gone down, and I'd dropped my flashlight on the climb up. But I was there, and I wasn't going back; the bell had rung and it was then or never. I checked the gun I'd bought on the street in Philly—boxer or not, I wasn't going to bring just my punch combinations to a mobster's house. The Feds reckoned Foster to be high up in the Philly organization, a caporegime, a captain, so I figured he'd have a couple of soldiers around. Still, I stuck the gun behind my back in the waistband of my pants; I didn't want to kill anyone if I didn't have to—at least not yet. I just wanted my wife back. The door to the sunroom was open, so I turned my hands into fists, and walked right the hell in."

+

James smelled Old Spice before he heard the voice.

"Mr. Miller. How good to see you."

The lights in the sunroom came on, and James froze (in the upright stance) except for his blinking eyes. The white-haired man stood maybe twenty feet away, sipping from an ornate mug.

"Tic-Tac and Ox: would you please escort the champ to his basement quarters?"

James started for the gun, but the two men were already crossing the room before he could reach it.

It took less than a minute.

Lift the lead leg and push with the rear leg. Jab. Jab. Right cross. Keep moving. Jab. Feint to the body. Left hook to the head. Crab guard. Jab. Jab. Uppercut. There it is. Straight right.

Tic-Tac, a squat man with crossed eyes, was out cold, his eyes probably straightened. James knew Ox was going to be a problem. Ox weighed three-fifty easy and looked immovable. Of course, the bigger they are, the harder they—

James picked himself off the ground. He could feel his left cheek swelling up to the size of a grapefruit. He had to keep moving and maintain the distance.

Bob and weave. Slip. Fade. One-two combo. Time for the hay—

James was down again, and he was having a hard time seeing out of his left eye. He cursed himself. He'd telegraphed the haymaker.

"It is so much easier if you do not fight it, Mr. Miller," Foster said. "Pugilism is the sweet science, but in any science, you need to be aware of the constant, which in your former profession is that, in time, everyone loses. There's always someone with a longer reach or a better inside game. For instance, in our situation, there will come a time when the amusement has been exhausted, after which, Ox here has been instructed to shoot you—preferably in the face. Now I would hate to do that in my sunroom, and honestly, I would hate to have you shot period, Mr. Miller. We have been expecting you, yes? We've been very much looking forward to your visit. You and I have much to talk over. The final bell may have rung for this bout, but the games have just begun. Ox, take his pistol and turn his lights off."

+

James thought of a dream he'd had a couple of years before. In the dream, he couldn't find Laura. She wasn't at work, she wasn't at home, she wasn't at the law library. Then he realized she was buried in the backyard. Desperate, he stuck a piece of plastic tubing in the earth for air, and he dug and dug and clawed at the dirt, but he could never reach her.

He wondered if he was dreaming now.

If so, he hoped he wasn't narrating his dream out loud.

Because it felt like he was. It felt like his guard was down.

+

When he awoke (or regained consciousness), he was in a police station—at least he thought it was a police station. The cops or the Feds must have raided Foster's house on the bluffs. Ravenwood. He was in an interrogation room that was dark except for a single intensely bright light that appeared to illuminate only the spot where he sat. There was a large, beat up-looking table and some mismatched chairs. (His chair defined uncomfortable.) He could make out very little of the surrounding area, but he could see a camera mounted in one corner. He wasn't handcuffed but he no longer had his gun. His face throbbed. He'd heard of fighter's who'd been KO'd and had temporarily lost their sense of taste or of smell. James thought something similar was happening to him, but it manifested itself differently: he could smell, but the aromas and odors were very faint and quite jumbled: sage and cinnamon and other spices on top of something moldy, damp, and decaying. When the detective entered, he brought with him two Advils and a towel packed with ice. The detective's right hand had two almost matching semi-circular scars. In the glaring light, James was unable to make out his face, but he seemed friendly enough, concerned, though occasionally brusque and slightly impatient. Still, James figured there'd been some sort of trouble. Had he killed Tic-Tac? Or Foster maybe? Even so, this had to be just a formality. The gangsters were the bad guys after all. The important thing was this: where was Laura?

"Comfortable, Mr. Miller?"

He gently laughed. "Except for the light in my eyes and this hard-ass chair?"

"Beverage? Water, tea, something stronger?"

"No, I'm okay, detective."

"Detective. Good, good. Let us begin."

"Thank God I came to here," James said; he could have ended up in pieces, stuffed into Hefty bags and dropped into the Neshaminy.

"Thank God indeed, Mr. Miller. But we have a lot of ground to cover, so let us begin, shall we? Let's start with the events that led you to breach Mr. Foster's house."

+

They talked and James told him about just about everything—except he didn't mention Laura's letter to Foster. Something made him hold back his knowledge of its existence and his familiarity with the contents, including Mei's real name. As his sense of smell returned, his wariness grew, but he felt that his brain was still too scrambled to explain why; it was working overtime trying to process the scents. After a while, he just wanted to go to sleep right there in the interrogation room. He hoped he didn't have a concussion.

"Where's Laura? Did you find Laura?" he slurred. "Am I being charged with something?"

The hand with the dental x-ray-like scars reached out of the gloom and patted his arm.

"You need to conserve your energy, champ."

The light that had been shining in his eyes went out.

After a disorienting number of seconds, overhead lights were switched on and James blinked, but he knew now whose face would materialize once his eyes adjusted. Foster sat across from him wearing a cream-colored turtleneck, his hair whiter than the lights, his face clean-shaven, Old Spice liberally applied. They were in a basement whose mustiness battled with the cologne for supremacy. It had a dirt floor and little else besides the table and three chairs, the third of which was on his left. James had no idea if they were still in Ravenwood. He became instantly alert and was on his feet in the orthodox stance in seconds—until he used his peripheral vision to take in his surroundings, and there was Ox and a fully recovered Tic-Tac. (A bruised nose with bloody tissues stuffed into his nostrils and a somewhat swollen cheek were the only evidence that James had ever laid the short, thick man out; he looked like he'd been in nothing more than a schoolyard scrap; these were tough motherfuckers.) They moved behind Foster, one on either side, both brandishing firearms, Ox a semiautomatic pistol and Tic-Tac a revolver. James sat back down. The rest of the basement was dark. The section they were in had cameras in *every* corner.

Think, James, think, he whispered to himself. No—don't think. Use instinct. Follow your feet, not your head. He started to rise again. He needed to at least be in position.

Rear foot a half-step behind the lead foot, legs shoulder-width apart.

"Mr. Miller, you are thinking aloud," Foster said. "Just as a courtesy."

Had they drugged him while he was out?

"Fuck you. Where's Laura?"

"Little Katydid? She is snug as a bug in a rug, Mr. Miller, I assure you."

Tic-Tac issued a congested snicker.

"I want to see her."

"She is closer than you think."

"Then bring her out, cocksucker."

Foster gestured with his hands for James to fully return to his seat, and he did. The lights felt extremely hot, and the smell of cologne was stifling but not strong enough to fully mask the dank, fetid smell of the basement. James thought he would either pass out or throw up or both. "Feet not head, lad," Father Mac had told him. "There'll be time enough for the head. Just enough time, as it turns out. But you can't very well strategize when you're off your feet, can you?" It was a lesson in grounding. To be off his feet was to be out of position, and a properly trained boxer only fell out of position and ignored the basic theories when he was lost in his head and off his breath or if he allowed himself to be overwhelmed by emotion. The boxing mirror wasn't for refining or checking position; it was for looking two moves ahead, which could only be accomplished if he initially put his feet before his head. So beneath the table, James placed his feet in toe-heel alignment, shoulder-width apart, relaxing his hips as best he could from his seat—he had to work with the hand he'd been dealt—and the nausea and light-headedness passed as his feet prepared the way for his head.

"Are you a betting man, Mr. Miller? Let me save you the embarrassment of a response, verbal or otherwise. I know who you are. I know your secrets, your vices. There doesn't seem to be a type of gambling that you don't indulge in, except maybe nickel slots. That's how you got into such a hole, isn't it, one that led you to your friendly neighborhood loan shark? You needed to cover your gambling losses, and you went from a hole to a pit. Then you were scrambling each week to make your loan payment, and this was the situation when you were approached with a way out of this mess, so you bet on boxing, did you not? Specifically, you bet on your own matches—two of them—with more money than I know you had, money fronted by your new sponsors: Genovese *cafoni*, in case you were wondering who was pulling your strings."

James forced himself to unclench his jaw.

"They saw a mark, someone who *needed* to make extra cash and came at you with a small proposal for your next bout. Just a one fight deal, they said, right? To prove to you they could come through and that they had your best interest at heart, they clued you in to a couple of sure things, fronted some cash for you to play with, *and* "offered" to manage it for you, which was nice of them. They got a couple of beards to place your bets, spreading your action by playing different books—including mine incidentally—and they made you a little money at first. That's called the Convincer: they showed you that they could make you some dough, so their proposal, which promised to be more lucrative, as long as you came through, would seem more viable and they would appear less threatening. But because you're Southie trash, those Wonder Bread wops, the Patriarcas, hold an interest in you, so New York should never have approached you without asking permission; however, that was the Patriarca family's problem. But the Genoveses shouldn't have played with the money line, and that was my problem, and they should never have fucked with my fix, not in South Jersey, and that became their problem. Your friends were dealt with accordingly. It's safe to say that the WBC and the authorities were more understanding or more willing to turn their heads than I was. Sometimes when you stick your nose where it doesn't belong, you're no longer in possession of it when you go to take it out."

James could feel his testicles contract. He was played by a Genovese crew? The Boston faction of the Patriarca family had a stake in him?

"For your next bout—against Tyrell Mosley, an up-and-coming buck—they tickled your balls with an over/under bet, a grinder favorite: merely predict if the fight will last shorter or longer than the number of rounds posted by the sports book. You bet on your own match—through them—and took the under, as they advised, which was giving better odds. Now all you had to do was finish the contest in less than seven and half rounds but carry him for a few 'cause they had a prop bet for the whole thing being over in the sixth. Suddenly you developed an uncanny ability to switch styles and knock that eggplant out in time. It was a neat trick; you'd always seemed content to win by decision, a real out-boxer. Nothing wrong with what you did, going for the quick buck. However, you played a risky game; that fronted money could have become another loan real quick, with the meter running from the word go, if you'd slipped up and gone over or even just missed the desired round. But you didn't and you were hungry for more, so hungry, in fact, that you were probably ready to agree to just about anything presented to you. Such is the lure of money: its pull is stronger than that of pussy; you'll never run out of pussy, but there's only so much money. You didn't hit it rich with the Mosley fight, but you didn't have to lay anything out either; you were probably flush even after covering your nut, plenty left over for gambling. So you were either too desperate or too stupid to see their play. Your friends were just biding their time, but they didn't have to wait long. You may have been happy as a dog in shit with your pile of shekels, but it was pocket change, and these Genovese *coglioni* weren't looking for chickenfeed. When your next fight was announced, you were the heavy favorite. The opening line had you at -2500 and your opponent at +800. Naturally, the line would be adjusted over time, but the initial numbers were indicative of just how favored you were. And like that, the game changed and the 'question' was put to you, the one that had been in your new friends' back pockets since day one. After all the foreplay, they were going to fuck you in the limo outside of the prom and leave you holding your soiled panties. And what did you do? You spread your legs and gave them what they wanted, pride be damned. But I wonder: did you feel a twinge of guilt, a dollop of shame?"

If James had been a pawn and Foster had handled his beef with the New York gangsters, what was the point of all this? To humiliate him? That had already been accomplished in the sunroom. And what did this have to do with Laura? But Foster was enjoying himself, gesticulating as if he was holding court, not verbosely annoying a captive audience of one.

"But all that debt! How could you not go through with it? So what if you had to dissemble, feign, pretend to insure an outcome so you could bag the big score instead of chase it? Rent and utilities don't pay themselves, and there was that pressing loan to consider, three points on top of the vig, according to my associate in Boston— who could blame you? Who doesn't want to find a way out from under? As I'm sure they told you, the Genoveses were planning on betting heavy on the underdog as late as possible so they could get the best odds. Included among the wagers they'd place would be bets made on your behalf using the generous amount they said they would front you. I'm betting they also convinced you to hand over the unused portion of your recent winnings, which they said you'd be better off using to invest in this scheme than simply giving it your local bookie. A big payoff, like the one dangled before you, could pay off your marker. As if to underscore this point, it appears that they stopped feeding you sure things.

"Alas, your final exhibition in South Jersey was transparent and clumsy—but effective as far as the Genovese crew was concerned. The only thing you got out of it was a big fat headache; what you'd believed were your winnings, you found, weren't yours to collect. If you had not met our Katydid—your Laura Katherine—and quit boxing, as your story goes, the WBC and the other boxing organizations would have had no choice but to ban you, not just for your, ahh, performance, shall we say, during the night in question but because of the known 'element' it exposed to outside eyes, for there were whispers, champ, almost immediately. The loud kind. The kind that makes the press *and* the authorities take notice and review footage. The latter did poke their noses in briefly, but I guess they thought you were too small of a fish to reel in, not even worthy of wearing a wire; even the Feds knew you'd never see your friends again, in part, because you didn't really know who they were and you weren't connected yourself. I'm sure this relieved the boxing organizations who were probably afraid that if the Feds had landed you, they would have found more than just a sad, debt-riddled palooka at the end of their line. So if you had not hung up your gloves, they would have taken them from you. All this is true, is it not, Mr. Miller?"

James nodded his head. He'd had a little gambling problem which had led to a sizable street loan with an outrageous vigorish. When he could no longer keep up with his payments, he began some questionable associations and started making extremely poor choices that he could still barely own. Father Mac would have called it eating his own tail.

"I never threw a bout."

Foster raised both of his hands in front of him.

"Perish the thought. Never entered our minds, did it, Tic-Tac?"

"Never entered our minds," Tic-Tac affirmed, in between spitting blood on the dirt floor. "Never, ever, swear forever." He grinned a crimson-toothed grin.

At least he'd done more damage to the goon than just swell his cheek a little.

"Not even when you fought Escovar?" Foster asked.

James felt his neck turn crimson and fought it from spreading upward.

"The one where you paid the beaner to hit the canvas, skipper, but this mick, here, beat him to it?" Tic-Tac asked.

Jesus.

Ox giggled. "Beaner." It was the first James had heard the colossus speak; he sounded like a little girl.

Foster spoke to Tic-Tac like a teacher instructing a student. "A necessary expenditure: the bets on Escovar to win became *extremely* heavy in the days leading up to the bout. Surprisingly heavy, if you remember, in the final hours. So we reach out to Mr. Escovar."

Jesus Christ.

"You know how it is, Mr. Miller, and as you are a betting man, I have designed this evening's activities to accommodate your habit. Since your wager is predetermined, as you will see, it will come down to choice. I'm afraid the action is all on our side of the gun. We even have a side bet going on. I have a C-note says you go all Butch and Sundance in Bolivia. Tic-Tac says you're going to suck on the barrel. But gambling is all about choices, isn't it? Choices and on occasion trust. Sometimes, if you're outside of a state-controlled environment, you're also betting that the other side will hold up their end of the bargain. For instance, even after she sent me a most derisive letter, I gave Katydid a choice when she came charging up to Ravenwood looking for the chink girl. You or her. That's what I told her, that's the choice. And you know what your sweet, idealistic Laura Katherine chose? She chose to become Katydid again. Oh, I'm sorry, I can see from your face that you didn't know that she spent part of her youth working for me—on her back or on her knees or on all fours. Of course, I thought she would be a trifle old now for my clientele's taste, but her tits are holding up, for what it's worth. And that ass—*merda!*—I would eat it just to see where the shit comes from. Does that make you angry, Mr. Miller?"

James' hands curled into fists under the table, and he calculated how many steps it would take to tap out Tic-Tac again and deck Foster. His feet were still in position, so it was time to use his head and stay one move ahead of his opponents. But Ox would probably remain difficult to topple, and he would still be holding a pistol.

"Suicidal," Foster said, as if reading his thoughts. "Ox would mow you down before you clocked back that golden fist of yours even once. He's much faster than his size would suggest."

James unclenched. Foster was right. The only way out of here, the only way to rescue Laura, was to buy his time, lie back.

Duck. Turn. Fade.
Bob and weave.

He was an out-fighter, for Christ's sake. Defense, defense…

"…defense," Foster finished.

"Fuck you."

"Maybe. But I doubt it. I'm rarely the one who gets fucked."

"What's this goddamn wager? And what do you mean Laura is a katydid again?"

Foster smiled and his teeth were as white as his hair.

"What I mean, Mr. Miller, is that Laura Katherine took my offer, her body for the little chink's, and she wagered her wares on me honoring the deal. And what do you know—sometimes a loser wins, because true to our word, we dumped the slant-eyed cunt on the Pike where she could hitch her skinny yellow ass back to freedom down in celestial town, and in exchange, Laura is once again my Katydid, as she was those many years ago, on a soiled mattress, legs behind her head, asshole gaping. You know the drill. Only it's more vociferating than stridulating, if you follow, champ. Quite to my surprise, she's already developing a client list. A very small one, true, but it's better than I expected out of the gate. I figured we'd be taking her out behind the barn before too long. My customers are usually inclined towards the pre-or-just-menstruating type or the fallen prom queen, Catholic school girl's uniform optional, but who knew? Middle-aged pussy works the same as new pussy, turns out. Just needs a little Crisco."

James lunged across the table, but Ox had him pinned on top of it in a quick second, and Tic-Tac held a gun to his head. He hadn't waited for his time; he'd let anger get in the way. He knew better than to try to land a roundhouse when he was thinking so much, when his emotions were so clearly gurgling to the top. He'd forgotten the basics.

"Let him go, Ox."

James slumped back into his chair and straightened his shirt. Foster was lying. Laura would never—

"Now about our wager…"

James nodded, buying time.

Duck. Roll. Fade.
Bob and weave.

+

"It's not so much a wager as an experiment in human behavior. You might say that I'm offering you a choice similar to the one I offered Katydid—similar but not the same, as I have no business interest in you: you're not twelve and hairless or a hot piece of mature ass like our still-lovely crusader. Nevertheless, this is an opportunity to lay it all on the line, so to speak, and bet on yourself, so it is a game, however we choose to refer to it. Or you could just say no and Tic-Tac'll turn your lights out now."

"I'm listening."

James could feel his muscles tense; his temples throbbed. Bet, choice, deal, fucking Monopoly—Foster was trying to play with his head, psych him out before the match, nothing more.

"Good, Mr. Miller. I'm glad I have your complete attention because I want you to fully understand the rules."

Foster placed a black revolver on the table.

"Yes, there are bullets in it. Go ahead, pick it up. Tic-Tac and Ox would put one in your brain before you so much as thought about pointing at me. So I am not afraid. Pick it up. Good, good. It's not the gun you arrived with, obviously. That was a pussy gun I wouldn't give my mother. This one is aesthetically pleasing and very accurate."

The revolver was heavy and cold, and James wondered how many murders had been committed with the weapon.

"Eighteen, would you say, Tic-Tac?"

Tic-Tac said nothing as he popped a Tic-Tac into his bleeding mouth.

"Just joshing, Mr. Miller. Pulling your leg. Tickling your sack."

Ox giggled as Tic-Tac took the gun from James' hand and placed it back on the table.

"The wager, Foster? The game?"

"Dispensing with the niceties. Fine, fine. Here's the game. There are only two bullets in that gun. You spin the chamber, put the muzzle in your mouth or against your temple, and pull the trigger. If your brains decorate the wall behind you, if Ox has to go get the lime, then Katydid remains my possession. Prostitution is really a rookie's sport, but a veteran, at the right price point, might attract the meth crowd or frat boys looking for a gang bang. Anything to fill out her book. That is what will happen if you bet on black and it comes up red: she continues in my employ, at least until her contract is terminated, most likely behind a dumpster with a hot cocktail, the needle still in her arm when her husk is discovered.

"But if you pull the trigger and you still have a head—an intact one—and the worst that happened was you soiled your Depends, Katydid will be yours to release into the wild and you can go with her. Two bullets—easy enough, wouldn't you say? And you only have to pull the trigger once. That is choice number one: betting on chance. Show Mr. Miller what is behind curtain number two, Tic-Tac."

The cross-eyed man flicked a switch and a row of lights came on to James' right. He could see nothing but more dirt floor, something half in shadow leaning against the far wall, and some odd trash: a cigarette butt that looked chewed upon; a balled up, partially burned tissue; a straw that was planted halfway into the dirt. (Was it a bendy straw?) And there were more cameras.

"I'm still listening, jagoff."

James felt emboldened. Choice number one was a feint, a classic: punching at the air. It goes like this: punch at an opponent's head, he'll instinctively defend it; punch at his body, he'll do the same. The idea is to punch at the air *next* to his head, drawing his hands away from his face. Foster's Russian roulette was designed to get him to defend his life while something else went down—what, he didn't know yet. And defend himself how? By choosing option number two? He was fairly sure about one thing: *two bullets, my ass.* But he thought if it came down to it (and he was right about there being more bullets in the gun), he could take out at least one of these lowlifes—preferably Foster—before they clipped him. Maybe that was how they expected him to defend his life—by making a suicide move. But that would end the game too early for Foster. After all, the capo had designed this farce purely for his amusement.

"It may not look like much," Foster said, smiling again, "but the beauty of this choice is below the surface."

"I'm all ears."

"I am so glad. I like to call choice number two, Clutching at Straws. It goes like this. You still have the gun. If you can pull the straw out of the ground—"

"*If?* Is the bottom of it stuck in cement or...?"

As soon as the words left his mouth, he knew he'd fallen for another feint. A boxer should always look forward—seeking openings and paying attention to movement but reacting without losing awareness. "A distraction, boyo," Father Mac had told him, "makes you see the forest alright, seconds before you run into a tree."

"Are you quite finished, Mr. Miller? Listening to your thoughts spoken aloud is becoming quite tedious."

Fuck your mother then. Did that thought come out loud and clear?

Father Mac always thought outside of the box, and when James was having a problem with concentration, the priest had taught him Vipassanā meditation. So in Foster's dirt basement, James focused on his breathing, as he'd been taught, in order to look forward and achieve mindfulness—and shut his pie hole.

"I was explaining that if you can pull the straw out of the ground, Tic-Tac and Ox—who'll move back a good twenty feet before the game begins so they're not right on top of you—won't fire a single round until five seconds after the straw is yanked free. Then you can have an old-fashioned shootout with the boys—I'll leave before the proceedings begin. Die and your lovely wife stays where she is—and I guarantee you that she'd prefer sucking strangers' cocks than eating dirt. But if you manage to kill Tic-Tac and Ox, then you go free—and you can take Katydid with you. After you dig her out, of course."

"Dig her out?"

Foster ignored him. James set it aside—for now.

"Think of it like a boxing match, palooka."

"Against two guys, and according to you, with only two rounds."

"Ah, yes, you're an out-fighter. You need more than two rounds to play your game of attrition. But after the sunroom, do you think you have two rounds in you? Or do you really have more?"

Now he wasn't sure at all how much ammunition he had—or if he had any. He was letting Foster's verbal ploys take him off his breath.

"You only have to cock the hammer once if you go for the roulette. As far as the shoot-'em-up portion of the program goes, whether it's my men's weapons or yours, there are only so many bullets in a gun, period, and after that, it is hand-to-hand combat, is it not? So it's funny that you used the word 'rounds' just now. Hard to believe it would come to that at such close range, but your evasive training is just one of the things that makes this choice the more interesting one. In fact, it's the very reason it's so difficult to handicap, but then to do so would take all the fun out of it. What do you say, Mr. Miller? Now that you know the scenarios, are you still willing to wager your life for hers—or would you like us to kill you on the spot? I speak for all of us when I say, I certainly hope it's the former. So if you're still in, champ, what's your game?"

James weighed both choices. There'd be no proof of life, so seeing how he'd landed himself in this basement (and told them *almost* everything to boot), any shot he had at rescuing Laura, however slim, was worth the risk. What else could he do? But what Foster had said a few minutes ago—another feint or...

"What did you mean I have to dig Laura out?"

His head still pounded; he had to work to maintain his awareness.

"That is what the shovel is for, Mr. Miller."

The object leaning against the far wall came into focus.

"A shovel? Is she—?"

It felt as if his heart had dropped into his stomach.

"Oh no, no, she is quite alive, I believe."

James counted his breaths, he checked his position—anything to prevent him from again suicidally diving across the table at the twisted son of a bitch.

"Then where am I digging her out from?"

Foster pointed at the straw.

"From there."

And for the first time, James saw the area of recently disturbed dirt, about five or six feet long, that ended in a low mound with the straw sticking out of one of its slopes. It looked like a hastily dug grave—how had he not noticed it before now? *A distraction, boyo, makes you see the forest alright, seconds before you run into a tree.* Other things came into focus. The dirt under Tic-Tac's fingernails. The dark stains on Ox's trousers. Panic struck his body like a rabbit punch. His throat constricted and his fists readied themselves to do battle.

"You motherfucker..."

His voice was a whistle and his curse died in the stale basement air.

Foster stood up, and Tic-Tac pushed in his chair.

"Your choice, Mr. Miller. I do not know how long she will last under there with only a bendy straw for cold comfort. So, what will it be? A little Russian roulette, where if you put a bullet into your frontal lobe, I'll have the pleasure of putting Katydid out to pasture once the cellulite and the sagging *really* kick in—or a fight to the death with her straw as your flag. I can see why you've come all this way to rescue your ladylove: despite becoming somewhat frumpy, she's still surprisingly tight."

He started to rise but Foster's button men raised their weapons.

"Surely you don't think I'd make this generous offer, even to a trespassing, disgraced never-was like yourself, without personally checking her oil first."

James bit his tongue. Laura couldn't be buried in the dirt, breathing through a straw. That just didn't seem—

"Perhaps you're still a bit discombobulated from getting your bell rung, but what I'm sure you're missing is that with roulette, she lives even if you don't. Perpetually sore maybe, not inclined to sit down after a night's work, but still breathing. Then again, if you beat the odds, then you and Matron Marion, beauty and the boxer, can scamper off to Sherwood Forest or even Beacon Hill scot-free—after we excavate Katydid, that is, and ascertain that she's still breathing. And I'll answer your question before you ask: you can trust me to keep my word because it's my game; I must have some skin in the thing, something to lose—in either game actually—or watching Tic-Tac scrub your blood off the wall would lose all its inherent pleasure."

Foster walked over to the mound and placed a foot on it, bending down to tie his shoe. James was sure the mobsters thought that the pistols aimed at his head were what kept him in his seat during this latest indignity, but he was trying to look forward; his increased heart rate notwithstanding, the stillness that had always settled over him before each bout was returning. "The goal of Vipassanā practice," Father Mac had told him, "is to learn to pay attention—first to yourself, then to everything around you." Thus he kept an eye on the wise guys' movements, ready to react defensively, without losing sight of any opportunities, any openings. Foster brushed the excess dirt from his shoes and walked back to his side of the large table. James could tell that the bastard was taking a lot of pleasure in this, and he guessed that he was not the first person forced to wager his life on an impossible game. He might not even have been the first to play for someone else's life as well.

Foster stared at his watch.

"I wouldn't expect a boxer of your record to go out *Deer Hunter*-style. But that's just fear talking, fear of exiting by your own hand; it may already be at play in your subconscious. Perhaps it will be pride that will prevent you from placing the muzzle against your temple or the barrel in your mouth—there's so much debate as to which is more effective. Or maybe you really are the aggressive cocksucker you appear to be, the kind of antihero who'd rather go down in a blaze of glory than in a muzzle flash of shame, taking Katydid down with you by leaving her in the dirt. If you do choose to play Clutching at Straws and you win the battle, your freedom, and the girl, I'll even throw in the shovel. Minus the excavating tool, it's same end result as spinning a winning cylinder in choice number one, but you get to put up your dukes. And when you're not busy faking a fall, we know you like to punch and dance and pummel; we're well aware of your predilection for smashing and thumping. However, you'd better dispatch the Glimmer Twins here pretty damn quick and get to shoveling. Without the straw to breathe through, Katydid won't last kissing time, especially not with loose dirt collapsing the little hole where the straw had been. So I need a decision, Mr. Miller. Time is wasting, and we are all busy men."

Tic-Tac emitted a muffled chuckle. "Busy bees," he said. "Busy bodies."

Lead fist at eye level, held vertically six inches in front of the face. Jab. Jab. Right cross. Sway. Low guard. Rear fist beside the chin, elbow tucked into the chest. Jab. Left hook. Slip. Tap the cheek. Mixed guard. Lift the lead leg and push with the rear leg. Jab. Jab. Uppercut.

Controlling the pace would be impossible. It would come down to strategy. And defense. He had to maintain the distance.

Duck. Parry. Fade.

Bob and weave.

Father Mac had told him that it was a writer named Pierce Egan in the early nineteenth century who coined the phrase "sweet science" to describe boxing, relating it back to a time when young gentlemen were schooled in the "sciences" of sword fighting, gunplay, and fisticuffs, and Mr. Egan was right: it is, "a branch of knowledge or study [of] a body of facts or truths systematically arranged and showing the operation of general laws," which was the definition of science in his old dictionary. Boxing is a delicate balance between adroit strategies and forethought on one hand and the practical application of brutal violence on the other. It was a science of how to align your feet and your hands and your head to achieve the desired result. Calculating the necessary combinations and anticipating an opponent's move when he climbed into the ring was not all that different from playing chess—except in chess, there was no need to literally take out an opponent or wear him down to nothing before he could get to you.

The only way he would win in the basement was to exploit every aspect of the sweet science.

Russian roulette was a shot in the dark—no pun intended. Yes, Laura would go free if he lived (assuming everything Foster said was true, and he had to believe him; there was nothing else to go on), but he could easily end up being buried in the thick woods of the watershed, a nasty hole in his head. He'd be leaving everything up to chance. In traditional Russian roulette, there was only one bullet in the gun. He had two—or so Foster claimed.

If he pulled the straw, Laura would quickly lose oxygen—if she was even down there and if she was, if she was even alive—but he'd have a fighting chance to get them both out of the basement (even if his firearm skills weren't as sharp as his boxing ones). He'd have to rely on his ability to read the other guy (or other *guys* in this case) and move at a moment's notice, if not staying a beat ahead; he needed to avoid getting caught in a corner (for as they say in chess, a knight on the rim is grim) and balance that strategic defense, which would only get him so far in this situation, with a well-timed, well-executed, savage offense. Wearing down his opponents and winning by decision weren't options with choice number two; he had to go for the KO, then dig Laura out before Foster returned to devise more sadistic events. But applying those aspects of the sweet science presumed that he understood the nature of the game, which he believed he did not. There had to be more to it than had been revealed, and he was sure it was rigged. He was also now beginning to think that the gun was at least halfway loaded, to cover any eventuality: ensure the end result of Russian roulette or spice up the second option, at least briefly, for the pleasure of the master of ceremonies.

"Five seconds *after* I pull the straw. Then Frick and Frack are free to ignore the slaughter rule, correct?"

"Precisely, Mr. Miller."

"Or I take my chances with the grim version of chicken."

He was buying time again, measuring the distance between himself and the mound, discretely lifting up the front of the now vacant chair across from him with his foot—barely half an inch—to estimate its weight. His strategy would only work if the goon squad remained standing on the opposite side of the table but back twenty-odd feet as Foster said they would. As soon as he snatched the straw, he'd have to turn the large table on its side, scramble behind it, and hope the top was thick enough (it was certainly large enough) for a little temporary cover from their initial rounds—it looked like it was. He'd also have to use one of his bullets to shoot out the light switch—maybe his only one, for his thinking had changed again: if Foster put all of his chips on James going for the straw (*I wouldn't expect a boxer of your record to go out* Deer Hunter-*style*), he wouldn't have given him even two bullets. Maybe he'd been partially right all along: choice number one *was* a feint, one designed to get him to defend— and here's where he'd been wrong—his pride, not his life. It was set up to insure he went with the straw game. And the old prick was right: James *was* the aggressive cocksucker who'd rather go down in a hail of bullets than commit suicide, and it made him sick to think he was that predictable.

With the lights shot out, he thought that if he bobbed and weaved from a crouched position behind the table, he could throw a chair their way to cause a little confusion before the Dynamic Duo's eyes grew used to the dark. (Although Foster had made it clear that he would not be in attendance, James knew he would be watching; all those cameras weren't just for show, and more than likely, they had infrared capabilities, something his thugs did not—nor did James, but the darkness wouldn't be a surprise to him.) The chair wouldn't distract Tic-Tac and Ox for long—these guys committed murder for a living—but it might be long enough for him to dart forward and knock Tic-Tac on his ass. Then, if he did have more than a single bullet, he'd put one in the thug's brain. If not, he'd pick up Tic-Tac's revolver to finish the job (if he could find it in the dark) before hightailing it back to the table. This maneuver was contingent upon Ox being at least temporarily unsure which of the dark figures to shoot, especially since he would expect Tic-Tac to be the executioner. Not exactly the sweet science, but the operation required the same dexterity and mental processes. Then there would be two: the boxer and the Ox, who soon enough would start shooting at anything, even his own shadow. Once the lug figured out that his life partner was the one lying on the dirt floor, James hoped that Ox would quickly empty his clip, firing at a dancing out-fighter in the dark, one constantly moving even while crouched behind the table, but if not, he'd aim at the muzzle flashes (if he actually had bullets left or if he'd grabbed Tic-Tac's weapon) and blow a hole through the brute's perpetually perplexed expression. Of course, Ox probably had more than one clip, but before he had time to slam a fresh one home, James would be on him, and he'd land the haymaker of all haymakers. If a woman under duress could lift a car to rescue her child, then surely, James believed, his right fist would be nothing less than possessed, especially once he had the straw. He'd rather knock Tic-Tac and Ox out before killing them; he wanted to feel this battle in his knuckles.

"Boxing requires an economy of motion," Father Mac had said. "Timing is efficiency, accuracy is effectiveness, and opportunity is everything."

He prayed he wasn't thinking out loud again. If he was, the Mafioso's face didn't betray a hint.

"Still undecided?" Foster asked in a dulcet tone that James thought sounded forced. "Let me help you, Mr. Miller. This gun lying before you, this black beauty, holds six bullets. So I'll come clean in the hopes of expediting matters. There are actually *four* bullets in the gun. I know, I know. I wasn't playing straight. Just feeling you out, champ. While it does make choice number one exceedingly more difficult, it also gives you a decent shot with choice number two now, doesn't it?"

He was lying. He could have forced James in a myriad of ways to make any wager or play any game. For that matter, he could have just had him shot in the back of the head after the sunroom scrap and been done with it. But the capo was practically drooling over his machinations; he was having a good time, despite his growing impatience. James already knew that Foster, who didn't have a subtle bone in his wicked body, wanted him to play the straw game (which was beginning to seem more and more absurd), but the depraved fuck also just about sprouted wood whenever he brought up Russian roulette. He got off on it all. But he was lying now: leaving him with two bullets or even four wasn't enough entertainment for the depraved son of a whore; no, the gun was fully loaded, James concluded. Foster couldn't resist. If out of fear of the unknown, he took the pussy way out and went for the roulette, the gangster would have the sick pleasure of watching James sweat it out while spinning a full cylinder, and if he went the way it seemed that Foster knew he would go, he would want James to have a fully loaded gun to face Tic-Tac and Ox; choice number two was the Mob version of a gladiator game.

Jab. Jab.
Fade.
I am brute force and the calculated maneuver.
I am the punch and the evasion.
I am muscle memory and mindfulness.
Jab. Jab.
Slip.

"How about *ten* seconds after I pull the straw? What are five more, fellas? I *am* playing for two lives here, so five seconds for each life."

Quick—his time was about to run out. *I am awareness.* Memorize every detail of the room, note the way Ox leans his considerable weight on his left leg, determine the—

Foster made a slight gesture with his head and Tic-Tac cocked his pistol.

"I grow bored, Mr. Miller," Foster said, tapping his watch. "There's a time to reap and, of course, a time to sow—now is the time to choose, *your* time, before I decide that reaping is more interesting than bantering, which will happen in exactly two minutes. If you don't choose by then, Tic-Tac and Ox will fill you with so many bullets that even your mother wouldn't recognize your face—if your body was ever found. As for our Katydid, although my own tastes run younger, the first thing I'm going to do to her after the boys dig her up is to nail her in the ass—again—before introducing her back into the open market. Lord knows that no one's going to bid to buy her like they do for my little ladybugs and the occasional puppy dog tail, so her customers won't mind a ripped—"

James stood, picked up the gun, and pointed it at Foster in one swift movement. *An economy of motion.*

"What if I just rip through your face instead, Foster?"

The white-haired man looked unconcerned, unflappable even. "Tic-Tac and Ox will still kill you and then pull the straw."

James placed the gun on the table and sat down. Father Mac had taught him, "Feet not head," but James had acted with feet, *no* head. Why hadn't the Neanderthals opened fire the second he'd aimed at their captain? Had Foster predicted this desperate, suicidal move as well and ordered his men in advance to hold back until their boss had his fill? He forced himself back to his breath. He'd missed his opportunity. Who knows what would have happened after he shot Foster, but at least the murdering pedophile would no longer be enjoying pasta braciole at the best restaurants and sipping Manhattans at the club while running a human trafficking ring and a train of underage prostitutes.

Foster smoothed his trousers and ran his hands through his hair several times as if he was primping himself for a date.

"Ah, you'll choose, Irish Jimmy. They all do."

They? He was right: he wasn't the first contestant, and the dirt floor behind Foster seemed to him now to be dotted with low mounds or maybe it was just his mind playing a trick on him, a result of all the adrenaline galloping through his body, for only the areas around the table and Laura's mound were lit; the rest of the basement was dark.

"I'll pull the straw." He was quiet but firm.

"Of course you will," Foster said even more firmly, as Tic-Tac and Ox each handed him a C-note. "I had no doubts."

Foster nodded to Tic-Tac, who walked to the wall switch and flicked on the rest of the lights. They had not been figments of his imagination: several small mounds were spread across the large basement. There were cameras mounted everywhere.

"Now, if you'll excuse me, I'm going to retire upstairs to enjoy a late dinner with my family. My youngest son just received his report card. First honors. We couldn't be prouder. But don't worry: the basement is completely soundproof. If you win, you and your beloved, after she shakes off the dead soil, can exit via the back door and we shall never meet again—as long as Katydid keeps her antennae attuned to something other than my business. Oh, and you'll need to find some way to cover her up, for you don't think we buried her still dressed, do you? The other girls always need clothes, and we are not savages, after all."

Foster extended his hand, the one bearing the scar Laura gave him with her teeth. "The pleasure has been all mine, Mr. Miller."

James ignored the gesture. "Let's go. Let's do this."

Foster climbed the stairs, then stopped.

"Saint Jude is the patron saint of the impossible, champ. May I suggest a short prayer. Good night, gentlemen. May the best thug— or thugs—win."

+

James forced himself to continue to look forward rather than stare at the barrels of Tic-Tac and Ox's guns, as Laurel and Hardy moved back the promised twenty feet or so (which didn't any further away). He tried not to think about the Escovar fight and how it had exacerbated the situation at hand. True, Laura had come right up to Foster's door in her hunt for Jiao, but maybe without a dual reason for torture—Laura's perceived insolence and the Escovar match—the caporegime might have just brushed her off (after ascertaining that she wasn't working with the Feds). Instead here they were: him above and her below.

Tic-Tac gestured to the mound.

James stared at the squat man like he would an opponent before a fight.

"Keep your pinky ring on."

So, four bullets in his gun. He didn't relish a gunfight in such a confined space, but it was just another square circle, another boxing ring, which is about as tight a space as he could imagine and one with which he was intimately familiar—and that was how he was going to approach it: merely another match but with the largest purse he'd ever fought for and the biggest downside. Father Mac used to say, "The ring is just big enough for one man." What would the priest say about the kind of boxer he became at the end, the kind who allowed the science to be tainted with dirty money? For he *had* thrown a bout, hadn't he? He'd thrown the very fight that more than likely had made everything worse even before he stepped into the sunroom, for Foster seemed to imply that his book had lost a great deal of money on the Escovar fight. It wouldn't surprise him if the white-haired pimp had kidnapped Laura just to lure James to Ravenwood; he'd sensed an underlying anger when Foster had gone over the events of James' moral decline and his involvement in a criminal enterprise, especially when he discussed the Escovar bout and the Genovese family crew's involvement.

In the seconds he had left before he had to snatch the straw, his brain replayed his downfall, going over it millisecond by millisecond to remind himself how he got there and to convince himself, that although this was an entirely different, even more fucked up situation, this time he knew how to get out. He couldn't help it; it was as if he needed to wallow in defeat before rising in victory over the Mickey and Sylvia of the Mafia set and rescuing Laura.

Love, love is strange (yeah, yeah)
Lots of people take it for a game

His trouble came when three loan payments in a row were late, the last one severely so; he wasn't even sure he'd be able to scrape anything together for the next one. His "loan officer" was understanding to a point, but James was sure his people would approach him about throwing a fight sooner or later. He owed a lot of money. However, it was entirely different group of men who would eventually broach the subject. But first they brought him up to date on his loan—they called it an investment—and even made his next payment (as an advance). Foster was right: they didn't ask him to take a dive right away. Instead, they further ingratiated themselves by staking him and betting a few "guaranteed" winners for him, and James began to think he could get out from under and square his loan (if he didn't blow it all on the upcoming Patriots-Eagles game or at the floating all-night poker game in the West End). Then they suggested what appeared to be (mostly) on the up and up, if somewhat risky for James: finish his upcoming match with Tyrell Mosley at the appropriate time in order to win the over/under. There was no margin of error; he needed to perform as expected and knock Mosley out rather than win by decision, which was his MO. Adding to the pressure, he had to end the fight in the sixth because of a proposition bet. But Father Mac had told him, "Potential is to belief as a forest is to a rainstorm: one cannot exist without the other."

Once you get it
You'll never want to quit (no, no)

He was an out-fighter through and through; he was too tall to be an in-fighter, a swarmer, and he didn't have the punching power of a slugger or brawler. But he'd been well-trained and found he had the ability to adapt the style of a boxer-puncher. The approach of boxer-punchers wasn't that far removed from his own, but they possessed the devastating power of a slugger; it was a hybrid style. Boxer-punchers tended not to be quite as fast on their feet as out-fighters and were more willing to fight at close range like sluggers. They tired out opponents with long-range jabs, as well as an array of combinations executed from the inside, before going for the knockout. That was the major difference in their endgames: like sluggers would, boxer-punchers focused on the KO more often than not, while out-fighters largely won by decision, emphasizing distance and mobility. After some intense training, he internalized the boxer-puncher approach; he even worked on the power of his punch by maximizing the lessons of Father Mac and combining them with those of his current trainer: control the energy flow of every useable part of his body, exhale sharply on each punch, and stay inside his range, no matter what style he was using. The priest had told him, "Moving your whole body one inch, boyo, hits much harder than moving your arm one foot." He thought of the Mosley fight, the whole experience, as a refresher course; in training he'd discovered that he'd become too complacent. Father Mac's lessons resonated with him more than ever—*speed is not power; power is force, and force is acceleration times mass*—and he recovered his mantras.

> *After you've had it (yeah, yeah)*
> *You're in an awful fix*

The night of the fight, he saved the boxer-puncher transformations for those moments when it was strategically advantageous. (It could only be a surprise once.) Mostly, he stuck to his familiar high-speed jabs and his ingrained sense of maintaining distance. Both approaches were designed to wear down the man who didn't belong in the ring. So he played a largely defensive game and was difficult to catch; there were even some chants of Coinín. He laid back when necessary or took successive hits to lure his opponent in and deliver a series of power combinations. But he only threw enough punches to add to the ongoing debilitation before quickly retreating, visions of dollar bills dancing in his head. He wanted to come through not only on the over/under but also on the prop bet; he had a lot riding on this match, even if most of what was riding wasn't his; he needed the dough. He took it to the sixth round. By then, Mosley was good and tuckered (it hadn't taken much), and when the bell rang, James came out like a full-on slugger to put him away.

> *Many people*
> *Don't understand (no, no)*

"Boxing is a mental game," Father Mac had said, "and those that don't know the board don't deserve to approach it. Only a winner gets to knock the king over." There had been a couple of fights that he'd lost to someone who *did* deserve a place on the board. When it was obvious that a guy had figured out his routine before he'd even finished rolling it out, his mouth always tasted like pennies (whether or not it was filled with blood). He used to wonder if that was what fear tasted like, because it always spooked him when someone was easily two moves ahead of him from the get-go. But after the Mosley bout, forget about being spooked—he was about to be castrated by his new backers, and he went to the surgery willingly. It was foolish to believe that the Mosley fight would be it, but the payout was enough to make him cocky and greedy, and being desperate, he was easily taken in, emboldened and encouraged by men he should have known better than to listen to—the kind of men who always hung just outside boxing circles, hustlers and shucksters and men like the professional criminals aligned before him in the basement.

They think loving (yeah, yeah)
Is money in the hand

But all had seemed good and his new friends never asked him to lie down—until it wasn't and they did, as soon as the odds for his next fight were posted. Only one time, they told him. Three points on top of the vig, they reminded him, as if he needed reminding. (That was the day he knew he'd be making payments for years to come—he still made them today, though without Laura's knowledge.) The cock of the walk had been reduced to a dancing monkey. He was to go down—for the first time in his amateur or professional career—in the third against Demián Escovar, a journeyman usually hired to fight up-and-coming prospects to pad their records.

It got strange quickly. Even in the first round, Escovar seemed ready to hit the canvas at the slightest jab, so James barely threw a punch in the second, and when he went down in the third after a weak hook by Escovar (James barely felt it), he tried to ignore the rock that had tumbled into the pit of his stomach and was distressed to find that he no longer heard Father Mac in his head, just the incessant booing of the crowd. In the days that followed, the boos, which continued to echo in his ears, gave way to the whispers Foster had mentioned. Before the whispers became murmurs that became something much louder, his shadowy partners disappeared. Foster would discover their identities anyway.

It never occurred to James that Escovar had been told to lay down and stay down too. Since James had never been KO'd before, it made sense that his fall would have set off bells for someone like Foster, even if the mobster hadn't paid or intimidated Escovar to take a dive in order to offset heavy last minute betting. It didn't help that to everyone else it was painfully apparent that Escovar probably couldn't knock out his own mother.

It wasn't long before the WBC began asking questions, and two Feds even came around talking "criminal conspiracy." James retired because he had to, not because of Laura, as he liked to tell himself and others. Not quite disgraced but definitely tainted, he hung 'em up because he was told it would all go away if he did. Now he was back, facing the kind of scum whose family was no better than the Genoveses or the Patriarcas; like them, they controlled bookies and loan sharks, and their shady crews circled boxing rings, evidenced by the Escovar situation, just as James was sure they haunted stables, floating poker games, and whatever legitimate activity in Atlantic City they could corrupt. He was betting on himself now because he had no other choice. Preacher Roe, a major league pitcher from the '40s, was infamous for his spitball and his uncanny ability to throw the illegal pitch without getting caught—at least not too often. After being thrown out of a game in the second inning, Roe observed that, "Sometimes you eat the bear and sometimes the bear eats you." James knew it was time to find out which it was going to be.

Rear foot a half-step behind the lead foot, legs shoulder-width apart. Bob and weave. Jab. Jab. How to hurt another man without suffering injury himself was all muscle memory, which left plenty of room for strategizing; it was that seemingly incongruous mixture of the sweet and the lethal. *Lead fist held vertically at eye level six inches in front of the face. Jab. Jab. Right cross. Sway. Rear fist beside the chin, elbow tucked into the chest.* He was going to approach this dirt room like he'd always approached the ring, calculating as many moves ahead as he could while striving to draw blood and cause abdominal bruising early and often.

Father Mac had said, "Losers rely on providence rather than their fists. Winners enter the ring knowing they have to fight for it."

James knew he could do this; they were his. He stood up slowly, as the guns were still aimed at him.

"I'm taking the straw now."

Tic-Tac nodded and looked at his watch.

Instead of going directly to the mound, James went around the table as if he were nervous and hesitant. (It was a ruse that Foster would have seen through in seconds, but James knew that Steve and Eydie wouldn't view his behavior as anything out of the ordinary, considering the circumstances.) He held on to the tops of the chairs as if he needed the support during this emotional moment, surreptitiously sliding each one away from the table, enough that they wouldn't impede his turning it over. He knelt on one knee next to the mound, and as he touched the dirt, it hit him like a sucker punch: Laura was buried alive in there. *I'm coming, babe. Just hold on a little longer.* He wasn't surprised at the tears coming down his face, and he could hear Laura standing on their bed, wearing only her underwear, singing Elvis Costello's "Alison" at the top of her lungs after drinking a little too much wine: "*But I heard you let that little friend of mine / take off your party dress!*"

James and Tic-Tac stared at each other for a few seconds. In his peripheral vision, he saw Ox check his magazine before firmly pushing it back into the hand grip.

Always look forward, boyo. Seek openings and pay attention to movement but react without losing awareness of your breath. If you don't know where you are, you can bet your opponent does.

"You fucks," James said as he pulled the straw. "I love you, babe." *I'm sorry.* He held up the straw before sticking it in his shirt pocket.

One…

Was it even possible to survive by breathing through a bendy straw, he thought as he moved back towards the table. It would have to be a pretty shallow hole—this wasn't one of those long novelty straws, and it had been stuck in the side of a mound of displaced—

…two…three…

It was as if someone had pulled the plug on a radio: "Alison" violently stopped mid-verse, and James knew that she wasn't here. The straw in the dirt was a sick hoax, and he'd swallowed it whole. Laura was already dead. Whether she was buried in the watershed or somewhere else didn't matter. She'd been dead the entire time.

…four…five.

He knocked over the table and ducked behind it before aiming for the light switch, but three quick shots forced him back down. His heart thumped to beat the band, and his mouth tasted like pennies. He knew he was a sitting duck, a vulnerable pawn, until he could shoot out the lights; the table wasn't meant to be a shield, just temporary cover, and it was more difficult to move defensively while crouched and ducking than he'd expected. More gunshots—*bob and weave.* The table top held. He sprang out and assumed a kneeling position to shoot motherfucker number one, Tic-Tac, in the kisser.

Click.

He dove back behind the table as bullets busied the air, while others peppered the wood. What rotten luck. The gun wasn't fully loaded after all. (There hadn't been time to check.) So much for his intuitive skills. If Foster had told him the truth and there were really only four bullets, then out of two empty chambers, he'd gotten one. He was sure, though, that if he'd chosen Russian roulette, his luck would have been just as bad after he'd spun the cylinder. His opening gambit was a bust, and he was only alive because of his speed and his still-reliable reflexes. He moved to the right side of the upturned table just as Ox opened fire, but his shots went wide—unbelievable in such a small space. Ox was a made man for other talents obviously. James raised his head for a shot at the behemoth.

Click.

What the fuck?

More fire from the Hardy Boys. He switched back to the left. *Slip. Fade.* He got down on his stomach and rolled over to shoot Tic-Tac's ankles from around the table.

Click.

Jesus fucking Christ.

He covered himself defensively (as if that would help) during the fusillade that followed, but amazingly the tabletop withstood all their bullets, sustaining only minor splinters. Thick goddamn wood, he thought, but it wouldn't hold forever. To go the distance, he needed at least a *couple* of bullets; either that or both Tic-Tac and Ox would have to run out of ammo so James could do when he did best and lay them out on the dirt canvas. He'd fired three times and come up blank. He flipped the cylinder open, spun it, and peered inside the chambers. All empty. There were no bullets in the gun. None whatsoever. He hadn't protected himself. *Low guard. Mixed guard.* Oh fuck.

He'd been outmaneuvered; he'd been checkmated while he was busy worrying over an isolated pawn. Why then hadn't Tic-Tac and Ox just walked to the overturned table and punched his ticket? Because they didn't know what was in the gun either—that had to be the only reason. But that didn't explain why they just stood there like toy soldiers, firing from their stationary positions—unless they *did* know and were having a little fun, dragging it out at Foster's behest.

Tap the cheek.

Not only was he predictable, but he'd lost a step. Despite all of his best efforts, he hadn't been looking forward; he'd been lingering and obsessing too much in his own head. He'd allowed himself to get hit below the belt, and he was about to walk into a roundhouse.

While he was shadow boxing blindly in the recesses of his brain, his opponents were arming themselves to the hilt and digging a hole just his size.

"In the boxing mirror," Father Mac had said, "you need to see what you hope to see before you look." The weak don't dare to peek into the glass, and out of shape club fighters no longer even make an approach, for they've lost the ability to see what isn't there yet; they can no longer look two moves ahead. You need to believe. The boxing mirror is not for evaluation. It's for seeing contenders and champions, your vision being a conduit for belief. It's not shadow boxing, with its emphasis on stance and technique visualization, which gave the fighter an idea of how he would look against his next opponent while training; that's all about *showing* and barely tickles the mind's eye. Father Mac used to say that with shadow boxing, which had its place, there was nothing to truly see except images on a shiny surface; it was all reflection without reflection. In the boxing mirror, you fight only yourself, no imagined adversary, because in order to enter the ring a winner, a calculated savage, the boxer you have to defeat is yourself, and to do that you need to break through any long-standing mental constructs. There is no other way to genuinely believe in what you see and see what you believe. As Father Mac would often remind him, oftentimes you need to beat the belief into yourself; it won't happen hitting the bag or jumping rope or sparring. In the boxing mirror, you *need* to see what you hope to see before you look, and that belief must follow you into the ring, into the street, and into a gangster's house. The more it becomes ingrained, the less you remember that the belief is not based on skill, which by now you either have or you don't, but on something as dangerous and slippery as hope.

And he believed again. Despite being bulletless and trapped, his hope had returned and with it a realization: he had to put the straw *back* in the side of the dirt mound, for what he believed was now as real as his reflection had been, matching him blow for blow. He'd been wrong: Laura *was* here, for that was what he hoped (not that she was buried alive but that she was alive and in this basement), just as he'd hoped for a chance to rescue her.

Sylvia...
Yes, Mickey?
How do you call your loverboy?
Come 'ere, loverboy!

Crouched behind the increasingly cracked and splintered table, dancing as best he could from that position, he knew he had maybe twenty seconds, maybe less, before the mobsters stopped toying with their prey and just ended him for the pleasure of the cameras. But if it was the last thing he did, he was going to put the straw back in so Laura could breathe. Even if he was killed, at least Laura would live and have a chance of finding a way out of this life. She was a smart woman. What she was doing with him was a mystery for the ages.

And if he doesn't answer?

Ohh, loverboy!

And if he still doesn't answer...?

He threw another chair and scurried towards the mound.

Bob and weave. Parry. Break. Rotate the body so that incoming punches slip by. Watch your feet. Keep your hands up. Bob and weave. Block. Fade.

The first bullet ripped into his shoulder, and his body twisted away from the mound. Out of the corner of his eye, he saw one of the cameras move as if focusing on the action in the ring. *Why hadn't they just filled him with lead?* He turned back around, ready to return to the fray, his hands fists, though he could barely lift his left arm. His adrenaline battled the pain. The next bullet caught his right leg above the knee and he screamed as he fell forward. *Don't disturb family dinner. Junior just got his report card.* His mouth seemed to be continually open, emitting a cacophony of harsh tones—*worry not, the basement is soundproof*—but no words. He took the straw from his shirt pocket, and with his right hand, tried to reach towards the side of the mound and replace it, but his mind was off his routine.

Focus. Focus. Focus.

Push with the rear leg. Forward motion from the guard position without hesitation, for timing is efficiency, accuracy is effectiveness, and opportunity is everything.

Reach. Reach. Reach.

Someone fired and the bullet exploded into the side of James' stomach, and he could feel something inside of him deflate.

"Your aim is for shit, you mammoth mook," Tic-Tac said. "You know that?"

Now or never. Do or die. Shit or get off the pot.

Blood filled his mouth as James pushed himself up a little. "Would you look at this persistent motherfucker," Tic-Tac said as he nodded to one of the cameras and came around behind him. "Thinks he's a contender." James used his right forearm to crawl closer to the mound, then lay prone, his right arm stretched above his head. He lifted his hand up just enough to have some force—*an economy of motion*—and planted the straw back into its hole. *He was Irish Jimmy; he was Coinín.* The last bullet entered the back of his head and exited through his left orbital cavity, his hand bending the concertina-like hinge near the top of the straw before joining the rest of his already-collapsed body.

"I told you it was a bendy," Tic-Tac said. "This *stronzo* bent it just right, and he was dead. You can't manage to keep your money in a roll, and you're breathing. *Stunad.* Hand me the shovel and go get the lime."

What was rattling around James' brain the couple of seconds before everything went deathly quiet was Laura singing: *"'Alison, I know this world is killing you.'"*

Tap the cheek.

Just as everything went from bright to the deepest dark, he thought the mound was a mirror where he could see what he hoped, and it was Laura that he saw in the glass and she was smiling.

Rear foot a half-step behind the lead foot, legs shoulder-width apart.

Jab. Jab. Right cross. Jab. Left hook. Jab. Jab.

Haymaker.

KO.

"No more Good Son
He lost his sense of space
His beginning froze
Under the weight of the Sun"

Alejandro Escovedo, "The Boxing Mirror"

-end-

The Divine Lorraine

Seamus had started out at the Wendell Arms, but it was more run-down than the Temple University dorms, which he'd briefly investigated. Both only received one channel: static. From the Wendell Arms, he tried the YMCA, but there was no working television there at all. When he passed the Divine Lorraine Hotel, its ten-story glory intimidated him. True, most of the other tall buildings in Center City Philadelphia were still standing; the force of the blast had only felled a few, but there had been some collateral damage. The Divine Lorraine was old, Seamus knew, built in the 1890s, one of the first high-rise apartment buildings in the city, and while there may have been older buildings along the Broad Street Run, none were as majestic. It had been abandoned, pre-Event. More intriguing, it had *her* name, and on the way back after his second run to the Navy Yard, he'd heard the sounds of a radio or a television coming from one of the upper floors. That was how quiet it was—quiet enough to hear a radio in the Divine Lorraine from the middle of Broad Street; he'd come through the shadow of City Hall (with the scorched statue of Billy Penn watching over no one from its top), but he was still some eleven hundred yards from the august hotel. He heard whatever it was the next day as well. So from the Wendell Arms to the YMCA to the Divine Lorraine. But he decided not break his way through the front doors until he'd finished the official race, which was set to begin the next morning. He spent the night in the credit union, catty corner from the hotel.

Now the day was here—the day that would have been the start of the Broad Street Run, a ten-mile race that began at Central High School in the Logan neighborhood and ended at the Navy Yard in South Philly. Over thirty thousand had been expected to participate in the race with a high number of spectators. Seamus was a runner and he'd completed the course three times since the Event; he was ready for today even if he was alone. There were eleven water stations along the route, digital clocks at each mile, not to mention port-a-potties, first aid stations, and a bandstand with a full PA system, all intact. (Seamus had thought about using the PA to find other survivors, but electricity was spotty at best.) There was even an empty ambulance sitting at an eastern corner of Broad and Spring

Garden. There were also all the unoccupied cars that, suddenly ownerless, had smashed into poles or rammed into each other; some ended up sitting in the middle of the street or on the pavement unharmed, keys still in the ignition. It made the course a bit of a maze, but one he was used to now. If the Event had happened four days later, Seamus would have been one of the pack running the ten miles, losing himself in a mixture of adrenaline, sweat, and pain. And losing himself was exactly what Seamus had in mind after he'd discovered Rainy had slept with that biker back in Mondauk. She came back home but barely lived there, and the time she returned one of his frantic late night calls—he pleaded his case on a static-filled cell phone connection until she hung up—was the last time he heard from her, he lied to himself. Unless he counted the evening she returned to the apartment after work to tell him she was going away with the biker for a week. Unless he counted that evening—the one where she called him a good friend and gave him a peck on the cheek. Getting lost with bad whiskey, colored pills, and wanton women seemed like a good idea when it was all over. He'd been practically majoring in the use of fermented or distilled beverages and street pharmaceuticals anyway before briefly sobering up in an effort to win Rainy back, so when she was gone for good, stepping it up a notch or two from where he'd left off had been just like turning up the hot water in a shower from warm to scalding; after a while, he didn't even notice the difference. Except now, he told himself, he truly no longer wanted alcohol or pills and there weren't any women as far as the eye could see. (He was alone; there didn't even seem to be even any animals, birds, or bugs.) So he ran, beginning the day after the Event, and when he'd finished his third race in forty-eight hours, his calves ached, his feet throbbed, his entire body hurt (especially his left hip where he'd connected with a Hyundai), and it was exactly what he needed to keep away his own divine Lorraine.

"Those maggots there, you can eat them too," was what the homeless person had said to him yesterday as he came up behind Seamus rifling through a hot dog stand. At least he looked homeless, smelled like it too, but since he was the first person Seamus had seen since the Event, who really knew? All the buildings in the immediate area were more or less intact, so homes were for the taking. Still, his presence unsettled Seamus, even when the man (who called himself Little John, and little he was) asked Seamus back to his lair in the lobby of Temple Hospital. (It felt like rain.) There on a bulletin board, the man had pinned up soiled fashion ads torn from magazines, all featuring busty models, each of whom had an X over their face. "Bang 'em and hang 'em," his host explained. Around an unnecessary fire in a trashcan (it was May for God's sake), Little John pontificated on the cause of the Event (theories included aliens, the government, the Christian right) and what actually happened to the citizens of Philadelphia. "Vaporized, they were, friend," Little John said. "Zap, zoom, zimmy, betcha betcha, Jimmy." This hypothesis was followed by a brief but bloody coughing fit. "Maybe they're all in hiding," Seamus said, but he knew that was a ridiculous thought, one he'd abandoned an hour or two after coming out of the old PNB building's sub-basement. "Maybe it was only here in Center City and South Philly. Maybe the Great Northeast is okay…maybe the suburbs too, Bucks, Montgomery…Mondauk." Rainy lived in Mondauk County with him. (*Had* lived.) There was no way the Event, which sounded like a detonation that lasted for hours, had disappeared *every* human from the planet, leaving only Seamus and the toothless and odorous Little John—and what would make people and creatures go away but not buildings? A neutron bomb? The Rapture?

"Can you hear the rain?" Little John asked, and that was when the homeless man's ticket was written—even before he pulled out his penis.

"What the fuck did you say?" Seamus asked.

Little John smiled conspiratorially, and a little red-tinted drool slid down his chin.

"I asked if you could hear the rain. Problem, bud?"

Seamus felt his body clench up. "What about Lorraine?" It was getting hot in the lobby. Steaming really.

"Sounds like she's really coming down."

That was when Seamus hit him and didn't stop hitting him, not even when Little John whipped out his little john as a peace offering. And when the hitting ceased, when all the images of everything he'd ever done with Rainy, sexual and otherwise, were out of Seamus' head, Little John was littler than before and no longer breathing, his face half-burned away from where Seamus had held it over the flames.

When he woke the next morning in the credit union, Seamus didn't give it much of a thought. It was the official day of the Run. Sure, he should have asked the man how he'd managed to survive the

Event. He should have asked him if there were others. But he didn't. Rainy, as always, burned brightly.

That was what he had called his Lorraine: Rainy. It fit. Rainy could be morose, like she stepped out of a Poe story. She was prone to mood swings, which after a while, he realized had little to do with him. Rainy was a brooder. In short, she was a rainstorm on a sunny day, a thunderstorm on an overcast one. So he called her Rainy. She never minded or commented on it, other than to tell him one night that even rain comes to an end.

"But it will always rain again," he'd replied. "It's always raining somewhere."

He leaned across her to grab the remote and turn on the Weather Channel to prove it.

She was out of the bed before a single button was pressed, brushing her hair, flossing her teeth.

That was another of Rainy's quirks or tricks: evasion. He'd go to put his arm around her, and she'd duck and focus her attention on anything else. It wasn't like they didn't sleep together. They did, but they didn't have sex very often, which only served in making Seamus want Rainy more. She held hands like girls shake hands: limp and uninspired. Even her kisses were tentative, as if she were afraid of a more full-throated experience. Rainy was a mystery. Her passion was reserved for two things: her job at the firm, though her work ethic struck Seamus as obsessive rather than ardent, and Shakespeare—she was like a groupie, spouting lines and re-reading heavily creased paperback editions of the plays. Other than her books, about the only item she brought with her to the apartment when she moved in was old poster detailing different species of sharks that she said she'd had since she was a kid. He didn't know much about her family (in fact, he'd seen them only once at a funeral for Rainy's aunt, where the interaction between Rainy and her relatives had been more awkward or aloof than cordial) and knew little about her past, other than that she'd been hurt, both physically and otherwise, by past paramours. He gathered that she'd also had a penchant for older men when she was younger. From the more recent stories he was privy to, it sounded like Rainy had acquired a taste for "bad boys," a mold he definitely didn't fit into—he felt he was more of a fuck-up.

Sure, he'd been a Mondauk County Police Officer, but he'd left after only five years. The job wasn't for him. He'd wanted to make detective grade, but the number of hoops he would have had to jump through to get there seemed endless. As a result, he grew less motivated when it came to police work, and being of a restless sort, he found more and more creative ways to be increasingly self-destructive in his extracurricular activities. (His exit from the force was preceded by some trouble with IAB concerning missing evidence.) He couldn't resist making a little extra scratch, and when he became a civilian again, he wasn't above the occasional B&E, which landed him in hot water more than once, but he was never charged with anything, largely thanks to his older brother, who was well-liked in the department and carried a gold shield. He returned the favor by shaking down dealers in Paradise Lakes Trailer Park, wielding his brother's name until they started offering him free shit. Generally, however, he tried to stay on the straight and narrow (if not always sober) path, and he had a job as a custodian—a glorified janitor. An honest living, one where he knew all the pitfalls. But dirty hands and an inclination for getting loaded still did not make him a bad boy. Not like the biker. Not like who knew how many others.

As he rubbed his legs with a sports cream he'd lifted from a drug store, he pondered the situation: despite everything, despite the evasions, the infrequent sex, the bouts of melancholia, and yes, the eventual cheating, he loved her. He'd looked for her everywhere after she left. (Lie.) Maybe she somehow escaped the Event like he did. (Lie.) Was it such an impossibility? (Yes.) He wished she could have been here today, watching him navigate the Broad Street Run. (Truth.) It was literally a race against himself, but it was funny: the surrounding stillness along the route was louder than any crowd he imagined. He even thought he heard his name called out once or twice, but he didn't stop to look around.

He checked his digital stopwatch: 53:07—he was slowing down. But what did he expect for his fourth race in three days, he thought. He should be grateful for 53:07. All during his run, his thoughts alternated between Rainy, the radio, and the man he'd murdered not twenty-four hours ago. If this was the new world, it was going to be tricky navigating the moral course without a social compass. Did the old laws still apply if there was no one to apply them to, no one to avail oneself to in order to redress a wrong? Considering the number of laws he'd broken before the Event, it was a surprise he even cared, but being the last man standing could do that to a person.

The old laws certainly didn't apply when he broke into the Divine Lorraine through the front doors—none of the cellar door jimmying he'd majored in during the early part of his post-law enforcement career. Moving into the hotel (even its grand red signs were still intact) was just a way of getting closer to Rainy. He could have lived anywhere he wanted. He could even walk the ghost highways all the way back to Mondauk County. In his post-Run elation, he felt his battered legs and feet would be up to the task once he gave himself enough time to rest. But the Divine Lorraine, he was sure, would feel just like home—and he hadn't even stepped through the doorway.

And there was also the radio or whatever had been playing in one of the higher floors. He'd heard it twice, so there was no mistake. Either it was running on batteries (all of the batteries he'd been able to find had gone bad from the Event) or, even better, electricity, although why would a building long empty before the Event have power? Maybe there was even a survivor already checked in. He just had to be careful not to mention Little John.

He didn't know what to expect when he gained entry, but what he found wasn't decay as much as years and years of dust. (The Divine Lorraine had closed its doors fourteen years ago.) But he knew he'd made the right choice; even the dust smelled familiar. At one time, this grand example of High Victorian Gothic architecture had been a working hotel run by Father Divine and the Universal Peace Movement. Father Divine began life as George Baker before adopting the more glorious title of the right Reverend Jealous Divine and mutating into a charismatic religious leader considered to be God incarnate by his congregation and a notorious charlatan by the authorities. He was also an early civil rights activist, although some found this appellation controversial because of his claim that he wasn't black. But it was his claim to divinity that caused the most fuss. In 1948, he turned the formerly secular Lorraine into the first fully racially integrated hotel of its class in Philadelphia, where men and women slept on separate floors and referred to each other as brother and sister. For all the good his movement did, many outside of his small circle believed he was simply another fruitcake in a long line of fruitcakes. Seamus didn't have an opinion one way or the other. He'd been raised Roman Catholic in Northern Ireland (a time he didn't much remember) before his mother moved the family to the States when he was just a wee lad. If he'd ever had any real religious beliefs, they had been left behind in Downpatrick. Now he just shrugged, took his mother to Mass when she asked him, and attended the various baptisms, First Communions, and confirmations of his nephews and nieces without feeling elation or enmity.

The stretches of custodial downtime (often self-imposed) and the significant amount of space he gave Rainy when her moods were at their worst left him with a lot of time to kill, which he did by drinking more and reading (whatever was available), so Seamus was familiar with the good Father Divine and the Universal Peace Mission Movement. And as he wandered about the hotel, marveling at the grand marble staircase and tinkling the large room keys hanging behind the front desk, everything thickly covered in fourteen-year-old dust, he recalled the ghost stories that had surrounded the Divine Lorraine since its closure: the sounds of music and laughter in the Great Banquet Hall and the wronged woman who roamed the halls of the seventh floor. Seamus shivered. If ever there was a building to house such spirits, it would be this one, but then again, *every* building as far as the eye could see would now more than likely embody the same spectral feeling: breakfasts beginning to mold on kitchen tables; book bags and lunches by the door; wet laundry in the dryer. (The city was one big haunted house, if he really stopped to think about it—something he tried not to do; he found the dog leashes that littered the sidewalks the most disturbing.) What was there to fear then in the Divine Lorraine? Everyone had disappeared. *Everyone in the whole goddamn city it seemed!* If there were such things as ghosts (more believable to Seamus than the concept of God), they had to be all around now. Hell, he could be a ghost. Little John certainly had potential, even before his misfortune.

It was a depressing thought, one not made better when he read the posted notice of Father Divine's Modesty Code. It was no surprise that the members of the Peace Movement were forbidden to drink alcohol. It was more difficult than he thought, trying to stay on the sober side—and he didn't like being reminded of it, ghost or not. But he could always get take-out, BYOB, he told himself: anything he wanted was readily available if he planned to dive off the wagon, which wasn't on the events calendar, not yet anyway—it was best he stay as sharp as he could post-Event.

He tried to clear his head of all the negative nonsense but stopped. It wouldn't do any good, he knew. From the moment he entered the old hotel, the cautious optimism of yesterday had been replaced by a sense that everything he held to be true was just a semblance of reality, approximations, and that all the stimuli to be offered by the Divine Lorraine would bring him terribly close to what was real. That he'd dared to believe it would feel like home seemed like an affront that required a significant amount of penance to erase. It was not enough to survive a massive disappearance. He sensed that being corporeal meant little within these walls.

He also increasingly began to believe what he'd only feared: that the effects of the Event had carried beyond Center City, which meant his mother was gone, his sisters were gone, their children too. His big brother Feargal. And quite possibly Rainy. (Lie.) True, she could have been on one of her business trips to New York or Boston, but more than likely she'd been right here in Center City. (Falsehood.) She'd been bucking for a promotion when they were together, and he figured she must have gotten it because he heard she'd moved to Society Hill not soon after they'd broken up for good. (Complete and utter fabrication.) He'd driven by their old apartment in the town of Mondauk Proper a few times even though he knew she wasn't there. (Absolutely true.) The lights were always off, which he found disappointing each time for some reason. He didn't know who lived there now, if anyone. He'd broken the lease when Rainy departed, because no matter how hard he tried, he couldn't get rid of the image of Rainy in their bed with the biker, his grease-covered hands soiling her best skirt, his bearded mouth on her nipples—even though she'd sworn they never done it there. In the past four days, with hope as ephemeral as his fellow citizens had turned out to be, he'd combated thoughts like those by pretending that she'd be waiting for him at the finish line today, and he'd pick her up and spin her around just like in the movies. But Seamus guessed there were no more movies. And maybe no more Rainy. (True, true.)

Seamus moved up the marble staircase. (He wasn't even going to try the elevator.) He assumed room keys wouldn't be necessary. It was a disturbing tour. Many of the rooms had neatly made beds. Some had wrapped bars of soap in the bathroom. One had a pair of shoes next to a shine box. It was eerily similar to the domestic scenes, outside the hotel, of those lives suddenly interrupted by the Event, but the rooms at the Lorraine felt like carefully arranged museum pieces. He walked softly, listening for the radio, and when he finally heard it, he fell backwards onto a dusty bed.

"Deliciously healthy convenient snack…"

Seamus stayed perfectly still like he'd been taught in the academy. Listen, assess, formulate, implement. He ignored the nervous flutter that suddenly appeared in his stomach and focused. He was on the fifth floor. It sounded like it was coming from only a floor or two above.

"Deliciously healthy convenient snack…"

Before he left the room, he snapped off a bedpost—just in case his visit wasn't welcome.

The sixth floor was as quiet as a tomb. (Seamus allowed himself a little chuckle at that one.) There wasn't a radio in any of the rooms.

The seventh floor seemed just as quiet. The dust in the hallway had been disturbed, but that could have easily been the work of long gone mice. Gripping the bedpost, he began a room-to-room search like he had on the floor below.

"Come out, come out, wherever you are."

The first two rooms: nothing.

" *Radio is sound salvation,*'" Seamus sang softly. " *Radio is cleaning up the nation.*'"

In room 707, it overcame him, the bone-weariness from having survived the Event, climbing out of the sub-basement, and subsequently racing the Broad Street Run on four occasions while still finding the time to beat and burn a man to death. He plopped down on a fastidiously made bed and was briefly consumed in a cloud of fine, dry particles of matter from the past. He leaned the broken post against the nightstand, upon which was an open Bible. Seamus leaned over and blew the dust from its pages. It was open to John 11:11: "Our friend Lazarus sleepth; but I go, that I may awake him out of sleep."

Well, good luck trying to wake ol' Seamus Finnerty, he thought. He planned to follow Lazarus of Bethany's lead and sleep the sleep of the (nearly) dead right here on this creepy bed. He'd find the fucking radio tomorrow. His feet were blistered, his knee still burned from the fall he'd taken at Broad and Pattison. If Rainy was still alive, she'd be thinking about him, about his safety after the Event, not some biker's. If Rainy was still alive, she'd be looking for him, alone if she had to. Then again, that wasn't true—Rainy didn't like to diverge from her rigid schedule. Not that it mattered. Rainy wasn't really—

Seamus awoke to a scream—not his. A woman's. He sat up in bed and wiped the dust from the side of his face. Had he dreamt the scream? Real or Memorex? He grabbed the broken-off piece of bedpost and crept towards the door. Had he closed it before he'd retired for the evening? He couldn't remember, but it was closed now. Goose pimples had broken out all over his skin. The nervous flutter was back. What if it was another survivor? What if—?

The second scream was reverberating in his ears before his brain could process the information, as if he'd been wearing headphones and someone had suddenly turned the volume up so that he couldn't recognize the song.

That was no survivor, he thought as he listened to the ringing in his ears slowly cycle away.

"Deliciously healthy convenient snack…"

Seamus spun around—and there it was, tucked away behind a curtain on a windowsill: the radio.

"Deliciously healthy convenient snack…"

Oranges—oranges were the deliciously healthy convenient snack being advertised in the commercial. Oranges were Rainy's favorite. Oranges and strawberries. Seemed like she ate them every single—

"Strawberries, strawberries! Two boxes for a dollar! Strawberries!"

What a fucking coincidence, Seamus thought. Of all the 246 rooms, he'd chosen the one with a radio playing commercials for oranges and strawberries.

"Strawberries, strawberries! Two boxes for a dollar! Strawberries!"

He stared at the radio, waiting for the next dispatch. Then his ears picked up the melody. It sounded as if it was coming from somewhere far away but accompanied by the clearly identifiable hiss and crackle of a vinyl record.

"When I was seventeen, it was a very good year…"

Seamus began to feel something he'd given up on since the Event (maybe even since the biker): hope. Commercials could be played on a loop, but if someone was playing vinyl on a local station, that meant someone else was alive, which meant Rainy might still be too. (Big lie.) Sinatra—this DJ couldn't be all bad.

He placed his ear to the radio—nothing. Where the fuck was the music coming from?

"When I was twenty-one, it was a very good year…"

Downstairs! Someone was playing music downstairs. He ditched the bedpost, which seemed superfluous now that he was chasing a song, and opened the door without hesitation. It wasn't just any song that he pursued; it was the song that had been playing on the radio the night he and Rainy first made love. As he started down the hall, he thought he saw a woman's skirt flutter around the corner. It looked as if it were translucent except he wasn't sure what he saw beneath it. The vision only slowed him down for a couple of seconds. He was on an urgent mission, and he ran down the stairs, taking them two at a time.

Sixth floor.

Fifth floor.

His shins screamed.

"And it came undone—when I was twenty-one…"

Fourth floor.

Third floor.

His calves threatened rebellion.

"When I was thirty-five, it was a very good year…"

Second floor.

Ground floor.

Unbelievably, he was winded; on top of that, many of his blisters had broken open. But the music was loud here. It wasn't a Sinatra record—it was a band. The music was coming from the banquet hall. Seamus limped towards the doors. He heard laughter and glasses clinking—glasses filled with water, no doubt. *Mind the Code please.* What the hell—Seamus could use a big glass of water right about now. Join this party of survivors, find Rainy, get back to living.

"But now the days grow short; I'm in the autumn of the year…"

He pushed at the big double doors with both hands.

"It was a very good year…"

The Great Banquet Hall was empty. Floating dust motes rode drafts caused by the many cracked windows. There was mouse shit scattered all over the floor. No band, no record player. He had partially expected this. Call it some sort of aural mirage brought on by too little food and too much exercise. (He frequently had to remind himself to eat in this post-Event world.) But it had seemed so real—he thought could almost smell perfume in the otherwise dead air and just the hint of a cigar, except smoking was another vice forbidden by Father Divine. Maybe the party hadn't involved the Peace Movement and the denizens of the Divine Lorraine, but instead the wealthy elite who lived in the Lorraine Apartments during the 1920s—and who had the foresight to play "It Was a Very Good Year" roughly forty years before Frank recorded it. But it didn't matter much—his little hallucination was over. The remaining revelers consisted of him and the ghosts of several thousand shitting mice.

Instead of going to back to room 707, he continued climbing the marble stairs, despite the pain in his ankles, and stopped on the tenth floor. Here was the sect's chapel, almost like a mini-auditorium, pristine except for the dust. He sat in the first row, a place he never would have taken during the times he'd accompanied his mother to Mass. He looked down, and there was blood on his socks.

He didn't care very much for the sight of blood, especially his own; he was not a violent man. (Lie.) Even as a cop in Mondauk County, he'd never seen a dead body. He'd never even drawn his service revolver. Little John was…an aberration. (Falsity.) Some slight disturbance of his character brought on by the disappearance of apparently millions of people. (Prevarication.) Perhaps, just perhaps, it had been the result of previously latent behavior traits exacerbated by the biker situation. (Bingo.) Rainy's thighs wrapped around some hairy deadbeat from Paradise Lakes, violating the sanctity of the bed Seamus shared with her—sure, that thought alone could make him want to kill. And he had. Not seventy-two hours into this little emergency state, he'd taken the law into his own hands—literally. For the crime of commenting on the weather, he'd beaten Little John to death. Because of Rainy. All because of Rainy. (*Bad girls, bad girls, beep beep!*) What if he'd never seen that Trojan floating in their toilet? What if the biker had remembered to flush? He'd pray if he knew how anymore, but he didn't know whom he'd be praying for: himself or Rainy or Little John or the whole goddamn human race. He'd burned a man's face half off; all the praying and repenting in the world wasn't going to erase that sin. (Or his other biggie either.)

He made his way quietly back down to the seventh floor, simultaneously listening for the band and the radio. Once there, he entered the communal lavatory in the hallway that had a painted sign above the door: "Brothers." He chuckled at the plurality as he entered. There were no more brothers, no more sisters. No more golden retrievers for that matter, probably. His dog had been his life since discovering Rainy's indiscretion, her psychological aberration. He supposed Desmond, with his soft fur (more brown than golden) and expressive eyes, was also alone and possibly starving if the borough of Rhawnhurst was a town of shadows as well. Unless Desmond had been disappeared, a distinct possibility, he admitted, thinking of all the empty dog leashes. He stared at his eyes in the mirror and was surprised to find his hair had become significantly grayer since the last time he looked. Well, at least he still had his health, he laughed to himself as he pushed open the first stall door, and there, staring back at him like a demon's eye: a used Trojan. Recently used. Trails of semen floated upon the fetid water's surface.

He pulled himself through the lavatory door like a cripple, found his sea legs, and ran down the hall to room 707, making sure he was the one to close the door this time. Fuck it—he'd pee out a window if it came to it. He was Irish; he could piss anywhere. And goddamn it if he couldn't use a pint right about now. Too fucking bad the Divine Lorraine was a dry hotel—wasn't that a mouthful of truth, as his old da used to say. Of course, according to Rainy, it was his alcohol consumption that had led her to spread her legs for the biker. (*Bad girls, bad girls, beep beep!*) And the truth was, he'd never meant to hit her. He slipped, his shoes were slick from the rain, and Rainy had answered the door wearing an old t-shirt and nothing else. He'd lost his key, and his banging had finally woke her up. He could see her pubic hair for Christ's sake and so could anyone else staring their way at three in the blessed a.m.—and he slipped. Afterward, that was it, he promised, no more pints, no more shots, no more drugs. He may have already lost her, but if not, he could no longer sit idly by and watch their relationship up and disappear, his only reactions being to increase his alcohol intake and slap her off her feet. He even quit cigarettes and took up running, which seemed to alienate Rainy even more. What did they have in common? Certainly not age (Seamus was ten years her senior) and certainly not sex anymore. (His new prescription of Celexa, which was supposed to aid him in his battle with alcoholism, had fairly quickly diminished his ability to perform.) All that was left was—

"Deliciously healthy convenient snack…"

He jumped then twisted around in an almost cartoon character movement. The radio…but it was the same commercial …he heard no DJ, no call letters, no Sinatra…just—

"Deliciously healthy convenient snack…"

It was a simple black AM/FM radio with a broken antenna and two gouges in its only speaker. When Seamus picked it up, he saw the battery door had been broken off. There were no batteries inside.

"Deliciously healthy convenient snack…"

So if there were no batteries, that meant the Divine Lorraine had electricity. As far as who was paying the utility bill, he hardly gave it a thought.

"Deliciously healthy convenient snack…"

He followed the worn black cord down behind the radiator and was surprised when he lifted the plug straight up. He stared at it as if it held all the answers. Could he have pulled it out of the socket? He peered behind the radiator—no socket. No socket, no batteries—

"Strawberries, strawberries! Two boxes for a dollar! Strawberries!"

That was when it hit him: this wasn't a commercial for strawberries. This was what the produce man had cried from his truck, through a little speaker, as he drove up and down the streets of Rhawnhurst when Seamus was young. He was a tiny man who combed his few remaining grey strands of hair straight back. Their mother would give them a dollar, and the Finnerty clan would gorge themselves on fresh strawberries as they sat on their patch of a front lawn. This was America! But there came a time when the old produce man stopped coming around, or at least stopped driving down their street. Now why was that?

They hadn't even bothered to lie to their mother, who, bless her heart, never turned them in. It would have been difficult to lie to her anyway: he and Feargal were covered in red strawberry juice and deep blueberry stains mixed in with a bit of blood, a blend of their own and the produce man's from when they pulled him from the cab, which they'd done after the truck plowed into the stop sign at Stanwood and Frontenac. It was only meant to be a gag—Feargal's idea. God knows why they went through with it. The produce man always drove ten miles an hour or less through the side streets until he was hailed down. The plan was for the Finnerty brothers to hop on the back of the open truck and carefully toss Jersey tomatoes, ears of corn, and boxes of strawberries and blueberries to their friends following behind. Then as the old man began to brake for the stop sign (which he always did early), Feargal would boost Seamus up the wood rails onto the top of the cab and hold on to his ankles. Seamus, armed with berries, would smear them on the windshield. And the plan worked perfectly until the old man turned on his wipers, spreading the whole mess across the glass. Yelling that he couldn't see, he hit the gas and smashed into the stop sign. The force of the crash slid Seamus off the top and down the windshield. (Feargal had fallen backwards, letting go of his brother's legs.) His head throbbing, Seamus scrambled off the hood, and he and his brother pulled the street grocer out of the cab. During the hasty extraction, they managed to smack the old man's head on the way out, opening a gash on his forehead (his face was already covered in little cuts), and Feargal slashed his arm on a bent coil, for there wasn't a front seat, just a kitchen chair cushion atop a bed of springs. But he and his brother ignored their injuries, and once they ascertained that the produce man was still alive, they hightailed it to one of their secret hiding places, turning themselves in to their mother only when the rumble in their bellies became too loud to ignore and their wounds felt too neglected. Seamus used to tell this story when he explained why both he and Feargal had entered the police academy. (The hurdles to advancement were never an impediment to his brother like the way they were for him, and Feargal ended up a homicide detective.) On that day, although their intention was to be criminals of the prankster variety, they ended up playing policemen, pulling the produce man from the smoking truck. Seamus never told anyone, but the incident also had another formative effect. They may have done good at the end, but they'd also gotten away with a crime: their friends, who'd wisely took off, did so with a decent amount of fruits and vegetables; it was a lesson Seamus, at least, never forgot.

"Strawberries, strawberries! Two boxes for a dollar! Strawberries!"

A toilet flushed in the hallway lavatory, and Seamus abandoned the ghost radio and rushed down the hall. The Trojan was gone. The sink was wet as if someone had just washed their hands. As he ran his fingers through the drops, he heard footsteps coming from the hall, but when he opened the door, the corridor was empty, just a glimpse of a translucent skirt turning the corner at the end of the passage.

Seamus was wiped out. He leaned against the wall and slid down to his haunches. Was it only four days ago that he'd fought his way out the sub-basement of the old PNB building through rubble, bent iron rods, and wire, expecting to see, if not other survivors, at least the occasional human limb? Was it yesterday or today that he killed Little John? Now radios without power played the produce man's cry plus one looped commercial hawking oranges. Oranges and strawberries. Rainy's favorites. Was the evening she came home from work to tell him she was leaving—not leaving for good, but going on vacation with the biker—only two months ago? God, she told him so casually, as if Rainy and Seamus were just fuck buddies, not lovers with potential. She even turned on the radio while they spoke, tuning in an old disco song like they were simply talking about where to go to dinner, nothing earth-shattering. And Seamus, acting on some remote control, told her he'd check the oil in her car before she left for her trip. Like he always did. The oil and other fluids. Rainy stared at him, then shrugged and told him she was going to his place that night and that she didn't know if they were taking her car or his bike on the trip. He nodded but barely heard her. And in the fading light of day, he checked the oil and the transmission fluid and coolant. And he'd cried when he crawled under the car and cut the brake line. Oh, and the tears he shed later when he got the call at home and rushed to the scene. She was trapped in the car, the front of which looked like an accordion. The other vehicle, a small hatchback, didn't look nearly as bad as Rainy's, but it was totaled nonetheless. The driver was safe and was being treated for cuts to the head by the EMTs. Rainy had blown a red light, drove headlong into traffic, and plowed into the hatchback, pushing it into a traffic light. All that was missing were the strawberries. When he arrived, the police were trying to clear the crash site, but Seamus had been on the job and most of the uniforms knew him on sight. (It was a cop that had called him.) And he sobbed when they pulled Rainy from the car. The rest played out achingly slow. As the cops held up a tarp to shield her body from public view, Seamus' hopes swung back and forth: did he want Rainy and her complications and his reactions to them back in his life or did he want her to remain still? And all the while, the same old disco song that had played in their apartment blasted from her car radio or at least that was what he heard. Soon it became apparent that the EMTs' efforts were of no use: Rainy was gone. He went into self-preservation mode; there'd be time to mourn later. His shitty Camry was blocked by squad cars, and he began to map out what the quickest route on foot to the train station would be. His anxiety was ratcheted up a notch when, after quiet debate, it was decided that they wouldn't cover Rainy because they didn't want to contaminate her body while they waited for the Medical Examiner—which meant someone felt that foul play was a possibility. He breathed easier when his brother arrived and had a couple of uniforms take Seamus to one of their sisters' homes. In the squad car, he whispered to himself, "It's not raining anymore," and was surprised to find that there wasn't a drop of blood on him; he felt he should be stained with it. But it didn't matter. The biker took the fall. Had a record a mile long and coincidentally was already a suspect in a case involving engine sabotage. Because of the cut brake lines, it was Feargal's case, and the light of suspicion never fell on Seamus, not even a beam.

So maybe he had murdered before.

Someone was typing a few floors below.

Seamus was down the stairs before the pain in his ankles and knees and calves had a chance to impede him. He thought he glimpsed the translucent skirt before he left seven—he also caught a whiff of familiar perfume, but he was in a hurry. He followed the typewriter sounds to the third floor, and he went down the hall, throwing open doors, disturbing critters large and small. (These animals—which he'd heard rather than seen—had escaped the vanishing, it seemed, which meant there was a possibility that Desmond had too, maybe even the shitting mice.) In room 303, the clacking stopped the moment the back of the door hit the wall. The typewriter was an old Royal, covered in dust, but there were impressions on the keys, like footprints on sand. A piece of paper was rolled in the platen; it looked new, the ink on it fresh. Whoever had typed it had used a red ribbon, which was nowhere in sight.

It read:

Deliciously healthy convenient snack...

Strawberries, strawberries!
Two boxes for a dollar! Strawberries!

> *Down here, it's always rain rain rain.*
> *Down here at the Divine Lorraine.*

Zap, zoom, zimmy, betcha betcha, Jimmy.

> *"So full of artless jealousy is guilt,*
> *It spills itself in fearing to be spilt."*
> *So sayeth the Bard.*

You can stop running, babe. You can't just disappear.

> *Down here, it's always rain rain rain.*
> *Down here at the Divine Lorraine.*

Enjoy your stay.
Mind the Code please.

> *Beep beep!*

Seamus tried to take the stairs in record time but he was accompanied by the hard-to-ignore howls and groans of his lower extremities, which hampered his progress. He had no idea why he was running back up the stairs instead of down them and out of the building. The radio—maybe he could find some place with electricity or come upon some batteries that hadn't gone bad. He'd take the radio and leave the Divine Lorraine. His mind was clearly playing games with him. He was good at pretending—always had been. *Like pretending Rainy was still alive when the Event occurred?* Like that. *Like pretending Little John was his first murder?* Exactly.

The closer he got to the seventh floor, the more his body betrayed him. It was like swimming against the current in a viscous ocean. They'd catch him for sure if he so much as lost a step or missed a beat. Whoever *they* were. The woman in the skirt. The typist. The condom enthusiast. The ghost radio DJ.

In room in 707, written in the dust on the bureau: *You can run, little boy, but you're covered in strawberry juice. And we can smell you.*

He grabbed the radio and headed back down the hall.

There she was.

At the end of the corridor, wavering on some invisible breeze: Rainy.

She was wearing the skirt she'd worn the evening she left for the biker's to go on their trip, the evening he fixed her car but good. It wasn't just her skirt that appeared to permit the passage of light; it was all of her. But despite being translucent, Rainy looked as pretty as ever, her shoulder length brown hair nicely framing her ice-blue eyes. (Except there were no colors now, were there?) Even as a ghost, she was still a busty girl, he noticed. She was dressed conservatively with only the top two buttons undone on her blouse. The skirt was too long to see her footwear, despite its translucence; there wasn't much light in the Divine Lorraine.

"Rainy…" he croaked. "Rainy, what happened to you?"

"You did what you did for nothing, Seamus," Rainy's ghost said. "But I couldn't be kept, so I suppose that was your way of removing the problem you couldn't solve. The thing is, I was never in love with you. I tried, for your sake, but a reef shark needs to stay in constant motion; the coral does not."

"You were never…I thought there was a time when—"

The ghost shook her (its) head, which wobbled as if it would fall off at any moment.

"But I was inside you." He hoped it didn't come out as a whine, but considering the circumstances…

"And so was the biker. Did you think you were scent marking? In both cases, I was lonely and needed warmth, however temporary. Still am and still do. Only now I am inside of you."

So the nervous flutter in his stomach had a name. He tried to steady his voice. Was there a splinter of hope lodged between her words?

"So we have a chance, you and me? Now, I mean. You said you're inside—"

"We only get one chance there, babe. We had different wiring, different vices."

"I see…"

"I *am* lonely here. But it's a matter of what you're willing to accept."

"So you know what happened?" Seamus asked, gesturing around with his free hand. "With the Event? With everyone disappearing? Are they all dead? Are they all…well, ghosts, no offense?"

Rainy looked him up and down, and her head bobbled somewhat. It was making him a little seasick.

"No," the specter answered. "I was dead before *your* Event, remember?"

"I'm truly sorry, Rainy. I really am. If I could take it back…I was just a little angry. Need an anger management course or something. It's just when—"

"You know," Rainy's ghost said, pointing, "you're covered in strawberry juice."

He looked down and indeed he was—or maybe it was blood. He wasn't sure which would be more alarming. The radio slid out of his hand where it fell into the little red pool developing around his running shoes.

"Deliciously healthy convenient snack…"

He tried to ignore his constricted throat and the damp spot in his boxers, as he had tried to ignore the translucence and the wobbly head, for to truly acknowledge the existence of those things would mean he'd traveled far beyond auditory hallucinations—but dread had crept into the darkest, most hollow parts of himself, settling like a stubborn moss, and he was aware that an element of his brain remained willfully oblivious at its (his) own peril.

"How do I know this is really happening?"

Rainy's pretty little head lurched unnaturally to one side, a ship upon choppy waters, and her body ceased wavering briefly, a port waiting for her flagship to return.

"Dip your finger into the strawberry juice and taste it," she said.

"How do I know it won't be—?"

"Blood? Either way, you'll know it's real."

"I'll take your word for it," he decided.

"At the sound of the bell," the radio squawked, *"the time will be…"*

Rainy tilted her head again, listening. (Seamus thought her noggin was going to slide right the hell off.) A bell rang.

"…time to go, time to go, time to go…"

"It's time," she said.

"Time for what?"

"To come with me."

His heart palpitated like a wild, runaway horse. His muscles twitched, and he experienced chest and neck pain. His temples had been assailed, and they pulsated with a stabbing effect. He was talking to a ghost. There was a metallic taste in his mouth, as if he'd been sucking on old quarters. This wasn't the life he'd envisioned for himself. Back when the produce man used to come around their neighborhood, before the mischief of the Finnerty brothers, he thought his life would be so different.

"But it isn't—different, is it?" Rainy asked. "Come with me, Seamus. Join me willingly, and all your sins will be forgiven. And I do mean all. It's not so bad, and this hotel is mine. They were waiting for me. And now I'm waiting for you."

"What would I do? Rattle some chains? Haunt a fireplace? There's no one left to scare."

"Kiss me, Seamus. Kiss me like you used to, babe, just the way I liked it. Kiss me and you'll be one of us, and all your transgressions— yes, even your murders—will be wiped off the books."

"Does it hurt?"

"Did kissing me hurt before?"

He thought carefully before he answered—it sounded like a trick question—but the shade had sincere with him thus far.

"No. No, it didn't."

The truth was it only hurt when he thought about her kissing someone else. It hurt so bad, he had to make her disappear, but the pain didn't stop; it just moved to a different part of his black, black heart.

"Kiss me, Seamus."

The funny thing was he wanted to, despite the terror that seemed to shutting his body down piece by piece. But he had a boner developing. (That part of his body was still quite functional post-Celexa.) Ghost or not, it *was* Rainy. And if he kissed her, he could be with her forever. No biker. No cheating. No killing. Rainy and Seamus together forever in the new world.

"What do I have to do?" he asked.

"Have you forgotten how to kiss?"

"It's usually just with live girls." He was just being honest.

"Close your eyes, tilt your head, open your mouth a little...there, that's a good boy. Now kiss me."

Seamus did as he was told. He closed his eyes, he titled his head, he opened his mouth a little. Her perfume was light at first, then grew heavier, intoxicating even. He could feel her tongue gently play with his, could feel her teeth lightly bite his lips. There was a bad taste in the back of his throat. It wasn't metallic anymore; it was something worse. It was on Rainy's tongue now too. It was like licking grave dirt. But it was Rainy, and she was his again, she would be his forever, and she would never—

Seamus looked up at his body. He was not surprised a bit to feel a burning sensation around what he guessed was his soul. Eternal heartburn, he thought. He was lying dead in the hallway for a week before a small group of survivors found him; at least he assumed they were survivors. They took his clothes and radio and buried him in the basement. Some of the survivors reported seeing a woman in a skirt—a translucent woman, a couple of them said—going down the seventh floor hallway with a spring in her step. She was alone and appeared to be smiling to herself. But the survivors had seen enough horrors not to worry about a peaceful ghost who haunted the halls of the long forsaken Divine Lorraine. They moved on as a new dawn beckoned, eager to begin their lives again, the unknown future absolving all their past sins.

-end-

Gulager

Gulager always had a fairly big stride, but that was because he was a fairly big boy. Some of the children on the island called him giant. Those that didn't called him freak. Gulager didn't have any friends—not human ones anyway—except for his mother, and a boy's mother shouldn't be his only friend. Many of the island's animals scattered when they heard his footsteps (which they could hear a good half-mile off), but the armadillos that lived in the northern part of the island were quite fond of him. Gulager would sit on the banks of the dump and watch them root around the garbage, and on occasion a 'dillo would bring him a chicken bone with a small piece of chicken still clinging to it, as if the armadillo thought a boy as large and scary as Gulager needed nourishment. That was as far as the friendship went. Gulager never tried to pet one, and they never followed him home for a cup of stew with him and his mother. But it was enough of a friendship for Gulager. He loved the armadillos and envied them their suits of armor. He could use a bit of armor sometimes. The island was a tough place to live.

This particular island was located in the middle of Neshaminy Creek, which was more than a creek, but smaller than a river. From the eastern banks, Gulager could spy the town of Coryell's Ferry, and indeed, Monday through Friday, a ferry shuttled across the bay between the mainland (Coryell's Ferry, Mondauk County) and the island (also considered part of the county, the seventh town of seven). The ferry rarely brought visitors to the island, just the occasional repair man and the mail. Mainly it was used by those islanders who worked in one of the other towns. It was large enough, it appeared, to accommodate almost everyone on the island, but it was nearly empty between nine and five and on the weekends. The ferry did bring copies of the *Mondauk Common*, the county's newspaper, and Gulager fervently read every edition. He'd already gone through most of the contents of the island's small library. The *Mondauk Common* was all he had to look forward to, even if a good part of it was over his head. (He was very intelligent but was still only in grade school.) He liked to sit and read the paper at the end of the rock jetty when the weather was nice; no one ever looked for him there.

It must be noted that the name of the island was Gulager and that Gulager the boy was named after the island when, in a fit of unchecked pride after his birth, his late father declared that he would be as big as the island. And it seemed that most people believed his prediction had come true. Gulager's father died in a bizarre accident while working at the dump. A large pile of refuse had given way, and his father was trapped beneath it. Gulager always imagined the chicken bones the armadillos brought him were actually his father's bones (minus the pieces of chicken), and while this thought may seem morbid, it was actually comforting to Gulager, who was never quite comfortable with the thought of his father's remains being buried in the ground at the cemetery, his dad being the kind of person who liked being outside, even if it was working in the dump. So Gulager's father never lived to see his son grow up…and up…and up. Gulager was six foot one in fifth grade, and now in eighth, he was nine feet tall and weighed almost four hundred and fifty pounds (but because of his height, he was never seen as being heavyset). His uncle came from the mainland to enlarge all the door frames as much as he could and strengthen the staircase. (Gulager still managed to bang his head on various ceilings several times a day.) Gulager's mother stopped letting out the hems of his trousers or inserting panels of fabric on the sides of his shirts as he grew. Instead she started making his clothes, even once fashioning an old school flag into a pair of pants (a sartorial decision that did little to endear him to an already hostile student body). She could no longer find shoes that fit him, so he wore sandals, even in winter, but only after she wrapped his feet in beach towels. Gulager's hands were almost a foot across the palm, a sign, his mother said, that he had a ways to grow.

Gulager's mother was a quiet woman (some would say meek) with a tough exterior (some would call her calloused—but none of these people knew her very well, if at all). She didn't brook much horse hockey. Some of the women in the cheese shop or at the butcher's would stare and whisper, but Gulager's mother went about her business just the same. Her son's size bothered her not one bit. So what if he was a big boy? That meant he had a big heart—not just big feet. And so what if he didn't have friends right now and spent all his free time clomping around the island? Friends would come in time; Gulager would have to fight them off. All these things Gulager's mother thought, but mostly she thought about how she would defend her son, which seemed funny, someone of her size (five foot four in heels, and when was the last time she had worn heels?) defending her monumental boy.

Now Gulager did like to walk around the island (he could circle it twice before supper if he walked fast), and he liked to spend time with the armadillo knights. But what he really liked, or rather *whom* he really liked, was Becky Strunk. Becky was in Gulager's class. He'd sat behind her in fifth grade, but now he was too big for the desks so he sat on the floor in the back of the classroom. Still, he could see Becky's profile, and Gulager found himself lost in her creamy skin and flaxen hair and sea blue eyes. Mean Mrs. Meany would call on Gulager, and Gulager wouldn't even remember what the subject was. All the kids would laugh, Gulager would blush (looking like a volcano about to explode), and a fresh round of schoolyard teasing would begin at lunch. Bigfoot, they called him; freak, they screamed. Gulager would sit and eat his lunch by himself, as he did every day, ignoring the occasional tossed acorn or rock; he would think of the armadillos and their armor and their friendly, non-judgmental snouts. He would think of his mother's inner strength. Gulager loved his mother, adored her really, and he kept very little from her, but how he felt about Becky was one of the things he kept for himself. So he never told her about being scorned or about once having a rotten tomato hit his head because he'd been staring at Becky.

The Day to End All Days started out normally enough: his mother packed his enormous lunch and then climbed the stepladder to kiss Gulager's cheek. But the Day to End All Days was also a Becky Strunk Day. Mrs. Meany rotated seats every day to discourage cliques from developing, and most every Friday (including this one) Becky Strunk was seated at the back of the class, directly in front of Gulager. The Day to End All Days was also school pride day (Color Day), and the students were given breaks from the normal curriculum to work on signs and banners for the big rally that was to take place after school. Gulager, who was almost swooning from the smell of Becky Strunk's shampoo, was given a poster board and several pieces of construction paper, as well as the biggest pair of scissors the school had and a tub of paste. Gulager tried to lose himself in the project, but he was naturally clumsy, and soon he had paste everywhere: his clothes, the floor, his cheeks. Soon too his attention began to wander—back to Becky Strunk. He could see her ankles and they looked strong. Her arms, sticking out of her short-sleeved blouse, were white like birch limbs but toned and defined. (Gulager knew she played basketball.) But it was her hair that fascinated Gulager most. How perfectly flat and yellow it was. How it shone whenever the light squeaked through Mrs. Meany's half-closed blinds. If he could just touch her hair. Gulager closed his eyes. If he could just touch Becky Strunk's beautiful yellow waterfall hair. If only, if only, if only…

Gulager opened his eyes when he heard someone scream.

He was doing it—he was touching Becky's hair! He could barely believe she was letting him. How soft it felt, how wonderful, how incredibly wonderful.

Gulager wanted to whisper sweet somethings in Becky's ear and tell her that he loved her. He wanted to buy her chocolates and hold her little hand in his at the movie house. He wanted to ask her over for dinner to meet his mom.

When he moved his hand, the screaming grew louder.

He was stuck—his hand was stuck. The paste! He tried to remove the offending appendage, and Becky Strunk screamed some more, and Mrs. Meany clobbered Gulager on the head with an umbrella from the coat closet.

Gulager tried to explain. He opened his mouth, but his words were drowned out by Becky's screaming. She touched his hand—clawed at it—and the contact led Gulager to experience an incredibly brief moment of complete joy before Mrs. Meany's umbrella came down upon his head once more. It would be his last moment of complete joy ever. And Gulager knew it.

Someone shouted, calling him a freakazoid, and others took it up and began chanting it in unison.

Two husky boys, football players, tried to tackle him, and Gulager swatted them away with his free hand (his right). Another boy attacked from behind and tried to choke him, but Gulager grabbed one of his wrists and squeezed for a couple of seconds, turning the boy's arm purple, and his assailant quickly withdrew. Gulager was surrounded. Before anyone had time to make a fresh assault, he grabbed Mrs. Meany's umbrella and while still sitting on the floor, hurled it like a spear through one of the tall windows, shattering it. His fellow students' anger over what they perceived to be his intentional abuse of Becky Strunk was momentarily interrupted by their awe at his forcibly taking something out of a teacher's hands and his subsequent destruction of school property. Becky's renewed cries broke the silence and the violence resumed. Mrs. Meany's next weapon was a large history textbook, but Gulager lifted up the old woman, put her into the coat closet, and shut the door. Meanwhile, the footballers had recovered and waded back in. Gulager punched one in the stomach and the other in the groin. Both writhed on the floor like fish out of water.

It was time to escape. The school fire alarm was going off, but Gulager couldn't smell any smoke; he knew it was for him. A police siren wailed, growing closer. Gulager finally stood up (as much as he could), and in doing so, lifted Becky Strunk right out of her chair. He tried to apologize, but her screaming had become a banshee's wail. Gulager froze for a moment, Becky dangling from his hand by her hair. More attacks were imminent. Joey White had a bicycle chain in his hand, and Helen Hacker was helping Billy Phelps break off a chair leg. Gulager was unsure of his next move—until he spied the scissors on the floor. He apologized once more to Becky Strunk and cut off a large chunk of her hair, freeing his hand and plopping her back in her seat. He reached the other side of the classroom in half a step, then covered his eyes and jumped through the tall window he'd shattered with the umbrella, scuffing his hands on the schoolyard asphalt.

Instinct led him home, although he wanted to go to the dump and visit the armadillos. Becky Strunk would never like him now, not with the large piece of her hair that he had cut off still attached to his hand, smelling not of intoxicating shampoo but of non-toxic school paste. Propelled by the tremendous lengths of his strides, he was almost home before he heard the mob, a ways behind him, heading towards his house. (He had a keen sense of hearing due to his large ears.) His mother was outside hanging the laundry (he was always embarrassed whenever he saw his large drawers flapping in the wind), and he was explaining what happened before he even reached the gate. His mother didn't ask too many questions. She helped Gulager remove Becky Strunk's hair from his palm, and Gulager sadly watched her pretty yellow locks float away, down the rivulet towards the creek. His mother told him to wash up and change his clothes and stay in the house no matter what. She could hear the mob approaching now too, and Gulager did as he was told.

Sunset was drawing near when he finished changing, and when he looked out the window, the mob was at the top of the road. His mother was in the backyard, her hands on her hips, laundry basket at her feet. Although it wasn't dark yet, some in the mob carried lit torches. Two policemen were with them, but they appeared to be leading the mob rather than encouraging them to disperse. (Gulager Island did not have a large police force; the two officers constituted half of it, so the authorities weren't going to be much help.) Gulager could see many of his classmates in the vanguard. Some of them had weapons shaped from school desks and chairs. Billy Phelps held a torch made from a chair leg. Mrs. Meany had retrieved her umbrella and waved it menacingly. Workers who'd been enjoying an early happy hour must have left the pub to join the throng, for they hoisted blackjacks and metal poles and mugs of ale. Volunteer firemen, in full gear, held axes above their heads. And Gulager understood. How else to fell a giant but with axes? Gulager was truly sorry from the very top of his head all the way down to his toes, and he was prepared to pay the penalty for his misstep. There was no need for axes, blackjacks, and mugs of ale. He'd surrender peacefully, and if Mrs. Meany banned him from ever using paste again, Gulager thought that was appropriate and fair.

But that's not what happened.

The first rock hit Gulager's mother square in the forehead. So did the next one. And amidst cries of, "Slay the giant! The giant must crumble," a third rock hit her in the same place as she was falling. When Gulager reached the yard, a hush descended on the mob. His mother wasn't breathing. There were large dents in her forehead. One of the policemen, who was creeping towards the yard, told Gulager there was nothing more that could be done for her. Gulager picked his mother up and backed towards the door, telling the policeman in no uncertain terms that he would kill all of them if they came any closer or tried to break into his house. Once inside, he laid his mother on the couch, propped her head on a soft little pillow, the one with the tassels, and covered her body with her afghan.

That day's *Mondauk Common* lay on the coffee table, and Gulager snatched it up, as if it was a security blanket, before rushing up the stairs. He squeezed into his closet, which took some doing even though it was oversized, and there he sobbed and shook and sobbed some more until he was sitting in a puddle of his colossal tears. His mother had been the one person in the world he'd always thought of as being taller than him, and now, inside at least, he felt very small. His eyes became red and raw, and in time, he (temporarily) ran out of tears, the demand exceeding production. To keep himself occupied until he could resume crying for his mother—a manifestation of grief that he believed had no end—he read the *Mondauk Common* by the dim glow of the closet bulb. There, cramped and wet from his tears, he read an article. An important article. One that gave him an idea.

This article was about the Maldives, an island nation (1,192 islands to be exact) in the Indian Ocean. Gulager knew where the Indian Ocean was. He blocked out the growing noise of the mob to concentrate. According to the *Common*, the Maldives "might just as well have been built on a lily pad, so low does it ride in the water." The average elevation was just three feet above sea level. The people there were always worried about the next disaster, which could be lurking just around the corner. They worried about the greenhouse effects that caused sea levels to rise higher and higher. Gulager wondered about the water level surrounding his little island. He thought about his mother's lifeless body stretched out on the couch as if she were listening to one of her shows on their tiny radio. Gulager knew what he had to do.

Gathering whatever courage he possessed (which ended up being quite a bit), he left his closet of mourning, descending the creaking stairs with care. He realized how empty the house was without his mother's living presence even though he took up more room. Gulager straightened his mother's blanket and kissed her goodbye on the cheek. The noise outside was deafening. It was as if the whole island had encircled his house with torches and clubs and other instruments of terror. Gulager climbed the stairs again and peeked through all the windows. In his old playroom, the windows faced south, looking over a side portion of their yard. There were only a few people along the fence line; he knew from his reconnaissance that most were congregated either by the front or back doors and that the majority of the rest milled about restlessly on the north side of the house where the mob had originally halted to slay his mother. Gulager thought of the armadillos, then kissed them goodbye too. His old playroom had casement windows, and he turned the cranks slowly until they were both open, letting in a gasoline-scented breeze. No one looked his way. He swung one foot out, followed by the other, and squeezed through the frame until he was sitting on the ledge…then he jumped. He landed with such a thud that the few people nearby scattered like rabbits with hot feet. Gulager hopped the fence and headed towards the western shore.

As he strode across the island, the air felt good on his tired face, drying his tears almost as soon as they emerged. It didn't take long to get there, not with his immense stride, and when Gulager reached the beach, he kicked off his sandals. He needed to do this without footwear; he needed to feel Gulager Island sinking with his own bare feet.

Years later, people spoke of how lucky it was that the ferry was heading back towards the island just as the first shudders hit, the captain having left his lunch pail on the dock. They spoke of how welcoming the people of Coryell's Ferry were and how that spirit of inclusion led to a referendum renaming the town New Hope. And of course, they spoke of the armadillos.

The future was the furthest thing from Gulager's mind. He started with just a few big, heavy steps along the beach, then followed it with a couple of leaps and a few minutes of jumping up and down. Nothing. He began to walk more forcefully, each step clobbering the ground with a dread purpose. He was all the way to the southern end of the island when he felt it: a subtle shift in the earth. Gulager took even bigger steps, putting all of his weight into them—and it happened again. He could actually hear it this time: a seismic shifting, an unmooring of something ancient.

Gulager began walking faster, adding a leap or two when the feeling struck him. He tried not to think of Becky Strunk. He hoped she wasn't part of the mob with her family. Their time together had been sweet if short and it had come with deadly consequences. Still, he wished he would have been brave enough to talk to Becky during recess or after school; his only words to her were the apologies he made while she was dangling from his hand.

He was almost through his second turn around the island, and he could feel it shudder every couple of steps. They'd killed his mom. They killed his mommy right in front of his eyes. She died because of him, because he was a giant, a behemoth, a freakazoid. He quickened his pace, and he could hear shouting coming from the mainland. But they weren't coming for him; they were feeling his power, they were feeling the island tremble and shake beneath his feet. The freakazoid's bare feet. Gulager began to whistle while he worked— then stopped. There was nothing fun about what was about to happen.

People later said it felt like an earthquake. Others thought it was the end of the world and dropped to their knees rather than run for the eastern shore where rumors of the ferry's presence had spread from man to woman to boy to girl. No one spoke of Gulager. No one remembered being part of the mob that had stoned his mother.

As the island began to sink, slowly at first, then more rapidly, all anyone thought about was reaching the ferry and whether everyone that showed up would fit. (They did.) No one noticed Gulager was not among them. Even the birds were flying east towards the town of Coryell's Ferry. Soon any creature without means of escape would drown in the turbulent Neshaminy.

From where the rock jetty used to meet the shore (the structure had already tumbled into the Neshaminy), Gulager watched the ferry depart. The water was up to his neck. He surveyed the damage around him; all he could see were a few treetops and rooftops, a couple of confused birds. He'd done it; he'd destroyed the place where his mother had been murdered. He'd sunk his namesake island whose inhabitants had labeled him with any name but his own. And he was about to go down with the ship.

The water was up to his chin.

He was happy that the people had escaped on the ferry, but he was sad about the animals. He never meant to hurt or kill. He just didn't want his mother's death to go unnoticed. He hadn't planned on dying himself, but those were the breaks, as his mother used to say. You break it, you bought it. And he was about buy it. Big time.

The water was almost up to his eyeballs when he saw them—a most wondrous sight. He had to blink a few times to make sure he wasn't seeing a mirage. The armadillos—the armadillos were floating towards Coryell's Ferry, their little legs paddling, their shells floating upon the surface of the Neshaminy. Gulager watched his friends until he submerged, then he just waved, and from beneath the water, he thought he saw the last of the 'dillos turn towards him, but then Gulager was gone, and the great story of the sinking of Gulager Island came to an end.

The armadillos never forgot their only human friend, the only one who didn't call them rodents or rats with shells, and once on the mainland of Mondauk County, they continued to tell the story of Gulager the Great and the day he sunk an island, the Day to End All Days.

-end-

About the Author

Michael-Patrick Harrington lives in Ambler, PA.

His top ten books (at the moment) are:
1. *A Prayer for Owen Meany* by John Irving
2. *To Kill a Mockingbird* by Harper Lee
3. *The Sun Also Rises* by Ernest Hemingway
4. *The Great Gatsby* by F. Scott Fitzgerald
5. *As I Lay Dying* by William Faulkner
6. *The Lord of the Rings* by J. R. R. Tolkien
7. *Mrs. Dalloway* by Virginia Woolf
8. *The Secret History* by Donna Tartt
9. *The Age of Innocence* by Edith Wharton
10. *A Christmas Carol* by Charles Dickens

His top ten albums (at the moment) are:
1. *John Lennon/Plastic Ono Band* by John Lennon
2. *Revolver* by the Beatles
3. *Horses* by the Patti Smith Group
4. *Darkness on the Edge of Town* by Bruce Springsteen & the E Street Band
5. *Let It Bleed* by the Rolling Stones
6. *Zen Arcade* by Hüsker Dü
7. *Music from Big Pink* by the Band
8. *The Velvet Underground & Nico* by the Velvet Underground
9. *Rumours* by Fleetwood Mac
10. *Ten* by Pearl Jam

His top ten films (at the moment) are:
1. *The Godfather* directed by Francis Ford Coppola
2. *West Side Story* directed by Robert Wise & Jerome Robbins
3. *Rear Window* directed by Alfred Hitchcock
4. *Mean Streets* directed by Martin Scorsese
5. *Hannah and Her Sisters* directed by Woody Allen
6. *Casablanca* directed by Michael Curtiz
7. *The Wizard of Oz* directed by Victor Fleming
8. *Star Wars* directed by George Lucas
9. *Almost Famous* directed by Cameron Crowe
10. *Jaws* directed by Steven Spielberg

www.michaelpatrickharrington.com

www.ingramcontent.com/pod-product-compliance
Lightning Source LLC
Chambersburg PA
CBHW070908260626
47162CB00007B/2600